MARKED

THE BOYS OF BISHOP MOUNTAIN
BOOK ONE

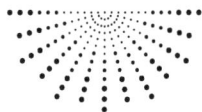

LEXXI JAMES

Marked: The Boys of Bishop Mountain
Copyright © 2022 Lexxi James
www.LexxiJames.com
All rights reserved. Lexxi James, LLC
Independently Published.

Edited by Pam Berehulke
Proofreading by The Ryter's Proof

Cover by Okay Creations

No part of this publication may be reproduced, distributed, or transmitted in any form or by any means, including photocopying, recording, or other electronic or mechanical methods, without the prior written permission of Lexxi James LLC. Under certain circumstances, a brief quote in reviews and for non-commercial use may be permitted as specified in copyright law. Permission may be granted through a written request to the publisher at LexxiJamesBooks@gmail.com.

This is a work of fiction. Names, characters, places, and incidents are the product of the author's imagination. Specific named locations, public names, and other specified elements are used for impact, but this novel's story and characters are 100 percent fictitious. Certain long-standing institutions, agencies, and public offices are mentioned, but the characters involved are wholly imaginary. Resemblance to individuals, living or dead, or to events which have occurred is purely coincidental. And if your life happens to bear a strong resemblance to my imaginings, then well done and cheers to you! You're a freaking rock star!

INTRODUCTION

For fans of the Alex Drake Series, this book takes place long before Alex meets Madison. This is a standalone story of billionaire tycoon Mark Donovan and the girl who nearly got away.

Someone once said that giving love a second chance is like giving them an extra bullet because they missed the first time. But maybe, just maybe, it's not a bullet at all, but an arrow. A Cupid's arrow that can only be given once your soul is ready. Ready to scale impossible mountains, walk through fire, slay every dragon, and crawl your way back for round two.

Because when you hand them that arrow and truly expose yourself, they only have two choices: annihilate you by driving that arrow through your heart or plunging it into theirs . . . and loving you.

PROLOGUE

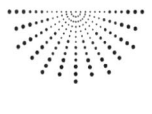

MARK

When I was a kid, my parents made me believe I could be anything. To my younger self, it was music to my ears. I could be Batman.

Come on. Who wouldn't want to be Batman? (A) He was good and righteous with killer fighting moves and witty banter. (B) He had a treasure trove of insane gadgets that made his average human ass capable of anything. And (C) With a bitchin' signal that would light up the sky, he could be summoned at a moment's notice, just in time to save the day.

Fast forward two decades, and I stand by my decision. But I didn't need to be Batman to do all that. Instead, I enlisted as a soldier. I pushed myself harder, ran faster, and shot straighter than anyone. Even my best friend, Brian, thought I often conceded the point to avoid him pummeling me for sport.

Being a soldier meant I didn't have to be a superhero to be a badass protector. I could be good and righteous, have serious combat moves and well-timed snark, with the coolest weapons on the planet. Being a sniper came as naturally as breathing. It was like it was in my blood.

The cold metal of a rifle tamed in my hands—a mistress who would mold to my every move and respond to my very thoughts. Precision timing. Unparalleled targeting. All I had to do was breathe. A smooth exhale before I fired—the snap of release, the high of a hit. It gave me everything I ever wanted. Valor. Honor. Service. Protection.

And maybe, in some ways, I was avoiding Jessica Bishop because of all of that. Well, that and guilt.

Like any hot-blooded American male, when I see a woman from behind, news flash, I'm looking at her ass. And not because I don't respect her as a person and don't want to get to know her on a deeply spiritual level, but because the locked and loaded weapon between my legs has needs. Dark, dangerous needs that two back-to-back deployments aren't exactly helping.

Is it my fault her jeans wrapped her curves like melted on denim? Or that her shirt lifted just enough to show the silky skin of her back when she bent down? How was I supposed to know who it was? Until she plucked up that fuck-saving dandelion, I had no idea. Hell, I was a stone's throw from a filthy suggestion that started with my tongue and ended with her—

Argh. Her. My best friend's baby sister. A girl I haven't seen in years. And, oh yeah, the only woman in the world to say straight to my face, "I hate you."

Granted, she also said she'd marry me, circa age six, and that I had the prettiest eyes in the world—a fact backed up by my mother. But it was the *I hate you* that lingered like a foul fart in an elevator. Those three little words were enough to set me straight.

It's not my place to cross a line with Jess. Any line. Christ, she's eighteen. I'm twenty-four. If I had an eighteen-year-old sister, the last person I'd trust her with is me. Anything shy of a football field between us is my funeral in the making, and trust me when I say, the last thing I want is her brothers lining up my balls for target practice. I'd like to see age twenty-five, thank you very much.

I even gave her a nickname as a big, fat DO NOT ENTER chastity belt. A reminder that no matter what it takes, she's a thousand percent off limits.

Even if it makes me the villain.

I wait for her to head into the restaurant before I slip around back. My big brother, Ty, heaves a pile of empty crates into the loading truck, and, *thank fuck*, he's alone. Perfect timing. "I need a favor," I say, grumbling the words that will undoubtedly bite me in the butt.

"Is this where I name my price now, or will you owe me?" He pops a brow, giving depth to his malevolent grin.

I hop to the inside of our mid-size delivery truck, lending him a hand as the two of us form an instant assembly line. "I'm covering the restaurant for you tomorrow. Isn't that enough?"

He chuckles while handing over an extra-large cardboard box stuffed with recycling. "You did that for yourself. You and I both know that between missions, the last thing you want is to haul your boneless ass out of bed an hour before the cold ass crack of dawn."

He's got me there. "Fine. I'll owe you." *Whatever.*

Clapping dust from his hands, Ty leans against the opposite wall of the truck. His loud, maniacal laugh cracks the air, echoing. *"Bwah-ha-ha-ha-ha,"* he howls, rubbing his crafty hands with glee. "Name your favor."

I kick a ragged pebble away from the tire. "Tell Jess she's got tomorrow off."

Intrigued, his smile lifts. "Well, well, well . . . Is something going on with you and Ms. Bishop?"

"Absolutely not." My denial is as calm as a duck gliding on the water. Above the surface, steady as a rock. Below the surface, I'm backpedaling my ass off from the mouth of hell.

"Okay, okay." His hands raise in small surrender. "You don't want your best friend's baby sister around." His expression lifts curiously. "Why?" He studies me, knotting his arms with keen interest.

I do exactly what the military taught me. Evade and avoid. "Because I do. End of story."

His voice lowers salaciously. "She's, *uh*, not a little girl anymore."

I glare.

He chuckles. "Is this because of that time she threw your clothes in the lake?"

"That lake was ice cold by the way, and no, it isn't."

"Then what?"

I stare back hard, glazing past my guilt. "Like I need a reason to avoid the one person who always manages to claw her way under my skin. I have exactly one day at the restaurant. Keep her away."

He tugs the cell from his back pocket. "And what do I tell

her? You know as well as I do, she can use the tips. And I need someone in her place."

How this man manages a restaurant, I'll never know. "You don't need a play-by-play. Figure it out."

"But—"

Oh, for fuck's sake. "No but's. I'm offering my balls on a silver platter for you to roast, deep fry, or flambé at a time of your choosing. You want them or not?" I hold out my hand, ready to shake.

His mouth twists to one side as he plots my demise while his hand locks a firm grip on mine. "Deal."

CHAPTER ONE

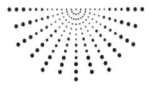

JESS

*H*ave you ever believed that if you wished for something hard enough, you could make it happen?

I did. It all started when my mom used to say, "Never underestimate the power of a wish." Then she'd hold the fluffy-white dandelion in front of me as my cheeks puffed with air. "Blow, baby girl!"

And I would. Wasting a universe of wishes with reckless abandon on books, candy, and toys. It's like slots for toddlers: The more you wish, the more chances you have of one of those wishes coming true.

It took a few years before I got serious. Doubled-down on just one wish. What was it Hannibal Lecter said? We covet what we see every day? Who knew the words of a fictional psychopath could ring so true?

And see Mark Donovan, I did.

My brother's best friend. Yeah, try not seeing him. Dark, carefree waves that melted down to eyes that changed with his mood. Golden caramel at his happiest. Moody winter green when he was brooding.

He was it. My first big wish. My first epic fail.

Every night for a month, I wished I would grow up to marry him. And then I did the unthinkable. With my little-girl outside voice, I said it. "I am going to marry you." Said it straight to his beautiful boy face.

Considering I was six and he was twelve, it went over like a loud fart in a packed church. What started with a wince morphed into uncontrollable laughter, culminating in Mark doubling over on the floor.

Oh, that last part wasn't from laughter. It was from my angry little-girl fist jabbing a full-force punch square at his balls.

This cautionary tale taught me two things. First, boys apparently can't breathe without their balls. And second, wishes aren't meant to be trite or trivial. If only a few wishes are meant to come true, make each one precious. Make them count.

When my dear, sweet parents made their way to heaven—a pain so raw, it hurt just to breathe—I had faith. For every dandelion I plucked, I wished messages could make their way up through the clouds, delivered by the wind.

I wished Nana Winnie was as happy as a lark, cutting out crazy patterns for her latest quilt. I wished our old Labrador retriever, Saint, was with them, running fast and free to catch a Frisbee from my dad. I wished every time I sang to the clouds, my mom could feel the love I poured into every note. Knew how much I missed her. Missed them all.

When my brothers moved away, lured by the military, I

wished them back. Brian showed up the next day, the Rock of Gibraltar by my side ever since.

How? I have no idea. Considering he's a sniper at the beck and call of the Army, I can't imagine how he worked that out. But we both knew it couldn't last forever, and the lifeline he cast me was beginning to strain.

In five short days, he returns to the other side of the world, and the last thing he needs to worry about is me.

So, today's dandelion is for a job. Not just any job. Just a small promotion that keeps the lights on and cements me in place, home on Bishop Mountain.

On my day off, and armed with the fluffiest dandelion I could find, I close my eyes and imagine my mom holding it out. My small smile makes way to a gust of breath. I blow all my fears and doubts away, letting the feather-soft wisps fly free on a breeze.

One wish. One shot. And one man who can make it all happen.

CHAPTER TWO

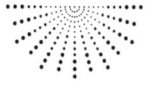

JESS

"Have you seen Tyler?" I ask, standing a respectable distance from the customer side of the bar.

Anita frowns as she side-eyes me while flipping a shaker with finesse. "I thought you were off."

I shrug. "I am." Though I have no idea why. I pause for a beat. "But I wanted to pick up my check." I can't help my envious stare at her nametag. Anita Mae, Bartender.

She nods, her smile knowing. "And call dibs on my job?"

I scrunch up my face. "Too obvious?"

"Uh, it's called initiative. You're a Bishop. I'd expect nothing less." She notices the space I've created between me and the bar. Bartending in the great state of New York at eighteen? Totally legit. Taste-testing even one drop of alcohol? Not so much.

And as I am the last of the Bishop children to work in this establishment, let's just say I don't want to be the one to eff it all up with the liquor authority.

"You're not a kid anymore, Jess. Step on up!"

Proudly, I do. With a lighter, she demonstrates a technique called *flaming an orange peel*. With the strike of a match and the flick of her fingers, a fireball showers the drink, then vanishes behind a small trail of smoke.

"Doesn't that burn?" I ask.

She shakes her head. "You're not really lighting the peel as much as spraying the orange oil against the flame into the glass." She walks me slowly through the motions. "See?"

I nod. Rumor is, her promotion is in the bag, which leaves her job up for grabs. It's a long shot, but I've been practicing. Thank God for YouTube.

She peers over thick-framed glasses. "Master this trick. People eat it up, and the tips flow like water." She gestures grandly to the wall of liquor and art-deco accents. "This will all be yours someday."

Fascinated, I glance around. "There's so much to learn."

She tosses a small notebook on the glossy wood. "Here. You want the job? Memorize this."

Flipping through, I realize it has to be fifty pages of customized cocktails from the *Adirondack Sunset* to *Donovan's Deadly Twist*. But when my gaze hits *Bishop's Breeze*, I pause, and my eyes well up. I expected it to be a drink created by Brian, Rex, or Cade—any one of my brothers—but it's not. It was written by Henry.

Henry James Bishop, my father. My fingers skim across the page as I inhale pride and exhale sadness. Vodka. Lemon. Honey. Club soda with a splash of Moscato. I choke up. I can almost see him making it for mom.

Anita's warm hand covers mine. "Anything I can do?"

Rewind time. Stop them from getting in that car.

"No," I say softly. *Not unless you can bring my parents back.* It takes a breath before the pain subsides and a few blinks to dislodge an annoyingly stubborn tear.

"Lunch?" she says kindly.

I decline with a hopeful grin. "Rain check?" Considering I'm blowing all my money on my gift for Brian, I will absolutely take a free lunch IOU.

Sharp, jabbing pains erupt in the lowest point of my gut. *Not now.* I suck in a breath to stave it off. A hard pinch comes again, a tight twist. I hug both arms against my belly, wrestling the pain away, grateful that Anita's too busy to notice.

"Hmm . . ." She fills a thick glass mug with whatever's on tap. "Tyler?"

She thinks for a moment while I try not to double over in pain. Or cry out *"Mercy"* to the gods of pain.

Month after month, my periods are ten times worse, and over-the-counter medications are barely making a dent. With any luck, the extra-extra-strength medication I got at the drugstore will kick in any second now.

While I bite my lip like a bullet, Anita ponders on. "Tyler . . ."

Maybe it's the repeated knife jabs to the gut talking, but if one more person says they haven't seen Tyler Donovan, I'll throw down like a toddler. I'm two seconds from unceremoniously face-planting onto the questionably clean floor, arms and legs flailing about in full-on meltdown mode.

Anita sets a pink-and-purple drink at the pickup station

and a mug of beer next to it before sliding her glasses to the tip of her nose.

"So, you have to see Tyler?" she sings suggestively. Or hopefully. I swear, the woman is vying for the official title of Cupid.

The knife jab below the belly subsides to a dull ache enough for me to play along. "Obviously, because Tyler knows how to make a girl truly happy."

She gives me the hairy eyeball. "You're lucky you're legal," she says, smirking as she waggles her brows.

"All I need is a few minutes alone with him. Just me and Tyler so he can"—I deadpan— "pay me." I lower my voice and clasp my hands in prayer. "And pitch him a dozen reasons for why I'd be perfect for your job."

By her outrageous yawn, she's underwhelmed. "Boring." She leans in confidentially. "Moment of truth . . . which one?"

"Which one what?"

"Which one of the Donovans melts your butter?"

Which? How can she ask me that? I mean, they're all friends with my brothers. *Which* makes it weird.

Wide-eyed, Anita smiles expectantly as I think it through. Anything to take my mind off the pain, though it's eased up enough that I'm no longer tasting blood from my lower lip.

Ignoring my childhood faux pas of a wish, I run through the list.

There's Tyler, who's inherently sexy because he has my paycheck. He's the older, wiser, kinder of the Donovan brothers. His sandy-blond waves are always as carefree as his soul, and his twenty-seven-year-old smile warms you from the inside out.

One day in the not-too-distant future, this business will be his kingdom, an attractive quality that the vagina of every eligible bachelorette in the tri-county region has zeroed in on.

Hunk-worthiness? A ten and a half. On the date-worthy scale, I can't even go there. He's almost paternal. Or a really hot uncle you hope will find his forever match. Whenever I come in, he's always checking to see how I'm doing and if I've eaten. Thanks to this place, I have.

Then there's Zac, the youngest and three years older than me. A young McDreamy in his own right; his looks are totally wasted. The man has been my BFF since forever ago, but he never dates. Between studying at New York University and launching his own mogul career, you'd think the man was thirty-one, not twenty-one.

Over summers and holiday breaks, he returns to Saratoga Springs to shake things up. Moving the inventory system from the caveman era into the next millennium. Shifting the ordering to the cloud and ensuring it takes everything from Venmo to Bitcoin. And launching a spruced-up website with candid shots that always manage to blow up Instagram, which he often credits me for.

Every chance I get, I snap outrageous photos and videos, and at Zac's insistence, they've posted every single one. Food photos. Tyler clowning around, serving a bachelorette party in nothing but a black apron. Well, he had shorts on, but you couldn't tell from the front. Even simple things like Anita plopping dry ice into drinks at Halloween.

Zac says I have raw talent. I call it an obsession with Mrs. D.'s food.

Zac will forever be my biggest cheerleader and best friend,

but something more? Let's just say our one and only test-the-waters kiss was all we needed to be eternally friend-zoned. Plus, I'm not sure he'll ever settle down. Core-of-the-Earth-level hotness? A thousand percent. A compulsive workaholic? Ten-thousand percent.

And last, but not least, there's Mark. The very same Marcus Evan Donavon my child mind thought I could marry. Silly girl. I couldn't possibly marry an ass, and make no mistake, that man is an ass.

As if reading my thoughts, Anita asks, "Ooh, is it Mark?"

Heat flares up my neck to my cheeks as I scoff. "Mark? Mark hates me."

"He does not."

"He even gave me that stupid nickname."

Anita coos at me. "It's adorable."

My palm is affronted before I am, and it flies in her face. "Don't even."

Her hands raise in surrender as she smartly backs up a step. "Okay, okay. Just saying, he's not terrible on the eyes."

When Anita gets googly-eyed for Mark, I gag. She grabs a ticket and pulls a highball from the shelf to work on her next drink.

All I can think is . . . Mark? Really?

I mean, to look at, yes. Agreed. If Mark had a mute button, he'd be the perfect man. The problem with him—or rather, the biggest problem with him—is that his looks far overshadow his tiny, little pea-brain. That and his two-sizes too-small heart.

Have you ever seen a man too beautiful to exist? Sure, in and of itself, it's not a reason to hate him. What I hate is that

Mark wields it like a weapon. Whenever he walks into a room, I feel the need to dispense chastity belts with reckless abandon.

Again, I'm not talking about your garden-variety good looks, as in he looks great in a pair of jeans with an insta-swoon dimple that could launch a thousand ships. I'm talking about a legs-locked, knees-weak, heart-stopping level of sex appeal that would stand out in a sea of Hemsworths. The irony is that with all that heat, Mark is too cold.

Anita pops the cork on a bottle of Moscato and works on a Bellini. "Well, if your heart's set on Tyler or Zac, you're SOL. I just remembered that Tyler isn't here. He and Zac went fishing with their dad before Zac returns to school."

I nibble my lower lip again, worry twisting my gut.

"Nope. Don't do that," Anita says, frowning.

"Huh? Do what?"

She waves an accusatory strawberry-margarita painted fingernail in my face. "That thing where your brows pinch so hard, they nearly touch. Trust me, you're too young to start with the permanent angry line." She wipes down the bar. "You worried about Brian leaving?"

"No," I lie, lifting a defiant chin. "Brian has been here long enough. Having him take care of me since my parents—"

My mouth dries, sand filling my throat before I can say the words. I breathe through it until words come out.

"Anyway, the military gave him all the leave they could. I'm an adult. I've graduated. I'm a big girl, and my brother's a big boy. We can take care of ourselves." I say this out loud at least a dozen times a day, because any day now, I'll believe it.

Anita places a bowl of mixed nuts between us and pops a few into her mouth. "Then what is it?"

Deflated, I sigh. "I have five days to get Brian his going-away gift before his deployment."

"That should be plenty of time."

"I need to be able to afford it first. It costs my entire paycheck."

She lifts a brow. "All of your paycheck?"

I nod. "Along with the engraving, yes. I caught him drooling at the jewelers over some stupid-expensive tactical watch. After an insane amount of searching, I found a pre-owned one, but I have to pick it up today. The owner already has other buyers." I'm about to show her on my phone, but my battery's already low, and I still need to use it to find this guy. Wiggling my fingers at her, I say, "Give me your phone."

Anita hands it to me, and I pull up the Laney Jewelers website, then scroll to the right photo. With a two-toned whistle, she approves.

I smile. "And then hopefully, I'll have time to get it engraved before Brian leaves."

"You mean Brian and Mark. What, no gift for his bestie?" she teases.

My lips quirk as my narrowed eyes respond for me.

"Hey, if push comes to shove, girl, I've got you." She holds up a paring knife. "Seriously, how hard can it be to scratch two Bs on the metal band?"

"What I had in mind is a little more than his initials, and this watch is worth weeks of my life," I say indignantly as I lower her knife-wielding hand. "As skilled as you are with slicing and dicing, how about we leave the pretty letter carving to the experts." I tap the counter, not sure what to do. "Who can I get my check from?"

"You can get it from Mark."

"What? Mark's here?" My brows pop up as the name of my arch-nemesis rings through the air. Or is it just nemesis? "Mark never comes here. And why isn't he fishing with everyone else?"

Smiling, she shrugs. "Mrs. D.'s working out the details for the Whitney wedding. I guess he's filling in."

"Perfect." I let out a frustrated sigh. "Any idea where he is?" Anita shakes her head as I slide off the leather stool. "I guess I'll stop looking for Tyler and hunt down Mark."

"Hang on." She fishes cash from the tip jar and hands it to me.

Blinking, I stare at her. "What's this?"

Her hands grab mine, shoving the bills into it. "A bunch of tourists went all out at brunch. Take it. I don't want you not to have a paycheck. You'll be working this side of the bar soon enough."

Emotions overwhelm me as I stare down at the twenties, tens, and fives. This isn't just how Anita is. It's how everyone is here. Always looking out for me when I suspect it least and need it most. Everyone here cares for me. In return, I have to care for them back.

Counting it quickly, I split it right down the middle and toss half back in the jar. "Thanks," I say, rushing out of there before I'm a blubbering puddle in the middle of the floor.

Sternly, I wipe my cheeks and make my way down the hall. I can cry when I'm at home. That's what showers are for.

Scowling, I mutter under my breath. "Yoo-hoo . . . Satan. Come out, come out, wherever you are."

Where Tyler and Zac are wholesome goodness wrapped up in sunshine and smiles, Mark is the polar opposite, ready to fight, run, or fornicate at a moment's notice. His brothers are easygoing sails on tranquil waters, while Mark is a storm. And those eyes. Shamefully, I've stared at them more than once.

Some men were meant to build castles while others were born to slay dragons. That's Mark. A hot-blooded fighting machine who can't turn it off. It's what makes him the best. And the broodiest.

When Brian entered the Army, Mark rushed in after him, besties since their stupid blood oath in the fifth grade. Seriously, how deep did they need to cut? They both required five stitches each. But that was them. Two beautiful idiots pridefully counting every last scar.

It's the reason why no matter how hard I try, I can't avoid Mark. Like my brother's shadow, he's always around. A personal tormentor, ready and eager to strike at will.

I pop my head into the break room. A few waitresses are eating a late lunch and gossiping about customers.

Gasping, Kara looks up at me. "I thought you were off," she says, offended at my very presence. "Tyler said you needed a personal day." Her eyes roll to a resentful stop. "Must be nice."

Why would Tyler tell them that? I ignore her, and not just because Kara's an ass, but because convincing Kara that Tyler is wrong would be as fruitful as convincing Mark I should be a bartender. There's no point. It'll never happen. But I still need to pick up my check. "Have either of you seen Mark?"

"Oh my God," Starr says as she whips back her pink hair. "Is Mark *Danger Zone* Donovan here?"

Kara claps and squeals like a seal, while I rub my temple, praying that the migraine she just spurred up goes away. High-pitched and hopeless, she carries on. "He's so lickable. I heard he now holds the record for the most confirmed kills."

Confused, I stare. "How does that make him hot?"

She smirks. "You wouldn't understand." She scans me up and down before dismissing me with her eyes. "You're too young."

"I'm only a year younger than you, Kara."

She scoops her breasts into her crossed arms, forcing cleavage that even her overstuffed push-up couldn't tackle. "There's a world of difference in a year."

Perhaps to a dog.

"Trust me," Starr says. "His brothers are princes, but Mark Donovan is a full-fledged demi-god." She licks her spoon suggestively. "I've got something that sharpshooter can aim at."

She sucks her finger, amplifying the point. I dry heave and leave the room. Only God knows where that finger's been.

Kara calls after me. "Tell him we're looking for him, too, okay?"

Their giggles echo wildly as I shake my head. *Sure. Why not? Because maybe if I offer two semi-virginal sacrifices to your demi-God, he'll give me that promotion I desperately need.*

"Jess?" I hear Mark say. His deep, gravelly voice flows effortlessly down the hall, though I don't see him.

As I approach his office, the door is ajar. I slide a hand on the handle, pausing as soon as I hear, "What about her?" Because Mark isn't talking to me, he's talking *about* me.

The door is cracked ever so slightly, an obvious invitation to listen in. His heavy footsteps move farther away, and I nudge the door a hair, wide enough to peer inside.

Framed by the large picture window at the other end of the office, Beelzebub stands in all his glory: dark blue jeans, crisp white shirt, and chestnut-brown hair mussed to perfection. The million-mile stare he sports is fixed somewhere off in the distance as he presses the cell phone to his ear.

It's wrong of me to stare. But I can't not stare. I mean, it's hardly the first time I've seen Mark Donovan. It's just the first time I've dared to unapologetically stare at his ass.

He shifts in place, and the move is hypnotic. Did he bulk up . . . his butt?

I knew he did some heavy lifting, but this is ridiculous. I mean, once, when traffic was blocked, he and Brian lifted a fallen maple to the side of the road. By themselves. So, yeah, I get it. Muscle mayhem. But now, his arm bulge alone has his shirtsleeves within an inch of their lives. It's as if he graduated from bar-belling trees to tanks.

"What?" he snaps indignantly.

I shouldn't hang on his every word, but I do. Who's he talking to? Is someone complaining about me? Because I've been crushing it. Taking double shifts. All smiles. Amped up like an Energizer bunny. Nobody works as hard as I do, and not just for the tips. I have the Bishop legacy to maintain.

And yes, I may have mixed up an order here and there, or spilled one tiny little kid's milk. But I fixed every last mistake. And the *milk spill Boomerang clip* the kids posted got a ton of love on TikTok. Granted, the putrid dairy after-smell was wafting about for weeks, but thankfully, it's gone. Almost.

"No. No way," I hear Mark say, chuckling. I frown hard. I know that laugh. That's his evil laugh.

It's the laugh he had when he and Brian set a rope snare and trapped me in it, which, in my defense, I was eight. It was also the laugh that accompanied that nasty bowl of foul-tasting jellybeans and his insistence that girls couldn't eat them. He knew what he was doing. Throwing down a double-dog dare in the face of the female race. Well, I ate every last one. And whoever decided that vomit and boogers were palatable should be shot.

He also had that very same annoying laugh when he came up with that stupid nickname—

"Choir Girl?" he says with a scoff.

Fire fills my face as my grip on the door handle tightens.

This is the same man who tosses nicknames like *babe* or *princess* at every walking vagina in town, but for me, I'm simply Choir Girl. I mean, sure, I was in the church choir. And not just because everyone there was nice or that they handed out cocoa and cookies after every performance, which I lived for, but because Mom was there, too. It was our space as much as anyone else's.

"Me with Choir Girl?" He says it as if disgusted. By this point, I'm already inappropriately one foot in the office and charging straight at him. But Mark doesn't notice and just keeps going.

"Not with a ten-foot pole," he says with another scoff, and half of my heart shatters as he goes from being cold to cruel. "Make that a hundred-and-ten-foot pole. She's too"—he pauses for a moment for just the right word, the wheel in his mind landing on—"Jess."

Seriously? It's bad enough that he's banished me like a dwarf planet in my own brother's solar system. Why talk about me at all? Oh, that's right. Because he's Mark.

I bite my cheek, my face burning with more emotions than I can count. Frozen with indecision—to leave or to knee him in the groin—I blink away my stubborn tears just as he turns around. "Not even if the fate of mankind was dependent on my dick connecting with her vag—"

His mouth snaps shut, and I narrow my eyes.

He hangs up. For the longest second in history, I stare down the first man to make my *Vow to Hate for All Eternity* list. And that's not just my period talking.

"Jess," he says with a huff, annoyed. "Ever hear of knocking?" He walks over to his desk.

He did not just say that. *Ever hear of not talking shit behind someone's back, butt-munch?*

My mouth falls open, and I can feel every last one of my freckles catch fire. "Oh, I'm sorry, Your Royal Highness. Is that the proper etiquette? Knocking so I don't disturb you being an asshat?"

"Asshat?" His steps stop cold. He spins, facing me. "Well, this asshat happens to be your boss for today, Jess. That is, if you were working, which you shouldn't be. How about you come back tomorrow?"

Is that why Tyler told me to stay home? Because of Mark? When I could've used those tips? I feel my anger rise to a dangerous high as I stand my ground. "How about you give me an apology?"

When he rolls his eyes, I poke him in his dumb, stone-hard chest. *What am I doing?*

His eyes dart to my finger, then to my eyes. "I—" I take a breath, my chin defiant. "I deserve an apology," I snap.

He edges closer into my space. "Haven't you heard? In life, you never get what you deserve, Jess. Only what you can negotiate. Move it along, Choir Girl."

Again with the name? "Make me," I say in total stupid-brazen disregard for my stand-in boss. But I can't back down. Instead, I step up to him, toe-to-toe. I'm keenly aware of the childishness of my action considering the man has, oh, I don't know, a yard of height on me.

My stare-down is feeble, pathetic, really. I blame his eyes. They're gold now—charged and deadly—like some wild exotic cat I'm stupid enough to be in a staring contest with.

Two knocks chop at the door.

"Come in," he barks.

"Hey, hey, hey." Brian's voice is too familiar to both of us, but neither of us budges. My brother wraps a casual arm around me as if the death-glare crossfire isn't happening at all. He pulls me back and leans over to Mark. "I thought we had a talk about this."

I whip my head to Brian. "A talk about what?"

"Nothing." Mark's reply is quick. Too quick. He retreats behind his desk. *Coward.*

I turn my attention to Brian, breaking down his resolve with my angriest angry eyes. "What talk?"

He shrugs, his guilty smile on full display. "Nothing," he says, rushing me out of the room with both hands on my shoulders. "Mark and I need to chat, sis. See you later."

Before I get too far with a protest, the door slams in my face.

"*Argh.*" I stomp my foot. I still need my check. Maybe if I'd taken Anita up on that lunch, I wouldn't be consumed with hangry rage. Between my hunger and my period, there's only one solution: full-blown annihilation. Crazed, I plow down the door, guns blazing.

"Why'd you hang up on me?" Brian asks Mark.

"What?" I glare down my enemies, Tweedle Dumb and Tweedle Asshat, trying to make sense of why Mark's dick and my vag would ever come up in their conversation.

What the hell?

When Anita asked me about Mark, did I say, *"Me? With the dildo of the century? Not even if my vagina was on fire and his dick was the only way to put it out."* Wait, that came out wrong. And of course, I didn't. At least, not with my outside voice.

Instead of being a half-decent person, Mark clasps his hands and cocks his head in that arrogant way he always does. "Remember our little talk about knocking, Jess?"

It's as if his balls are begging to be kicked so hard, they lodge in that vacant space where his brain should be.

Fire licks at my good senses. I'm so ready to hand him that perfect ass of his on a platter, but the second I open my mouth, he adds, "I'd hate to see you lose your job for something as trivial as manners."

Stunned, I stare. *He'd really fire me over this?*

And what about Brian? Instead of standing up for me, my idiot big brother is just standing there. Like a big, dumb oaf, he's doing nothing but warning me with his eyes and a slow shake of his head.

Brian's right. I know he's right. He's leaving in a few days and taking this worthless sack of shit with him.

I should stay calm because I don't want this job, I need it. And not even for the money. Without it, I'm more or less alone. Rex is stationed in New Jersey. Close, but never close enough. And Cade is away in some god-forsaken part of the world that feels as unreachable as the moon.

Tears threaten fast. Too fast. As soon as he says, "Well, what do you know? Even choir girls have manners," no-holds-barred atomic anger wins.

I see the stack of checks on the desk, miraculously in alphabetical order. Mine's right on top. I snatch it up and stuff it in my pocket.

"Go to hell, Mark Donovan." And once again, when faced with the most beautiful man I've ever seen, my brain snaps in two, and I do the unthinkable. "I. Quit."

Pulse racing, I rush out of the room, determined not to cry like a girl or beg for my job. How did today end up like this?

I should've spent today planning the sendoff of the century for the brother of the year. Instead, I'm stuck spending the better part of it finding a new job and hating the both of them.

Asshat, one.

Choir Girl, zero.

CHAPTER THREE

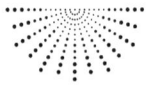

MARK

A fist of fucking titanium flies from out of nowhere and slams me square in the chest. "Ow." My tone is pure *what the hell?*

It's true, I know better than to pick a fight with Jess. And I am technically the grown-up. Well, with her being eighteen and all, I guess she's a grown-up too. But I swear to God, that woman gets under my skin like lava-coated chiggers. Or maybe it's the guilt.

Brian and I know the price of his extended leave. It was a deal with the devil. Saying our next mission will be dangerous is like saying the Pope sometimes prays. There's a good chance we'll never see our families again, and the last thing I needed was to face off with Jess and her big, blue, soul-searching eyes. Hell, I can't even bear to look my mother in the eye.

Guns blazing, Brian lays into me. "You fire my sister five days before our next deployment?"

I didn't fire her. She quit. But with Brian glaring me down, there's no use arguing that technicality. Flustered, I point a finger at him. "This is your fault."

"My fault?"

"For giving me the fucking third degree and accusing me of making a play for Jess. Which she overheard. Thanks a fucking heap."

"Ah." He flicks a speck of dust from the desk. "How was I supposed to know you'd have that conversation with the door opened?"

I wave both arms in the air. "Now you know. And Jess was eavesdropping. *Again*. Her own bad habit brought this on."

Brian gives me a *don't fuck with the Bishops* face. "I can't have your back if things aren't square with Jess."

I rub at the ice pick driving into the base of my neck. "Well, technically, she quit."

When Brian hits me this time, he doesn't hold back. The man packs a punch like a battering ram. "Fix it, fucker."

I look at him as if a dick sprouted from the top of his head. "How? You know your sister. She's earned every last flaming strand of that red hair of hers. Fuck, we haven't spoken in years, and this is our reunion." I huff and lift my chin to the sky. "She hates me."

He shrugs. "Well, considering your first conversation in years is to threaten her job, her hating you seems validated."

"Is it my fault you made me say I wouldn't make moves on your sister with my outside voice?"

"Is it my fault you'll hump everything from a hydrant to a lamppost, and it wasn't exactly a stretch?"

I gesture at the door. "Clearly, you had nothing to worry

about." I adjust my pants from behind the desk. *Yeah, that's a bald-faced lie.*

"Clearly." Brian shakes his head. "You can't talk to her like she's twelve. She isn't."

Duh. One look at her ass told me that.

I remain stone-faced as Brian continues to lambast me. "You don't understand. Jess is stressed, too. With all the shit she's going through—" He clams up.

My ears perk up. "What's she going through?" I ask, tiptoeing as I pry.

He shakes it off. "Nothing. Just, *er*, woman stuff."

Enough said. The last thing I need to hear about is the world of Jess's uterus, though it does explain her flying off the fucking handle. With Jess, Moody is her middle name. Plus, with how full her breasts are and—

Where the fuck did that come from? I scramble to wipe the image from my mind. *Can we change the subject already?*

Brian drones on. "She's not a child anymore. And you're only filling in for the day, dickwad. Don't make me call your mommy on you."

"I know she's not a child."

While the very full-grown woman was busting my balls, it took every sheer ounce of willpower to avoid staring at those full, pouty lips. *Fuck*, she can't come back here. At least, not while I'm here. This is my funeral in the making.

Hmm. I think it through. Because I also can't *not* bring her back. Brian would murder me—*Saw* movie style.

I offer a solution. "She can consider herself on paid vacation until we leave. This way, the two of you can spend some time together."

And she'll be far the hell away from me.

Brian socks me again. Playfully, this time, but considering he gave it all he had the last round, I wince. "I guess you'd better find her and tell her that."

My eyes shoot wide. "You're her brother. Why don't you find her and tell her?"

"Because it's not my mess. It's yours. And we have our entire next mission to clean up after each other." He winks, the smartass, and heads for the door. "You know my baby sis would love to tend bar," he sings at me on his way out.

I throw a stress ball at his head. And miss.

He chuckles. "And they call you a sharpshooter," he calls out as he closes the door behind him.

Fucker.

I scroll through my phone until I find Jess's number, filed under "CG." I shoot her a text and wait her out.

Can we talk?

An hour later, after a thorough review of Zac's new inventory system, I check my phone. Still no response from Jess, so I try again.

I really need to talk to you.

By the time I've finished reviewing next month's menus with the staff, getting the seating arrangements for the Whitney wedding changed to accommodate nearly two hundred people instead of one hundred people, and reconciling the accounting for the month, my brain is fried.

I blow out a breath. Not a word from Choir Girl.

So, I do the unthinkable. I apologize.

Sorry I was an asshat. Please call back.

A text pings back, but the small surge of relief is instantly snuffed out. It isn't Jess. It's Brian. Even his text looks unhinged.

Did you talk to Jess???

Brian sends me a screenshot. Her phone finder app has her pinned on possibly the worst street in Albany. Without even speaking to him, I know Brian's about to lose his shit. Hell, my heart's beating out of my rib cage, and I'm half a breath away from losing my own shit.

What the fuck is she doing there?

Keep calm, I tell myself. If I'm panicked, Brian will panic tenfold.

I lock my voice into casual mode and call. "I've texted her several times. She hasn't returned my texts, but that's nothing new, considering her nickname for me is sometimes Satan. Have you tried calling her?"

"Yes, dumbass. Tried that first. I'm heading that way, but I'm home." The Bishop home is buried in a southwest pocket of Adirondack Park—at least an hour and a half from Albany. His voice rises, unnerved. "I need you to—"

"I'll take care of it. I'm leaving now."

I grab the nearest keys and rush out the front, nearly plowing down Anita. "Sorry, I'm in a hurry."

"Wait." She blocks my path. "Did Jess find you?"

"Yes," I grumble, irritated. Now I just need to find her.

"Oh, good. I know she was worried about getting that watch for Brian."

Impatient, I mutter, "What watch?" as I move around her and make my way to the truck.

Anita keeps pace, shoving her phone in my face. "This watch."

I check out the price tag. All her paychecks for two months wouldn't cover that watch. "How is she paying for a four-thousand-dollar watch?"

"She isn't. Some guy is selling his old one."

Of course. Because that's what people do. Sell four-thousand-dollar watches for a fraction of the price. It happens every day.

I get in the truck, slam the gas, punch the dashboard, and shout, *"Fuuuck!"*

The sun is nearly gone, and a small part of me is relieved to find Jess's clunky little hatchback car.

It's parked in front of what seems to be a house converted into a bar. There are a dozen bikes outside—Harleys, mostly. A few people are lined up at the end of the block. By the looks of them, I can only assume that's where the line starts for hookers and your hardcore drugs of choice.

Shit.

I reach under the seat and grab the Glock, a move that could get me arrested and dishonorably discharged as neither the gun nor the vehicle is technically mine. They're my father's. Still, I untuck my shirt and shove the weapon in the back of my waistband because I have no idea what I'm walking into, and this gun is the only thing watching my six. Determined to the core, I ignore the blaring warning signs going off in my head.

Jess first. Consequences later.

I head inside. It's dark and reeks of asscrack and beer, with the aroma of cigars and weed floating through the air. Here's hoping they don't pee-test me before I deploy.

When my eyes adjust, I study the room, quickly assessing the occupants, potential weapons, and exits. The place is filled with a few dozen men, but no Jess. Ice water drips down the back of my neck, and my heart drums louder as I make my way around the space.

What if she isn't here? Where else can she be?

I pull out my phone, eager enough to ask if anyone's seen her and gauge their honesty by the look in their eyes. I'm sure there's a recent photo on our website, and when I pull it up, I freeze.

Red tendrils frame a smiling face that's all lips and eyes and a sprinkling of freckles that skyrockets her beauty. What the hell?

No wonder Brian is worried. He should be. She's a fucking wet dream wrapped up in a girl-next-door smile, and this is no place for her.

Like a hawk, I circle the room in a dizzying spin that comes up empty. Desperate, I scan the bar full of hardened men. If Choir Girl is here, I need to get her the fuck out.

Going person to person? Probably the quickest way to get

my ass kicked if I rattle the wrong cage. I make my way to the bar, in the hopes that a few twenties might jog the bartender's memory. I take the nearest seat at the far corner and wait my turn.

"I'll be right with you," I hear from the other end. Her voice is angelic and sweet, and music to my fucking ears.

Bathed in relief, I exhale and text Brian.

I've got a lock. She's fine: I'll make sure she gets home safe.

Brian's text is cutthroat.

Return without her and lose your balls.

I smirk. As if I would leave her. But I'm not about to poke the bear.

Roger that.

"What are you doing here?" Jess asks as she approaches me, half-surprised, half-confused, her big blue eyes staring me down. She nibbles her lower lip, and that's the spot. The one I'm suddenly dying to taste.

Who said that?

This is Jess. My best friend's sister. His baby sister. And, for the most part, my arch-nemesis. A girl who curses the very ground I walk on.

I take a beat and breathe through the swell in my heart and the twitch in my pants. *What the hell is wrong with me?* I mentally shake myself. This is Choir Girl.

No. Just . . . no.

"What are *you* doing here?" I spit out in accusation.

Two crystal-blue eyes narrow hard. "I needed a job."

I feel a grin emerge, wide and goofy. "Well, I'm here for the asshat convention." I look around in jest. "Am I early?"

Arms folded, she blinks at me, deadpan.

Wow. Not even a smile. She really does hate me.

"You weren't answering your calls or texts. Brian was worried." So was I, but no need to bring that up now.

Regret fills her face, and she pulls her phone out of her pocket, pressing the button hard. "It must have died." Businesslike, she says, "Well, as you can see, I'm fine. What can I get you, sir?"

I huff out a laugh. *Sir.* As if she can create a professional distance between us with a sir. Jess is going to make this way harder than it has to be, and there's nothing I can do but sit back, eat every ounce of crap she slings my way, and compliment the chef.

"I just wanted to make sure you were all right and—"

Her lips purse as she shakes her head. "Sorry. This seat is for paying customers."

I swear to God, ditching her or fucking her would be easier than this shit. I mentally thrash myself about the head and shoulders with a two-by-four for even thinking the latter.

Annoyed, I grumble and check out the bar. I need to place an order because, at the moment, I'm out of options. I happen to be very attached to my balls, so there's no way I'm leaving without her. "Whatever's on tap," I reply.

A second later, a tall lager is presented before me. I admire it for a minute. Thick collar of foam. A perfect pour. I sip, blown away by the flavor.

"It's good. What is it?"

"Chocolate lager. A combination of light and sweet malt gives it a richer, nuttier flavor, with a smidge of chocolate. I recommended it a month ago, but no one listened."

I take another long, satisfying swallow and raise a brow. "You've tasted it?"

"I read about it. It's a huge trend in upscale dining. And there's a local brewer who can private label it for the restaurant. But what do I know?" She sighs and taps the bar. "That'll be three dollars when you're done."

When she walks away to deal with other customers, I plant my ass deeper in the seat. Little does she know, I'm not going anywhere.

By the time I've had two beers, a mediocre club sandwich, and a large plate of cheese fries that Jess eventually nibbles at, she's speaking to me again. More relaxed, less ax-murdery. I know her weaknesses and can feel the barbed wire slowly melting away.

Chatting with Jess like this is just . . . weird. I've known this girl all my life, but up until now, it's like I've never known her at all. I mean, beyond the whole *hate you* thing. Hell, I didn't even realize how many of Donovan's social media images were her work. Why didn't I know that? Oh, yeah, because I'm gone two years at a stretch, and whenever I'm around her, I'm a dick.

She holds up her wrist. A large, clunky watch dangles from her thin arm. "I'm having it engraved," she says, almost daydreamy. "It'll say, 'Our path may change as life goes on, but our bond is ever strong.'"

I eye the narrow links skeptically. "Will all that fit on it?"

Nodding, she shows me the clasp. "Right here. In very small print," she says, and we both laugh.

"It's a beautiful gift, Jess."

Her smile is wide and full of teeth, sporting an adorable overbite that I never get to see. "Did you just give me a compliment?"

Did I? Bring Jess a bouquet of kudos instead of a ton of shit? Wow, how times have changed.

I ignore her question and stack another compliment on the pile. Why not? I'm on a roll. "So, you got a watch and a job from the same guy? You're quite the multitasker."

She beams with a shrug. "It's just for tonight. He was shorthanded. But I can now officially say I've tended a bar."

Part of my heart squeezes. Jess should have had that at Donovan's, not here. Zac said we should give her a chance, Tyler was undecided, and I was fucking Switzerland.

Well, no longer.

An old man wheels his way behind the bar. By the tattoo on his neck, he's a Marine veteran. His chair is narrow enough to maneuver the tight space, and he does it with practiced ease.

"Thanks for filling in, kid." He hands her an envelope—probably full of cash. "You can take off. These last customers are like family. They can help themselves."

She shakes his hand. "Thanks for the opportunity, Mr. Adler. I really enjoyed it."

"Buzz," he says insistently. "Everyone calls me Buzz." He frowns. "I wish I had a regular job for you, kid."

"That's all right," I tell him. "She's got a job waiting for her in Saratoga Springs. A bartending one."

"Really?" she asks, not masking her excitement at all.

"Really," I say with a firm nod. "After you take off on a short paid vacation. Spend a few days with your brother."

Jess's star-lit eyes capture mine, and I feel it to my soul.

This girl is gorgeous, and I'm a goner. And that's not beer goggles talking. That's a little too much Jess time sinking into my heart. Regret swims through my chest. She makes me wish I were sticking around.

"Come on," I say. "Your phone is dead. You'll need a navigator. I'll lead you home."

For nearly the entire drive home, Jess's car stays at a tight distance to mine. I know she's nervous and probably has no idea where she is until we hit the familiar road past Donovan's. She passes me, waving as she mouths a thank you.

I could easily veer off at the next road and head home, but I can't. Instead, I follow Jess for forty-three minutes until she arrives safely in her driveway.

I've spent more nights in this part of the Adirondacks than I can count. And despite what Jess usually says, I can count pretty high. With no city lights to outshine the stars, the sky twinkles brightly, a sea of diamonds against a backdrop of velvet night.

Jess parks, but I keep the engine on. *This isn't a date, dumbass* I remind myself. It's just a best friend looking out for Brian's baby sis.

I roll down the window and paint on a scowl. "Bartending on a trial basis. You'll start next week."

Cocking her hip, she crosses her arms. "How long of a trial?"

I huff, feigning irritation. "I don't know. Do you think you can last more than a month without spilling chocolate milk all over the rug?"

Her smirk is adorable. "No promises." After a long beat of her standing and me staring, she breaks the silence. "You didn't have to look after me all night."

"Well, I needed to make sure you were safe." Did that sound weird? I quickly add, "Since your brother threatened my balls and all."

She nods with a soft smile before leaning down until we're suddenly face-to-face. Eye to eye. *Fuck*, any closer and we'd be mouth-to-mouth. Thunder pounds my chest, and—what the hell—are my hands sweating?

I swallow hard. "Jess—"

"I need something from you, okay?"

Frowning, I say slowly, "Okay . . ."

"I know your next mission is dangerous."

I sweep the impending danger under the rug. "As dangerous as any of them," I say with a weak shake of my head.

"Liar," she breathes, and, *fuck*, what do I do? This girl knows when I'm lying, and right now, I'm telling her the lie of all lies. Her sad blue eyes hit mine. "Look out for Brian. I can't lose him, too."

Her request hits me like a wrecking ball to the gut. I feel her parents' funeral all over again. I miss them, and it hurts, so

I can't imagine what she's going through. I need to talk to Tyler and Zac. Make sure they look after her.

Before my tightening heart makes me a basket case before her eyes, I steel my resolve. "I will. I swear. I—"

But before I can say another word, her lips press against mine. Kissing me. Choir Girl is kissing me, and it's . . . everything. With each soft caress of her sweet mouth on mine, I die. And live. Any second now, my heart will pound clear out of my chest and take flight. And don't even get me started on the relentless throb in my pants.

I feel things for Jess that I don't want to feel—that I shouldn't feel—but I can't stop feeling. And when she pulls away, it rips the oxygen from my lungs. I summon every ounce of willpower and strength not to keep her. Lock her in my arms. Never let her go.

Her words are a whisper. "It's not a blood oath, but a swear sealed with a kiss will have to do." I blink through a haze until she giggles. "I'm not getting stitches," she says jokingly.

We both laugh, and I want to kiss her again. Touch her. Taste her. Tell her . . . tell her what? In five days, Brian and I are gone. There's not a promise I can give her that's worth the breath it's spoken on.

Still, I can't leave it at that. I have to give her something in case I don't—

My voice is gruff. "Hold out your hand." She does, her smile wary as she watches with curious eyes. I reach into my shirt. "I've got one better," I say before yanking the dog tags from my neck.

She tries pushing them back. "What are you doing?"

I place them in her hand, closing her fingers around them.

"Giving you my word that I'll watch after Brian. And every time you wonder, I want you to look at these and know I've got his back." I wipe a rogue tear from her cheek and steal one last innocent kiss. "Good night, Choir Girl."

"Good night, Sharpshooter," she whispers. My nose rubs hers as she murmurs, "Watch your six."

I stare after her as she heads into the house, watching her sweet six as my little arch-enemy strolls away with my heart. I don't know where or how or when, but I know this.

That kiss was not our last. It can't be.

Or maybe that's just me, clinging to hope beyond hope that this next mission won't be the death trap we all believe it to be. That Brian and I will watch over each other and return home safe and sound.

That I'll keep my promise to Choir Girl. And maybe even earn myself another kiss.

CHAPTER FOUR

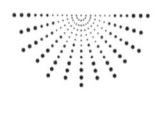

JESS

Eight years later

"What the hell?" I say, horrified.

A large box has just arrived with two dozen prosthetics. Arms. Legs. Hands and feet. It's not the prosthetics that bother me . . . it's the fact that they're here. They're supposed to be at a clinic over sixty miles away. A dozen vets of all ages are waiting for these.

So much for squeezing in a late lunch. Looks like I'll be doing a two-hour round trip to deliver them where they belong instead.

Russ Hensen pops his head into my office. He owns the building and sublets the space I'm renting. As it happens, he's been trying to kickstart his own nonprofit and always wants to pick my brain. It's tough, though, considering there's no real purpose to the nonprofit he's inventing.

His mission is sketchy, and his vision seems to shift slightly every time I ask, though the only thing he's fixed on is the dollar figure. One million dollars, I say with a mental maniacal laugh. That's the figure.

In the past year, I've been able to raise a little over thirty thousand for my venture, which barely keeps the lights on. But I have a major fundraiser coming up, and if all goes well, I might actually be able to quit one of my many part-time jobs.

I quickly put all the anatomical parts back in the box. "Oh, thank God, you're here."

On cue, he straightens his tie. "Exactly how I should be greeted. Now, start chanting my name."

I smirk at his suggestion. "Help me get this in my truck, will you?"

Skeptically, Russ examines the contents, grabbing a hand and scratching his head with it. "Sure. What's going on?"

I snatch it from his grip, careful as I set it down. "I need to rush this to the Hartford Clinic."

He hefts one side of the box as I grab the other. "But what about our date?"

Confused, I look at him. "Date?"

"You know, to go over our strategies." He motions to his backpack. "I brought all my stuff. You said we could put our heads together. Collaborate."

Of course. Collaborate. With no notice whatsoever.

Since Russ is doing most of the heavy lifting of a box that might as well be filled with lead, I don't argue. I'd be happy to help him search for grants, but it's definitely not a date.

Russ is tall, blond, and built like a linebacker. Good-looking by any standards. Persistent in a charming, *I'd be a great boyfriend* sort of way. So why can't I get into him?

Maybe it's because as much as I could use a date, I'm too busy. Or, too focused. Or too stuck on . . . the past.

Without breaking a sweat, he hoists the refrigerator of a box from my hands and places it gingerly in the bed of my truck. "So, about that date—"

I give him a small smile. "I'm sorry, Russ, but this was delivered by mistake. And between the vets and the technicians, they're waiting—"

He raises both hands in surrender. "Say no more." He opens the driver's door for me. "Get out of here and go save the universe."

I hop in. "Thanks."

The windows are down—permanently so—and as I stick the key in the ignition, I say a small prayer that the engine starts. With a rough *clunk*, it turns over and revs up. I relax with relief. "Bye, Russ."

"Bye, beautiful." Without warning, he kisses me. I'm not sure what comes over me, but I jerk back in response, a move that pinches his brow and crushes his smile.

I feel the need to apologize, but before I can get the words out, he's gone. A second later, his sleek black sportscar is a pinprick in the distance, and I'm left with my head still spinning, wondering what the hell just happened.

We aren't like that. We've never been like that.

I don't have time to decipher the mating rituals of men, or figure out why I'm completely immune to them. All I know is I have a truckful of limbs and not a lot of time. I jerk the truck into gear and drive, hopeful that no matter how colossally messed up this day starts out, it'll all be better tonight.

Three men have come to save me from my hamster wheel of overthinking. My brothers. They're all back, and I can't wait to see them.

～

"I'm here," I call out as I walk through the door of Brian's place, an hour later than I hoped to be. But a dozen grateful vets telling me how wonderful I am when I delivered the prosthetics was totally worth it.

The delicious scents of marinara and fresh breadsticks hang in the air as I take a few steps inside. Considering I'm half-starved and could eat a small child, pasta night with my brothers is a welcome alternative.

"In the kitchen," the trio calls out loudly. Brian's voice is loud and boisterous, easily drowning out Rex's and Cade's.

I ditch my coat and purse and hold tight to the chocolate ganache cake that none of them will get without a hug.

When Cade instantly goes in for the grab, I whip it away. "Hug me before I eat this all myself."

My demand is met with a shallow smirk. "That's only because you didn't make it." He gets an elbow to the gut for that one, but he laughs it off. "Besides, I'd pay good money to see you eat that entire cake."

Rex swoops it from me with one hand and pulls me into a hug with the other. "Looks like I get to have my cake and eat it, too."

"Dumbest saying ever. If you have the cake, you eat the cake. End of story," I say defiantly.

Rex's bright blue eyes are a perfect mirror of mine, though we all share variations of what Mom referred to as Bishop Blue. And his dark brown hair holds the faintest highlights of my red. I'd kill for his hair.

I muss up his shag that's at least two inches longer than normal and tug at his lumberjack scruff. "Does this mean you're sticking around?" I ask, filled with hope.

He and Brian exchange a quick glance.

"We'll see," Rex says enigmatically before shoving me over to Cade, the blond of the bunch.

Cade's power hug lifts me clear off the ground. "If you play your cards right, kiddo, we all might be sticking around through Thanksgiving."

"Really?"

"Cart before the horse," Brian says, remaining focused on the stove. He shifts his weight, adjusting to the new prosthetic. His first years back from service were a blur of surgery after surgery.

I wrap both arms around him from behind, grateful for every single day that he's here. "Spoilsport."

"That's me. Here." A wooden spoon slathered in sauce is presented over his shoulder. "What does this need?"

On cue, I take in a mouthful... and die. "*Mmm.*"

Brian chuckles. "I'll take that as it's another masterpiece and doesn't need a thing."

"It needs to be on the table already."

I drain the pasta and pour it into a bowl as Rex and Cade reach over my shoulders to pick at it.

Brian loses it. "Can you all stop acting feral for half a second and get it to the table?"

Giggling, I sneak a few noodles into my mouth. "Nope."

Cade sets two bottles of red wine in the center of the table. They're far too fancy for us, but the label makes us smile. There's a pitchfork engulfed in flames behind the words DONOVAN'S RED.

Rex grabs a mishmash of wineglasses as Cade opens a bottle. "I ran into Zac. Donovan's is expanding. He hoped you might be willing to drop by and take some shots."

My smile widens. "And you all thought nothing would come of my obsession with foodie photography."

I set a bottle next to the bread and line up a shot that fades the spaghetti behind it. After a few more candid shots of Cade pouring and us raising our glasses in a toast, Rex hogs the screen.

"Can we eat before midnight?" he says with a pout.

"Fine," I relent as we all sit down. I send Zac the candid shots while Brian fixes me a plate that's twice as big as I want. When he tops it off with not one but two perfectly grilled Italian sausages, I protest. "Hey."

"Hey, nothing. You and I both know you'll pack that away and still have room for dessert. I'm guessing you skipped lunch again."

"And breakfast," Rex says, pointing his fork at me.

It's frustrating how well my brothers know me. "This social media hustle is helping me launch the nonprofit. A few clicks here, some blog posts there, and I'm halfway to making my little veterans' support nonprofit a reality."

Brian's hand falls to mine. "Mom and Dad would be proud." Out of nowhere, he smacks my hand playfully. "But you need to eat."

"Not a problem," I say, fully prepared to dig in.

Cade points a breadstick at me. "Zac was curious why you haven't hit them up for support." When I shrink a little in my chair, he continues. "He knows you're having a pretty big fundraiser."

"I can't," I say defensively. When they all stare back, I roll my eyes. "It's hard enough asking strangers for money, but he's a Donovan. They've done so much for all of us, and Zac is already my biggest client." I shake my head. "It feels wrong to ask for anything more."

I sip the wine and hope we can move on to something else. I can't ask them for money. Not after—

Cade pipes up. "What's the big deal? You're asking for money from the entire world but not the Donovans? The wealthiest family in the area?"

Rex lifts his fork in the air. "I heard Mark alone is worth hundreds of millions of dollars." He elbows Brian. "Well?"

"Well, what?" Brian glares at him.

"Is it true?"

Brian takes a breath. "I'm one of his military strategists, not his accountant. Technically, I'm not even on his payroll directly. I'm just a consultant."

We all look around his new place, an upscale luxury condo in a tower overlooking the river. Contemporary furnishings. A computer system that probably costs more than my truck. And considering you could park said truck in his kitchen, he's now the envy of us all.

I smirk. "Lay it on me. Is"—I do air quotes—"*military strategist* code for his personal hitman?"

Brian rubs his scruff. "Maybe." He winks and hands me the grated parmesan.

I add it to my mountain of pasta. "But you're at the cross streets of Donatello Avenue and Leonardo Way. If you're not with the mob, then I'm guessing your lifelong dream of becoming a Mutant Ninja Turtle finally come true."

Brian chuckles, but his smile quickly wanes as he polishes off his wine and clears his throat. "About living here, Jess. There's something we wanted to talk with you about."

I don't like the sound of that. And I hate it even more that Cade is filling my glass to the rim.

I twirl a forkful of spaghetti endlessly on my plate. "What is it?"

Hands clasped, Brian meets my gaze. "A developer made us an offer on the land," he says carefully, and I go from zero to furious in under a second.

Heat fills my cheeks. "Don't even." I take a healthy gulp of the wine, and then another. How can they even consider selling? "This land has been in our family for generations."

"And it's a bear to maintain," Rex says, always the voice of reason and logic. I just want to shake him. "You're here all by yourself."

"I'm doing just fine," I say, raising my voice a notch. "Have I asked any of you for anything?"

Cade scoffs. "No, not even when the roof caved in. Rather than call for help, you nailed up a tarp in the hopes that, I don't know, shingles would miraculously heal themselves."

"I don't want to call you all for every little thing that breaks."

Rex points to the sky. "The roof is not a little thing."

"I can use the fresh air."

He tosses his napkin aside and doesn't hold back. "How many more things have to break before you wave the white flag? Weren't you without electricity for four days?"

I shrug. "Reminds me of our roots."

Cade leans in. "At the most, you've got one more good year before the well dries up."

Chained to my stubbornness, I double down. "If and when that day comes, what I haven't devoted to the nonprofit, I've socked away. I have almost enough now to connect to the city."

"By working four jobs," Cade says, frowning

"It's very fulfilling." And exhausting, but it'll be a cold day in hell before I admit it.

"Fine." Brian takes a controlled sip of his wine, a move that reminds me of our father. We all wait for him to speak. The oldest. A sage spirit. The voice of reason. "And when's the last time you went on a date?"

What? I flail my arms. "What does that have to do with ... anything?" Whatever fury I feel fizzles under the weight of the embarrassing truth. Fumbling for words, I mutter, "I, uh, date. I just went out last—"

His palm flies in my face. "Zac doesn't count."

He's right. I'd do anything for Zac. And he'd do anything for me. Except for sex, of course. He's more or less my fourth brother. The meddling one who nags me about dating more often than Brian does.

God, why couldn't I have sisters? This is the sort of thing

you can explain to sisters. Heat and chemistry can't be manufactured, no matter how hard you try.

"I'm building my nonprofit," I say firmly, leaning on my career like a crutch.

Irritated, Cade huffs. "You're twenty-six, not eighty-six. When you're not working, you're hiding away in the mountains like a hermit. Seriously, Jess, all you're missing is a knitting needle and about nine cats." He tosses back the rest of his wine. "Your life is slipping through your fingers. The last thing Mom and Dad would want is for this land to be a burden."

Outraged, I jump to my feet. "The land isn't a burden," I shout, my palms hitting the table. "Bishop Mountain is ours. Why am I the only one to remember that?"

Cade's voice rises to match mine. "Because we're all moving on with life while you're clinging to the past like a goddamned security blanket."

Rex places a hand on Cade's shoulder to calm him down. "It's a good offer, Jess. Cade's thinking of his future. We all are. If I leave the service, this will help. And Brian—"

"Brian would never sell," I snap back. "Would you?"

His eyes avoid mine as he helps himself to another glass. He doesn't answer. He doesn't need to. It's all so obvious.

I glare at them all. "I see. I come for what I think is a family dinner, and trip into a well-orchestrated ambush." I chug the remainder of my wine, slam the glass down, and wipe my face. "I'm. Not. Selling."

Furious, I rush out of the room as stubborn tears make their way down my cheeks. I grab my coat and reach for the door.

"Halt," Brian says in a commanding voice, military to the core.

I freeze on the spot, not wanting him to try to chase after me. But I'm not backing down. Arms folded tight over my chest, I turn around, but I don't look at him. I can't. *Traitor.*

Gently, he rests his big hands on my shoulders. I know he won't start talking until my eyes meet his. Brian has the patience of a saint, just like our dad.

When I finally come around to look at Brian, his blue eyes are darker, and the knit in his brow is hard. Still, his tone is tender.

"This isn't just about me, Rex, or Cade, Jess. Cade was a dickhead for how he said it, but he wasn't wrong. You're all by yourself up there. What if something happens? What if you're hurt? In good weather, you're forty-two minutes away from civilization, the nearest ambulance, or me." He takes a cautious breath. "Mark reviewed the proposal—"

I push him away. "So, this was Mark's idea."

"No. I asked him to review it as a favor. Jeez, what is it with you and Mark?" Brian asks with a raised brow.

"*Me* and Mark? Why would anything be between *me* and Mark?" Instantly, I regret my tone. It's snappish and defensive, and now it sounds like something *does* exist between us. "The only thing that exists between me and Mark is two hundred miles of New York distance."

"I don't know," Brian says as he rests his weight against the wall. "The mere mention of his name sets you off like fireworks under your ass. You never said what happened at the hospital when he was sent home from overseas."

What's there to say? A voluptuous blonde nurse told me he

didn't want to see me but that she'd take extra-good care of him. Then when he was discharged, he went from nearly losing his life to taking off for New York City without a word.

Brian would probably strangle Mark bare-handed if he knew about our kiss. Granted, I was the one who gave him that kiss, but he gave me his dog tags. His *dog tags*. It was significant. It meant something.

Or maybe it just meant something to me.

"Nothing happened," I say to assure Brian.

A true statement. Disappointingly true.

"This . . ." I point between the two of us. "This isn't about Mark. Or the Donovans. This is about us. Our family." By this point, I'm sobbing. "Don't do this," I choke out. "You can't."

Brian wraps a tight hug around me and kisses the top of my head. "I've spent too many restless nights worried about you all alone up there."

"You don't have to worry about me. I'm a mountain woman, raised by a brood of military brothers," I say, giggling softly through my tears.

"You're killing yourself, trying to make this work."

"But I am making it work." I wipe my face and plead with my best puppy-dog eyes. "I've saved enough to fix the roof. And Mr. Lewis is selling me his old generator."

"And what happens when vagrants and folks up to no good show up at your doorstep?"

"I'm damn handy with a shotgun."

Brian's chuckle is mild, but it's there. "That you are."

I clasp my hands around his. "Please don't evict me. It's our home."

"You're hanging on, and I get it. I miss them, too. But the

damned place is crumbling around you." He motions down the hall of his house. "The back guest room has a walk-in closet and a garden tub. It's all yours, Jess. This could be your home. At least until you find what you want."

I smile. It's a hell of a consolation prize. I don't even want to tell him how I've had to take baths because the shower stopped working months ago.

"This is a beautiful place, Brian. But it's not my home. I need fresh air and views of the lake. Trails I can run blindfolded because I've skipped down them since I could walk. I want the fireside where Dad taught me how to make a s'more and Mom taught me to sing." I reach up and cup Brian's cheeks. "I have a home. Don't take it away from me. Not yet." My breath shudders. "I need to hold on to Mom and Dad just a little longer."

His head shakes slowly. "Jess—"

"Not forever," I say quickly. "Just a little longer."

Brian's growl is playful. I smile, knowing I've worn him down.

He pins me with a squint. "If you swear on a stack of bibles that when the next thing goes wrong—anything that puts you in harm's way—we sell. Deal?" He holds out his big hand, anticipating mine.

With no room to negotiate, I shake on it, determined that nothing else can go wrong. "Deal."

He yanks me into a hard hug. "Now, go to the bathroom, take all the time you need cleaning up your face and doing whatever the hell girls do in bathrooms, and come back prepared to polish off your tower of pasta and eat a quarter of a cake."

He's trying to make me smile, so I do. A little. Brian shoves me off to the bathroom.

I close the door and don't even bother with the mirror. Instead, I sink to the floor, my back against the wall, and set free every last tear as I feel my parents being ripped away from me all over again.

CHAPTER FIVE

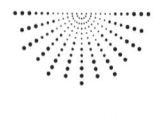

MARK

Two knocks sound at the door. Before I can say anything at all, two men barge in.

Lance Anders, Esquire, my lead attorney, rushes to my desk ahead of Dean Emmerson, my chief financial officer. Seeing them in custom-tailored suits with near-matching blue-striped ties, I have to laugh.

"Did you two call each other this morning to coordinate outfits?"

They do a quick once-over of each other, and Lance scoffs. "What can I say? The man has impeccable taste."

Dean nods to accept the compliment, then dumps three newspapers on my desk.

I stare up at him. "Is it crossword puzzle day at The Centurion Group?"

"No," Dean says, almost cooing. "It's Pick Your Arm Candy Day, Mr. CEO."

"My what?" I ask as Lance fans the papers across my desk.

Dean takes a seat and points his steepled fingers at me.

"With the initial public offering in less than two months, the more we can do to rally stock interest, the better."

Lance lifts a brow. "We all need to do our part, *PlayerMark-Donovan*, and that includes you."

Annoyed, I glare. He knows I hate that fucking hashtag.

He ignores me. "Our last hundred-million-dollar deal for The Centurion Group barely made a blip in the headlines. But every time a bachelor billionaire is spotted with a woman, the media go into a frenzy."

"Multimillionaire," I say, automatically correcting him.

"Close enough." Lance points to the first paper. "Here you are spotted in Ibiza with a supermodel."

Agitated, I huff. "She crashed a private party I was invited to and snapped a selfie. We were not on a date."

He ignores me. "The point is her Instagram got forty thousand likes, and our sales went through the roof."

I roll my eyes.

Dean grabs the second paper and holds it up to my face. "Exhibit B," he says.

It's a shot of me with Ariana Farer, a wealthy socialite who offered to snort a line of cocaine off my dick and then suck it clean. After I politely passed, she snapped a shot of us and sold it to the media. But by the look on Dean's face, relaying this would do no good. All he can see are dollar signs.

"When she announced your status as a couple, we gained ten percent. In one day."

Seeing where this is going, I pinch the bridge of my nose. "Your point?" I say, rolling two fingers in the air, insisting they move it along.

Lance drops a folder on my desk and opens it. There are

two photographs of women, both equally beautiful, both vaguely familiar. "Pick," he says with too much enthusiasm for eight o'clock in the morning.

"Aren't you supposed to blindfold me, hand me a tail, and spin me around?"

Lance points to the brunette with pale lips and a minimal smile. "This one is an activist. Well-traveled. Speaks four languages. And she doles out more money on global policy than the Gates Foundation. She's looking for a mutual partnership and has more than twelve million followers worldwide."

I give him a droll look. "What's wrong with her?"

He shrugs impishly. "She might be overcoming a small scandal."

Wide-eyed, I snap my fingers. "I recognize her. The woman who was all over the news for fucking a senator backstage while his daughter performed 'Somewhere Over the Rainbow' and his wife sat in the audience with their newborn. Didn't the media dub her *The Catastrophe?*"

Dean shakes his head. "No, it was *The Dumpster Fire*. Because they set off the fire alarm. But," he holds up a finger, "her followers doubled overnight."

I shake my head. "How about we avoid homewreckers outright? Next."

Dean taps his finger on the second photo. The woman is blonde, with plump red lips and enormous breasts that look as real as an iceberg off the shores of Turks and Caicos.

"My vote is for this one." His smile widens. "With twenty million followers and a family net worth that rivals several countries in Europe, she's a cash catapult. She's an influencer who's invited to everything from club openings to Broadway shows."

I give the image a scrutinizing glare. "Where do I know her from?"

"You might recall her viral video," Dean says.

I stare back.

"TikTok," Lance says, as if that would mean anything at all to me.

The last time I saw a TikTok, it was a video of Choir Girl singing her heart out to a bunch of vets at some fundraiser. What was that? Six years ago? Seven?

Annoyed, I blink, which prompts Lance to continue.

"She was in a bikini, wearing the captain's hat. You can hear him banging at the door in the background, demanding to be let in." He winces behind his smile. "She crashed her father's yacht right into the dock."

Dean clucks his tongue, with pity in the shake of his head. "Such a pretty yacht, too."

"But," Lance taps his finger on the page, "no one was hurt."

By this point, I'm done. I collect the papers and sweep them from my desk, dumping them into the trash. Satisfied, I beam from ear to ear. "Decision made. Anything else?"

Both men frown at me as if I just shut off the Super Bowl before the end of the game.

"I'll take that as a no."

My cell phone rings. The name *Badass* lights up the screen as "Macho Man" by the Village People blares loudly. Fucker's been messing with my phone. But he's saving me from matchmaking hell, so he gets a pass.

Stone-faced, I dismiss them with, "I really need to take this."

As Lance and Dean march from the room, I answer. "What's up, Brian? Or should I say, *Badass?*"

A hearty chuckle fills the phone. "When tech giants leave their phones unlocked, they suffer the consequences. Hopefully, I wasn't interrupting anything important."

"Just Lance and Dean concocting some asinine plan to jettison our IPO." I click it to speakerphone and walk over to the window, looking out on the gray stacks of Lego towers below me—Manhattan in all its glory. "Let me guess. Jess hated the proposal."

"Hate is a strong word."

"Is it?" I pocket my hands. "Did she kick each of you in the balls as I predicted?"

"No," he says defensively. "She was very civilized. At least, once I got her away from Cade the moron."

"Did you at least give her a bite of food before you ambushed her?"

"Two bites. And some fine Donovan wine."

I blow out a frustrated breath. "How many times do I have to tell you? If you want to stay on Jess's good side, don't attack when she's hangry."

He chuckles. "You would know."

I smile when he says that. He's right. No one could push Jess's buttons like I could. As she could mine.

Damn, what is it about her? I haven't seen her in years; she abandoned me in my time of need, and just the mention of her has me grinning like a loon.

Fuck, I need to get laid.

"So, the offer is killed?" I ask.

"This one is, but there will be more. I made her a deal. The next catastrophe that happens at the property, and we're out."

"She agreed to that?" I rub my chin. "Seems too mild of an exit for her."

"You'd be surprised. Her red hair and temper have really tamed down since you last saw her."

I laugh out loud. "The lies."

He laughs, too. "You're right. Her red hair still heats her to the core."

Jesus, I'll bet it does.

I grab my phone, tempted as I always am to take a look at today's version of Jessica Bishop. And then something stops me. I don't know if it's pain or sadness, anger or rage, but I do what I always do. I set the phone back down.

"Jess knows what's coming," Brian says. "She's not avoiding the inevitable, just prolonging it. If she gets one last Christmas there, maybe she can finally let go of the past and live a little."

Live a little? Jess is, what, twenty-five? Twenty-six? Fuck, why isn't she living a lot? Choir Girl needs to live it up.

I catch a glance at my reflection in the window. A scowl of judgment glares back at me. I'm at the cusp of being a billionaire. If anyone should be living it up, it should be me.

I turn away. I have my excuses. Choir Girl has none.

Checking out the calendar, I make an executive decision. "Hey, with the holidays coming up, why don't you stay off the grid?"

"Huh? I work virtually. My life is on the grid."

"Not today," I say. "It's time you had an all-expenses-paid

vacation. Through Christmas. We'll hit the ground hard and heavy the last week of December."

"But the IPO—"

"I've got a million guys working the IPO. You should spend some time with Jess. If this really is her last Christmas up there, she shouldn't be there alone."

"Thanks," he says before hitting me with, "And what about you?"

"What about me?"

"You haven't been home in years."

"Hello? Important CEO with an initial public offering coming up."

"You said it yourself. You've got a million people working on it. Your family would lose their damn minds if you dropped in. It would be great to have you back here. The festival is coming up..."

Brian goes on and on about fall cookouts and bonfires, while I stare off into a steel city of cold skyscrapers.

"And Jess has this charity event—"

"Sounds great," I say automatically, my voice distant and unengaged.

"Seriously?" His tone perks up. "You're coming?"

Wait. What? No. I—

"God, if I could have one more day with my folks," Brian says with heartfelt emotion, and a solid gut punch of guilt hits me hard.

Here Jess is, hanging on to every sentimental shred of their parents, while I push mine aside, year after year.

Brian roars with delight. "Your parents will freak the fuck out when they see you. Hell, how long has it been?"

I puff air into my cheeks. "I don't know." Which is a lie because I know exactly how long it's been. Nearly eight years, almost to the day . . . the day I left the hospital.

"I'm sure your family will insist on putting you up, but as I'm now going to be crashing with my little sis, you're welcome to stay here. Not a preppy-boy penthouse, but it's all yours if you need it."

I hadn't even thought about a place to stay. Mom and Dad will have every bedroom filled with aunts, uncles, cousins, and kids. And the last thing I need is to share a bunkbed with a kid who will badger me endlessly about my morning wood. It doesn't matter that it happened a decade ago. I consider myself permanently scarred.

Never again.

"Sounds like a plan."

CHAPTER SIX

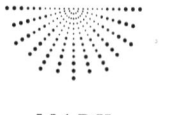

MARK

"You look ridiculous," Zac says with disapproval. I've been in Saratoga Springs for exactly one hour, and he's already busting my balls.

I push the dark glasses farther up my nose as we head up a busy street toward the restaurant. I wanted to take in everything. Breathe the air. Incognito, of course.

"I don't want to be recognized. I know you're going to find this hard to believe, but women always want something from me. For once, I want to walk down the street, free of selfies and claw marks."

He rolls his eyes. "I'm not sure why. It's not like you're good at making women happy."

I stop in my tracks. "Meaning?"

Zac huffs. "Meaning that you tend to use women like tissues. Grab them when you need them and toss them out when you're done."

I grab my heart. "Harsh."

"Yet true."

I kick a small pebble along the cobblestone path. "It works both ways. Women use me as much as I use them. It's not as if *the one* has come along."

Amused, he scoffs. "How would you know?"

The darkness in my chest brightens for a second, and the softness of the memory of a kiss breezes through my mind.

"Because I do," I tell him as I take a casual glance around. When a group of passersby makes their way around us, I shift my ball cap, lowering it to cover my face.

Zac whips off my cap and tosses it into a tree. "You're home, butthead. You can relax."

I wrinkle my nose and think about it for a minute. Maybe he's right. "You really think so?"

"This isn't New York City. Here, you're just an average schmuck. Trust me, no one here wants anything from you. I'd bet my car on it."

Considering he drives the latest Ferrari Spider, I take that bet. I tug off my sunglasses and place them on top of my head.

Instantly, I hear, "Mark? Mark Donovan, is that you?"

Zac shrugs with a smile.

I cringe and slowly turn around. I know better than to flee from fans. Enough people caught me on video a while back when I tripped off the curb into traffic and almost got plowed over by a cab. I nearly lost my life, while Dean played the viral video of it on repeat for months. *Bastard*.

I turn around. I'm face-to-face with an older woman with tight silvery-gray curled hair, her apron covered in flour.

Relieved, I smile. "Mrs. Haverty. Hello."

Memories of cold winter days flood my mind. Mrs. Haverty always welcomed us into her bakery with warm cocoa and a cookie each. She's been the Donovan's restaurant baked-goods supplier for years.

She wraps a warm hug around me, and I gladly reciprocate. "Your mom didn't tell me you were in town."

"It's a surprise. We're just making our way there now."

"Oh." Mrs. Haverty frowns.

"What is it?"

"I need to get a large cake to Saint Andrews, but my delivery man called out sick. I know it's in the opposite direction, but the church is only three blocks away, so I was wondering if you and Zacky could—"

I hold up a hand. "Say no more. We'd be happy to."

Relief lifts her smile as she leads us into her shop.

I elbow my brother in the ribs as I mutter, "You can sign over the car anytime."

"What?" he asks, feigning confusion.

I wave my hand toward Mrs. Haverty as she disappears into her shop. "I told you," I say with a smirk. "Women always want something from me."

He narrows his eyes. "If she leaves a single claw mark, my car is yours."

I smack him in the gut. "The day is young."

We file into her shop and willingly take a cookie as we strategize. The cake is a tower, though not horribly wide. Her absentee driver uses his own van, and any suggestion of this buttercream nightmare going anywhere near Zac's car instantly earns me a death glare.

I wheel a large cart from the corner. It's sturdy. Industrial strength. "I think this will work if we go very slowly. It's only a few blocks up."

Mrs. Haverty claps her hands and jumps in place. When she kisses my cheek, I snicker at Zac.

"See, I can make a woman happy."

She hands us each a flyer. "Drop by my booth at the fair tomorrow, and you can have one pie each."

Zac and I give her a hug and stuff the flyers in our pockets.

Carefully, we roll the cart down the street as the light foot traffic parts to give us plenty of space. Stepping back into my old life feels good. Feels almost like myself. No racing pulse. No jitters. Just the crisp air filling my lungs and a sense of pride into helping out.

The minute we round the corner to Saint Andrews, my ears perk up, and I freeze.

Zac snorts out a laugh. "Don't tell me. Leg cramp, old man?"

"*Shhh.*" I press a finger to my lips.

The song is beautiful, and the voice, haunting and familiar. An Adele song, "Make You Feel My Love." The way that she sings it tugs at my chest. I know the woman singing, perhaps better than I should. She's not singing to an audience. She's singing to her parents.

Her voice comes from an open window in the church. I'd bet she thinks she's alone.

Zac whispers in earnest, "Can we drop this off already? I'm starving and two minutes from taking a big, fat bite out of this cake."

"See if the back door is unlocked," I whisper. "I don't want to interrupt her."

"Her?"

"Choir Girl."

Zac's forehead furrows hard. "Who?"

"Jess."

Unamused, he raises his brows. "Why? Is there something going on with you and Jess?"

"No." My response is quick. Too quick.

He narrows his eyes, hard. "Listen up, asshole. You want a fuck-girl, get one in New York."

Now I'm the one darting an angry glare. "Is something going on between *you* and Jess?" I ask, pointing a finger at his chest.

"No," he says flatly. "Jess and I agreed eons ago it wasn't like that with us, no matter how cute wedding invitations with ZAC AND JESS would look." He props his hands on his hips. "But she's a good friend and a good person. She needs someone to take care of her, not some player to fuck with her head."

Why do people keep calling me that?

I cross my arms. "I am not a player."

Zac scoffs. "The headlines say otherwise." When I roll my eyes, he glares at me. "Try me, butthead, and I'll take Jess up on her promise."

I huff. "What promise?"

"That when she turns thirty, if neither of us is married, I'd buy her the biggest, fattest diamond and marry her."

What the fuck?

I wave my hands like a madman. "You don't even like her. Not like that. Not in a wifey way. You said so yourself."

He shrugs sadistically. "It doesn't matter. We have enough in common to make the perfect match."

"Are you forgetting that neither of you has the faintest

attraction to each other? If you did, you probably would have married her in the tenth grade."

My brother gives me a patronizing grin. "It's called a marriage of convenience for a reason. We'll support each other the way we always have. Fully. Non-judgmentally. Mom and Dad adore her, and her brothers are practically family already." He leans in. "Mom's always said we'd make the cutest fucking couple."

I shove the cart at him and nearly rack him in the balls. "Oh, I'm sorry . . . did I almost smash your balls like an accordion? The cart must have slipped." I smirk.

He smiles obnoxiously, but at least his big mouth stays shut.

We make our way down the church's corridor and to the kitchen. The place is clean and well-kept, and except for some modern computers, it hasn't changed at all. A bleached-blonde walks in wearing a tight-fitting sweater that shows off her midriff.

Zac and I exchange a glance.

She looks down her nose at us. "You'd better not have messed it up. The bride paid a gazillion dollars for it, and it had better be perfect."

"No one wants to ruffle Bridezilla's feathers," Zac says with an eye roll.

"The bride?" I ask, unsettled. "Is that the woman who was singing?"

"What?" The blonde scoffs. "God, no."

I relax, though I'm not sure why. Jess was the one who abandoned me.

The woman elaborates. "That's the cleaning lady. At least, that's what she's doing today."

I tilt my head in curiosity. "What do you mean?"

"She's always begging for work. The word is she'll do anything for a buck. Says she's trying to start a charity. Pathetic," she says as she swipes a finger along the icing at the base of the cake. "Today, she was crying." Her tone is judgmental as she licks her finger clean. "What kind of loser does that? Cries for no reason?"

"She was probably lamenting your mother's poor choice in birth control," I huff under my breath, annoyed.

"Hey." The girl points her wet finger my way, and I cringe. "Don't I know you?"

Oh God. Here we go. I slip on my sunglasses. "No."

She gasps and covers her mouth. "You're that guy. The one who was in the hospital for, like, forever, and then became rich." Her eyes turn bright with excitement. She smacks my shoulder before clasping her hands over her chest. "Oh my God. I saved your life."

My face falls. "Excuse me?"

"I mean, the surgeons did their part, but I was your nurse." She leans in, reeking of menthol cigarettes. "I gave you a sponge bath when you were weak and frail."

Zac smothers a laugh.

Horrified, I back up. "I must have blocked it out."

"With the elephant tranquilizers they had you on, I'll bet." She snorts, laughing as I make hasty steps for the door. "Where are you going?" she asks, pouting as she blocks my path. "You could be my date for the wedding."

Not even if Jesus Christ himself was officiating.

"Sorry, I'm unavailable."

She pins me against a wall, aggressive like a she-hulk. "You can't be upset about Jeff."

By this point, Zac silently howls with laughter.

I try squeezing around her without touching her breasts. "Who?"

"Jeff. The guy you kept calling for when I nursed you back to health."

God, this woman is psycho.

When her hands press against my chest, the gloves are off. I grab her by the upper arms and plant her to the side of me.

"I kept everyone else away," she calls out as I bolt. Even from the hall, her voice carries. "It's not my fault Jeff never showed up."

Zac and I race away.

"Who's Jeff?" he asks.

Stunned, I halt in mid-step. "Holy fucking shit," I mutter, then rush back.

Behind me, Zac roars hysterically. "Holy crap. You're going back for seconds? Fuck, I need to get this on video."

I race into the room to find the woman smoking a cigarette, snapping selfies with the cake. "I said I didn't want to see anyone?"

She flicks a few cigarette ashes on the cake. "Uh-huh."

"But I was asking for Jeff."

"Yes," she says, stepping into my space.

"Could I have said *Jess*?"

When she shrugs, my face falls into my hands.

She moves on. "The wedding starts at six."

I look up, appalled to watch her snapping half a dozen selfies. *With me.*

Goddammit.

I reach for her phone, but she shoves it down her blouse. Stunned, I stare. *There's not enough hand sanitizer in the world . . .*

"I'll give you a thousand bucks to delete every last photo."

"One thousand dollars? Try ten, rich boy." Something inside me snaps because I'm seriously considering it until she adds, "For fifteen, I'll take it off of Insta."

Instagram? "Are you fucking kidding me?" I shout.

"Keep your voice down," she says, shushing me. "We're in a church." She frowns as her cigarette is once again flicked on the top tier of the cake . . . as if it were a fucking ashtray.

I hear a series of sounds erupt from her breasts—an onslaught of horrifying pings that mean people are liking her post.

I pinch the bridge of my nose. "What hashtags did you use?"

"#WeddingDate. #PlayerMarkDonovan." She beams with sadistic pride.

I try and fail to laser her into a million points of ash with my mind. When a dozen more pings hit the air, I storm off to avoid wringing her neck.

CHAPTER SEVEN

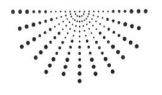

MARK

"Welcome home," Mom says, squeezing me within an inch of my life. She hugs Zac next but quickly returns to muss up my hair. It manages to make me smile. Sternly, she pinches my cheek. "Do not stay away that long ever again, mister."

"Yes, ma'am," I say as she stares up at me. Her dark hair is in a messy bun at her nape, and her smile is infectious. When tears well in her eyes, I know coming home was the right decision.

My dad's hand lands on my shoulder. "Now you've done it," he says jokingly. "Your mother is getting emotional. Look out. I see a feast in your future."

She bats his chest playfully and pinches her fingers together. "Perhaps just a little one."

They lead me into a home where, with the exception of newer furnishings and an updated kitchen, nothing has changed. Everywhere I turn, the walls are lined with photographs of our family, and the lingering scent of vanilla comforts me more than I can explain.

Zac gives my mom two dozen roses we picked up in town as I hand each of them a box. "Don't open these. They're for Christmas," I say, straight-faced.

Mom's shoulders sink hard. "Christmas? That's weeks and weeks away." She shakes the gold gift-wrapped box. "This gift won't make it that long."

"Fine," I say, feigning exhaustion with a huff. "Go ahead. Open them."

For Mom, I got an original collection of recipes from famous hotels across Manhattan. They're all handwritten by the chefs, and if they invented the recipe, their signatures are on the bottom.

She fans through the cards in a rush. "Ooh, this one." She holds up the iconic Waldorf Astoria Red Velvet Cake. "I'm doing this one."

Dad opens a hand-carved wooden box. Across the top, DONOVAN is inlaid beneath a sword, a serpent, a shield, and a coat of arms—the original Irish Donovan family crest. Since his 23&Me test, he's become obsessed with our ancestry.

"It's for fishing tackle," I tell him.

"Nonsense," he says with a laugh. "I'm filling it with cigars. You know, in case there's something to celebrate." He looks at me expectantly, and so does Mom. "Something you want to share, son?"

I hesitate, feeling like it's a trick question.

Mom pulls up her phone. "Who's your wedding date?" she asks and shows me Menthol's Instagram.

For fuck's sake. "She is not my wedding date."

Confused, Mom looks at the phone. "But you look so happy together."

"They do look happy," Zac says, laughing.

I threaten to kick the shit out of him by just narrowing my eyes.

Zac takes a closer look at the caption. "Apparently, *PlayerMarkDonovan* is on the prowl. Twenty thousand likes."

"What?" I snatch the phone, dismayed at the train wreck in progress.

"Well," Mom says, "I'm guessing playboying works up an appetite."

"I'm not a playboy, and *playboying* is not a word," I say, correcting her.

She loops an arm around my waist. "Come on. I'll rustle us up some lunch while you tell me all about your social media scandals."

"You sound way too excited about this." I lay an arm across her shoulders, squeezing her against me. "I'm not a soap opera."

Zac pats my back. "You are today."

CHAPTER EIGHT

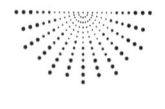

JESS

The light casts shadows along the wall as I lie awake in the darkness. I've seen the shape of a puppy. A cow. Fairies. I imagine the fairies are helping me keep that damn tarp in place.

It lets in a dewy breeze. Shivering, I tug the quilt higher against my chin.

It's past two in the morning, and I'm no more tired than I was when I lay down an hour ago. I should be exhausted, but I'm wide awake. Mostly because Brian's snoring rattles the walls like the subway. But also because I thought I saw Mark today, which is impossible.

And it wasn't like I saw his face. The man storming from the church wore dark glasses—I couldn't really tell who he was. But there was something about his broody jaw. It was squared and hard, and his dark scruff made me want to cup it. Feel it. Maybe rub my thighs along it.

Stop it.

Frustrated, I throw an arm over my head. *What's wrong with me?*

Hmm, let me make a list.

I'm burning the candle at both ends and searching for more matches.
I believe I can change the world with a nonprofit organization that has no resources and gnats' chance at survival.
I'm using duct tape and rubber bands to hold a hundred-year-old house together.
I work myself to exhaustion and still can't sleep.
I'm obsessed with a man who doesn't know I exist.

I toss and turn and give up on sleep entirely as I reach for my phone. There was a wedding at the church today. Not for anyone I know, but it gave the church an excuse to hire me again. Every penny counts, right? All I have to do is fix the roof and adopt nine cats, and maybe my brothers will leave me alone already.

I search for images of the wedding. The bride is Ann Jenson. I don't know her at all, but she looks beautiful. I do know that her family spent a fortune on flowers, and don't even get me started on the cake.

It was nearly as tall as me. I know because I sneaked a peek.

A gorgeous cascade of buttercream peonies and roses, it was divine. There was even some trendy glitter on the top that was probably chopped and shredded hundred-dollar bills. Yeah, it was that kind of cake.

I stalk the church's Instagram. Gorgeous people in candid shots, without a care in the world. I stop at a photo of a man in dark glasses and a face full of scruff. The man from the church is with that woman. The nurse who never leaves home without a cloud of menthol-smelling smoke. The one who shooed me away from Mark's hospital room all those years ago.

I snap to a seated position and flip on the light so I can look closer. Is that Mark? He's a little out of focus, though the tower of buttercream cake is crisp. I rub my eyes and zoom in. It's too hard to tell.

Then I read the caption.

#WeddingDate #PlayerMarkDonovan
What the fuck?

I screw up my face, angry at him and her, and at the world, for that matter. But mostly at myself for being an idiot. All these years, I've been holding on to some inkling of hope that there had to be feelings between us. Some . . . spark.

I tug at the chain around my neck. My security blanket. My leash. My fingers feel each letter of his name stamped into the steel. MARCUS E. DONOVAN.

My secret obsession.

For years, he's been a nagging little wound over my heart. It never heals, and I never want it to. I want to see it. I want to feel it.

Obviously, I have issues. The only feelings Mark had were for the overinflated assets of his ever-diligent nurse.

Argh . . .

With an angry huff, I scroll through my phone and stop at

the last text message I received. It's from Russ Hensen. He sent it last night.

> *Let's do coffee? Swap notes.*
> *Drop by anytime.*

I haven't responded to him at all lately. But then I think of Mark lip-locked with Nurse Ratched, and all the grief my brothers have given me about holing up like a hermit, and I do the unthinkable.

I reply.

> *I'm working at the fair all day.*
> *Drop by anytime.*

CHAPTER NINE

MARK

*A*t five in the morning, my phone lights up like the Fourth of July. Lance is the first to have a fucking freakout. Thankfully, it's via text.

#PlayerMarkDonovan? WTF???

I wipe a hand down my face and text him back.

I did not go out with her.

My phone rings. I answer and have to hold the phone an arm's length away.

"Well, your little *wedding date* has notified three major magazines that, for the right price, she has a scoop for them." His voice ratchets up a notch. "This is not an IPO-worthy date."

I growl. "Can you at least wait until I've had a shower and a cup of coffee?"

"No."

"Fine." I sit up and throw my legs over the side of the bed. "I don't know her. I looked up. She snapped a shot. End of story."

"Really?" he spits out. "So, everything she says is a fabrication?"

"Yes."

"Total lies."

"One thousand percent."

"I see. So, her stories about her rescuing you from the brink of death eight years ago are completely unfounded? Sponge baths and a tattoo in the shape of—what did she say? A Hello Kitty?"

Furious, I jump to my feet.

"Oh, for fuck's sake. She may have been working at the hospital back then, but considering I was actually on the brink of death and heavily medicated, I don't exactly recall. And I swear on a stack of bibles and my mother's blue-ribbon lasagna that I never dated her. Hell, I don't even know her name. And what the fuck? Do I look like the kind of guy who would have a Hello Kitty tattoo on me? It's a skull with two rifles behind it. I was a sniper, remember?"

There's a long pause. "I might be able to fix it for you."

Since the bastard never does anything for free, I rake a hand through my hair and brace for impact. "And what do you want in exchange for your selfless act of good Samaritanism?"

"Good, powerful publicity. In the form of a real date. With one of the women we showed you yesterday."

"I can't," I say, making any excuse to get out of this. "I'm back home through Christmas."

"Not a problem. She'll come to you. Meet you anywhere, anytime."

God, I hate Lance's motherfucking hardball. "She gets an hour."

"It will take her twice as long just to get glammed up. Two hours before you're paroled. She gets all the selfies she wants, and you get a skyrocketing IPO."

"Two hours? And you make psycho nurse go away?"

"So, will it be the Dumpster Fire or the Yacht Destroyer? Take your pick."

I blow out a breath. I really need this nightmare nurse to go away. My family already thinks I have the worst taste in women. And what if I ran into Jess? I shake my head. What if Jess really had turned up and was turned away because she wasn't *Jeff*?

"Fine," I say through gritted teeth. "Does Yacht Destroyer have a name?"

"Brie. Brie Withington, of the Long Island Withingtons."

I look to the ceiling and pray for a lightning bolt.

"Where will you take her?" Lance asks. "I'll send you a list of her preferences."

"Her what?"

"You know. Her food, wine, and water preferences."

I laugh. "Did you say water preferences? Because, to be clear, whether she eats or drinks is her decision. I'm not going out of my way." The flyer Mrs. Haverty gave me stares up from the nightstand—a beacon of hope. "Tell Cream Cheese to leave her heels at home. For two hours, we're going to the fair."

Lance audibly chokes. "Her name is Brie, and you can't be serious."

"As a heart attack. Nothing stinks up a pair of Louboutins like a cow pie. Now, I'll send the address. You arrange for her transportation. One p.m. to three p.m. on the nose. After which, little Miss Trust Fund goes back home. Hopefully, in that time, she'll get all the likes, fans, thumbs-ups, or fucking whatevers to make you happy."

"But—"

"But nothing, Lance. And I want that nurse's stuff down today."

I can almost hear his teeth gnash. "Consider it done," he says before disconnecting the call.

I look around. Brian's place is neat as a pin, with several thriller and suspense books stacked on his desk. I notice a picture of the four of them—Brian, Rex, Cade, and Jess, front and center. She had to be nineteen—maybe twenty.

I look closer. *Is that my chain around her neck?*

After a good, hard stare, I shake my head. It has to be a shadow.

Next to the frame is Brian's old watch. I hold it sentimentally and flip it over.

Our path may change as life goes on, but our bond is ever strong.

The day Jess first showed me this watch was the last day I saw her. Unless Brian said something to her, which I doubt, she'll never know its true value.

I look at it again, wondering why he isn't wearing it. It's scuffed but works. Is it because he's with Jess, and he doesn't want it to upset her?

I look again at the photo. At Jess. She's like a depraved pastime I'm ashamed to admit to. I shrug it off as her picture stares back at me. Why should I be ashamed?

Oh, maybe because she's young. Or my best friend's little sister. Or because I've beat off more times than I can count to the thought of her lips wrapped around my dick.

Fuck.

I wipe a hand down my face. I need Choir Girl out of my system. I set down the photo and come up with a plan. I've dreamed up a million ways to get over her. Over her lips and that kiss. Now, it's time to move on.

My phone pings with a text.

Brie will be on-site at 1:00 p.m. on the nose.

**Sending pic and digits.
She insisted.**

He sends me her phone number and the picture of a blonde bombshell with tits up to her eyeballs and legs that go on for days. She's suggestively licking a banana.

I look down at my dick.

Nothing.

"Nothing?" I suck in a breath, offended. I hold the image to my crotch. "This is a sure thing. A voluptuous trust-fund vixen with sex on her mind and followers out her firm, round ass. She will let you do dirty, nasty things to her all while tripling your IPO. Learn to like her."

Again, nothing. The fucker is playing possum.

I take a good, long look at Choir Girl. Instantly, I get an image of her mouth on mine and her skin bare of everything except my dog tags.

My jaw clenches, my pulse thrums, and my dick is as hard as a titanium missile.

Frustrated, I pocket my phone and throw back my head.

I'm so fucked.

∽

The fair is alive with loud music, kids' laughter, and vendors selling everything from roasted corn on the cob to deep-fried sticks of butter, which taste better than they sound. My arteries will curse me tomorrow.

Brie clings to my arm for dear life because, despite my warnings, she's in six-inch heels. After the third person recognizes me, I buy the first ball cap I find. FAIR HAIR, DON'T CARE, GET ME A BEER is embroidered across the top, but it'll do since Zac got rid of my favorite one. *Bastard.*

I slide on my sunglasses as we make our way to the games.

"Oh, I want one." Brie points excitedly at a small stuffed animal at a shooting gallery.

Amused, I lead her over. I never thought I'd use my Special Forces sniper training again.

I pick up the toy rifle and gauge its weight. It's light and feels like a Nerf gun in my hands. I stick the butt of it into my shoulder. The sights are old school, and the alignment blurs in my vision.

Or is that me?

I shake it off. A row of downrange duckies moves at varying speeds. This time, I dig the weapon in deeper as pain sears my shoulder. I don't care what the shrinks say. After four shoulder surgeries, I can still feel the pins. It's not in my fucking head.

Sweat beads on my brow, and as soon as my finger slides onto the trigger, my hands go numb.

Make the shot. Make the shot. Make the fucking shot.

I don't remember my finger squeezing the trigger. Still, I jolt, anticipating a crack in the air that never happens.

The duckies keep rolling on the conveyor belt. Not one of their little yellow bodies falls back. Not a single one. And it doesn't matter. A sheen of sweat forms on my neck and face, and all I can do is stand there.

Someone removes the rifle from my grip. Gentle strokes are on my hand. It's enough to blink me back to the present.

A cat woman stares back at me. "You okay?" she whispers.

Her voice is soft and compassionate, and it stings like a slap. Is she pitying me?

I look her up and down, then glare at her. She's wearing another enviable ball cap—HOT MESS—DOING MY BEST prominently displayed across the top. Should I tell her she's failing miserably? How about a gun that actually works?

Her hair is pulled beneath it, and bright carnival paint covers every square inch of her face. A pink cat nose and black whiskers are accented with bright red hearts covering her cheeks like a drug rash, and her eyes are hidden behind dark oversized glasses. If anyone needs pity...

Her hand rests on my skin, her touch burning like ice. I whip back my hand and clear my throat.

"Why wouldn't I be okay?" I ask, annoyed. "Oh, I know why. The game is obviously rigged."

She takes a step back, her sweet expression souring. "No, it's not," she says, her voice lowering to a kitten growl as she gestures to my hat. "Maybe you've had one too many."

The nerve of this woman.

Brie rubs my arm and chest, as if mauling me is the solution. "Aw, baby, you gonna try again? I really want that cute, little elephant. It reminds me of you."

It what? Obviously, she's never seen a grown man's trunk.

Brie's body presses against mine as her bust spills over. Which I barely notice. I'm too busy inspecting the alignment of this worthless kiddie gun.

Without warning, she jumps up and down excitedly, nearly taking my eye out with one of her breasts as she squeals, "Popcorn!"

The popcorn does smell good. And I am hungry.

No, no, no, no, no.

There is zero chance I'm leaving here without knocking down one of those fucking baby ducks. I empty my wallet, handing her a thousand dollars in cash.

"Here." I shoo her off. "The sky's the limit. Eat popcorn. Ride some rides. Buy shit. Enjoy."

Brie wraps both arms around my neck and plants a kiss on my cheek as she shoves the hundreds into her cleavage—a vast crevasse so deep, I doubt she'll find it all again without breadcrumbs and a treasure map.

Her teeth graze my ear. "Thanks, hot shot."

Oh, Jesus Christ, just go away already.

Brie finally leaves as I make stern faces at the gun.

I look up to find cat woman making herself busy clipping stuffed animals high overhead. Her white T-shirt is wrapped in a light-pink sweater as the rest of her body pours into a pair of body-formed jeans.

When her back arches, it pushes her tantalizing breasts outward. A pair of perky nipples outline the stretch of fabric, and my dick takes notice.

Hallelujah, it actually works for someone other than Choir Girl.

Her hair swings from a thick ponytail that trails down her back. Dark amber. I adjust in my pants. I'm rock-hard. The damn thing can sniff out a redhead like a drug dog zeroes in on coke.

I'm ogling her like a sex-starved creeper, while she's barely aware of my presence. What kind of customer service is this?

I snap my fingers to get her attention. "I'd like to try again."

Even behind those costume glasses, I can feel a barrage of mental darts pelting my head.

Once out of ammunition, she speaks. "I think you've had enough."

"Really? I didn't realize there was a legal limit to circus games."

"There is for you," she says without missing a beat.

Who does she think she is? She has no idea how many women would rather lick my asshole than ever once tell me off. I stare her down, and fuck me, I must be a sadist because I'm enjoying every second of this way too much.

"There's something wrong with your equipment," I say matter-of-factly as I egg her on.

"Did you just say faulty equipment is your problem?" she asks with a snort too adorable for words.

I swear, that smart mouth of hers is begging to be pumped and punished.

She steps over, strumming delicate fingers on the counter. "The gun's fine. They all are. Tested them myself this morning."

Tested them herself? Now she's the Queen of Quality Assurance? *Liar.*

She folds her arms across her chest, and I have visions of pressing my cock between her smooth breasts while she tells me off. *God, I'm a sick fuck.*

"Now, listen here." I wave a finger in her face. "I didn't do ten contingency deployments throughout the Middle East and other god-forsaken areas of the world to get my ass kicked by an unscrupulous, rickety fair game. Dying to make a buck? More power to you. But I'm playing again."

"I tell you what," she says with a smirk. "How about I try? With that very same rifle. If I make the shot, you owe me three bucks. And if I don't, you and your lady-friend get any prize you want, including Dumbo. Deal?"

I eye the woman, then the gun, then the innocent ducklings downrange. Then her breasts again because her angry crossed arms are squeezing them to oblivion. "Any prize I want?"

"Yup."

I feel like the devil salivating over a soul-binding contract. My dark glasses meet hers. "Deal."

We shake hands, and when we touch, it's electric. Fire courses through every vein in my body. Her full lips part, and I know she feels it, too.

"Fine," is all she says as she exits the booth and gets into position.

I step aside, grandly gesturing to her place, center stage on the platform. Gentlemanly, sure. Relishing in the cheap thrill of laying my eyes on a deliciously round ass. Oh, hell yes. It's taking every ounce of self-control not to fall to my knees and kiss her there.

Suspiciously, she checks the gun. "Just making sure you didn't stick gum in it or anything."

I smirk her way. Sass swirled with paranoia. My new personal favorite.

Rifle in hand, she leans her firm body forward. I watch as she takes aim. Her tresses fall seductively over one shoulder, exposing the nape of her neck. I see a chain. Dog tags. Is she a vet? *Hmm.* Getting a firehose of pure smartass would be fitting from a fellow vet.

My gaze trails down her body, and all I want to do is follow the line of her curves with my tongue. I need her name. Her number. Damn it all, why is it that the first woman to do it for me in years lives here? I need this, but from a New York City girl. Not a small-town girl.

Small-town girls are tied down. She'll want too much. Weddings. And children. Evenings at the dinner table and a kiss before I go to work. I'm a guy who barely eats or sleeps, works until two a.m., devotes every non-working moment to running or workouts or anything that will shut my mind the fuck off. I'm not a relationship guy.

I can't be.

Ding.

Huh? I look downrange. Duckling down. *What the fuck?*

Proud as a smug, little peacock, she's all smiles as she sets the rifle aside and leans against the counter. "You owe me three dollars."

Defeated, and ready to get her number, I feign an exhausted breath. "So I do. A deal is a deal." I tug out my wallet. "Three dollars..."

I stare at the empty cavity of leather. No cash. Because I gave Trust Fund Barbie all my money. What was I thinking?

No matter. I reach for the one thing that never fails me. My black card. It's also the only other thing I have on me other than a driver's license.

Confidently, I hand it over. "Do you take plastic?"

"Sorry, Toto. You're not in Bloomingdale's anymore." Her fingers tap the CASH ONLY sign on the wall.

Cash only. A trademark of fairs and brothels. How inconvenient.

I paint a little charm on my smile. "I'm sure we can come to some arrangement."

"Arrangement?" she purrs seductively, her smile dancing with delight. "That's exactly what we need. An arrangement like you," her hand brushes my chest, "handing me," her fingertip taps her chin, "three ones, twelve quarters, thirty dimes, sixty nickels, or three hundred pennies?"

I think of my internationally recognizable name and impending billionaire status. Oh, how the mighty have fallen.

It's like she has an invisible wall around her, shielding her from the love potion of my charm or wealth. It's like a cruel joke of nature that it makes her ten times hotter.

Desperate, I hand her my wallet. "Here. It has my driver's license in it, and the leather alone is worth more than all your stuffed animals combined. If I'm not back in half an hour, call the cops. I'll find an ATM."

She tosses the wallet back at me. Did she not just hear me say how valuable the leather is? "The nearest ATM is out of order, and a pretty boy like you wouldn't last a night in the pokey."

I can't resist a chuckle. "The pokey?"

"You know. Jail, prison, the big house—"

"The pokey," I say again.

"You'd snap your manicured fingers at the wrong inmate and become his bitch for the next three to five years." She releases a meditative sigh. "I couldn't have that on my conscience." She leans across the counter. "Tell you what. Say I'm a better shot than you, and we'll call it even."

Oh, she is the devil.

I lean my body in, too, my stance mimicking hers, my dick ravenous. We're nose to nose, my eyes dark on her clown glasses, her chin tipped up, defiant.

I breathe out the words she just agreed to. "I'm a better shot than you."

And there we stand in a seductive face-off, soaking up rays of raw, intoxicating heat. I'm under her skin as much as she's worked her way under mine. Both of us are too stubborn to admit it or walk away. It's fucking delicious.

I take in a breath, the scent of vanilla sinking into me like home. "I'm Mark," I say softly to her lips.

I can't imagine how or why, but it's as if handing her my name was a slap across the face with my business card. Equally perplexing is how much I hate the thought that I might have wounded her. Hurt her, a woman who treats me as if I deserve all the good graces of an undesirable vagrant. I couldn't pick her out of a clown-car lineup, so why does it matter?

I don't know why, but it does.

She latches on to a giant pink flamingo and clips it overhead. Her back arches beautifully, and I catch a glimpse of bare flesh beneath her shirt.

"What's your name?" I ask.

She turns away from me to find another toy. I almost think she hasn't heard me when she finally speaks. "Kitty Catamarca."

"Your name is Kitty Catamarca?" I scoff playfully. "Liar."

Her snicker assures me I'm right. "It is my name," she says without missing a beat. "My porn star name."

"Your what?"

She giggles, a melodic sound that goes straight to my dick. "Take the name of your first pet and add the name of the first street you lived on."

I think for a moment, recalling a lovable Saint Bernard and a modest house that's now been converted into an insurance agent's office. "Pleased to meet you, Ms. Catamarca. I'm Bucky. Bucky Morehead."

We both roar with laughter. Maybe my luck's turning up.

"Bucky Morehead. What a surprisingly perfect name for you."

She mocks me as if she knows me. Does she?

Our laughter dies down, and she makes herself busy again, putting pen to paper to capture her inventory in a notebook.

"Is there a man in your life, Ms. Catamarca?"

"Actually, there are three."

My eyes pop. "Reverse-harem porn?" I ask, intrigued. "As a matter of fact, I happen to have recently entered the porn business myself. I'd love an application."

Her smile widens, and mine falls. I want an answer.

"Seriously, is there a man in your life?" *Please say no.*

"Seriously, there are three." When I frown, she relents and explains. "Brothers," she says as she hands me a cold bottle of soda. It's a local brand of root beer I haven't had since childhood. Barton's Best. My favorite.

Brothers. Thank fuck. I relax and swallow a mouthful as she sips an orange soda of the same brand.

"Good," I say, approving.

"And why would that be good?" Her question is genuine. She can't be this naïve.

"Well, your shooting skills are as impeccable as your taste in soda." I clink my bottle to hers. "Who knows? Maybe one day, I'll take you away from all this and make an honest woman of you."

"I believe you already have a plus-one at the ball, Prince Charming. Someone's got harem delusions of grandeur."

"I'd like to take you out."

"How mafioso of you."

"Seriously, I'm asking you out to dinner."

"Seriously, don't you have a blonde to chase?"

With awful timing, a family of four steps up to the booth. I step aside to give them room, but I'm not giving up. Not by a long shot.

The mom and dad study the game, as though trying to figure out if their little ones can play. Two boys. They look way too small for most of the rides, and considering the popgun is bigger than they are, it might be too much for them to handle.

Ms. Catamarca pats the counter in invitation. "You can pop them up here and help them hold the rifles," she says helpfully.

It fills my heart with how good she is with them. Not that kids are remotely close in my future.

The parents each grab a happy toddler and lift them up, letting their legs dangle freely over the edge.

When their mother takes a curious glance at me, I tighten my ball cap and slide the glasses higher up my nose. I don't know why but I don't want them to know who I am. Not yet. And certainly not Kitty Catamarca. Nothing good comes of a near billionaire leading with his wallet.

Certainly not now.

My phone pings. I lean my back to the platform as I glance at the text. The unknown number has to be from Brie, because everyone else I know is programmed in.

Please don't let it be her telling me she's crashed a go-cart into a tiny human. Or a vag shot.

Can't find you.
Meet me at the front.

Ready to go.

She drives her message home with a lip emoji, eggplant emoji, and peach emoji. I'm staring at a clear invitation to any of her Brazilian-waxed holes, and my dick couldn't care less. *Is this thing on?*

Frustrated, I scold my finicky cock. Though I shouldn't be too hard on the sex-starved guy. Who can blame him? The Bries of the world aren't nearly as interesting as a cat-sassed porn star.

Speaking of which, I look over my shoulder to see how it's going. Horrified, I find her standing behind me, reading the text over my shoulder.

I snap my phone to my chest. "Has anyone told you it's rude to snoop?"

"Rude but fruitful," she sings, her words sardonic.

I stare her down, admiring her plump pink lips, wondering if they taste as good as they look. They part to release a few choice smart ass words.

"Well, seeing as you've got yourself a produce emergency on your hands, you'd better get on that. Or in that. Whichever." She pats my shoulder, and I'm tempted to take her over my knee.

I pocket my phone. "I'll be back with your money first thing tomorrow," I say, needing an excuse to see her again.

"Your money's no good here, Mr. Donovan."

Now it's me who's smiling. She knows who I am. "Considering you have me at a disadvantage, aren't you going to tell me your name?" I sweep her hand into mine. "Or will the stalking commence?"

She stays silent, a rare quality for her, no doubt. The air crackles between us. In this moment, it's just her and me and—

Ding.

The family of four roars in excitement, all of them giddy with applause. One of the two tiny kids has just nailed a ducky.

Really? Is there anyone who can't outshoot me today?

Ms. Catamarca lifts a giant tub of small stuffed animals to the delighted kids. "We're running a special," she says sweetly. "Two for the price of one. You both get to pick."

The children squeal with glee, and their parents thank her. I stare at cat-faced Catamarca, her identity completely concealed, and I'm enthralled. She's three wishes in one. A gorgeous, dick-approved heart-tugger—the redheaded trifecta.

I wave, not wanting to pester her too much for one day. Small doses with this one. "See you tomorrow," I say with a smile as I head off.

"Hey, Sharpshooter!" she says, and I stop and whirl around. "Catch."

A streak of gray arcs through the air, bouncing off my chest before landing in my wide-open hands. The little stuffed elephant toy stares up at me. A gift for Brie.

Stunned, I stare back. She called me Sharpshooter. My pulse thunders as my gut does a triple-axle somersault. My smile lifts to the sky.

Choir Girl?

I do a double-take. This is Jess? No, it can't be. This

woman is light years from the girl I last saw. Last kissed. The girl I gave my dog tags to.

Or is she?

I blink a few times as my gaze unapologetically roams every inch of her. Her curves. Her hair. That smartass mouth. And, oh my fucking God, my dick was right. It is her.

I'm half a step from rushing over, sweeping her into my arms, and fucking her against the nearest beer stand when a man steps between us. He's tall, blond, and Webster's definition of boring.

He gives her a hug. I hate him already. He proceeds to kiss her hastily on the cheek. My jaw tenses. Obviously, the man has no value for his life. I'm half a second from breaking up their little love fest when Jess backs away from him.

But she also doesn't send him away, or kick him in the nuts, which kind of pisses me off. Aghast, I pop both hands to my hips and glare at her. I mentally will her to look at me, and she does. Her bright blue eyes zero in on mine, and there is nothing but us.

"Sorry! Excuse us." A swarm of people and a baby stroller collide into me, hastily making their way around me because I'm hogging the damned path.

I move to the side. When I look up again, both Choir Girl and the man are gone. A sign that says BACK IN TWENTY MINUTES is tented on the counter.

Oh, no, she doesn't.

I pick up my phone and click on Z, tapping my foot as Zac takes his sweet time picking up.

"What's up?" he says.

"I—"

I can't be too interested, or Zac will make this ten times harder. Bribes. Perpetual taunting. Watching me like a hawk every time I'm within a foot of Jess.

So, I clear my throat and start again. "Didn't you say there's some event for veterans going on soon? Something to do with Jess?"

"Yeah. Saturday night. Why?"

Why, why, why ...

"Because my company needs more public presence with nonprofits."

That sounds convincing, right?

"With the IPO coming up, we're looking for avenues to get some good publicity. I thought it would be a win-win. Throw a spotlight on a worthy local cause and get heralded in the press as a do-gooder."

"Right. With your luxurious Manhattan penthouse and chauffeured cars, you're a real man of the people." Zac exhales heavily. "Is this your way of telling me you're using Jess to improve your social media status?"

"Maybe." *Damn, it sounded better the way I put it.* "And the pendulum on trending swings both ways. It's good for her, too, butthead."

"Agreed," he says. "It's also good for the restaurant and Donovan Wines. Mom and Dad are her biggest sponsors. I'll make sure you have a ticket."

Saturday? Uneasiness settles in the pit of my gut. I scroll to my agenda for Saturday and screw up my face.

"Actually, can you make that two tickets?"

"Consider it done."

"What happened?" Lance shouts at me over FaceTime, red-faced and way too angry.

For a man in his forties, he needs to calm down before he has an aneurysm. I search through Brian's selection of wines and take Lance's backlash on the chin.

"Brie said you didn't even kiss her goodbye!"

In disbelief, I stare back. "Why would I kiss her goodbye? This was a publicity stunt, not a booty call."

"Had you played your cards right, it could've been both. Ever heard that a photo is worth a thousand words? Well, a kiss shot is worth ten thousand likes. We would've nailed our quarterly earnings before the IPO."

My head tilts in confusion. "How so?"

He gives me a look as though I'm stupid. "Brie posted a shot of you and her in the car. Our earnings jumped half a percent. Do I need to tell you what half a percent of nearly a billion dollars is?"

I find a bold red and treat myself to a healthy pour. Sighing, I say, "You're driving me to drink."

Lance pulls out his flask and swigs. "Ditto."

"Brie is a very special girl," I say, my well-rehearsed speech long since memorized. Considering I've wrapped up dozens of breakups in it, it's had more shares than a Grumpy Cat meme. "She shouldn't squander her heart or talents on me. She'll make one man, and his social media accounts, very happy someday."

"Considering you've been holed up in a monastery for the past year, a spin around her block would've done wonders for your grumpiness."

I swing my legs to the ottoman and cross them at the ankles. "I'm not interested in riding the town bike, no matter how many followers she has. I don't need training wheels . . . I need a challenge."

His brows tighten with scrutiny. "Who are you, and what have you done with Mark Donovan?"

He's right. A year ago, I'd have been all over Brie like a puff pastry. But now?

Lance shakes his head in disbelief. "Did you see those selfies I sent you? She's double-jointed and obsessed with yoga, Pilates, and dance. Cirque de Soleil level of flexibility."

He bombards me with a series of texts. The man isn't wrong. In one pose, she has an ankle around her neck with the caption, "Saving myself for my future husband." Nice.

After I glance through them, I give him a deadpan look.

"You can still change your mind," Lance says quickly. "She's very eager for a happy ending, if you catch my drift."

"Oh, I've caught it all right. Now I need a vaccine to get rid of it."

Exhausted, I drain my glass and rest my head on the back of the sofa. An image of Choir Girl riding my cock flashes through my mind, and I sit up.

"Back to business. We need to balance out our portfolio. Bring on some charitable giving. For PR sake," I say.

Lance nods. "I couldn't agree more. Anything with kids or dogs is sure to go viral. The more, the merrier."

"And vets."

"Veterinarians?" he asks, absolutely serious.

I blink. "Veterans. Like me. We need to give back."

Unconvinced, he frowns. "I'm telling you, dogs and kids."

"No, I'm telling you. It's for . . ." I try to think of the name of her charity. Hell, I don't recall. "A local charity here in my hometown. I'll send you the details. I'll need a check."

He takes several notes like a good little lawyer. Then he hits me with, "They're not a start-up, are they?"

"They are," I say, and when his lips tighten to a frown, I blow out a breath. "Who cares if the nonprofit's still in its infancy—"

"Nobody." Lance glares at me through the screen as he taps his pen on his notebook. "Nobody but shareholders and the media."

I adjust a pillow behind my back. "I like newbies. We were new once, remember?"

Lance shakes his head. "The dark ages. I try blocking it out."

"They're a little hungrier. Eager to make a dent." I think of Jess, and it hits me. "Passionate."

He eyes me quizzically. "Passionate?"

Why does he always assume the worst?

"To succeed," I say.

"I see." He takes another swig. "Does Ms. Passionate have a name?"

I laugh. "As a matter of fact, she does. Choir Girl."

That gets a rise out of him. "You? With a singer in the church?"

"Actually, her name is Jess. Jessica Marie Bishop."

CHAPTER TEN

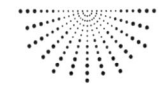

JESS

"*Jessica* Marie Bishop, what a turnout!"
Mrs. Donovan always greets me with all three of my names, and I love it.

She fusses with the appetizers. The banquet hall is filled with stylish people, and the Donovans didn't skimp one cent on their donation. Shrimp cocktail, chicken croquettes, and sliced filet mignon are just the beginning. There's a wall of desserts and an alcohol station proudly serving Donovan's wines.

"I'll bet there are three hundred people here," she says, beaming as she claps her hands with delight.

"It must be your food and wine pairings," I tell her sincerely. "I can't thank you enough for your generosity, Mrs. D."

"Anything for our vets, and call me Delilah."

"Delilah," I repeat humbly. I pick up a bottle. "I didn't know you had your own champagne, too."

Mrs. D. beams. "They just came in. The Donovans are red,

white, and bubbles." She lowers her voice. "It's not made in France, so technically, we can't call it champagne." When I set the bottle in her hands and snap a shot, she says, "Thanks to your photos, we got a call from a distributor. Starting next week, we'll be in five states and branching out."

"That's amazing. I'd better get you more content."

I snap two more shots. The better one goes up on Donovan's Instagram first. I use the second one for the social media feeds I set up for the charity and use the hashtags #Bubbles4Vets and #ANightofGiving.

I'm immediately scolded. "Stop that. This is your night, Jessica." Mrs. D. holds my hands out, getting a good look at me. "I hope you raise as much money as how you look, because you look like a million bucks."

I smile bashfully. "Thank you for loaning me this dress."

It's an elegant periwinkle halter that hugs every curve and fits like a glove. The skirt flares so I can move freely, and with my deep amber hair loosely curled and swept back, I feel stately and elegant, perhaps for the first time in my life.

Smiling, she pats my hand. "It's yours, dear." She pauses for a moment, choosing her words thoughtfully. "Your mother helped me pick it out."

It must have been when I was young. Back when Mom worked at the mall. When Mrs. D. continues, I blink rapidly.

"And seeing you in it," she says, "I know in my heart it belonged to you all along."

To avoid a cascade of tears, I give her a big hug. "Thank you," I whisper.

She gives me a kiss on the cheek and shoves me off to work the room.

By the end of the first hour, I've made my rounds, shaking more hands than a congressional candidate. The music, courtesy of a local band, keeps things upbeat, playing jazzy renditions of Cole Porter and Ella Fitzgerald. People dance and chat, eat and laugh. The entire venue pulses with an energy that's almost surreal. People are here to happily support this cause.

My eyes meet Zac's across the room. He lifts his drink in a toast to me and taps his watch.

Reluctantly, I nod. I both love him and hate him for reminding me that my big speech is coming up.

Why can't I just enjoy myself? I mean, I love the thought of publicly thanking everyone for making this pipe dream a reality, but public speaking? I'd rather have my vagina tattooed.

Singing in front of people? Not a problem. In a choir, it's easy. I can fade away behind some tall person. But speaking when all eyes are on me? I'm queasy just thinking about it. Like a buck-naked deer pinned in the spotlight, ready to puke on cue.

My nerves prick beneath every inch of my skin, and my fingertips are going numb. I scratch my neck a few times before stopping myself. Hives on a freckled redhead are the work of Satan himself. Instead of listening to my speech, people will be too distracted, wondering if that poor girl is breaking out in rubella.

I check my watch. Half an hour. My breaths are too fast, too panicky. Clutching my chest, I make a break for the balcony. Full-blown hyperventilation is not what I need right now.

Though I could use a Valium.

"Is that Mark Donovan?" I hear in loud whispers as I make my way through the crowd.

I turn and spot him. It's not exactly hard. The man stands out like the statue of David in a Florentine art gallery. He drips with an innate sexual energy that's hard to put into words but could spread a million legs. The man makes not noticing him impossible. Now I definitely need a Valium.

People step back to make room for him, like the sea parting for Moses. He's in a black suit that should be illegal, with his zero-fucks-given hair that's turning women's heads from every corner of the room . . . including mine.

Not that it matters. I'm still a red-headed mountain girl struggling to make my way in the world while he is the billionaire-in-the-making Marcus Evan Donovan. And, of course, he's brought a date.

From behind him, a woman emerges, if you can call her that. She's got long, blonde hair and a dainty pink dress, and, holy hell, she looks like a girl. If I didn't know better, I'd swear she wasn't old enough to drink. Or to bartend. He wings out his arm, and she takes it giddily. They practically skip through the room, making their way to the food.

His mother is meeting him now. Mrs. D. gives him a big, swaying hug. Then she hugs the girl and cups her cheek sweetly. It's endearing. And annoying.

I wrap my arms around myself, trying to shake off a million things I'm feeling.

Mark hasn't changed one asshat bit, and I will not pine for him. I push past the crowd—a salmon swimming upstream.

Once I get to the balcony, I suck in a needed breath, determined not to look back.

CHAPTER ELEVEN

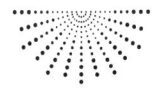

MARK

"There you are!" My mother pulls me into a hug, squeezing me hard. So hard, I kick myself for being away for so long.

Why did I stay away?

She quickly moves from me to my "date" and cups Ella's cheeks. "Let me look at you. Oh my goodness, I haven't seen you in four years. My, how you've grown." My mom whispers in her ear. "Got a boyfriend yet?"

Ella giggles as she rolls her eyes wistfully. "I wish. Between Dad and Papa Mark, I'll be an old lady before I'm even allowed to look at a boy."

I tilt her chin and give her my fake mean face. "A very old lady. No boys until you're thirty-five. Forty if you keep this up." I tap her nose with my finger and then kiss her forehead.

Her eyes widen in delight. "Maybe I'd be okay with that if I had a teensy, tiny sip of champagne." She snatches a large bottle from a display and looks up at me adoringly.

Ha! She has no idea how immune I can be against big puppy-dog eyes begging for alcohol.

Amused, I cross my arms.

"I'm not okay with it, even if you are," Mom says to me as if I'd give in. "No booze to minors. It's the single fastest way to lose a liquor license."

I grab the bottle from Ella's hands and admire the label. "Bubbly?" I say, surprised. "When did we start this?"

Mom's smile widens from ear to ear. "*We* started this week, though it's been in the works for months. And thanks to Jessica, *we* just got picked up by a major distributor." She holds up all the fingers of her hand. "We're about to launch in five states with the rest of the US not far behind!"

My own toothy grin breaks loose. Not just for the way Donovan's grows like a magical beanstalk, but because in a weird way, I'm proud of Choir Girl.

I scan the room. *Where is she?*

"There must be three hundred people here," I mutter half to myself.

"Last count," Mom says proudly, "three hundred and fifty-two!"

I don't know which Mom is more excited for—Jess's success or the fact that hundreds of the most influential people in the area are trying our food and sampling our wines. Knowing her, probably a bit of both.

Ella waves frantically across the room. "Oh, Andrea is here. I haven't seen her in forever. Can I—"

I nod. "Go on." Pocketing my hands, I watch the two girls as they head to the silent auction items.

Mom latches on to my arm. "How's Davey doing?"

Davey would be Jim Davidson, or Cousin Davey. Whenever I needed anything—a ride to New York City or a good, swift kick in the ass—Jim was more like an uncle. And I've been that little girl's godfather since the day she was born.

"Halfway to Georgia, I imagine. He said he'll only be gone a few days, and he sends about a million thanks."

"We love having Ella over. She's quite the baker. And every parent needs a getaway. Single parenting is hard with his wife away. A weekend away with the boys will breathe new life into him."

I check my watch. "I promised I wouldn't keep Ella here too late."

"I've got the guest room ready for her." Mom jabs an elbow into my side. "Since *somebody* didn't want to stay with their mother."

"Hey, if *somebody* didn't selflessly take Brian up on his offer, then Ella would have no place to stay, and Davey wouldn't get his desperately needed fishing trip." I shrug modestly. "I'll bet you had no idea you gave birth to a superhero."

Laughing, she shoves me away. "Go have fun before your head suffocates all these nice people."

I make a hasty lap around the room, searching for Jess. I find Brian instead, and we instantly bro-hug.

"Thanks for loaning me your place."

"Get on my boss's good side while hanging with my baby sister? Anytime." Brian motions to his new prosthetic, which I hadn't noticed under his suit. "I'm up to six miles in this one. We should run sometime."

"If you want to laugh hysterically at me heaving up a lung,

let's." I notice his cufflinks and remember his watch. "You left your watch behind."

He snaps his fingers. "I knew I forgot something. I'll grab it tomorrow."

A group of women waltz by, giggling and waving at me, and Brian is all grins.

"Fan club?" he asks.

"At functions like this, I avoid women like gently used flashlights." I look around. "I won't be able to stick around too long. I wanted to compliment our hostess, but finding Jess is like trying to find a guppy in the Atlantic Ocean."

Brian scans the room, as well. "It doesn't help that she's as big as a pixie. If I see her, I'll let you know."

I spot Zac hanging out against the far wall, but he doesn't see me. I grab two bourbons from the bar and head his way.

"Check this out," he says as he takes his bourbon, pointing with it outside of the French doors.

We both sip and watch. Out on the balcony, Jess is with a man. Mr. Boring. He's wearing a white tux, and by the look on her face, reeks of Aqua Velva. When his hand slides down her arm, she moves away. Any moron can see she's uncomfortable.

When I see red and take a step for the door, Zac smacks the back of his hand on my chest. "This is Jess. Or have you forgotten?"

I fume, but my feet stay planted in place. In my junior year, I watched Brandon Emerson slap her ass at a game. I rushed off the field and socked that asshole square in the jaw—an action frowned on by my coach. Not because he was opposed to violence. It was a full-contact sport, after all. But because it was his quarterback that stopped the clock.

In the heat of that moment, I couldn't have given two shits. How many people remember their high school games with vivid recollection? I do. And it always brings a satisfied smile to my face. Until I remember Jess in the aftermath.

What did I get for my selfless act of chivalry? A big, whopping *I hate you*. At least, I think that's what Jess said. It was hard to hear over the booing crowds and the ref screaming in my ear.

Still, my restraint only goes so far. I text Zac Lance's number.

Zac checks his phone. "What's this?"

"My attorney. You'll need to call him if that son of a bitch lays so much as a finger on her again."

I watch as Jess frowns before a fiery glow lights her cheeks. I don't know what's happening, but maybe Jess doesn't need help after all. The dipshit in the white tuxedo looks two seconds from getting kicked in the balls. *Where's the popcorn when I need it?*

He drops something to the floor. I don't have to know what he's saying, but it's hurtful. I can tell because she's on the verge of tears.

"Who is that guy?"

Zac takes another sip and lets out an irritated breath. "His name is Ross. Or Russ. Hansen, I think. He's been sniffing around Jess for about a month. Met her at some seminar for nonprofits. I caught him rummaging through her office once. Said he was looking for a pen. When I told Jess, she brushed it off. Said it wasn't like there was anything of value there." He shrugs. "She had a point. Most of her records are electronic."

I narrow my eyes. "Is he her date?"

"No," he says with a smirk. "She'll never be that hard up."

Thank fuck. I relax into another sip.

"Besides, Jess doesn't date."

What? "Why?"

Zac takes a sudden interest in his drink, avoiding my eyes.

My blood rolls to a boil, and I have to know. "Did someone hurt her?"

He shakes his head. "Nothing like that." He tosses back the rest of his bourbon. "But it's not for me to say."

My mind is a clusterfuck of a million questions, but I don't ask. I'd have better luck breaking through Fort Knox with a toothpick than getting any more out of Zac "the Vault" Donovan.

I pull my phone from my breast pocket and send a text to Lance.

Need a background check.
First name Ross or Russ. Last name Hansen.
All of New York. And any associated companies.
AVOID BRIAN BISHOP.

His reply is swift.

On it. And I know you didn't ask,
but there's something you need to know about your Choir Girl.
Something I don't think she wants you to know.
I'll send my full report.

It pops through instantly, not that anyone asked him to go prying into Jess's private life. I make a mental note to throat punch him later. I barely skim through the highlights before my attention turns.

White-tuxedo guy is finally leaving. Before I make a step in any direction, Zac holds out his fist. Of course, he's not just going to *let* me check on her. The bastard has to make me work for it. And if I lose, he goes to her rescue, and another day ticks down without me seeing her.

We bounce our hands in tandem. My confidence peaks as I sour my expression. I've never let on how easily I can read all this fucker's tells.

Tight lips: *rock*. Slight squint: *paper*. And the one he's exhibiting now, a near imperceptible tick of his left dimple: *scissors*.

I stifle a chuckle. Someone should really tell him to stop blowing his money on poker.

I smash my rock over his scissors and head for the bar.

"Hey." Zac pockets a hand.

Another tell. This is something serious. I pocket mine, as well, and prepare for a lethal warning.

Instead, he checks his watch. "Her speech starts in fifteen minutes."

I nod and make haste, stopping short to grab two drinks from the bar. "What can I get you?" the bartender asks, his smile chipper as he waits for my reply.

I open my mouth, but nothing comes out.

This is Choir Girl, and I swear to God, she's got me fucking second-guessing everything.

CHAPTER TWELVE

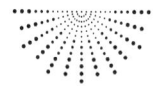

JESS

"Ladies and gentlemen, I—"
I breathe in. And out.
"I—"
My voice catches in my throat.
I clear it and curse. "Dammit!" Why am I so tongue-tied? With an unsettled sigh, it's increasingly apparent what I need isn't more practice. *What I need is a good, stiff drink.*

Frustrated, I toss my handwritten notes on the table. I've practiced this speech a million times. Why am I so nervous?

Oh, I remember. I hate public speaking. What's worse than public speaking? Begging perfect strangers for money.

I look out in the distance, grateful I'm all by myself. There's a magical gift to twilight, when day is night and night is day, and I can lose myself in the scenery. Fireflies dance in the forest in the distance, and right around that bend is where my father first taught me to fish. And . . .

Ugh. And nothing. *Seriously, Jess, get your head out of your ass and focus.*

This is the first step in a long journey to building something incredible, brick by brick. Making sure every veteran has the resources they need and in the way they need them. Brian's prosthetic isn't one from the VA. It's a high-end model a tech company was willing to test out. With a lot of phone calls and a whole lot of persistence, I opened that door. How many more doors could I open?

None, if I don't get my shit together and nail this speech.

Determined, I grab my speech and stand proud and tall. I take in a breath and imagine I'm back in school, giving this speech to Mom and Dad. "Ladies and gentlemen—"

A single person applauds, and a man's voice breaks my concentration. "I'd give you all my money."

Surprised, I turn. "Russ," I say as he steps over and kisses me on the cheek. It's awkward, but it's over quickly enough. "What are you doing here?"

He flashes me a million-dollar smile and pockets his hands. His sandy-blond hair is slicked back, and though it's black tie, he's opted for white, which only confirms he never saw the invitation. Not that I didn't briefly consider inviting him, but space was limited, and I needed every donor I could get.

"I heard you were going to be a big deal tonight. I wouldn't miss this for the world."

Ah, he's party crashing.

His dark brown eyes take their sweet time looking me up and down, and a smile emerges. Suddenly self-conscious, I wrap my arms around my waist.

He steps closer, reminding me of yet another reason I

didn't invite him. "You look ravishing. Good enough to eat," he says, waggling his brows.

I don't know what it is about Russ, but I'm just not into him like that. He's good-looking enough, charming in his own unique way, but when I look at him, I feel . . . nothing.

He glides a hand down my arm, the gesture too friendly. I need to have a chat with him, but not now.

"Don't be nervous," he says, empathy pouring from his words. "You'll get used to it."

"Used to what?"

"Making the rounds." He motions back to the banquet hall. "I've been doing this for five years, but I've never packed a room the way you do." He leans in. "But I guess I never looked this good in a dress."

I don't think he means anything by the comment, but it makes my skin crawl. He lets his breath linger on my neck, and I have to back away.

When he frowns, I know I've hurt his feelings.

I hold up the page filled with my chicken scratch. "I really need to practice."

He nods with a crooked grin. "Can I get you anything? There's one hell of a spread in there."

I shake my head. "I'm too nervous to eat. Besides, these people didn't pay good money to come here and watch me vomit from stage fright."

"Why don't I give the speech with you? Two causes at once."

What? I've spent months putting this together.

I'm sure he doesn't mean it, but it feels like Russ is trying to steal the spotlight. I need every cent of funds tonight just to get this nonprofit off the ground. I've got a tarp for a roof and have been relegated to ramen and tuna for months just to make this work. Sure, I could be living on easy street by selling my family's land to the highest bidder, but I can't. I'll be buried on Bishop Mountain before that happens.

How can he even suggest this?

Russ holds up some pages. "I've got a speech all ready to go. It's like I always say . . . two heads are better than one."

I pull in a calming breath. "Two heads are better than one, Russ. But two people holding their hands out aren't better than one. Not now." I don't want to hurt his feelings, and I can see he's getting upset. "Look, I'm more than happy to combine forces when it comes to how to strategize or submit our proposals, but I made commitments to people. To this charity."

"Do you hear yourself?" Nostrils flared, red blazes up his cheeks as he points a stern finger at me. "Look around, Jess. There's enough money in that room to fund ten projects. Why do you have to be so greedy?"

My jaw drops, and I stare at him, speechless.

He shakes his head. "You think you're too good for me, is that it?"

Too good for him? I don't even know what to say. Not that it matters, because he keeps going.

"My project is just as valuable as yours."

"It is," I say to assure him. "No one is saying it isn't."

God, I really don't need this right now, but I can't have a scene either. I've got to calm him down.

"I'm more than happy to help with an event for you, too.

But I really need to focus right now." Why can't he just go away? "Okay?"

Russ gives me a tight smile. He turns, ready to leave, but then faces me. This time when he looks me up and down, his brown eyes turn sinister, icy and dark. Cold pricks my spine.

"I noticed Donovan's is a sponsor." His smile flattens. "You must have done something—" he taps his bottom lip as he thinks of the right word, "*desperate* to get the richest family in the area to donate all that food."

What the hell does that mean?

Heat floods my face, and tension pulses through every vein in my system. I fist the speech in my hand and imagine balling it up and shoving it down his throat. I don't like where this is going, but I need to calm down. I can't let him frazzle me when I'm about to go onstage.

"They're friends of my family," I blurt. Why did I just say that? I don't need to justify myself to him or anyone else.

He smirks. "Sure, they are. I didn't believe folks when they told me about you."

Confused, I stare back blankly.

"Oh, come on. You know what everyone says about you?"

My eyes widen. I'm almost afraid to ask.

Defiant, I jut out my chin. "What, Russ? What does everyone say about me?"

His smile is sadistic. "That you'll do anything for a buck." He fishes a dollar from his pocket and tosses it at my feet. "See you around, Jess."

Stunned, I wince. It would have hurt less if he'd slapped me. I want to tell him off. Shout at him to go take a flying fuck. But I can't breathe. It's as if his words knocked all the air from my lungs.

Is that what people think? What they're saying behind my back? That I'm the town whore?

Before I can explain or shout or outright kick him in the balls, he walks off. And I'm left staring at the stupid paper in my hands. Months of exhaustion and hunger and putting up with everyone's crap—it's too much. I'm seriously a stone's throw away from losing my shit.

I step over to the large stone railing, my sanity shredded. I'm so tired of burning the candle at both ends just to have people pour lighter fluid over me. I stare at my hopeless speech, the words blurring as I wipe my eyes.

Defeated, I give up. There's no way I can go on that stage now.

"*Argh!*" I growl, tired and hungry and mad at the world. My movements jerky, I tear my speech to confetti, letting the breeze sweep it away. "I. Am. Not. A. Whore!" I shout defiantly to the darkness.

"Damn," a deep voice says from behind me. "And here I thought it was my lucky day finding you *and* a one-dollar bill."

My eyes wide, I freeze. I know that voice. And now I really can't breathe.

CHAPTER THIRTEEN

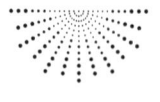

JESS

Mark Donovan's timing is impeccable. *If he wants a fight, he's got one. Bring. It. On!*

I whirl around to square off with the jerkwad. But as soon as I see him, I can't. I can't speak. I can't move. And I certainly can't kick him in the balls. I'm face-to-face with a god and in his core-drenching, take-no-prisoners presence, I'm rendered utterly speechless.

His suit cuts along his muscles in all the right places, and his dark hair is messier than before, to near just-fucked perfection. And those eyes . . .

"Hi, Jess," he says, and it takes me a minute to realize he's carrying an enormous tray of drinks.

Confused, I stare. His lips form a smile—a drop-dead gorgeous one.

"I didn't know what you liked," he says as he steps closer. "So, there's a little bit of everything. Booze. Cocktails. And, of course, Donovan's bubbly."

I'm still stunned, not really hearing a word he's saying. I'm just staring like a creepy stalker, and I'm pretty sure my mouth is hanging open.

"Mom's been bragging about you nonstop. Told me that you've brought her little bubbly out of its shell to overtake the US by storm." He nudges me with his eyes. "If you haven't tried it, I'd start there."

Flustered, I pick it up from amongst the myriad of glasses. He sets down the tray and grabs what I would imagine to be a bourbon or a Scotch and sidles up beside me.

After a long sip, he says, "I hope I wasn't interrupting you. If that was cathartic, perhaps I should try."

Huh? "Try what?"

He takes in a large breath, his chest stretching the integrity of his shirt, and now I'm really staring. Defiant, he shouts over the balcony.

"I am not a player!" He wrinkles his nose, seemingly dissatisfied, then bellows again. "I am not a man whore!" he shouts even louder, then nods, pleased as spiked punch.

I stifle a laugh. "Thanks."

Mark looks over with those captivating blue-green eyes. "I'm the one who should be thanking you. That did feel good." He clinks his glass to mine. "To you, Choir Girl. It's one hell of a shindig in there."

He sips, and I follow suit. Not drinking to a toast is bad luck. Or is that toasting with water?

It doesn't matter. I need all the luck I can get. I down the drink and examine the tray, searching for another.

He grabs my hand. "Oh, no, you don't."

When I attempt to take my hand back, he tightens his grip. Not painfully. Just enough to keep me locked in his hold.

I could yell at him. I mean, he's not here to babysit me. But if Mark Donovan wants to keep holding my hand, to hell with it. I'm letting him.

I feel the inkling of a smile warm my face. "I'm legal. I assure you."

With a wicked grin, he glances down the length of my body and back up to my face. "So you are." His brow lifts. "And I'll bet your nerves are as crisp as bacon, which means you haven't eaten a thing all day."

The way this man knows me is . . . what is it? Do I hate it? Love it? Oh, I don't know. I'm too edgy to play with Mark right now.

Indecisive, I eventually smile wider. "A day and a half, actually."

"Take it from the voice of experience—bad things happen when you're three sheets to the wind and giving a public speech."

He's trying to make me laugh. And again, still holding my hand. Which is waking every butterfly in my stomach and ratcheting my heart rate past a hundred beats per second. But I can't let this go on.

"Why are you here pestering me?" I ask, acting annoyed. "You have a beautiful date waiting for you inside."

His clasp on my hand doesn't ease up as he takes a dangerous step closer. "You noticed me when I came in." His smile is smug and arrogant, and the absolute death of my panties.

The door to the banquet hall opens, and a woman stands there. His date.

I snap to my senses and yank back my hand. In three steps,

I'm back at the table, creating some much-needed distance between us. As soon as I reach for a bright pink drink, his stern voice rises.

"Don't you dare, Jessica Marie Bishop."

My jaw falls to the floor. This is how he speaks to me? And in front of his date? Who the hell does he think he is?

Mark's child-date shuffles over. Her hair is a shade of golden blonde so perfect, it must be natural. And even without a trace of makeup, it's clear she doesn't need it. She's beautiful. And weirdly familiar. Where do I know her from? A magazine? Or a movie, perhaps?

Her smile is warm as her baby-blue eyes meet his. "I've been looking for you everywhere." Her voice dials up an excited notch. "Can I have some money?"

Money?

"Money?" he asks, repeating my thoughts. "Manners," he says under his breath.

Did he just say that? It's one thing that she looks like a child, but it's another thing to treat her that way. I grabbed the biggest, tallest drink I can find, a lager, fully prepared to dump the damn thing all over his misogynistic head.

"Sorry," the girl says, as if she has anything to apologize for. Before I can say anything at all, her arms are around me, squeezing me with a hug. *What the hell?*

"Hi, Ms. Jess. Thank you for inviting me." She corrects herself. "I mean us."

Her voice. As soon as she speaks my name, I know exactly who it is.

"Ella Davidson?" I pull back from her and get a good, long look.

God, how did I not recognize her? The last time I saw Ella, I swear she was half the size. "Did you and your dad move back?" I set down the pitcher-sized drink and look up at Mark. "Is Davey here?"

They both shake their heads, and Mark tugs her into a side hug. "She's Donovan property for the remainder of the weekend. Her mom's tending to Aunt Ethel while her dad catches a marlin off the coast."

"He said he nearly caught a shark."

"I wouldn't doubt it." Mark tightens his hug on her. "She's all mine until I take her to Mom's." He wrestles her into a playful headlock. "At least she was, until she started treating me like an ATM."

He releases Ella, and her eyes light up. "They have a photo booth, and Andrea and I want to do it, but . . ."

"How much?" Mark rolls his eyes as he takes out his wallet. Apparently, he topped it off before coming tonight.

"Twenty dollars," she says, her hands in a prayer-like clasp.

His eyes bulge. "Twenty dollars?"

His disapproving glance lands on me. I know every expression that ever crossed Mark's face, and this is his angry look. His fake angry look.

Crossing my arms, I play along. "Well, it is a fundraiser. And I'll bet all you have is a credit card." I pull a swipe card from my pocket. "Here, use this. You can have all the free photos you want."

"Nonsense." He whips out a ridiculous pinch of twenties, all while keeping his gaze on me. "After all, *it is a fundraiser.*" He hands the cash to Ella, and she wraps him in a quick hug and takes off.

"Look," she cries.

We both break from our gazes to see what Ella's excited about. She waves a dollar bill at us. "I found a dollar. A lucky dollar!" Her glee-filled expression vanishes as she hands it to me. "Oh, you could give it to the veterans."

"Nope," I say, pushing it back into her hand. "Finder's keepers. That's your lucky dollar, Ella."

Mark grins. "Go see if Zac can turn it into another twenty for you."

Grinning, she scurries off. We can't help but watch as she breaks through the crowd to Zac, who points a stern finger our way, mouthing, *It's on!* Of course, he pulls out his wallet and exchanges her single dollar for another twenty.

We laugh and make faces at Zac. When Mark begins unfastening his pants, I shout, "What on earth are you doing?"

"What does it look like? I'm mooning my brother."

With both hands pressed to his chest, I shove him from the door. The band is performing "Conversations in the Dark" by John Legend as electricity swirls around us like fireflies.

Without warning, Mark spins me out and snaps me back. A move we learned a million years ago.

I look into his eyes, which are so much darker, it feels like he's not looking at me, but inside me. Uncovering every secret thought I've ever had about him.

He pulls me against his body, his voice husky and deep as he says, "Dance with me."

Christ, what woman could say no to that? We fall into a natural rhythm that's strange and intoxicating.

And if I was worried he was about to seduce me, Mark

does what he always does. He pulls a one-eighty and throws me for a roller-coaster-size loop.

"You have no idea how much I enjoyed that."

"What?"

He chuckles hard. "The look on your face. When you thought Ella was my date."

I scoff, covering my embarrassment with a flutter of my eyes. "It was hard to see her from that far away."

He spins me back again. This time, my back lands at his chest. His hot, rock-hard chest. His deep voice is seductive in my ear. "Do I have to shout, 'I am not a lecherous bastard,' from the top of my lungs too?"

His breath is warm on my neck, awakening a ripple of goose bumps down my spine. I ignore it and shrug.

"Couldn't hurt," I say. "And you have no idea how I nearly enjoyed dumping an ice-cold beverage right on your head. It would've been a shame to mess up your pretty suit."

His lips graze my ear. "You have no idea how bad I want you to mess up my suit, Jess."

What the fuck?

This time, it's me who spins in his arms. Maybe if I face him, it'll stop the slow thrumming heat waves building between my legs.

Nope. Worst mistake ever. His eyes are playful, his smile mischievous, and his body is a hard, granite, cardinal sin wrapped in a tie. The heat of his hand drifts to the small of my back in a slow, seductive line.

I melt like lava in his hold. *God, those eyes . . .*

This is unchartered territory—me and Mark—too

dangerous to navigate now. I have to look away. "I didn't know your family was so close to the Davidsons."

"Davey and I served two tours together. I'm Ella's godfather." He goes on a little about a chubby-cheeked baby and changing diapers. For a second, my mind wanders off, thinking of how wonderful Mark would be as a father.

In the next moment, he pulls me even closer, his body in seductive movements against mine, swaying us in time to the music.

I pull in a deep breath and, oh my God, does he smell good. There have been many times over the years that I've smelled Mark Donovan. In his puberty years, he smelled like ass. In his later teens, like Irish Spring and drugstore cologne. But now, he smells like a double dose of man, with a hint of cologne and a twist of cigar.

I know it's wrong, but I take a deep, lingering whiff, and my knees go weak. I close my eyes as my thighs clench.

I'm in so much trouble here.

"Don't be nervous," he says.

Blinking, I try not to think about his arousal, which has been hard against me for half the song. "Nervous? Why would I be nervous?"

"Your speech."

Ah. We're going to ignore the Empire State Building prodding me from between his thighs and carry on with a conversation.

"My speech." I swallow hard. "What speech? I tore it to shreds in a fit of rage. I have no idea what I'm going to say," I say sheepishly.

He tugs my chin up so my eyes meet his mesmerizing ones. "Three hundred fifty people haven't come here for the food or the music. They came here for you, Choir Girl. Speak from your heart, Jess." He presses two fingers between my breasts for a dizzying moment. "That's all anyone wants to hear."

His hand sinks lower, and I hold my breath. He feels it. I know he does. My eyes search his as his search mine until a small chime sounds from his watch.

"Fuck," he growls under his breath.

He releases me, and I take a big step back.

Regret fills his face. "I have to go. I promised I'd get Ella home and—"

"It's okay. It's nearly time for me to go on."

"I'm sorry, I'll miss it."

"That's all right. I'd be more nervous if you were here."

He nods politely and removes an envelope from the inside pocket of his suit. "Don't open this until after the event." He hands it to me.

"What's this?"

"A small contribution from my company to yours." He takes a step toward the door, then pauses. "I'm only in town through Christmas, Jess."

Why's he saying that?

He pockets his hands and blows out a breath. "If that doesn't work for you, I understand."

"If what doesn't work for me?"

His eyes hold mine. "I'd like to see you. Away from anyone else. I'm staying at Brian's."

I try not to look too shocked when Mark says that.

"I know you have a key," he says. "Use it. Anytime."
And then he's gone.

CHAPTER FOURTEEN

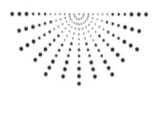

MARK

"You're the best, Papa Mark!" Ella squeals with joy as she looks over at me.

"Eyes on the road," I say.

I must have lost every last cell in my brain to let this girl drive my Maserati. True, she's not a kid anymore, and her driver's permit is valid, but I'm pretty sure her parents would lose their shit if they knew she was plowing down this country road at eighty.

"And don't tell your father."

"I won't," she promises, focused on the road ahead.

Davey wouldn't care that I let Ella drive. That I let Ella drive this beast before he had a shot at it, though? I'd literally never hear the end of it.

Maybe I should have driven and let Ella tackle the technology jungle. I concentrate hard. How the fuck does all this social media work? They're live streaming Jess's speech, and fuck me if I'm missing it.

I search for Jess's name, and the feed pops up. I bounce

glances between Ella's driving and Jess taking the stage. She looks stunning. And nervous.

"Ladies and gentlemen," she says, and the mic gives a high-pitched squeal. Not too loud.

"You've got this, Choir Girl," I say to the screen.

After a short pause, she lets out a breath, and I let mine out, too. My palms are actually sweating.

"I can't begin to thank you all for coming tonight. I just checked the donations, and that meager goal of ten thousand dollars—the one that seemed as achievable as touching the moon—well, we overshot that goal tenfold in the first fifteen minutes of this event. And I have every one of you to thank for it."

Thunderous applause hits the air.

I pound my fist to the roof. "Yeah!"

When Ella claps, too, I lose a year off my life.

"Hands on the wheel!" I shout.

"Oh." She grips the wheel with white-knuckle force. "Sorry."

I give my seatbelt a hard tug. "How about you ease up on the gas a little so I don't ship my car."

Ella does, giggling. That joke never gets old.

Jess continues for a few minutes, thanking her family and friends and my mom and dad. They've gotten even closer since I've been gone. She then makes a special mention of her parents. I can't imagine a dry eye in the house. Looking down at her, who wouldn't be proud?

When the applause dies down, she taps my envelope in her hand. I smile, knowing she hasn't opened it yet. "I'd also like to send a special thanks to a man who couldn't stick around."

Uh-oh. If she mentions my name, the New York City media will descend on this town like a locust plague.

"Don't say it," I beg, whispering.

"This man said that if I spoke from my heart, I wouldn't have to worry about my speech. Which was a good thing because I happened to throw it away."

The room roars with laughter.

"But he gave me the strength to realize that you're all here because, like me, you believe in this cause. You believe that no vet should go without. That together, we can change lives, one vet at a time." She holds up the envelope. "For one very special sharpshooter, thank you for reminding me what I was doing here in the first place."

I stare with a goofy grin. "Anytime, Choir Girl," I whisper. "Anytime."

Ella moves her gaze between me and the road. "What's a sharpshooter?"

"You did not just ask that." I pinch the bridge of my nose. "What's a sharpshooter? I swear, your father has taught you nothing."

As we cruise the rest of the way home, I share stories of how her father and I met. "It all started when I needed a new set of dog tags . . ."

CHAPTER FIFTEEN

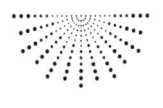

JESS

"So, this is where you work," Mark Donovan says as he strolls into my office like he owns the place. And for all I know, he might actually own the place.

Unnerved, I stand to greet him.

He gives me a stern frown. "What are you doing?"

I shrug and feel like an idiot for standing. I flail my hands near my sides. "I don't know." I wave the envelope at him. "How am I supposed to treat a man who just handed me a check for half a million dollars?"

"Like a god, I suppose." His gaze roves the small space, his nod of approval slight. "I have a bone to pick with you, Choir Girl. Two, actually."

He moves to my side of the desk and places both hands on my chair, urging me to sit down. When I do, he pops his butt on my desk, smiling as he fidgets with every single thing on it. For everything he moves, I move it back in place. He knows how OCD I am. It's his favorite form of torture.

Finally, he settles on a small Rubik's Cube. I know within a few minutes, he'll have my catastrophe of a cube decorated in some design. Those were always his favorites. He finishes and tosses it in my hands, the classic checkerboard. The red and orange side is face up.

"You haven't taken me up on my offer."

"I've been thinking it over."

"It's been a week. In case I didn't mention it, Jess, I'm leaving after Christmas."

"Actually, Mr. Donovan, you did mention that."

I grab my Rubik's Cube, spinning it until the colors resemble a paint-by-number craft. When his jaw clenches, I know his brain is two seconds from snapping like a twig. Two can play at the torture game.

Mark snatches it from my hands. "What's wrong with you?" he sneers playfully under his breath. The high school cube champion goes to work fixing the atrocity I've created for him.

"You also haven't cashed the check." He taps a finger on the envelope lying on my desk.

I don't say anything. Not cashing that check is idiotic, I know. But I can't take Mark's money. Not like this.

"Lunch?" he asks with a slow, sexy smile. It's really not fair how good-looking he is.

I straighten a small stack of paperwork. Mostly bills.

"I can't." I point to the brown paper bag on my desk. "Brian made it for me this morning, and I won't waste it."

Mark helps himself to the bag and takes a whiff. "Peanut butter and banana." He makes a pouty face. "I'm offering you a lavish lunch at Dante's, and you counter with peanut butter and banana?"

Is he crazy? "Dante's is nearly an hour away."

He straightens his tie. Why is he wearing a tie today? "They have a private room. No one will recognize me."

I lean back and cross my legs. "I can't."

Fire brims behind his gaze. "But I wanted to see you today." He straightens his lapels. "I'm dressed for Dante's."

I have to laugh. "Aw, is my pretty boy all dressed up with nowhere to go?"

"Your pretty boy noticed you in that dress at the bank this morning and seized the opportunity to wine and dine it off of you."

It's true, I'm dressed better than my normal jeans and T-shirt, but I needed my loan officer to take me seriously. Which he did. I now have a mountain of paperwork to get through.

I point to the bag still in his hands. "We can eat here. I'm happy to share."

"Share?" He scoffs as he opens the bag. "This sandwich will barely feed a toddler, and you need every calorie you can muster."

He takes a long pause to measure me up.

Look in my eyes, Sharpshooter. I'm dead serious.

Defeated, he loosens his tie and unwraps the wax paper. With his fingers on the top slice, he pries it open.

"Well, you're in luck. Chocolate chips."

"I love a chocolate chip PB&B."

He holds a diagonal slice to my lips. I don't know what comes over me, but I open. And somehow, letting this man feed me is perhaps one of the most sensual things I've ever done. I let out a deep, satisfied sigh of pure pleasure as I hand him the other half.

"You, too. I won't eat unless you do."

His gaze drops to the apex of my thighs. "There's something else I'd rather eat." When I stare blankly—determined not to let him know how wet he just made me—he relents. "Fine. Considering I invented the sandwich, it's one of my favorites." He grips my hand, forcing me to feed him as well. He licks his lips and chews like it's his last meal. "That's good. Got anything to wash down the bread pasted to the roof of my mouth?"

"Water?"

"Please."

I grab two bottles of water from the fridge and hand him one. "And excuse me, Mr. Donovan, but I believe it was I who invented that sandwich."

"Ha!" He laughs and holds the sandwich to my lips again. "You and your little girl fingers accidentally dropped the bag of chocolate chips all over our sandwiches. It threatened to ruin lunch for the entire Donovan-Bishop village. It was me, the benevolent and gracious King Marcus, who declared it was delicious and, indeed, a sandwich . . . thereby avoiding your beheading." His eyes dance in a caramel glow, the way they always do when he's happiest.

"Revisionist history," I say, chewing.

He leans in, his mouth barely an inch from mine. "I saved your life that day," he says, smirking as he stares. "You owe me, Choir Girl, and I'm here to collect."

I say the first thing that comes to mind. "Why? You said it yourself; you're leaving at Christmas."

A torturous look crosses his face, creasing the beautiful

lines of his brow. He stands and pockets his hands. "I don't do relationships."

This man is utterly dumbfounding. "Sounds like the perfect reason to see each other." I smile sarcastically.

"It is perfect," he says with a huff, his stance aggravated.

He moves to my chair, placing both hands on the armrests to cage me in. He's searching my eyes for something . . . empathy? Desire? Then he finishes saying what he has to say.

"It's perfect because you don't do relationships either."

"How do you know that?"

A sad smile forms as he clasps a hand around the nape of my neck.

Heat flashes against my skin, and I bite my lip to stay calm. I half-think he's about to kiss me when his fingers dust my collar . . . and draw out the one secret I've managed to hide from everyone. Everyone but him.

He tugs the chain from under my blouse until his dog tags are resting in his hand.

"You never take it off, do you?" He turns his hard gaze away. "That's how I know."

He's this close to me, calling me out on the one thing I never wanted out, and it's too much. Much, much, much too much.

I grab the check and press it to his chest, forcing him back. It breaks the spell. "I'm actually glad you dropped by. I can't accept this."

That got his attention. His expression stern, he rolls his eyes. "What? Don't be ridiculous. Of course, you can."

"It's too much."

"Too much?" He chuckles warily. "I've handed checks to

thousands of people over the years, Jess, and I'm not sure I've ever heard, *No, no. I couldn't. It's too fucking much.*"

His hands rake through his hair, and I'm sure he'll storm from my office any second now. Which is exactly what I need. Distance. Lots and lots of distance. He's seconds from losing it, while I'm scrambling for a retreat with no exit in sight. I need out. Now.

I scratch at my neck. "I'll feel—" I don't even think I can say the words aloud.

Mark looks down at me, his lips curled as he fights a smile. He places the last bite of sandwich at my lips. "I believe the word you're looking for is indebted."

I open my mouth. He pops it in, after which his thumb brushes against my lower lip . . . and I absolutely die. When he licks his thumb, I feel it clear down to my core.

He stands and straightens his suit. "This is a business arrangement. Nothing more. It makes my company look good while your company reaps the benefits." He brushes an imaginary crumb from his lapel. "It's not a big deal. People ask me for money all the time. This time, it's a gift. You didn't have to ask. I'm not here to make you feel indebted."

"Liar."

Mark chuckles. He's lying through his teeth. I know it, and he knows it. "Have dinner with me. We can discuss your hang-ups about taking vast quantities of cash for your charity."

"If I take your money, Mr. Donovan, you and I most certainly cannot date."

His mouth falls open in shock, and his voice rises. "We've

already released our charitable contributions to the press. It's a done deal. You have to take it."

"It's a free country. No, I don't."

"Free to be insane, I guess." He stands and pounds a finger on my desk. "Why are you always so stubborn?"

"Why are you always so arrogant?"

He paces a bit, his steps choppy. "Do you have any idea how many companies would crawl through crap for that check?"

"I know one that won't."

"Take the check."

"No, Sharpshooter, this is a hard line I won't cross. If you and I date, or hook up, or Netflix and chill, or do anything that remotely tips the scales from Brian's little sister to booty call, no money exchanges hands. Period."

Intrigued, he gives me a sideways glance. "So dating, hookups, Netflix, and booty calls *are* on the table?" He unbuttons his blazer. "Why didn't you just say so?"

I march for the door, opening it wide. "Get out."

He closes the door and props both hands on his hips. He's ruffled. I've missed this: ruffling his handsome feathers. "You have to deposit the check. Otherwise, it'll look like we lied. I can't have that before our IPO, Jess." His gaze is softer now, pleading. "This IPO is the pinnacle of my existence. One shot I've been building up to my entire life. Nothing can derail that."

"The last thing I want is to disrupt a millionaire's apple cart."

"Multi-millionaire," he corrects playfully.

"Multi-millionaire," I concede with a roll of my eyes. Smiling, I offer him a compromise. "You did give it to me. That's all people need to know. Your books might be on trial, but mine aren't." I take another look into those mesmerizing eyes. Big mistake. I have to level with him. "You said it yourself. People are always asking you for something. I can't be one of them."

I can see the gears turning behind those captivating eyes of his. He rubs a thumb to his chin. "And what happens if the press calls you?"

"I say what I always say when they call me, snooping for intel on the self-righteous and very important Mark Donovan. No comment."

"And good-looking. Don't forget good-looking."

"How could I forget?"

He pockets his hands. "The press has called you?"

I shrug. "Off and on. They've chased down everyone who ever worked at Donovan's, from what I hear."

Mark steps into my space until I'm backed up against the door. His jaw is clenched, his gaze dangerous.

"You're making this harder than it has to be, Choir Girl." His finger sweeps a strand of hair behind my ear as I swallow the lump in my throat. "So. Fucking. Hard."

God, this man . . .

His lips are like fire as they brush against mine. "Shred the check."

CHAPTER SIXTEEN

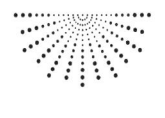

JESS

"Shred the check?" I repeat back, breathless. It's everything I can do to lasso back my runaway pulse. Is Mark Donovan really saying what I think he's saying.

His reply melts over me like hot honey. "You're all mine tonight, Jess." In a rush, he cups my face, pins me against the door, and kisses me. His tongue is desperate as it swipes against mine.

His arms wrap tightly around me, forcing my body against his, his hard, lengthy cock against me. My insides melt, and my body craves more.

All those walls I've put up—the bane of my resistance—evaporate as my mind snaps in two. I kiss him back. Sensual. Hungry. I kiss him like I've never kissed any man before, and God, does it feel good.

I press both hands against his solid chest, my breathing ragged. "What's happening here?"

"You're seducing me," he says through labored breaths. "Obviously."

I smile against his lips. His tongue takes it as another invitation, and I am not objecting. I grip his hair as his hand slides down my back . . . down, down, down. Arousal pulses through, full force. All I can feel is him tonguing my mouth, and I have a vision of that dangerous tongue between my legs.

I'm tired of holding back. Holding off. Fighting every feeling I've ever had for this man. It's my one chance with Mark Donovan: The Unabridged Version, and I'm not half-assing it.

My kiss turns urgent as all the raw need for this man breaks free. When he cups a breast and grinds himself against me, it knocks a brain cell loose.

"Wait!"

His mouth rips from mine as his forehead falls to the door. "Is this your game? Murder?" His lips press to my ear. "You're killing me here, Choir Girl."

"I can't have dinner with you tonight."

He growls. "Why not?"

"Did you forget what day it is?" He thinks hard. I throw him a bone. "Someone's birthday."

The bulb goes on behind deep evergreen eyes. "It's Brian's birthday." He grumbles low. "I vaguely recall Zac mentioning it." His eyes lower. "It's this damned dress. I must have forgotten. Hell, the way you look in it, it's a miracle I remember my own name or how the fuck to drive." His jaw ticks as he thinks it over.

I sweeten the offer. "I'm baking a cake."

His eyes widen with alarm. "I rescind my comment. You? Baking a cake? You're not a murderer, you're a serial killer."

The nerve of him. Giggling, I smack his arm. "I can bake."

He laughs loudly. "You poor, delusional creature. Whoever told you that?" He pecks me lightly. "Let's avoid Brian biting into a mouthful of eggshells."

"It was just that once."

"It was definitely more than once, and not a chance. It's too risky."

Mark takes another taste of my mouth, licking my parted lips like they're covered in buttercream frosting. If this is how he gets his way, sign me up. He breaks away as I cling to his neck for dear life.

"I'll bake the cake," he murmurs.

That's right. Mark bakes. Not in an amateur-hour sort of way, either. More like a *Cake Boss* way. How could I forget that?

"I'll also bring some champagne," he says.

"Bubbly," I say, to correct him.

He tugs my bottom lip with his teeth. "Bubbly. What time?"

"Seven."

"Seven it is."

CHAPTER SEVENTEEN

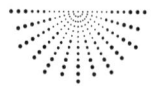

JESS

"The party has arrived!" Rex shouts and holds open the door.

Not only is Mark here, but so is Zac. He's carrying two gifts—I'm guessing one is from Tyler, who's probably too busy at the restaurant to drop by.

Mark has a beautiful cake in his hands—dark chocolate icing is decorated with caramelized bananas, a freckling of candied nuts, and yellow flowers dipped in sugar. It's ridiculously huge. Five layers, at least. Slung over his shoulder is a backpack, which is probably stuffed with bottles of red wine and bubbly heaven.

"Party crashing?" Brian meets them at the door and eyes the cake. "Flowers? It's my birthday, not my wedding."

Mark snorts. "It'll be your boot-up-the-ass day if you give me any more lip, birthday boy. And I had to fancy it up. After all, you are one of my best friends."

Brian slaps him on the back. "I'm your only friend. You

and I both know it's true." His fingers circle the air. "Okay, okay, Mr. Pillsbury, lay it on me."

Mark lifts the glass dome with an air of grandeur. "Voilà! This is a very special creation just for you. I call it *You Put your Peanut Butter in my Chocolate*."

"How original," Zac says with a touch of snark.

"It's five layers of dark chocolate cake separated by a concoction of peanut butter, buttercream, marshmallow cream, sliced bananas, and Bailey's. Lots and lots of Bailey's." Mark fires me a glance from the corner of his eye. "I was recently inspired."

Brian grabs Mark's bag and pulls him into a quick bro hug. "Fine. I guess you can come in."

They make their way to the table, and Mark sets the cake in the center.

"Still not wearing your watch?" Mark asks and motions to his wrist.

Brian snaps his fingers. "I knew I forgot something today. I'll drop by later and pick it up."

"I thought you did pick it up. It wasn't on the dresser." Mark rubs his chin. "Cleaning lady?"

He shakes his head. "You're looking at her."

Seeing as how that watch cost me way too much of my life, I have a vested interest in it. With zero shame, I barge into their conversation.

"Did one of you lose your watch?" My tone is laced with enough accusation to have both ex-snipers raise their hands in pathetic surrender.

"No," they say, having each other's back as always.

"Say, sis . . ." Brian wraps an arm around me. "You're the only one who hasn't brought me a present. Please tell me you're not going to surprise me with something like an actual pony."

"But it was on your wish list."

"Yeah, when I was eight."

I huff and throw my head back in fake irritation. "I wish you would just make up your mind already."

Over the next few hours, we drain every last bottle of Donovan's fine wines and double-dare challenge Brian to eat a quarter of the cake. In under ninety seconds. I'm pretty sure he got frosting up his nose and will hate the words *peanut butter* for the next year, but never let it be said that a Bishop backs away from a dare. I snapped enough shots to recap the moment for many a birthday to come.

When no one is looking, Mark slices my finger through the frosting on his plate. There was a time I would have kicked him in the groin for that. But not when he corners me in the kitchen and sucks my finger clean.

When Rex bursts through the doors, Mark inspects my finger and asks, "How could you cut your finger on the cake?"

Rex charges over, laughing. "You cut your finger on cake?"

Mark smiles sadistically and scurries out of the room. *Coward.*

I elbow Rex in the gut. "Of course, I didn't cut my finger on cake. It must have been an eggshell," I cry out.

The evening is hysterical and magical, and the way a home always should be. I miss these days. For so many years it was just me and Brian, and then just me.

I thought I'd gotten used to being by myself. But now, it

feels like denial. A cruel denial of warmth and happiness. And love.

I try not to smother Mark, but every once in a while, our eyes meet, sending every butterfly in my gut into an absolute frenzy. He isn't looking at me now, though. He's looking out the window, off into the distance, with a faraway, daydreamy stare.

Unable to stay away, I step close to him, but not too close.

"I forgot how much I loved it up here," he says, his tone sentimental.

For a moment, I stare out too. The mountain is bright tonight, with moonlight glazing every tree and shrub. Even with the full moon, the stars twinkle brilliantly, giving the wilderness a romantic ambiance. I take in a breath and relish the scents of juniper and honeysuckle.

"I hope I never forget."

Mark frowns. "Are you leaving?"

I don't want him in the middle of family business. And I certainly don't want him coming to my rescue. There are a million ways to die in this world, and I'm pretty sure embarrassment is one of the worst. This is Bishop business.

I shake my head. "Just saying."

He nods and sips his wine, and I'll bet he's dying for a cigar. Knowing my brothers, they all are. It's time for my birthday gift. If this really is our last time together on this mountain, I have to make it special. It has to be more than a gift. I want to give him a memory.

With a fork, I clank my wine glass. Their lively voices fall to give me their full attention. "All right, birthday boy, are you ready for my gift?"

Brian scoops me into a big brotherly hug. I know he said his prosthetic leg was easy for him now, but having him lift me clear off the floor makes me tear up.

"I have another year in my life with my family," he says with a huge grin. "What more could I need?"

That damn stubborn tear just won't go away. I swipe it from my cheek.

Diverting their attention, I point out the window to the old campfire site. "There's a box of cigars and a bottle of Four Roses waiting for you all."

"You're coming, too," Zac says. Or insists.

I never got the hang of cigars, but he keeps pestering me to try just once. I'm pretty sure it's just so he can laugh his ass off at me.

I shake my head. "I'm going to clean up in here. Go have testosterone-laden man time."

With a series of caveman grunts, they make their way over the hill as I get to work tidying up the remnants of birthday central.

~

By the time the boys return, it's late.

Brian kisses me on the cheek. "Best birthday ever," he says before heading to bed.

I kiss my brothers goodbye and give a hug to Zac. "Don't tell me Mark got eaten by a grizzly."

Zac looks back at the site, the campfire glow still visible from the hill. "He decided to crash there. You can take the mogul out of the country, but you can't take the country out of the mogul."

I wrinkle my nose. "I'll go grab a pillow and blanket for him."

Zac pockets his car keys. "I'm happy to run them up to him."

"Nonsense." I wave him off. "It's late, and you still have quite the drive."

He kisses me on the cheek, and his forehead wrinkles in an unsettled frown. It's as if he wants to tell me something but doesn't.

Instead, he pulls his keys back into his hand and shuffles along the gravel to his car. "Goodnight, Jess."

"Goodnight."

Zac clears the driveway, leaving me alone with nothing but Mark to preoccupy my thoughts. I take in the fire's glow along the hillside and wonder if his shirt is still on.

What? The man has always been a furnace, even during the deepest Arctic blasts of winter. Shirtless is as natural to Mark as poles are to strippers.

Ugh, let's face it. A pillow and blanket are just excuses to get closer to Mark *Danger Zone* Donovan. And proof positive that I am a masochist. It's as if I'm taking him by the hand and pointing out the exact location he can etch one more notch to his bedpost, as if there'd even be enough space left.

Warning bells go off all around me as I contemplate the risks of delivering a harmless pillow and blanket. What's all the fuss? I shake off a few insignificant worries and cling to the dog tags dangling beneath my shirt. There's nothing to worry about. I don't do relationships, right? And neither does Mark.

That should reassure me, the fact that Mark doesn't do relationship either. So why doesn't it?

My head falls back, searching the sky for answers. *This is Sharpshooter, and I swear to God, he has me second guessing everything.*

CHAPTER EIGHTEEN

JESS

Blanket and pillow in hand, I make my way to Mark.

The hillside is a beautiful illumination of dewy grass and majestic pines. Moonlight skips along the water, dancing across the lake to the tempo of twinkling stars and chirping crickets. This is my paradise. My home. And tonight, it feels magical.

I find Mark lying on his back. By his movements, I almost think he's awake, but he's not. His eyes are closed, though I can hear him mumbling something. I inch closer.

He tosses and turns in abrupt, jerky movements, like a wild stallion constrained by a dozen ropes. I'm almost upon him. A sheen of sweat glimmers on his brow in the moonlight, and every muscle in his arms, neck, and chest is tight and strained. I don't want to wake him, but it feels cruel to let him keep going like this, tortured by a nightmare.

I kneel beside him. "Mark," I whisper, and he twists

angrily. "Mark, wake up." My voice is still hushed, but I say the words louder.

I reach out, hesitating for a moment before my hand finally rests on his chest. He jolts to a seated position and grabs it. Hard. Hard enough to hurt. I wince from the pain.

He huffs out several breaths before he eases his grip on my hand, but he doesn't let go. His breaths are staggered beneath my palm, and thundering erupts in his chest. A moment later, it subsides.

"Jess?" His expression is pained and confused. He blinks rapidly at the dwindling campfire and looks around. "I'm home."

My gasp is slight. Something about him calling this mountain *home* does things to me. Squeezes my heart in a way that it shouldn't.

Silently, I nod, giving him time to get his bearings.

He examines my hand, caressing it with both of his as if it were an injured little bird. He rubs it tenderly, his eyes full of torment. "Did I hurt you?"

I shake my head and encourage him with a small smile. "No. It's fine. I was just—"

"Frightened? I know." He nods with heavy sadness and swallows hard. "My demons scare me, too."

We both sit there for a long moment—him with his demons, and me with my secrets. He's barely touching my hand, yet it's the closest I've ever felt to anyone.

When Mark regains his composure, a small smile emerges. "You brought me a blanket."

I nod and hand it to him. "And a pillow."

Then, in one swift, beautiful move, I clock him over the

head with it. He laughs out loud and yanks me into him as we both fall to the ground.

"Relax," he says, his voice gravelly.

His body is a wall of muscles, his arms thick and strong. But it's his heartbeat that captures me. A steady rhythm that connects to mine in a way I don't understand and can't explain.

My finger traces the line of his neck and chest as he kisses my head. He smells woodsy, with a hint of expensive cologne. I close my eyes and concentrate, memorizing this moment.

His fingers trail down my spine and ease into the small of my back, and he scoops me closer. I wonder if he's looking at the stars or if his eyes are closed.

His heartbeat is hypnotic in my ear. I never want to stop hearing this. His heart. His breaths. Him. Mark Donovan is a heartbreak waiting to happen, but I don't care. I nestle my head closer to his neck and slide a leg between his and sink into him.

His free hand moves up and down my arm before it works its way beneath my shirt. His fingers burn like fire against my skin. He works slowly at my torso, cupping and massaging my breast. My body grinds against his, momentarily satisfying the growing ache between my legs.

He slides his hand lower and stops exactly where I thought he would. He's clutching them in his hand. His dog tags. "Why have you never taken them off?"

I bury my face in the crook of his neck. "I did once. I was in a hurry and left them at home. It was the same day I got the phone call when I thought Brian was going to die. I put them back on, and Brian didn't die." I take a long breath, releasing it in slow, staggered waves. "I know there's no relationship. In my head, I know this. But I can't stop wearing them now."

Mark latches on to them hard. I can feel the strain of the chain against my neck. "What if I took them back?"

I grip his hand, full force. "Don't." When he doesn't move and doesn't let go, I sit up, glaring at him. "You have your demons and so do I. This keeps my demons away."

He finally releases the dog tags and cups my cheeks, soothing me with a soft caress. "Then they stay where they are."

My smile is weak at best. "It's a little hard to explain when you're on a date."

"I'm good with it," he says warmly. "The truth is, Jess, I envy you. I'd die or kill for what you have."

"And what's that?"

"A shield. Something to protect you from all the terrible things we hold inside." His words are so heartfelt, his expression so anguished.

"Is that why you're an insane control freak?" I ask, and his brow rises. "To cover for all those things you can't control?"

"Like you?" he whispers, kissing me. "Tell me you want this, Jess. I need to hear it."

My eyes connect with his. "I want you, Sharpshooter."

He kisses me again, only this time, it's possessive. He owns me and he knows it. He wastes no time sliding off my shirt and bra as I undo his shirt and unfasten his jeans. I want to explore him. Taste him. Lick him.

"Lie back," I whisper against his skin.

"Yes, ma'am," he whispers, smiling. "You're mine, Jess." His words are assured as his strong hand cups my face. I look at him for a forever of a minute. This man is gorgeous. I can't help trailing my fingers across his chest, the ripped muscles of his abs, the cut feel of his thighs. His erection is thick and large, the tip engorged, the veins protruding. I lower my head and swirl a lick around him.

"*Fuck.*" He hisses out a breath, and his eyes darken. "More."

"More?" My tone is coy and innocent as I flick my tongue across his tip.

Lust filled, his eyes narrow, with the grin of the devil himself. "Don't make me spank you."

I kiss the lowest part of his stomach, and with both hands wrapped around his base, I take him—all of him—into my mouth. He groans with pleasure, and my sex begins to throb as I take him deep into my throat. It's the deepest I've ever taken a man, and still, he's a lot of man to manage.

"That's it, Choir Girl. Let me fuck that smart mouth of yours."

This man is filthy. And, oh my fucking God, am I turned on. I've imagined being with Mark Donovan a million times. In reality, he's a hundred times hotter. It's as if a light switch that no one has ever touched has suddenly been turned on. I don't know who's more messed up—me or him—because when he talks like that, it drenches me.

He grips my hair, forcing my eyes to meet his. The lust in his eyes is raw. It's so fucking gorgeous.

"You like that?" he asks as he bucks through my lips. "Does my dirty little girl want to be fucked down the throat?"

I'm about to come just from how he talks to me, so I suck harder. Faster. Until his eyes flutter back as his hand finds my breast. He pinches my nipple with an unforgiving tweak, and I gasp for air.

"Get up here, Jess." His order is hard and militant.

This man has ordered me in one form or fashion a million times over the years, and not once did I ever get sex-crazed from it. But make no mistake, I am now.

I climb him like Mt. Marcy until the hard, purple head of his cock connects with my entrance. I slide myself, slick and ready, up and down his shaft.

"No," he snaps.

I heave out a breath. "No?" *Is he fucking kidding me?* "And you call me a murderer?"

His chuckle is dark as a strong finger loops the chain around my neck. Like a leash, he uses it to drag me up his body to position my pussy at his mouth. Christ almighty, he tugs on the chain until I'm seated on his hot, dirty lips. I could die like this.

Carefully, I ride his face at a slow, easy pace until a hand slaps my ass. His voice growls against my skin.

"Don't you fucking hold out on me." He swipes a lick across my lips. "Fuck me the way you fuck me in your dreams, Jess. I want the real you. Untamed. Unbridled. Un-fucking-believable."

And just like that, I give in. His thick tongue swipes through my flesh, and I let everything go.

Fear. Hope. The past. The future. None of it matters.

His hands grip my thighs, forcing deep, crashing fucks through my lips. Prying me open. Spreading me apart.

Our eyes lock, and waves of searing pleasure ripple across me. "Ahh," I cry out, like a wild animal in the dark.

My body clenches so hard that, for a second, I worry I've hurt him. I struggle for balance . . . for air . . . for sanity.

I just got tongue-lashed by Mark fucking Donovan, and he's ruined me for life.

Slow, penetrating tastes subside to licks, and then kisses. My vision clears. His eyes twinkling, his face full of me, the man is breathtaking.

Then he says, "My turn."

"Your turn?" I'm still trying to get feeling back in my toes, and this is what he says? "Is this a dream? You eat me to oblivion and want a turn, too?"

I brush my fingers through his thick mess of hair.

"I'm already at risk of diving headfirst into a Mark-induced coma," I say before he nips my inner thigh. "Ah! Mark!" I jolt, giggling.

"See? Not dreaming." In one swift, strong move, he rolls me beneath him. "Where are your manners, Ms. Bishop? You know, you get a turn, I get a turn . . ."

His lips take mine, and the taste is an intoxicating blend of me and him. My body hums against his, as if my entire being knows Mark Donovan isn't going to just give it to me good. He's going to give it to me mind-blowingly, too-good-to-be-true good.

"Now," he says as he lines his very hard dick against my sex, "don't be alarmed."

"Alarmed?"

He answers my question in one big, deep, balls-to-the-wall thrust. My eyes slam shut, my body quakes, and I cry out in mercy because if he does that even one more time, I'm going to come again.

He strains for a breath, his eyes rolling back. "Give me a minute."

"A minute?" I pant, still dizzy.

"Fuck, Jess, you're too good. This feels . . . so . . . good."

I scrunch up my face. "What kind of player are you?"

A massive growl erupts from his chest, and his dark eyes turn playful. "I'm a virgin. Can't you tell?"

When I burst out laughing, he punishes me with a series of thrusts that take me seconds from nirvana.

"Quiet," he murmurs, "while I figure out what makes a girl tick . . ."

He takes quick, choppy breaths and grinds his jaw hard. His slow thrusts turn meditative and serious. Deep. So, so deep. It's like watching a magnificent thoroughbred pick up speed in the final length of the track, focused and determined.

Mark's eyes are on me—my face, my breasts, my soul. I feel this man everywhere at once, and yet it isn't enough. He's stretching me so completely, giving me my fill of him for years to come.

I look up at him. Dark, damp waves sweep across his forehead as he moves one of my legs to his shoulder. His hand on my hip, he grips hard as he kisses my ankle.

It undoes me. I try to hold off, but I'm close. Too . . . close . . .

"Mark!"

He rams me harder. "I need you, Jess. Just like this. I've always needed you."

He's lying. He has to be.

I turn away and shut my mind off to anything but the possessive burn of his thrusts.

"Kiss me, Jess." His husky tone wraps a chain around my heart.

I shut my eyes and I do. I kiss him. All of him. The kid I grew up with. The boy I hated. The soldier I couldn't forget. The man I never wanted to love but did.

I tell Mark Donovan all of this in a kiss as our bodies collide.

CHAPTER NINETEEN

MARK

I wake to the smell of burned hickory and pine . . . and Jess.

Last night was a marathon of raw love and toe-curling sex. Choir Girl finished me. Her body is a fresh brand on my mind, every thought, a confused clusterfuck of pleasure and pain.

I thought if I had her just once, the spell would be broken. But it's not. I can tell by the way my heart, brain, and dick gang up on me. This isn't over. This isn't even close to being over. My titanium resolve is so bent out of shape, I doubt it'll ever snap back.

Which is a problem. Jess is . . . what is she? A pastime? My new favorite pastime that satiates the beast within? No. She's an addiction, and addictions are never over.

I pull in a tired breath and look up to the sky for a solution. Or a lightning bolt.

The more I think about Jess, the more I sink into a fiery pit of hell and wade in the heat. I want her—no-holds-barred and long-term, which is impossible. She's here, and I'm in the city. Hell, I'd have better luck uprooting a redwood than dragging Jess from Saratoga Springs. She'll never leave.

Or . . . would she? Maybe she just needs to give the city a chance. When a low draft sweeps across the terrain, I roll over, ready to move the flannel blanket over her soft skin.

There's just one problem. She's not here.

"Jess?" I jump to my feet. "Jess!"

Nothing but scurrying woodland creatures and a hungry hawk overhead. I look around. My clothes are noticeably missing as is my phone. What if a text came in from Brie? It's just like my little Choir Girl to go apeshit from Brie's relentless sexting.

I face the lake with grim discomfort. I swear to God, if she threw everything in there . . .

I have no control over the people who text me, nor thei innuendos, emojis, or images they may send. Trust me, what has been seen cannot be unseen, pornographic clips and all.

Angrily, I snatch up the blanket and wrap it around my waist. Who does she think she is? I chastise myself over and over again as I stomp over the hill to the house. That's my phone. My personal property with contacts, credit cards, emails, and a lot of important fucking shit. I mean, sure, it's all backed up on the cloud, and I could get a new one, but it's the principal of it.

What was I thinking? *This* would be my life with Choir Girl. Ignored. Frustrated. Alone on a hilltop, my dick swinging in the breeze.

I stomp across the hillside, rush up the porch, and practically kick open the door. When I shout, "Jessica Marie Bishop, get over here now!" it's clear I've lost every last bit of my mind.

Because Brian's still here and is the first to file in from the kitchen, followed by a wide-eyed Choir Girl, *what the fuck are you doing* written in every freckle on her face. When I notice my phone neatly placed on an end table, plugged in and charging, my heat dissipates, but not entirely.

Brian smirks over the rim of his coffee mug. "Something happen to your clothes?"

If by something, *you mean did your baby sister rip them from my body in a fit of lust and ride my cock until the wee hours of the morning? Then yes. Yes, it did.*

I cling to my self-control and tighten the blanket around my waist. "You could say that."

Brian's skeptical glance turns to Jess. "Let me guess. You caught him sleeping in the buff and decided that making his clothes disappear would be funny." He shakes his head. "Again." He hands her his coffee, collects his keys, and wags a finger in her face. "It's wrong, Jess. Funny, but wrong."

She breathes out a small, nervous sigh as he kisses her on the temple.

"And don't even think about getting me involved. The lake is subarctic at this time of day, and I'm not fishing his clothes out of it, no matter how big your puppy-dog eyes get." Brian checks his watch—then wraps a hand around his wrist as if remembering it's missing. "I'm gonna head over to my place. See if I can find it."

"Find what?" Jess asks.

The watch, though neither of us wants to drop that solid shit grenade and brace for the backlash. I've already turned the place upside down, but maybe Brian using the force will turn up more than my scavenger hunt.

He pockets both hands and gives me a death glare to stay silent. As if he has to ask.

"My, *uh*, journal. The one you got me to deal with all those annoying emotions you keep talking about."

Jess kisses him on the cheek, her gaze warm and tender. "I know it's not what big, rugged, tough men do when wrestling with their internal strife, but trust me, it works. It's backed by science, and every vet I've worked with swears by it. That and yoga."

Brian and I both roll our eyes.

She places a palm on his chest and lightly taps it. "Let me know how you like it."

"Will do." He moves to leave but turns to look between the both of us. "You two behave."

She nods, but I smirk. There's no way Brian is getting that promise out of me.

Brian steps through the front door, letting it shut behind him.

Heat bubbles over me until steam is pouring from every cell in my body, but I don't move a muscle in Jess's direction. I make hasty steps to the window. Brian shakes his head whimsically, no doubt wondering if leaving the barbarian dog and aggressive little kitten alone together was such a good idea.

Oh, it was. It was a very good idea.

My dick gives a maniacal laugh as I count down the seconds to his full departure. Once his SUV clears the drive—*one, one thousand; two, one thousand*—and is completely out of sight, the gloves are off.

And by the gloves, I mean the blanket.

CHAPTER TWENTY

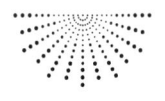

JESS

I stare at the magnificent man standing before me.

The lines of Mark's body are cut and chiseled to spectacular form, and that blanket is a lot thinner than I thought because I can make out the outline of every hot, bulging muscle beneath it.

He stalks toward me, and I take a wary step back. Something about the look in his eyes. Crazed. Deranged. Hungry.

"Why did you leave?" he asks.

I back into the kitchen, still awestruck. "Why aren't you wearing clothes?"

He pins me against the counter. "I asked you first."

"I couldn't sleep, so I thought I'd head back to the house and have breakfast ready for when Brian woke up, and—"

"Wait." Mark crosses his arms. It's meant to make him look hard and stern, but it only amplifies every last peak and crevice of his neck, arms, and chest. Mercy, this man is built. "What do you mean, you couldn't sleep?"

His words sound angry and hurt. I try to think of some

way of explaining without actually doing it. When I look into his eyes, I know the kind of woman he wants. The kind of life he wants. He wants a family and kids, and there's no way I can give him that.

I look away, avoiding those scrutinizing eyes. "I have restless energy. It's the reason I do yoga, actually. But I've skipped it the past few days, and I'm suffering the consequences." My words drift off as my eyes skim his chest and torso and— "Why aren't you wearing clothes?"

His beautiful eyes narrow, though his lips lift in amusement. "You know very well, why. Because they weren't there."

"Yes, they were. On the other side of the fire. Folded neatly and out of spark-igniting distance."

He studies me for a long, lingering breath. "So, first, you hide my clothes, forcing me to parade about, a half-naked show pony for your amusement." I bite my lip to stifle a laugh. "And then, Ms. Bishop," he grumbles low, his words feathering my neck, "you leave?"

His breath is like wildfire cascading over my skin. "I didn't want to wake you."

"Well, that doesn't work for me." He wraps his solid arms around me, working his stiff cock against my body. "You can't feed it all night and deprive it of breakfast." Strong fingers tangle through my hair, wringing me of sanity and willpower. His sea-glass eyes meet mine. "Where's my good-morning kiss?"

Mark is eyeing me like hot Belgian waffles slathered in syrup, and I melt into him. When his lips take mine, he takes everything. Tangling our tongues, this man is unapologetically stealing my breath. I'm just not sure he realizes he's stealing my heart.

When his hands start working off my jeans, I whisper into his neck, "I'll be late for work."

"Fuck work. You want to help a vet? You've got one right here who desperately needs your help."

Mark doesn't bother removing my panties. He's in too much of a rush. Instead, he lifts me on the counter, slides my panties aside and spreads my legs wide. And absolutely devours me.

I have to lean back and give him full access, my back arching with pleasure. The groans I make when I'm with him —I've never heard them before. It's as if he draws every sensual sound out of me with every slow, hard, erotic lick.

He carries me to a rhythm that my body has to take. Two fingers work their way in, finding that spot that makes me see stars.

My eyes flutter shut. He's given me an inch and I've taken a mile, sprinting to ecstasy. *God. Oh, God.* There are no defenses against this man. He's a Come-Master 2000, set to full speed, and I'm helpless to resist.

When he flicks his tongue on my clit and spreads me even wider, my gaze snaps to his face. A sheen of arousal coats his lips. It's the sexiest thing I've ever witnessed in my life.

The freight train of an orgasm rips through me, and I cry out. The roughness of his stubble against my sex and thighs eases as his feather kisses bring me back down to earth.

When he stands tall and centers himself between my legs, my own consciousness slaps me awake and my body stiffens.

"Condom?" I ask, confused. "You didn't use one last night. And you're not using one now."

Does he know?

His stance doesn't change as he works the untiring tip of his hard cock to split me only an inch. "It's fine," he says without explanation. "I've never been with another woman without a condom."

"But—"

His lips overtake mine as his cock thrusts inside me. I'm rendered as speechless as if he'd thrust himself into my mouth. With all of him spreading me, I can't breathe. All I know is this man is taking me over and over again on a dizzying roller coaster of lovemaking, and I can't stop it. I want more.

His hot breath whispers a devil's vow against my ear. "Trust me, Jess. Nothing will happen. I've got you." He kisses me again. "I promise."

This isn't just Mark saying flowery words to patronize me, to ease my doubts. He's a Donovan, and Donovans don't lie. They don't have to. He could have any woman in the world, but he's here, now, racing me to another mind-blowing climax, and I'm all in.

I want to try this. Try not to worry about every single consequence like they're the size of Mount Rushmore.

I want Mark Donovan. Damn the consequences.

CHAPTER TWENTY-ONE

JESS

It's been a strange, week-long challenge of Mark stealing me for slivers of time. Not long enough to stay together overnight, but long enough for him to nail my vagina to the wall like a perpetual sledgehammer.

Thankfully, Brian hasn't noticed my Jell-O legs wobbling through the door each night when I get home. If only Zac were so oblivious. With Mark having to return to the city suddenly, I was hoping Zac wouldn't notice anything out of the ordinary. Leave it to Eagle-Eyes Donovan to begin his inquisition.

"What's with you?" he asks me.

Zac and I have an understanding. In mixed company, mum's the word. But when it's just us—ride or dies since childhood—we have no walls. We are each other's safe space. How could we not be? Both the youngest of strong, male-dominated families, we had to have each other's backs. The truth is, I've never kept anything from Zac. Not until today.

I shrug innocently. "What do you mean?"

"Oh, don't give me that. My calls and texts aren't returned for an entire day, and I always find you smiling to yourself for no reason at all. Is someone in love?"

Love? Where did that come from?

"What can I get you?" the older man at the hot dog stand asks.

Zac and I discovered long ago that if we kept our standing lunches at the park rather than a restaurant, people would stop gossiping about us.

"One coney dog and one plain," he says to the vendor.

Zac always gets a plain hot dog. Because he's a psychopath. He also orders us two bottles of ice-cold Coke and a bag of jalapeno chips we'll both munch on.

Once he's paid, because he always pays, we make our way to our usual bench. It's shaded by a large oak, and every once in a while, a squirrel will come out. If I try to feed it, Zac will lift his brow with disapproval. But with winter coming, they need all the fat they can get.

"Well?" he asks again.

I smile sweetly at him. "Impossible. You're the man I'm destined to marry." I flutter my eyes and blow him a kiss.

"Deflecting. Wise tactic. It means I must be close, and you don't want to tell me who it is. Fine, I'll just stalk you. But heed my warning: If it's that Ross Hansen douchebag, we'll be in the Bahamas tomorrow getting married."

This is why I adore Zac, and why I agreed to that silly proposal. *If worse comes to worst, and neither of us can continue with the agony of dating, we'll marry each other.* I happily agreed.

In our defense, I was very drunk, and Zac was licking his wounds over one more in a long line of heartaches. I just don't understand why he can't find the right woman. He's kind of a perfect catch. Except for me, of course. Something about our friendship is almost like . . . siblings.

"Hensen," I say, correcting him.

Zac's eyes bulge, and two angry veins in his neck look as though they're ready to explode. "You'd better be fucking kidding. The two of you are dating?"

"What? God, no. You called him Ross Hansen. His name is Hensen. Russ Hensen. And trust me, if I ever see the D-bag again, the only thing that will be between us is my leg as I kick the living shit out of his nuts."

Zac crunches on a few more chips as he relaxes back onto the bench, winging an arm over the back. "Good. I really don't like that guy."

"I really don't blame you."

As he sips his Coke, he gives me a long, assessing look. "There is someone, though. You're practically glowing. And your smile is ridiculous these days. Like you've kidnapped a leprechaun and he finally gave up the location of his pot of gold."

I chew an extra-large piece of hot dog, mumbling, "I can't talk with food in my mouth," in incoherent gibberish.

Zac nods with a crocodile smile. "So, you *are* seeing someone, and it's someone I know."

I swallow the large knot of guilt lodged in my throat. It's not that I don't trust Zac with this information. The man hoards more secrets than King Tut's tomb. But I'm not ready for him to know yet. God, why does he have to be so good at this?

Deflecting again, I say, "Can we move on to the bigger issue at hand? You said you have work for me."

His lips curl with delight. "Sure, let's move on to business. I'll enjoy pestering you over the next few days and weeks about your secret lover."

"I'm so looking forward to it. Don't mind me, as I make a note to avoid you at all costs."

"Only until next week. Neither snow nor rain nor heat nor gloom of broken hearts shall keep us from our standing weekly lunch."

It's true. Unless Zac is out of town or I'm in the hospital, which was just that once, we never miss our lunches.

I wave my napkin in his face. "Business. Money. A girl has debts to pay."

"Only because you won't let me pay off your hospital bill."

"Your future wife would hate me forever if you did that. Seriously, she's going to expect a big, fat ring, and you can't afford both."

Zac chuckles as he chews. "Fine. Yes, I have a job for you. A big one. The bad news is that it's out of town."

My heart sags, weighty and deep. Just when things with Mark and me were starting. But money is money. And I know if the roles were reversed, he'd be on his private luxury jet or helicopter or whatever he takes, hightailing it back to the Big Apple.

I rub my chin as I wonder how far away it is. "I'm okay with that."

"And there's worse news. It's for Mark, and I know how you feel about him."

I cross my legs and squirm in my seat. If only he knew. "A job? With Mark?"

Zac nods. "It's just a week-long gig in the city. Mark mentioned that he had some need for social media assistance. I guess they're really in a bind."

I wrestle my smile down to the ground and paste on a look of professional interest. "Interesting. Go on."

Zac finishes off his Coke. "He'll have to tell you the rest. He was pretty vague. Only that he'd be grateful to be in your capable hands."

Oh, I'll bet he would. "This coming week? All of it?"

Zac frowns. "Is that a problem? I was pretty sure you were free. I might have overstepped by volunteering you." He shakes his head and rubs his temple. "Sorry, Jess. I'm an idiot. You're seeing someone. Of course, you're not available." He pulls out his phone and opens the contacts. "Let me talk to him—"

My hand flies out over his before he can press a button. "No, no. It's fine."

"You sure?"

"Positive."

CHAPTER TWENTY-TWO

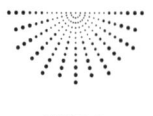

JESS

I pack my tiny duffel, stuffing it to within an inch of its life. The bed dips down with a foreboding creak as Brian sits on the corner of it.

I glare at him playfully. "You break it, you bought it."

He chuckles. "Gladly. This bed is a sad lump of broken sleep. I would have a new one here for you tomorrow if you would let me buy you one."

"This bed is perfectly fine for me. Just not for ogre-sized giants like yourself."

Frowning, I flick through my closet.

Brian trips over a dress I've tossed on the floor and makes his way to my doll-house-sized closet. "Problem?"

I shake the hangers in my hands, the dresses on them absolutely wrong. "I don't know what to wear. What do you wear when you're going to—" I cut myself off before I say *to see Mark*. "The city?"

My brother's face crinkles. "What do you mean? You've been to the city a dozen times."

Okay, so my cover wasn't the best lie I've ever told. It's not my fault. I'm not exactly seasoned about it. But I play through it the best I can because, unlike Zac, Brian won't let me off so easily. My big brother will literally sit on me until I tell him everything he wants to know. *Barbarian.*

"In school. Never as an adult."

"Never?" This seems to take him by surprise. "I figured you would have met up with Zac there every once in a while."

I shake my head. "The reason Zac and I are besties is because he loves it here as much as I do. He does the city for work. But the fresh air and big trees are his home as much as they are mine."

Brian leans his enormous body against the small frame of the door. "At the risk of getting thrown out, are you going to the city to meet someone? Like, on a date?"

I keep selecting clothes without meeting his eyes, and my heart pounds with a drumbeat of guilt. *Deflect, deflect, deflect!*

"Zac lined up this gig with Mark. I don't exactly know what it is, but the money is supposed to be pretty good." I shrug. "The Donovans seemed pretty happy with the social media campaign of their new wines."

Brian is unnervingly quiet.

I shoot him a sideways glare. "Why do you ask?"

He lifts a shoulder and heads out. "I don't know. A suitcase full of lingerie and mile-high heels seems perfectly appropriate for a week-long business trip."

I can't even stammer out a response. I'm too busy dying on the spot. I brave a look at my suitcase.

"I'm in a hurry," I finally muster out. "I wasn't even looking at the clothes I put in it." Though by the skimpy red lace bra and panties I bought on a whim four years ago, something in my subconscious definitely was.

"Don't do anything I wouldn't do," he sings from out in the hall.

"I'm pretty sure no such list exists."

My phone rings. When the name *Sharpshooter* lights the screen, that ridiculous smile Zac was talking about takes over every inch of real estate on my face.

I answer, holding it close to my ear in case Brian is just outside the door. Sibling paranoia at its finest. "Hello?"

"Hello."

Mark's voice is a low grumble of sex on toast. My body responds before I do. My heart races as energy zings through every nerve ending.

"I wanted to personally thank you for accepting my proposition."

"Actually, I was a little vague about your proposition. What was it, exactly?"

"You. Naked. In my bed. For a week."

I laugh out loud. "Those photographs wouldn't exactly be suitable for work, Mr. Donovan."

"I'm serious."

"So am I. What happens when I return after a week with no social media photographs posted on zero platforms? Zac will definitely know something is up and will pester us both relentlessly. We can't play house for the whole week when you've hired me for work."

Mark's growl is guttural and hungry. I know that growl. It can light my body on fire from a thousand yards.

His words are firm. "I'm not afraid of my brother."

"Are you afraid of mine? Because as soon as Zac tells Brian anything, he'll pound you first and ask questions later. You might have been able to outrun Brian before, but since he got the blade, he's been making ten-mile runs a thing. Olympic-quality running at its finest."

Mark hesitates, and I can practically see the cogs spinning in his beautiful head. "I was really hoping to keep you tethered to a bed the entire time, but perhaps certain accommodations can be made. *Hmm*."

I hear him clicking away at his keyboard and beam. Mark Donovan could have his pick of any voluptuous model or gorgeous fashionista, but he's trying to do this for me . . . for us. He's actually trying to make it work.

I want to make it work, too.

He clears his throat. "Well, Ms. Bishop, I believe we have no fewer than three campaigns coming up that we could use your keen eye on. In fact, one is actually perfect. My CFO has been pestering me about getting some candid shots. Me in the elements."

I frown at the phone. "How is it possible you don't have any?"

"People hound me relentlessly if I'm out and about. For the most part, I manage to stay incognito, but adding a photographer to the mix is the kind of trouble I don't want. However, I do intend to take you all over the city. You can grab the candid shots then. And feel free to throw in a dick pic for yourself."

I giggle uncontrollably. "I just might, Mr. Donovan. In fact, if I have carte blanche, I might just make a model out of you. Gray sweatpants. Calvin Klein underwear. All tasteful, of course."

"Of course."

"The possibilities are endless. I might need to get more memory on my phone."

His laugh is deep and husky, and it sets free a swarm of butterflies in the heart of my belly. "The car will pick you up tonight."

I check my watch. It's already four-thirty in the afternoon. I haven't showered or finished packing or . . . anything at all. A surge of panic runs through me.

"This is where our personalities clash. How can you possibly be a sharpshooter with this much spontaneity in your system?"

Mark chuckles. "It's the yin and yang of me. And I haven't been a sharpshooter for a very long time. Stop overpreparing and go with the flow. This isn't a spelling test."

I rub my chest to stave off full-on hyperventilating. "Go with the flow? Have you met me? I am not a go-with-the-flow girl. I'm a planner."

I scramble around the room, trying to decide if I need to replace anything in my suitcase. Or add anything. Or dump it out and start the hell over with my packing.

"What time is the car coming?"

"Six on the nose." His voice floats on a cloud of whimsy.

My eyes narrow. Mark loves sending me into a tailspin.

"Stop enjoying this so much," I snap out, unnerved. "You haven't seen me in a week. For all you know, I sprout hair like a Chia Pet, and south of the border is an Amazon jungle. You're rushing me, and you will suffer the consequences. I hope you've got your machete handy."

"I'm rushing you because I know you, Choir Girl. If I give you half a day, it gives you half a day to come up with excuses for why you can't go, or why you can't go for a week. You've already accepted with Zac, and you've got exactly," he pauses a beat, "one hour, twenty-two minutes, and forty-five seconds to be outside your front door, or else."

I stare at the phone incredulously. "Or else what?"

Mark's voice turns dark. "Or else I'll be on the next jet down there, dragging you from your home to mine—caveman style—where I'll thrash you mercilessly with my cock."

I swallow hard. Wanting to see that in action, I'm half-tempted to double-dog dare him. Instead, my gaze flies to the clock again. "How does this work, exactly?"

"My cock?"

"No, raging sex maniac, *this*. Is this car driving me there? Am I flying? Do I need a passport?"

"First of all, I'm only a sex maniac with you. Please don't attempt to pigeonhole me as being a garden-variety sex maniac. Second, the car will take you to a private airstrip not too far from your house. There, you will board my private jet. You don't need a passport since you're traveling in the US. Neal will be your pilot, and Clarissa will be your flight attendant. There will be snacks on the plane, but don't overfill yourself. I have something special planned for dinner."

A surprise dinner. I wonder what it could be. "If the surprise dinner is your cock after you've told me not to overstuff myself on the plane, you'll owe me a real dinner."

"Would I bring you all the way to New York City and not take care of my girl?"

His girl? My heart flits wildly against the cage of my chest. Did he really just say that?

I hear a knock from the other end of the line. Mark's voice is muffled as he replies to whoever has his attention. Then he's back to me, a slow, hushed tone falling over him.

"I have to go, sweetheart. Don't overpack. I'd like to take you shopping while you're here. I'll see you soon."

"Yes. See you soon."

The pilot greets me with a firm handshake and a warm smile as the flight attendant grabs my bag.

I'm entering a jet that looks like it just came out of a rich-people reality show, and I'm in a pair of distressed jeans and a plain white T-shirt. I pull my light fleece jacket a little tighter over my frame.

The flight attendant helps me to my seat, and when I look at the seat belt like I've never seen one in my life, she explains. "You can adjust the tightness of the loop here. Can I offer you water, soda, or champagne?"

My knee bounces relentlessly. "Champagne, please."

I didn't want to tell Mark I've never flown before. I'm trying very hard not to think of this jet as a death trap. Hopefully, the champagne will help.

Clarissa not only delivers champagne, but a small plate with elegant-looking chocolates, slices of fruit, and a white trillium in a sealed glass case. I laugh out loud at the sight of it as Clarissa points to each offering with her hand as she explains the plate.

"Here we have five handmade chocolate truffles with fruit centers. And strawberries and papaya slices, which are reported to be your favorites."

"They are."

"And a white Trillium. I don't know very much about this flower, but Mr. Donovan was specific as to it not being removed from the casing."

The three-pointed tiny flower looks up at me, bringing back a flood of memories.

"Mr. Donovan was right to say that." I lift the glass up to her. "This was my mother's favorite flower. She loved enjoying nature and going for mountain walks, but she never picked it. So, one day, I decided to get her a whole bouquet of them. I spent an entire afternoon selecting them and other flowers to go into a vase. I set it in the house for her to see as soon as she got home and went outside to play with my brothers and our friends. By the time Mom came home, our entire home reeked of these guys."

Clarissa's wide eyes dart to the bag. "They stink?"

"Stink is putting it mildly. They smell like raw meat after it's been sitting in the sun for a day. Flowers that attract bees smell sweet. Flowers that attract flies smell like the county dump." I eye the pretty white flower with a wry grin. "But I love it all the same."

She takes the seat beside me for just a second and keeps an eye on the pilot. "I'm not supposed to tell you this, but apparently, he spent all afternoon looking for it."

I offer her the plate. "Can I thank you with a chocolate?"

She shakes her head sweetly. "Mr. Donovan says he made them by hand specially for you."

I don't know at what point my legs stopped bouncing or my nerves eased up, but by the time we land, I've become relaxed enough to nod off.

A firm hand smooths over my forehead, brushing my hair to one side. I flutter open my eyes just as a warm mouth presses against mine. I'd know those full lips and delicious stubble anywhere.

Mark unsnaps my belt and unravels me with a slow, sexy glint in his eyes. "I have big plans for you and this jet when we return home."

Home. He probably means his family home. I try not to make too much of it. "And what would that be?"

He rubs his lips against mine as he shakes his head. "You think I'm just going to give up my secrets? You'll have to pry them from me." His hands clasp my face as he kisses me long and hard and achingly slow. He tears himself away as we both struggle for air. "Let's go."

He leads me down the flight of stairs where there's a car waiting.

A chauffeur has the back door open, and he nods. "Good evening, Ms. Bishop. Where to, Mr. Donovan?"

I slide across the back seat as Mark climbs in beside me. "Eleven Madison Park."

CHAPTER TWENTY-THREE

MARK

I knew that by giving Jess less time, she'd skip all the frilly dresses and opt for jeans. So, I wore jeans and a T-shirt myself and chose a Michelin-rated restaurant that still lets you dress down. Eleven Madison Park. I know my girl so well.

Huh. My girl. I've thought it over and over a dozen times in my head today before she showed up, then started saying it. It felt natural rolling off my tongue. Deliciously natural.

I could see the tension in Jess's body as she sat down, surrounded by four people waiting on us. What she doesn't know about this restaurant is that they customize each experience for the people who arrive. And for my Choir Girl, they brought her all the warmth of home. Wildflowers, rustic candles, and woodsy accents throughout. When her shoulders finally relax and I can see her relishing each bite, I feel a small sense of accomplishment. I'm bringing her to the dark side, one well-played meal at a time.

Later, we wander around Central Park so that it would

give her a sense of peace and calm to see big, lush trees in the heart of a concrete city. I'm in luck, because this year is especially warm, and instead of an icy wonderland, a fall-colored canvas still clings to each tree, the golds, oranges, and reds the perfect backdrop for my mountain girl.

I wrap my arm around her as we stroll, and when she melts into me, the hard crust around my heart crumbles away. I think I could love this girl.

No. I know I could love this girl. I just need to convince her to move here.

"Is it always this beautiful?" she asks.

"No. It's ten times more breathtaking in the spring." I point in a far-off direction. "Down that way is Lilac Walk. All season, it's a full palette of purples, and the air is thick with their fragrance."

Jess smiles quietly but doesn't meet my eyes. "And that way?"

I have to think for a moment. "In spring, that would lead to the cherry blossoms. The trees are a riot of pink confetti flowers."

She squeezes my waist. "Sounds like paradise."

I kiss her temple. "Anywhere with you would be paradise."

Anywhere? Fuck, who said that?

Reminder: Kick myself in the ass when we get home. I'm supposed to be convincing her to come here. Period.

After an hour of walking, day transforms into night. It isn't until Jess shivers that I realize her warmth has gone. She unleashes a small yawn.

"Ready to head back?" I ask and slide thick auburn hair from her face so I can look into her eyes.

She smiles sleepily. "I've been trying to keep my bearings, but I'm completely lost. Which way is the car?"

I jut out my chin straight ahead. "No need for one. I live right over there."

We make our way across the path to the entrance of my building. Francois holds the door open, anticipating our arrival.

But as we approach, my phone buzzes. By the ringtone, I know it's my chief financial officer. We pause before entering, and I tug Jess just a little closer as I answer.

"I'm on vacation, Dean."

"There's no such thing as a vacation for a CEO. We have a very important customer who needs your undivided attention. I'm not even kidding you when I say that they might bring in a billion dollars of work all on their own in the next seven years."

There are only a few customers with that kind of influence and wealth, and none of whom I can discuss on the phone. An annoyed growl erupts from my chest. "When?"

"I'll give you one guess."

Fuck. That means now. Which means they're halfway across the world and don't like to be kept waiting.

"I can be there in fifteen." I glance down, knowing Jess has heard my every word.

Doe-eyed, she peers up at me with a mischievous smile, trouble written all over her face. "Just give me the keys to your place, and I'll make myself at home," she says sweetly and bats those long eyelashes at me.

I kiss her lips, probably more passionately than I should,

considering that Francois is still holding a door and watching us keenly.

I turn to him. "Please see that Ms. Bishop gets a key to my place, and have the concierge show her up."

"Did you want me to call a car, sir?"

"No time. I'll grab a taxi. Attend to Ms. Bishop."

Francois holds the door wider. "Anytime you're ready, miss."

She pulls me closer to the curb and tugs me down so her lips are near my ear. "I was only teasing," she whispers. "I wouldn't dare dream of going in your place alone. I can follow you to work and wait in your lobby."

I take her hand to my cheek and kiss her palm. "My place is your place, Jess. Make yourself at home. If there's anything you need, you can call the concierge, and they'll bring it up immediately." With a finger under her chin, I pull her so her lips meet mine. "I don't know how long I'll be. If you get tired, crash."

With one final kiss, I lift an arm to the street. A taxi pulls to the curb, then I get in and take off.

CHAPTER TWENTY-FOUR

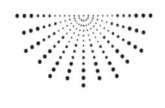

JESS

With a sigh, I wave goodbye to Mark and head into the building.

Francois leads me through an elegant hall to the concierge desk, where he hands me off.

"Good evening, Ms. Bishop." The concierge is a young man, perhaps thirty, with bold glasses in a striking blue frame. They set off his smiling eyes beautifully. "Mr. Donovan called and asked that I have a few things ready for you."

He called? "When?"

"Just now."

I must have the goofiest grin pasted on my face, but I don't care. Inside, Mark beats the heart of a beautiful multitasker. It's the most I've been taken care of since my parents...

"Here we are." The concierge hands me an envelope with instructions for how to program the door with my phone. When I stare blankly at what looks like Greek on the page, he says, "If you like, I can set it up for you now. It'll only take a moment."

I noticed his name tag. "Thank you, Ian." Willingly, I hand over my phone, grateful for his help. "Technology is definitely not my thing."

"Mine, either. I usually have my thirteen-year-old do it for me. I only know this much because it's my job." Half a second later, he slips it back into my hand. "Done. Let's get you home."

He wings out an arm and I loop mine in it, but I'm still tripping over what he just said. *Home.* Everybody seems to be calling this home all of a sudden. Or maybe everyone is just being hospitable.

We take the elevator up to the sky, it seems.

"Your bag arrived earlier," Ian says. "If you'd like me to send the butler up to help you put everything away—"

Quickly, I shake my head. It's bad enough that my brother saw what's in that bag. I really don't need a butler scrutinizing it, too.

When we arrive at our floor, the elevator opens, and I'm stunned stupid.

"Welcome home," Ian says, his hand pressing lightly to my back before the doors close, urging me inside the apartment. I step in and look around. "Punch number seven if you need me."

The doors shut before I can thank him properly, and now, I'm all alone. In Mark's lair. My steps are timid across the floor as I brave my way in.

The city is a sea of twinkling lights that take up every inch of the panoramic windows. I drink in the jaw-dropping sight for what has to be ten minutes.

No wonder Mark loves it here. His penthouse is huge. A

bachelor palace that could eat my little house in the mountains and spit it into the wastebasket.

As upscale as it is, though, it isn't trendy at all. Nothing is contemporary. Lots of beautiful leather furnishings are centered on magnificent rugs. Books and pictures are everywhere I turn. For a Manhattan playboy, he's managed to make a wonderfully warm home in the clouds.

"This place never ends," I mumble softly.

The great room is a vast space interspersed with textured pillows and expensive art. There are three televisions on the wall. I know Mark is a sports fan, but I have a feeling he mostly uses them for work. It occurs to me that maybe he never stops working.

Like me.

The kitchen is set up for a professional chef. Two massive islands span a large space boasting granite and stainless-steel surfaces. I see a recipe card on the counter and nearly lick it. It's for his mother's French silk pie. I've only had it a few times and nearly died. A traditional French silk pie is airy whips of chocolate. Hers sets those whips sky-high with only one secret ingredient: bourbon. It somehow magically makes the pie even more cloudlike and heavenly.

I check the fridge. Mark hasn't made it yet, but all the ingredients are front and center, and the promise of it is enough for me. I check out all the other goodies he has in here —which is stocked like a Costco—everything from gourmet foods to American cheese.

It's no secret that the man loves his grilled cheese sandwiches. Traditionally made. Even the suggestion of cheddar or provolone will seriously set Mark off.

I grab a chilled bottle of water. Considering it's the only drink available that won't permanently ruin Mark's gorgeous things if I spill it, it seems like the logical choice.

I make my way deeper into the Cave of Wonders, walking through a wide hall.

To my left is a study, or library, which connects to an office. To the right is a gym with state-of-the-art equipment, along with a wooden sauna and a huge Jacuzzi. I continue along and find several bedrooms in succession.

The man only has one butt. How many bedrooms does he need? A family of ten would comfortably live in this space with plenty of room to spare.

Within each bedroom is its own bathroom—or *en suite*, as I believe they're called. Marble countertops, grandiose showers, and unique, lavish bathtubs are featured in each and every one. Each room has its own theme, and I wonder how often they're used.

Who are his houseguests? Is this where Zac stays when he's in the city?

At the very end of the long hall is a set of double doors that are open so I can see inside. By the size of the bed fit for a king, this must be the master suite. It's just as opulent as the rest of the space is with one surprising exception: my scruffy little duffel. It's centered in the middle of the feather-soft, white-upholstered bench at the foot of the bed.

I giggle with stupid delight and do a ridiculous dance in place before slinging it over my shoulder. When I make my way to the closet, it's as if I've been transported to Barneys.

The entire place lights up the moment I stepped through. I could drive the length of it. There are huge windows across two walls, an island, another island, and neat rows of suits followed by more casual clothes. And don't even get me started on the shoes.

This is the kind of man I'm staying with. Wealthy. Sophisticated. With a doorman, concierge, and butler.

I'm standing at a crossroads with two options: dive in or run. Confused, I tug the duffel a little higher on my shoulder while I nibble my lower lip.

What to do?

CHAPTER TWENTY-FIVE

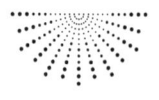

MARK

I never thought I'd be eager to leave work, considering work has been my steadfast mistress for years, but today is different. Jess is home waiting for me, and I feel it in every part of my soul. It's pushing nine p.m. as Lance and I make our way out of the building together.

"Oh, hey," I tell him. "I need another check for that charity I mentioned."

Lance nods. "Working your way up to a million-dollar donation?"

I would if I could. "It's a replacement check. Same amount. Same recipient."

"Should I cancel the first one?"

I shake my head casually as if it's no big deal. "No. The last one was accidentally shredded."

Lance wipes a hand over his face, impatience bleeding from the gesture. "Hundreds of thousands of dollars to a charity that can't even take care of a check. I know you're dick-struck by this *woman* . . ."

He says the word with enough frustration to make my jaw tense. Before I can explode at him, he holds up his hands.

"Look, I'm all for a righteous fuck as well as the next guy, but you need to be careful. This isn't Monopoly money."

I pocket my hands to avoid giving a friend an uppercut to the jaw. "Lance, I need you to hear me when I say this. Be very careful about the way you refer to or address Jess. Clear?"

His smile is mortared in place. "As the Centenary Diamond."

Lance dusts off his suit and straightens an already well-knotted tie, calculating his next move. I doubt my nose flaring and strained stance has escaped his keen observation.

"I'm sorry," he says sincerely. "I had no idea you could be so close to a girl, considering I suspect you're Satan himself."

"That's actually one of her nicknames for me."

He chuckles, his shoulders dropping as I relax, too. He pats me on the back. "I didn't realize she meant that much to you."

I puff air into my cheeks, braving the truth. "Until last week, neither did I." My driver opens the door to my Bentley as we approach. "Need a ride?" I offer him.

Lance waves me off with a sly smile. "I'm actually meeting up with someone for drinks. It's walking distance."

And people think I'm the player. Lance blows through women like breath mints.

I nod my understanding. "Have fun."

He lifts his smile higher and waggles his brows. "I intend to."

Jay holds open my door as I get in. "Where to, sir?" he asks after getting behind the wheel.

"Home," I say as I settle into the warm comfort of thinking of a home with someone in it.

Jeez, I left her hours ago. Lord knows what Jess is up to. Maybe enjoying the sauna or reading. God help us all if she's trying to cook.

Unfortunately for both of us, this is a city that never sleeps, and we're a hair above gridlock.

"Come on, come on." An impatient huff escapes my mouth. My knee bounces as the traffic inches along at a snail's pace. "I feel like I could army-crawl home faster."

Jay glances at me in the mirror. "Give me fair warning if you do. I want to have my phone ready to record."

This is what happens when you bring on a buddy to work for you. A dozen laughs at my own expense.

"I'll bet you would, *fucker*." I chuckle, welcoming every arrow he slings at me. It's why I hired him to begin with.

Jay is also an expert marksman with twenty-six hours in hand-to-hand combat training. A bullet to the ribs and two in the thigh took him out of the real action. But at six-foot-four and two hundred pounds of lean muscle, he's one hell of an intimidating presence, my chauffeur-slash-bodyguard whenever he's around. Saves me the hassle of having an entourage.

But that wasn't the only reason I offered him the job.

I brought him on to keep me grounded. Jay is a no-nonsense badass who doesn't give two shits about the money. He's here for me. Most people within arm's length of me are. It's too easy to get full of myself when everyone is telling me how great I am. When I'm suffocating from the swelling of my own head, I don't need kudos. I need an unyielding kick in the ass. Like my brothers would do.

It's probably why I like Choir Girl so much. I've got women beating down my door to stroke my ego and suck my dick. Jess would never let me get away with too much shit. I know my boundaries with her. I could never have her. I have to earn her, every step of the way.

And the challenge is getting me rock-hard.

After what feels like twelve years later, we finally roll up to the front of my building. Jay holds open my door. I notice the unsettled smile that hasn't left his face the entire ride.

"What?"

His hands rise in surrender. "Nothing, boss. I'm just not sure I've ever seen you, *eh*, happy. Your smile has been sky-high the entire ride here." He glances at the top of the building, and I look up, as well. "Must be one hell of a woman you've got there."

"She is. I'm just hoping I haven't left her alone long enough to burn the place down."

"Sounds like my wife. She only knows two settings: rare and charred."

I laugh and wish him a good night.

By the time the elevator reaches my floor, a thrill charges through me. I have no idea what to expect, but I know it'll be wonderful. Jess could burn the place down, and I'd just laugh hysterically and console her with kisses. Because that's who I am around her.

This isn't like before. She's not a kid, and I'm not a dumbass. Jess is a bright, beautiful woman, and I'm head over heels.

When the elevator dings, announcing the floor, I hold in a breath as the doors open. The entire place is oddly . . . quiet.

Dark and silent. Like the million and one times I've come home to be completely alone.

"Choir Girl!" I sing out.

Three heartbeats later, and her voice calls out from the other end of the hall. "In here."

I head in the direction of her voice, hard as a rock and straining just from the sound of it. It's gotten even worse when she sings, which she only does when she thinks I'm not listening. Foolish girl. I'm always listening.

I can see light flickering in my bedroom. Candlelight. I'm already working my way out of my shirt when I see her, and *holy fuck*.

She's in one of my button-down blue shirts with all but one button unfastened. A tie is around her neck, fitted like a bow. Mr. Gucci would be very disappointed to see how his silk ties are being abused . . . or would he?

I can't even pretend I'm angry. My smile is absurdly wide. "You've been playing in my closet."

She hops on my big Kluft mattress, with wanton disregard for it or the down comforter she's climbing across. Funnily enough, I don't mind at all. If Zac even looks at it with his shoes on, I threaten him with spending the night at a motel. But with Jess, it's adorably perfect.

She smiles, her eyes filled with glee as her hair floats with every bounce. "I needed a hanger. They all seem to be taken in that men's fashion boutique of yours."

She jumps about, staking her territory. I might mind if her tits weren't bouncing in hypnotic glory.

I slide off my shoes and remove my jeans. "The hangers are kept in a drawer, my precious Neanderthal." In nothing but my boxers, I hop up there with her. "And why do you need hangers? I told you not to bring clothes."

She giggles, and small fireworks burst in my heart.

I intend to make this woman giggle and laugh and relax and enjoy every single moment we're together. She may be my addiction, but I intend to be her love potion, convincing her to say yes to anything and everything I offer.

Jess gives me a mischievous grin. "Your shirt is remarkably comfortable."

I pull her slight frame into mine. "Too bad you won't be wearing it very long."

We tumble to the bed. First, my body is on hers, and then we roll until her body is on mine.

I tug at the tie. "Did you need the hanger for this, too? Your Windsor knot is atrocious."

She seats herself over my hips. My boxers are no match for her delicious heat. "I needed somewhere to hang my panties."

"Good. You're not wearing panties. Thank fuck you have some listening skills."

When she licks her lower lip, shreds of self-control peel away from me. I undo the single fastened button of the shirt she's wearing, and there they are again. My dog tags. My possession. Something in her eyes brightens when I drag the tags across her breasts.

I cup her cheek, grazing her lips with my thumb. "Have you done this before? Felt them here," I circle a breast, "and here," I press them against a nipple. "Played with yourself and thought of me?"

I press my thumb through her lips, and she sucks. Her eyes

flutter, and her body moves in a coaxing rhythm against my cock.

What did she use before? Her hand? A pillow?

My skin flushes with enough heat to combust at the thought of her getting off like this. If she goes on much longer, I'm going to blow.

Jess's eyes connect with mine, and I don't have to say a word. She knows what I'm thinking, what I'm wanting. She knows because it's what she wants, too.

Warm, tender kisses meet my chest and abs as she nibbles along the band of my boxers. I swear this woman is going to kill me, one titillating pleasure at a time.

"Take them off," I growl in demand, seeing a sly smile on her face. She wants to tease me. Torture me.

Her finger glides against the underside of the band, strategically avoiding my tip. Evil girl. It's as if she has to know how hard I am, how much I want her, because the battering ram of a cock rudely jutting her way hasn't given her the faintest clue. I tuck an arm behind my head and watch as she pries the waistband down.

It only takes a single lick before I slam my eyes shut. *"Fuuuck."*

Jess pulls the boxers down my legs, kissing and nibbling my thighs, her hair a sensual tangle of red that feathers my skin as it follows her. Her eyes are in a dream state when she looks up at me. Everything she's doing is turning her on, too.

And just when I thought she couldn't get any hotter.

I prop up on my elbows and take her in. "Touch yourself, sweetheart. Show me that you're ready for me."

Jess awakens a hunger in me, one I've never known with

anyone else. But when she lies with her back pressed against my pillows, spreads her legs wide, and wipes two fingers across her gorgeous pink pussy, I'm starving like I've never had a meal.

I lick her fingers and taste the sweetest arousal I've ever known.

My cock is impatient and makes its way to her entrance, forcing its way into her hot, tight fit. A snug lock welcoming the perfect key. I pause only for a moment to take it all in, and the sensation surrounds my skin like a glove.

A desperate squeak escapes her throat, her back arching as I take a breast into my mouth. My body thrusts full force, merciless in its rhythm. I bury myself in her over and over again as she writhes and gasps for air.

Good. Let that be a lesson to my bad little Choir Girl. How dare she play in my shirt? The one I'll never launder again.

Panting, we work together, our frantic pace gaining as my heart beats out *more, more, more.* I want more. I've never wanted anything from a woman, but with her, I want everything.

"Mark." Her voice is a sweet rush of warning, and it's my undoing.

It all feels so good. So . . . fucking . . . good.

I plow harder, electrified with excitement and fear. Exhilarated. Terrified. This connection is so much—too much. She knows me. Sees me. With her, I've been the biggest asshole and the bravest knight. I'm barreling into the event horizon where my past and future collide, and it's as if for the first time, I'm alive.

Her body shudders, and mine jerks with all I have in me.

With her, I'm not a broken soldier or a playboy multi-millionaire. I'm simply Mark, the purest form of me at tenfold the man I ever thought I could be. And I'm hers, locked in a connection I can never escape.

I know. Because eight years ago, I tried.

Now I can't imagine life without Jess. Without her, I'm not me.

CHAPTER TWENTY-SIX

MARK

For days now, Jess and I have been in this fantasy cycle of sleep, eat, and fuck. We're like animals, moving from one basic need to the next, with only a temporary satiation of our appetite for each other. But at some point, I had to release her from captivity, damn it all.

Today, we're shopping, walking up and down the streets, where I can't seem to let her go for more than a second. And if she feels the sudden urge to head home, Jay is never far. I've caught him circling the block a few times, but Jess hasn't. Close, but not too close. I don't want her concerned.

And if I'm lucky and she wants to cut the afternoon short, skip dinner, and dive right into dessert in bed, Jay will be here at a moment's notice.

We've stopped briefly, long enough so she can snap a quick shot of me looking in the window of a store. My hand already misses hers as I cup it around the back of my neck. "Do you have the shot yet?"

Other than the background mutterings of fast-paced New Yorkers, no response.

I glance in her direction. "Jess?"

It's only then that I notice her. She's gone inside the shop and is standing inside the window next to a gold-gowned mannequin, her phone targeting me like a creature in the wild. She checks her screen and smiles as bright as the sun. Her thumb rises in eager approval.

When a woman rushes over, lines furrow in Jess's face. I'm about to step inside and explain, but then somehow Jess has managed to work it out. All smiles, she shares with the woman what she's captured, which is really not fair, considering I've been her personal Calvin Klein model all afternoon and haven't even gotten a chance to look at the pics.

Jess reaches out, aiming her phone in my direction again, but she's not even looking at the damn thing. She's too busy getting a card from the woman with her other hand. Jess wastes no time getting one last shot before barreling out of the store and into my arms. Both legs wrap around my waist as my hands secure the beautiful mound of her ass.

"Someone thinks my photos are good enough to hire me on," she says excitedly.

My brows twitch. "Yeah. Me." I kiss that silly mouth of hers. "Are you telling me you were offered a job?"

A glimmer of hope brightens in my chest. I'll take any reason for Jess to stay in New York City, even if I'm not the one calling the shots.

"They've been hunting for someone who can give their social media campaign a fresh eye. She likes what she sees."

I nibble Jess's neck, ignoring every passerby like they're

invisible. "I know I like what I see." I make another move toward her lips when she manages to wriggle out of my hold. "Where are you going?"

"I just had to come out here to tell you I'm going to be in there for a few more minutes. She wanted to see what I could do with some candid shots on the fly. It won't take long—promise."

I snag a loop on Jess's jeans and pull her into me. I don't want to tell her, but I don't give a fuck how long it takes. As long as it keeps her here.

"Take as long as you need. I've got a few work things on my phone to keep me busy."

My lips press to hers with enough ownership in the moment. I slide a single finger to her belly and force her away. It's obvious by her pout she wanted to keep going.

"Either you're going back in," I say with a mock frown, "or I'm locking you in my bedroom for the rest of the afternoon."

It's adorable the way Jess takes her lip between her teeth as if she's thinking it over. "Decisions, decisions . . ."

I kiss her temple, taking a long inhale of her scent. The swirl of floral and vanilla seeps into me enough to keep me going until she returns.

With a smile that could light the city, Jess heads back inside while I find a bench and pull out my phone.

"Mark? Oh, my *gawd*, is that you?"

The clippety-clop of a nightmare in six-inch platforms heads toward me at lightning speed. Brie flops on the bench beside me and stops short of giving me a kiss when I lean away from her.

Has she lost her fucking mind?

My ass smartly scoots a mandatory foot away from hers, but I can't be rude. Her family's influence and wealth could seriously do me some damage if they wanted to, and I have a feeling she's a girl who holds a grudge.

My smile is forced and small. "Hello, Brie."

She reaches out to stroke the stubble on my cheek. "I missed you," she coos, as if I'm an infant or a Pomeranian. Apparently, a mandatory foot isn't enough.

I decide to stand. "We only had the one date, Brie."

She leans toward me. When her breasts nearly spill out, I have to wonder how much of my thousand bucks is still buried in there.

"You can't just end us like this," she says, pouting. "We were so good together."

At this point, I don't even know what to say. Between her unwanted advances and the overwhelming stink of Eau de BrewDog, it's clear she's not thinking. Not that I ever considered it her strong suit.

Frowning, I have to suck in a calming breath to avoid raising my voice. My tone is flat and uncompromising. "There is no us. We literally met that day, and I haven't spoken with you since."

Brie stands, practically tripping over herself as she acts *not drunk*. "Aww, you and I both know you're just playing hard to get."

I walk her to the curb and lift my arm to hail a cab. "You just need to get some rest, Brie. And maybe a bottle of water."

Her limp body falls into my arms. I'm not sure if she's fallen from grace in those ridiculously high heels or if she just passed out from the booze, but it becomes clear when her lips are on mine that nice and polite isn't driving the point home.

With no-fucking-way determination, I latch my hands on to her arms and shove her against the cab that's just pulled up. Not with enough force to hurt, but just enough to wake her up from this deranged state she's in.

"Get it through your trust-fund brain; I'm not interested." I stiffen my stance. No part of my expression is a welcome mat for this colossal mess of a woman.

Thoroughly annoyed, I shake my head. Lance was out of his goddamned mind to think this hot mess was worth a second of my time.

Brie's two-inch-long talon glides along my jaw. Her whisper is slurred and obnoxiously loud as she leans in closer. "Don't save it all up for that Choir Girl of yours. I can respect that a man needs to slum it."

At that, all traces of my patience are shot down quicker than a duckling at a toddler's hand at the fair. I swat her sparkle-manicured claw away. She giggles and tries it again.

Un-fucking-believable.

Thankfully, the cabbie earns a huge tip by wrestling her into the back seat. She's like a fucking octopus, all arms and legs that can't be contained. He finally packs her into the backseat, and I hand him a few hundreds.

"I don't care where you take her. Head toward the Upper East Side and drop her someplace nice. Tiffany's or a nice restaurant. Just get her far the hell away from me."

"Yes, sir."

Brie presses her lips against the glass, and a small amount of vomit worms its way to the top of my throat. *So fucking gross.* Considering that her lips touched mine, and I have no idea where they've been, I open the Amazon app and place a same-day order for ten bottles of Listerine.

Her voice carries from the other side of the glass. "Have your fun. I'll be waiting."

And I'll be doing triple-axel flips on a skating rink in hell before that happens.

∼

After spending the better part of an hour catching up on my emails, uneasiness rolls over me. I shake it off and stroll into the shop.

It's a quiet, little boutique. Dresses are lined up on hangers spaced about an inch apart, with shoes and purses on clear pedestals throughout the store.

A woman comes up to me, the same woman Jess was talking to. "Can I help you?" she asks, her smile predatory as she sizes up whether I could spend money in here.

What is this, Pretty Woman?

"I'm looking for the beautiful redhead you were speaking with earlier."

"Jess? She left."

Confused, I blink. "Left? When?"

The woman's head shakes in an *I'm not sure* fashion. Her shrug is slight. "Soon after she returned. She snapped a few shots, and we said our goodbyes. She walked right out the front door."

Realization gives me an uppercut to the jaw. *Goddammit.* She saw me with the Yacht Destroyer.

I bolt from there and wave for my car, already dialing Zac.

He answers on the first ring, but before I can get a word in edgewise, he says, "Nine one one. What's your dickhead emergency?"

Which means she's already called him, and he knows. About us. Me and Jess. As a thing. Which also means he's probably already worked out a way to get her the hell out of Dodge.

Fuck. "Tell me she's still in the city."

"Why don't you use your resources and figure it out, dickwad?"

I punch the seat next to me. "Goddammit, she didn't see what she thinks she saw."

"Really? I saw the video clip, dumbass. That girl was all over you like a roach on a Twinkie. And from what I can tell, it didn't look like you were doing much to stop her."

"She's a drunk, rich girl with delusions of attractiveness. She made the moves, not me. I was in the process of shoving her ass in a cab when she kissed me. Which, by the way, I'm still traumatized over and in desperate need of antiseptic. I'm not about to lie about a piece of ass."

"But you lied to me and said that you wanted to hire Jess just for quote-unquote social media photos. And you lied to her and said it's just for the week."

I make an angry wrinkle face at the phone, not that he could see me at all. "It is just for the week."

Zac's voice turns eerily calm. "I'm sorry. Did you say something? My bullshit detector is going off like crazy, and I can't hear a thing."

I stew for a moment, taking in the traffic as my driver

heads toward my place. Zac is silent as I slump my shoulders and throw my head back into the seat. The fucker is always right, and I hate it.

"What do you want me to do?"

"How about you tell the truth?"

"I have."

"About everything. Why you don't do relationships. Why you wanted her in New York. I wasn't kidding when I said I'd marry her. I know all her secrets and she knows all of mine. So, what if we don't have passion? We have love, and if you fuck up your chance, I'm taking mine."

Zac's words unsettle me like bugs crawling beneath my skin. And not just because I know he'd do it—he and Jess have been best friends for years. Our families love each other. Them getting married makes perfect sense.

His words also make me want to tear out my heart and toss it at her feet. It's taken me a while to come to terms with it, but the damn thing seems to beat for only her.

And the two of them together don't just leave a bad taste in my mouth. It would kill me. I can only thank my lucky stars that they share a mutual unattraction to each other. A square peg and a round hole.

Then, like a ray of light through a storm cloud, he says something truly prophetic. "Mark, you've been putting this off for eight years. Take the shot."

∽

By the time I return to the penthouse, I don't have to look

around to know that Jess isn't there. That electric charge that floated through the air like pixie dust has fizzled. She's gone.

So, I do what all living things do when they're deprived of the one thing that keeps them alive. Although I know she's gone, I search for her. With forlorn steps, I make my way through an enormous penthouse that feels cold and empty and ungodly big for one person.

In my bedroom, I find my shirt on the floor, the one she was wearing the first night she came. I grab it and take a seat on the edge of the bed. Even without smelling it, her sweet vanilla scent lifts to my nose and slices through me.

I close my eyes and shake my head. I swore I'd never wash it. Now all I want to do is burn it to ashes and erase the past week.

And along with it, my heart.

CHAPTER TWENTY-SEVEN

JESS

I stare blankly out the window, the tip of a pen at my teeth.

I should be getting to work, but my heart isn't in it. It keeps redirecting my brain. It's as if Mark's taken up billboard space in my mind. Dark, wavy hair. Eyes that capture me whether they're decidedly gold or piercing wintergreen. And that smile.

I can shake it off for a little while, but then it all comes spiraling back. Every time I close my eyes, he's in front of me. Crawling under my skin. His lips along my neck. Burying himself deep, deep, deep inside.

Ugh.

Ferocious, I snatch up my phone and glare at it. Not a call. Not a text. Not one apology.

Granted, it was me who walked out on him, but who can blame me? They were kissing. *KISSING*. In the middle of New York City for all the world to fucking see. So what if it wasn't the only reason I left? I don't need any more reasons.

Mark's a player. I'm an idiot. Case fucking closed.

Shaking it off, I stare at a pile of documents that might as well be written in hieroglyphics. I grab the first envelope on the stack and snap it between two hands. *Focus.*

It takes my brain a minute to re-read who it's addressed to. *Power Maker Unlimited.* Ugh, even the name sounds cheesy. This envelope isn't for me. It's for Russ, delivered here by mistake. But it's the return address that my eyes stay fixed on. *Renaissance Holdings.* Why does that ring a bell?

Before I can look it up, three heavy knocks sound so loudly, I jump from my seat.

Two men enter with dark glasses and *don't fuck with me* expressions.

I narrow my eyes, suspicion pricking at my neck as I notice their suits. They're either the men in black or with the IRS. Is it wrong that I'm hoping they're the former? I haven't even worked through all the donations yet, and a probe into my finances is the last thing I need.

Why are they checking my books so soon?

"Ms. Bishop? Ms. Jessica Marie Bishop?"

I shrink in my chair, the tone of the man's voice intimidating. "Yes."

One of the men unbuttons his suit jacket. The gun beneath it causes me to gasp.

He seems to notice and yanks the glasses from his face. His meek smile is surprisingly disarming. "I'm authorized to carry this, ma'am. I didn't mean to frighten you."

Now I'm wondering if they're undercover cops. "Am I in some sort of trouble?"

"No, not at all. I have a delivery that was to be made to Ms. Jessica Marie Bishop. I'll just need to see some ID."

I fish my driver's license from my wallet and extend it to him. He doesn't take it but merely glances at it, then nods with a tight grin. He removes an envelope from his inside breast pocket and hands it to me. Once I've taken it, they turn to walk out.

"Have a nice day," one says over his shoulder.

Have a nice day? Definitely not the IRS.

The envelope is plain, with that security print on the inside so you can't see what's in it when you hold it up to the light. But it's thin enough to just have a piece of paper in it, so I'm not sure what all the fuss was about.

I open it and pull out a check. A corporate check. For one million dollars, but it's not to my foundation. It's made out to me, personally. *What on earth?* The name THE CENTURION GROUP stand in big, bold letters at the top, and in true Mark Donovan form, the signature is barely legible. Like a psychopath.

And then, there's the note captured at the bottom.

For Services Rendered – xo

Services rendered? X-fucking-O? Are you kidding me? So, now I'm not just one of the millions of women he's played, I'm his prostitute?

With enough rage to light a city, I crumple the check in my hand like the Hulk. The nerve of this man. *The fucking nerve!*

Rapping sounds at the door. It's Russ. Just fucking perfect. Because when it rains, it apparently pours dickheads.

"Hi, Jess. Look, before you throw something at my head, I just want you to know that I'm sorry. I was way out of line at the gala. You've worked incredibly hard for what you have, and my ego was getting the best of me. If there's any way we can still work together, I'd really like that."

My crusty exterior softens. Not entirely, but enough that I feel like he's not the biggest jackass to walk the planet. No, that title is definitely reserved for someone else.

Besides, I don't want to burn another bridge. I'm still getting over the biggest one I burned to date. But I'm still leery, even if I can't put my finger on why. And I really do need to get out of here before I waste an ounce of my pent-up fury on the lesser ass.

I push to my feet. "Thank you for the apology. Look, I'm happy to talk about it another time, but I'm in a terrible rush."

Mark Donovan can shove this wad of a check straight up his didactic asshole, and that's a message I intend to deliver in person. Not that I want to see Mark. I have to. The words *services rendered* are enough to spike my pissed-o-meter past rage straight to ready to take on the fucking world.

I gather a few things into my purse and head for the door. Who tells a rich, arrogant prick off by phone or text? Chickenshits, that's who. No, I want to look that bastard in the eye when I tell him off.

A small, stupid part of my heart flutters at the thought of seeing Mark. But I pull in a fortifying breath and chastise myself.

Don't you dare. Vow to Hate for All Eternity—ring a bell? He's our enemy. Always has been and always will be.

Russ's hand flies to the door, opening it wide. I race

outside and screech to a halt, staring stupidly at the near-empty parking lot as my brain catches up.

Shit, Brian drove me in this morning. I don't have the truck. And double shit, that means it's Friday, and Mark is in Manhattan today. Which is over three hours from here. One way.

Damn it all to hell, because my determination doesn't waiver. That's right. The man has the superpower to render me psychotically insane.

"Is there somewhere I can drive you? I'm happy to." Russ bolts to the passenger side of his BMW and opens the door, bowing. "Milady," he says with an old English accent.

Keeping my eye-rolling to a minimum, I slip into the seat and buckle in.

"Where to?" he asks once he's settled in the driver's seat.

"My place." I can pick up my truck and leave a note for Brian so he doesn't worry.

The half-hour drive is peaceful. Mostly small talk. Nothing work-related at all. Neither of us seems ready to rehash the other night. Russ mostly has his eyes on the road because it's easy to miss my driveway, even with my directions, while I focus on the uncrumpled check.

I'm holding in my hands more money than I could imagine in a lifetime. Certainly more money than my parents ever had in all of theirs.

For a split second, I imagine cashing it. What do I care what he thinks of me? This money could change everything. No more tuna and ramen. No more scraping for work. I could fix every last broken piece of the house. And I know the truth. I am not that man's love slave.

Okay, that's a lie. But I'm definitely not in it for the money. And the sad fact is, I'd never be his for very long. Mark Donovan is always just a heartbreak away, so why not cash it?

After a meditative breath, I fold up the check and shove it into my pocket, along with the rest of my deranged thoughts. Thoughts of me telling off big, arrogant Mark. Followed by hot, sweaty, angry sex. And then, long, languid make-up sex. I close my eyes and run a finger along that dumb chain beneath my shirt, wondering just how truly fucked-up I am.

This is why I don't do relationships. If Mark and I became anything more, I'd have to tell him everything. And it's so much easier to keep sweeping everything under the rug.

Russ turns the corner to head up my drive, and my hand is already on the handle. "Oh." He pulls in close to the porch, right beside the door. "When you get back, maybe I can take you for an apology coffee."

When his car rolls to a stop on the gravel, I try getting out, but it's still locked. It's apparent he's waiting for an answer. I attempt to blow him off. "Don't worry about it." By his frown, that wasn't the answer he wanted. "I really need to go," I say with an impatient yank to the handle that nearly rips it from his precious car.

"Oh." He unlocks it, and I get out.

Before I shut the door, I add, "There is a letter that arrived for you. I can probably get it to you in the next day or so."

A flash of worry crosses his face before a smile masks his concern. "Thanks."

The drive to New York City is remarkably smooth and peaceful.

I never really tried long-distance driving before, not that this is terribly long, but it doesn't exactly ease up on the mind, does it? My brain fires on every cylinder. It takes overthinking to a whole new hamster wheel.

What if I've driven all this way and Mark isn't even there? Or what if he's with *her*?

Once I close in on New York City, I have a decision to make: where to go. It's painfully apparent I haven't exactly thought this through.

After a brief stop at a gas station and some mild debating, I decide his penthouse is out. So is calling Zac. Nope, I'm throwing all my chips on the workaholic being at his office. Which I've only seen from the outside, though Zac has told me all about it.

Their chief of security is Kevin. Or Devin. But Zac told me that if I was ever in the city, all I'd have to do is show my ID and they'd give me my badge. Apparently, I have one there.

I'm almost afraid to know what photograph Zac used for it. Ten bucks says it's the one where I tripped into his ice cream cone, ending up with chocolate-strawberry swirl all over my face.

The building is ridiculously huge, taking up an entire city block. I'm not exactly sure this is it, though that's what the gods of Google Maps told me. Two security guards are standing out front when I pull alongside the curb and roll down my window.

"Is this The Centurion Group?" I ask.

One of the men listens to something in his ear and nods to

himself. "Yes, sir," I hear him say. I'm half-expecting him to demand that I take my heap of a truck out of here when he smiles.

"You're in the right place, Ms. Bishop. Leave the keys in the ignition, and we'll take care of it. Mr. Donovan is expecting you."

My heart flutters wildly, thumping hard against its cage. I'm here to tell off the world's greatest reconnaissance mastermind, and not once did I consider he'd be waiting for me. Did I really think he wouldn't know I was coming?

I shake my head and release a heated huff under my breath. "Of course, he did."

CHAPTER TWENTY-EIGHT

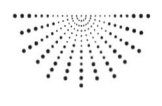

JESS

*I*nside, I'm greeted by a well-dressed man, probably in his early forties.

His suit is impeccable, his sandy-brown hair well-tamed, and he has an air about him that reeks of control freak. Every hour, every day. His smile is wide, but not entirely convincing.

He extends a hand with all the power and confidence his expensive watch can exude. "You must be Jessica," he says, his British accent crisp.

It's unnerving to have everyone around you know who you are when you have no idea who they are. I don't want to be rude, and not just because he's a stranger, and I'm never impolite to strangers. But because, by the looks of him, he could be a duke or something, and I don't want to inadvertently piss off a dignitary of a nation state.

"Everyone calls me Jess."

He squeezes my hand firmly and looks me up and down, not as much judging me as assessing me. Probably a habit he picked up after long years at boarding school. Or, what if *he* thinks I'm a prostitute?

His gaze drops to his watch. "You've had a long drive. Mr. Donovan is tied up at the moment."

I imagine Mark in some gilded office, surrounded by a flurry of blondes, quickly undoing hundred-dollar neckties from his wrists.

My smile tightens. "I'm sure he is."

The man leads me to an elevator that lifts us to the highest floor. As soon as the door is open, I'm not even sure what to think. It looks more like the lobby of an expensive hotel than an executive suite. The ceilings are at least two stories high, with glossy marble floors and fresh bouquets of roses everywhere.

"Can I offer you something to quench your thirst?" he asks.

I could eat. I mean, I didn't have lunch. And with every passing mile of the drive here, I got hangrier. I'd almost gnaw off this guy's arm if it weren't attached.

"If there's a water fountain nearby—"

"Water fountain." He chuckles, both brows raised. "Do they still make those?" His eyes connect with mine, and I can't tell if he's simply amused or being patronizing. "It's easy to see why Mark carries on about you."

He carries on about me?

He raises his hand and snaps two fingers in the air. My mouth falls open. It's about the rudest thing I've ever seen.

A man dressed in a white shirt and black vest rushes across the lobby with a tray. There's a tall glass of ice standing beside a bottle of Barton's Best orange soda. The disappointment I have in myself for surrendering to my weakness is overwritten by my swelling heart and goofy grin.

Now if they only had some vodka to go along with it.

I'd be perfectly happy drinking it out of the bottle, but the man beats me to it, pouring it into the glass as if it were an expensive drink, then waits for me to take it. I do, but before I can thank him, he's vanished into the woodwork.

My host leads me down a hall, and I drink as we walk. The first sip is thirst-quenching bubbles that tickle my nose and instantly reset my mood.

"Thank you . . . oh, I didn't get your name."

"Lance P. Anders, Esquire. Corporate attorney for The Centurion Group."

I nod. He looks like a man who would insert his middle initial into every introduction. A small, snarky side of me wonders if the *P* stands for pretentious.

As we make our way through the long corridor, he notices a man passing us. "Tighten that knot, Mr. Jeffries."

The thing is, I didn't see anything wrong with his tie. All I see is somebody who manages people like a series of mistakes to be corrected. Out of curiosity, I check the third finger on his left hand. Shocker, he's single.

When we arrive at two large double doors at the end of the hall, he opens one. "He'll see you now."

As if I've been summoned.

I want to scream at the top of my lungs, "Hey, he didn't bring me here. I'm just here to tell the bastard off." By the look on Stuffed Shirt's face, he's expecting me to walk in, so any tantrum I might have would do no good.

I hold my breath and step into the Donovan lion's den.

And it is a den. An enormous, state-of-the-art den.

Poured concrete floors. Contemporary furnishings. Stone and metal tables, along with sleek white leather sofas and deep, squared-off chairs. The colors are neutral, save for a few palm trees in planters and the rich blue fabrics of the drapes and chairs. Not at all the sort of office I would picture for a CEO. It's far too utilitarian to be comfortable. I imagine he's extremely efficient in a space like this, cut off from the comfort and the conveniences of the world.

But Mark Donovan is nowhere in sight.

I take a few irritatingly loud steps in, clicking my heels along the floor, which apparently, echo beyond these walls.

"In here!" I hear him shout from an ajar door against the far wall. I hadn't actually noticed it, and I'm sure once it's closed, it blends seamlessly into the pattern of the paint.

When I step through, it's clear I've fallen through the rabbit hole.

A far departure from the room I left, this one is bright and airy and reminiscent of a chef's kitchen. Floor-to-ceiling French windows are accented with irises and lilies. There's a huge marble slab in the center of the space with an eight-burner gas range behind it. Elegant stools line the island, which surrounds a large two-sided basin. Through a small archway is a table set for two.

The small, round table showcases a square porcelain vase of pink and cream roses, a delicate place setting before each chair, and two crystal flutes with a bottle of expensive champagne.

My mouth falls slack as I look at the label and realize just how expensive it is. It's not a Donovan's bubbly, which at a hundred dollars a bottle is light-years from cheap, but a Krug Private Cuvée. The last year I worked at Donovan's, I spotted one on the shelf and googled it out of curiosity. Roughly, it equated to hundreds of dollars…per glass.

Then it vanished.

Ever since then, every time I wandered near the empty space where it used to be, I couldn't help wondering if it had been sold for someone's extravagant birthday party or lavish wedding. Now I know where it disappeared to.

"Hello, Jess."

His deep voice sinks into me with too much force to deny—a match strike straight to my core. I turn, and it's like basking in the rays of the sun.

Mark's hair is combed back more than I'm used to seeing, and the black apron he's wearing seems out of place, but everything else is the same. A stark white shirt that clings to every sinewy muscle. Twinkling eyes the color of the sea. That smart, devilish grin that ignites his killer dimples.

He's carrying a three-tiered tray, but I'm paying no attention to it. When he locks me in the hold of his gaze, my body betrays me, cementing my feet in place.

We stand and stare as I catch my breath. Electricity crackles all around us as waves of heat lick at my skin.

Why does Mark always have this effect on me? The way he looks at me, I feel naked and vulnerable, and I hate it. I've always hated it.

My heart thumps hard in warning—*thump, thump, thump*—nearly breaking through my chest. This is a mistake. A bad, horrible, catastrophic mistake.

What was I thinking?

I could never one-up Mark Donovan. Not now. When I was a kid, it was easy. Kick him in the nuts and run. Now, when we fight, I bring a knife, and he brings his swaggering dick. As all the humming in my body reminds me, I have no defenses against this man.

I don't think. I act. Or better yet, I run, blinking away the bindings of his spell and storming past him to the door.

"Do you really think I would let you get away that easily?" he calls out after me. "I learned the first time, Choir Girl."

Two solid doors of the archway swing shut. They look white and elegant and come together seamlessly. When they do, a loud clank echoes through the room. I have to touch them to know for sure, but they're definitely metal.

Dumbfounded, I scrabble, but my search for a knob turns up completely empty. "What in the world?"

"Panic room," Mark says as he sets everything up at the table. "For the girl who likes to panic."

With the way this place is decked out? More like a panic room for Julia Childs. "Are you kidding me?" I give the door an annoyed swat and nearly break my hand. "Ow."

With two large steps, Mark stands before me, his hand taking mine. He caresses my skin in a way that I can feel everywhere. "There's that passion I love."

He inspects my hand and kisses my knuckles, setting off a chain reaction of me whipping it back, nearly losing my balance on this slippery-as-snot floor, before getting my ass hoisted over his shoulder.

I pound his back relentlessly and yell at his butt. "Put. Me. DOWN!"

I feel the crack of his large hand sting my right butt cheek.

I'll never freely admit the sensation it's sending to all the wrong places, but if Mark weren't carrying me, my knees would melt. Breathless and feigning shock, I simmer down.

"No." He takes bold, assured steps to the table.

Red-hot anger simmers up, rage overflowing and taking charge. My fists pound on his rock-solid thighs, and *ooh*—I'm not even thinking when my brain misfires. Enraged, my teeth sink into the lean meat of his tight, round butt cheek.

"Wha—ow—Jess!" His cries aren't in outrage. They're more of a chuckle. "Did you just bite my ass?"

Me? Commit a childish outburst as ridiculous as biting a high-powered CEO on the derriere? What an accusation. How dare he! I stifle my giggles. "Did I? Sorry, was that not on the Services Rendered menu?" I snark. Like a brat mid-tantrum, I pound the ass meat in question. "Marcus Evan Donovan, if you don't put me down right now, so help me, I'll—"

"Bite me again? If that's your idea of foreplay, consider me sold."

His words cut my tantrum short.

More gently than expected, or even deserved, Mark settles me gingerly in a seat and scoots into the chair. "I've done my due diligence, Jess. Gave you three days to stress-starve and stew in your righteous indignation."

He takes a seat opposite me as I consider all the items within arm's reach to throw at his colossal head. But then I take a good look at the tray, and I can't even begin to consider wasting one of the scrumptious items as ammunition.

Every bite on the tray, I know. They all tickle my heart for attention. It's my childhood on three tiers.

Heart-shaped grilled sandwiches ripe with white cheddar

and thinly sliced tomatoes are at the bottom, with two cups of creamy tomato soup and a matching heart shape of sour cream. The second tier is the best side order known to man: sweet potato fries with a dusting of cinnamon sugar. In the center is bibb lettuce filled with dark chicken salad with pecans, crowned by thin wafer crackers. And at the pinnacle is one of my mom's recipes—reverse s'mores, where the marshmallows are dipped in chocolate and rolled in graham cracker crumbs while they're still warm.

It's the most extravagant kiddie meal I've ever seen, and I can't help noticing all the flowers circling the plate.

My finger brushes a bright yellow petal. "Dandelions," I whisper.

"I washed them thoroughly. I can't think of you without one of them clutched in your little-child hands. Lucky for us, they're edible." Mark unties his apron and places it over the back of his chair before he pours me some champagne. "Don't pretend like you don't want to eat."

I open my mouth with a witty comeback. It's drowned out when my stomach interrupts with a *take no prisoners* growl. Before I can pretend it never happened, the damn thing does it again.

Hell, did the walls rattle? Horrified, I slam my eyes shut. *Kill me now.*

Having poured his own champagne, Mark chuckles and takes a seat. "Truce?"

Snarling, I cross my arms in front of my chest.

He reaches for a sandwich and dunks it in the soup before holding it to my lips. "If I go first, I can eat it all," he says in challenge, and then he tries to sweeten the deal. "We won't talk about a thing until you've had at least a sandwich and some soup. At the end of our discussion, you're free to go."

I lift my chin, narrow my eyes, and glare. "Fine."

"Fine," he says back, mimicking me, then reaches out to tap my nose.

The man nearly loses a finger when I snap at it the way I bit into his ass. He yanks back his hand, his smile growing. His sip of champagne dials up his grin to full-on smug, and those mesmerizing eyes turn playful.

"I love it when my Choir Girl turns feisty."

Oh, I'll just bet you do.

But the second I taste the food, savor the grilled, buttered bread and melty cheese, I moan. And not some dainty, subtle kind of moan, but an *Oh my God, this is the best thing I've ever had in my mouth* moan.

And I know it's game over.

That's the problem with trying to date someone who knows so much about you. If they choose to zero in on your weaknesses, there's no escape.

A small voice pushes out from the dark recesses of my heart. *Tell him.*

But I'm not ready to tell him everything. Not yet. Maybe not ever, if I can avoid it.

Mark has a few bites here and there, but it's clear he's leaving it up to me to decide how much or how little I'll eat. So, when I'm done hoovering it all up, which I do in record time, he pours us each a second glass of champagne and slides his chair beside mine.

Don't look at him. Do not look at him.

"I'm going to share something with you, Jess, which is

something I rarely do with women, so take it for the gift that it is. When you left, I was devastated."

My heart squeezes. *Did he say devastated?*

Keeping my gaze lowered, I set the smoothed-out check on the table. "Is this how a devastated man acts?" My words hold a small spark of anger.

"No, that was the act of a desperate man. I've never seen you run, Jess. Not from me. You'll spar till you're blue in the face, but back down from a fight?" He scoffs with a small laugh. "No. Not my Choir Girl. Not in a million years. So, if you ran, you didn't want to see me. I knew you wouldn't take my calls or texts."

"How do you know if you don't try?" I retort like a coward. He's right. I know he's right.

Mark presses a strong finger gently to my lips as his eyes latch on to mine. "It's not your turn to talk yet," he whispers.

His eyes are so tender, so full of emotion, my heart aches.

Then he says, "I know what the store clerk said to you, Jess."

I hide my shock and pretend not to know what he's talking about. But I do know. The clerk instantly recognized Mark as well as the woman he was with. But it wasn't the comments about what a cute couple they'd make, and it wasn't even their kiss, or rather, her kiss.

Plain as day, the woman threw herself at him, and in truly classy form to get her sloppy-drunk self impregnated on the spot. Not that he fought her off with any real amount of force —a fact I'm still justifiably peeved over. But Mark's right. It's not the reason I ran. It was what the clerk said next.

He'll finally get the wife and family he's always deserved.

A little voice inside nudges me. *Tell him.*

When his finger skates down between my breasts to that sacred spot he always manages to find, the metal of his dog tags, tears prick my eyes. I blink rapidly and look away.

Instead of fessing up, I shove it all aside. Emotions. Grief. The truth. I swallow all the millions of things I want to say to a man I've loved forever and deflect like a satellite dish.

"This isn't going to work. My home is in the mountains. Your world is here."

Mark silences me again, but this time with a rough, possessive, searing kiss. And I want this kiss.

His hands are on my face almost painfully, and my fingers find their way to his hair. I can feel every knot around my heart untying as hot tears stream down my cheeks. When he owns me, really, truly owns me, he finally comes up for air.

"You're not just another notch on my bedpost, Jess. You're mine, and I'm yours. Those dog tags aren't a trinket. They're the most meaningful thing I could give to the only woman I have ever loved. A woman I never thought I would see again."

His eyes are red and weepy, and everything he's saying is everything I've always wanted to hear. But he doesn't know. Know that if he loves me, if I let him love me, he will be giving up everything he's ever wanted.

And even then, I'm selfish. So greedy for his love, so desperate to be his, I do the unthinkable. His demand is a feather on the wind, one my heart can't help it follow it.

"Promise me, we will try this," he says earnestly. "We will both give it our all. And maybe you're not ready to share all your secrets or confide in me enough to tell me what really spooked you. But that's okay . . . for now. I have secrets too,

Jess. Secrets that I'm not ready to share today, but someday. We have time. We have to try. Baby steps."

He slides his hand under my shirt and wraps his fist around the dog tags. I feel the tug of the chain on the nape of my neck. He's prepared to rip it away.

My hands wrap around his. Panic surges as I wince. "Stop—"

Then Mark presses the warmest kiss to my lips. "Promise me, Jess. Or return these."

I know what he's trying to do. It's what he always does. He pushes me into a corner and forces my hand.

I could argue. Fight and scream. Kick and wail. Run.

But for the first time in my life, I don't want to. I want to believe in happy endings. To see what happens if we flip one more page to the next chapter. I want to stop wondering *what if*. And try.

This time, it's my lips that meet his. My heart that's reaching out. And my mind that's shutting down. I tell him what he wants to hear because I have to do this. For us. For me.

"I promise."

CHAPTER TWENTY-NINE

MARK

This morning, when I wake up, all is right in the universe. Jess is a sleeping goddess in my arms, her breath on my skin, and I'm at peace.

Her red hair is wild and free against my chest, her plump, pink lips slightly parted as she takes in each deep breath, her breasts heaving peacefully. With her belly full of food and a night of unrivaled passion, she's wiped out.

Deep satisfaction puts a wide smile on my face.

Keeping her here was a small victory. Well, not a *small* victory. A big victory. A huge, mountainous, Olympic-level victory.

But no matter what my cock thinks, and the damn thing seems to have a lot to say, I can't just go plunging into the deep end at fifty thousand feet. There are too many potential land mines between her heart and mine. Not to mention what getting together, just to be torn apart, would do to our families.

Baby steps. I take several meditative breaths. *Must take baby steps.*

Jess and I made love for hours last night. More than make-up sex. Everything about her skin, her touch, her whimpers, it was all so fucking combustible. We were giving in to each other, and it was the most erotic lovemaking of my life.

She barely stirs as I wiggle carefully from her hold. I grab a pair of flannel pants and stand there staring for who knows how long.

Jessica Marie Bishop is in my bed, and God help me, I intend to keep her there. And not just for the pockets of pure, unadulterated bliss. I want her here, period. My lifelong hostage.

After memorizing the lines of every curve and dip and stopping short of licking that delectable nipple that's peeking out from the blanket, I make my way to the kitchen, hard as an obelisk. I stare down at it, surprised the beast isn't satiated. When it wants to work, it really works, and it's definitely pulling out all the stops for Jess.

Once there, I stare blankly at the espresso machine. The damn thing cost me the price of a car, and I have no idea what to do with it. Not because I don't know how to operate it—I mean, you press a few buttons. It's not exactly rocket science. But because I have no idea how Jess takes her coffee.

During her weeklong vacay with me, she was the early bird. Hopping out of bed and into the kitchen at some ungodly hour, singing sweet notes of harmony all along the way. A songbird with the sounds of an angel and the footsteps of a Clydesdale.

As we naturally fell into our morning routines, she'd be

done with her coffee long before she made mine, which had been ready and waiting and made to perfection by the time I woke up an hour later.

Which is fine for the moment. I can fuss with breakfast until she wakes up. This is a special day. A new day for the two of us. I know she'll want pancakes in the same way I know she loves all things blueberry, an extra-large slice of butter, and enough pure maple syrup to drown the titanic. She'll also indulge in the strangest quirk of brushing her teeth before her first meal of the day.

Which, is it fucking weird, or is it just me? As with all things in life, I couldn't tell you the exact moment I learned these things about Jess. I just know them.

I whip up the batter, the power in my wrist giving it extra air. With Jess, the fluffier the better. Nothing too fancy like chocolate ganache swirl or stuffed with cream cheese. Nope. Just blueberries. That and a side of crispy smoked bacon should have her happy as a springtime lark.

I snap to the door. Footsteps are nearing, the slow yeti-like shuffle of a tired vixen.

Jess walks in, her hair like a freshly scooped-up bird's nest, makeup long gone, and the buttons of my matching flannel top completely misaligned. And let's not forget the small smudge of toothpaste still on the corner of her mouth.

This is her. My Choir Girl. Exactly as she is, she's the most beautiful woman I've ever seen.

My heart leaps to life, and yes, my cock springs into action.

Down, boy. You already wrecked her vagina mercilessly. Give the poor girl a little rebound time.

She makes her way to me, her eyes still blinking the sleep away. Our lips meet as I wrap her in my arms. She backs away just enough to look down between us.

"Does that thing ever go down?" Her light sapphire eyes meet mine. "Not that I'm complaining."

I kiss away the toothpaste on her lips. "Not around you."

Intrigued, she scans the counter. "What's for breakfast?" she asks as we kiss.

"Pancakes, if they're still your favorite."

Her smile reaches her eyes. "Aren't they everyone's favorite?" Her warm kiss on my chest is heaven. "What can I do to help?"

Her question is so sincere, I'm almost tempted to let her help with the pancakes. But then flashbacks of her accidental salt substitute for sugar a millennium ago return, and so I move her quickly along.

"Show me how you make your coffee."

"Okay . . ." Jess elongates both syllables as if my demand is silly. She slips behind the door of the pantry and returns with a glass jar in her hand.

I'm horrified. "Instant coffee? How is it possible I even have that in my house?"

She shrugs. "I brought it with me last time. It's really good. I tried using that transformer robot thing you call a coffeemaker. I don't think it works."

My mouth falls open in disbelief. "Wait. Are you telling me you were feeding me instant coffee the week you were here?"

"It was good, wasn't it?"

God almighty, I hate to admit it, but it was good. She's got to be fucking with me.

"Give me that." When she hands over the jar of coffee she probably bought from a gas station, I say incredulously, "You're seriously telling me this is the coffee you made me every morning?"

"Yup."

Jess goes to work making us two cups as I work on our breakfast. Once we're seated with mile-high towers of pancakes before us and an insane pile of bacon, I sip the coffee. Then I sip it again, swirling it around my mouth like wine, and finally swallow it and my snooty ways along with it.

"It is good."

Both hands around her mug, she looks over it as she takes a long, savoring sip. "You're still a mountain boy, Sharpshooter. You'll love this coffee till the day you die."

"So, for as long as I'll love you."

My breath screeches to a stop. Did *I love you* just fly from my mouth?

I sit back and grin. So it did. To that, she says nothing. She pours a near pitcher-full of pure maple syrup on her pancakes, cuts a fork through it, and stuffs her mouth in an abysmal attempt to hide the goofiest grin.

Which is fine. I don't need her to say it back. Not yet, anyway.

I just need her to hear it over and over again until it sinks into that stubborn brain of hers that we can actually work.

CHAPTER THIRTY

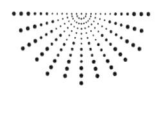

MARK

"Did you hear what I said?"

Brian and Zac are seated across the table from me at a small local diner. I came up to Saratoga Springs to tell them personally, and Jess and I drew straws for who would break the news.

I lost.

Brian grumbles into his coffee and hurls death glares over the rim of his mug.

Zac places two fingers on his temple and decides to speak first. "I'm not sure if I heard you or if my brain snapped. Because it sounded like you said you and Jess are moving in together."

Definitively, I nod. "We are."

He scratches his head. "When did the two of you start dating?" Before I can answer, he leans in and asks with his outside voice, "Are you two sleeping together?"

"Don't answer that!" Brian shouts, angry as a bear with a sore paw.

I sip my Coke. "Wasn't planning on it."

I kick Zac under the table and hurl a silent *what are you, a dumbass?* at him. He shrugs with a helpless apology.

The waitress brings over a selection of pie slices. "Here we are," she sings, handing us each a slice of pie and a can of whipped cream to share.

Brian grabs the whipped cream first and unleashes damned near the entire can on his slice of pie. Emotional eating at its finest. But, hey, at least I'm still alive.

We eat in silence for an eon of a minute before he asks, "And where will you both be living?"

Good. I know the answer to this question.

"Under the circumstances, and seeing how much Jess loves her home, I figure the only right thing to do is to give you back your place while I move in with her."

The two men glance at each other, then look at me like I'm crazy.

"Are you an idiot?" Zac asks. He earns himself another kick for that.

What? He's a black belt in aikido and a state-level boxing champion. He can take a little hit to the shin, though he points a stern finger at me.

"It's three, sometimes four hours. Each way. Asking if you're an idiot seems warranted."

I pull out my phone and show him a photograph of my latest purchase. An Airbus AS365 helicopter. "I've been licensed for a year. With this, I can come home every evening and be back to the office the next morning. I'll also have two pilots on standby in each city if I need to work during the flight."

Zac takes another glance. He's in and out of the city all the time and has been going on and on and *on* about how much I need a helicopter, which of course, he'd be using, too.

Impressed, he asks, "How long will it take to get from here to there?"

And just like that, I know I won my brother over. Still, I answer. "Thirty-six minutes."

Brian finishes scarfing down his food and eases back in his seat. "Look, the two of you are grown. I can't exactly tell you what to do or not to do. But there are things you don't know about each other. And I don't want to see you, either of you, getting hurt."

Before I can pry open the door he just gave me a peek behind, he slams it shut, holding his palm to my face.

"I'm saying nothing more about it. Period. She's my sister. You are my best friend. I love you like a brother, but if push comes to shove, I'll have her back over yours."

"I'd expect nothing less."

Zac nods. "And if you hurt her—"

I stop him right there, both hands up in full surrender. "Trust me when I tell you this woman has me by the balls. She'd slay me before I'd ever do or say anything to hurt her." I shake my head in disbelief that I'm admitting this. "The truth is I'm in love with her, and I'm scared shitless."

Brian levels his brows. "Sometimes we need a little bit of being scared shitless to be grateful for what we have."

I look at him, my chest swelling with hope. "Does that mean we have your blessing?"

Irritated, he waves me off like a fly. "Don't get ahead of yourself. It means I'm on a *wait-and-see* approach before I decide if I'm blessing this very bizarre union." He shakes his head. "Or if I need to string you up by your balls, sling you around like the blades of your precious helicopter, and hurl your sorry ass to the next county."

As he polishes off his coffee, I gulp and cross my legs, trying like hell not to grab my balls.

Then Brian and Zac give each other a knowing glance, after which my brother rolls his eyes and slumps as if exasperated.

"I hate you." The fucker is looking at me when he says that.

What the hell?

Zac pulls out his wallet and hands Brian a hundred-dollar bill.

Looking pleased with himself, Brian beams from ear to ear. The blue eyes he and Jess share land squarely on me. "I told him the two of you were shacking up."

We all crack up, chuckling.

The two of them put me through the wringer just for the hell of it. The way family always does.

∼

I grab the last of my things from Brian's and take one last look around.

There's a picture of the four of them: Brian, Rex, Cade, and Jess, all lined up on the porch in front of the house on Bishop Mountain. That's not the official name of the mountain, nothing you'd ever see on Google or find on a map. It's just what all of us called it the whole time we were growing up.

"There's one thing I don't get," I say. "You had me glance

over that offer? If Jess wants to hold, why would you want to sell? You're usually in her corner, even if she doesn't know it."

Brian takes a seat, ready to unstrap his prosthetic blade, when he looks up at me. "Do you mind if I—"

"Never." I can't imagine what it's like having yourself strapped to it for fourteen or sixteen hours a day. But he never complains.

He removes it and sets it aside. "I am in her corner. The truth is, I was all for helping her renovate. But last winter, I was a little bit of an idiot, tried working my way up the ladder, and fell. I don't know how long I was out. A few hours. Jess found me, and the pain in her eyes—"

I take a seat beside him. "I can only imagine."

"It wasn't just that she thought I was hurt. She thought I was dead. Apparently, there was some blood coming from the back of my head. Concussion. It wasn't that I couldn't help her with the property anymore. I needed someplace with better accommodations. Handrails. No stairs. Workable surfaces. When you offered me the job, along with a stipend since I'd be working from home, it was enough to afford this place."

It isn't until he mentions it that I notice all the adaptive changes around his home. Strategically placed handrails and hard surfaces for easy grip everywhere.

"I got this place with plans for Jess to move in with me. But she's the last of the Bishops to live there, and she carries that responsibility like a lead weight. Rex and Cade have their own lives to consider. Neither of us would ever weigh them down. But Jess will never leave. Except . . ."

He hesitates for a minute, working his thumb into a deep muscle just above the knee.

"You want me to get the icepack?" I ask, and when he nods, I grab it from the freezer. I know where it is since my favorite brand of vodka rests neatly on it.

As soon as the pack hits his skin, he leans back in relief.

Then I ask, "Except?"

Brian inhales a deep, remorseful breath, letting it out in an aggravated sigh. "Except that the boys own 25 percent apiece, as do I, as does Jess. The two of them want to sell. We get offers every other month—stupid amounts of money that go up with each new offer."

"But you'd never sell, right?"

"I wouldn't, but . . . part of me wonders if Jess is stuck in the past. Maybe if she's forced to let go, she could move on with her life."

I want to tell Brian *what the fuck?* You're supposed to stand by your sister. Thick or thin. Especially with everything she's gone through. Hell, she nursed him back to health single-handedly.

But then an ugly little twinge of guilt rears its head. It was like me, threatening to rip back the dog tags that she's been clinging to for dear life over the past eight years. She struck a deal with me, just like I know she struck a deal with him.

"So, how did the two of you end it?"

Brian wipes his face with both hands. "I said if even one more thing went wrong with that house, I'd side with them."

CHAPTER THIRTY-ONE

JESS

By the time Mark gets home—my home—I've done my best to lipstick the place up.

Everything is clean and tidy, with several drapes strategically placed to hide the unruly drafts and damage in the walls. Hopefully, he'll be too distracted by all the glasses filled with wildflowers to notice the enormous hole in the ceiling or the tarp covering it.

A lump settles somewhere between my throat and the pit of my stomach, and there's no swallowing it. There's no way I'm moving to the city. So the insane man I've decided to go full-speed ahead with opted to move in here. To a rickety old house with only one bathroom, no running shower, and sketchy Wi-Fi at best. Oh, and the entire place would fit in one corner of his master closet with room to spare.

But this place means more to me than the world, and Mark knows that. He's doing this for me, and I have to try. Plus, it's not like he hasn't been here before. He was just here for Brian's birthday. I'm not even sure why I'm so worried. I keep my mind occupied with tidying and cleaning and keeping calm, telling myself there's nothing to worry about.

Until I go to wash a few dishes. Then the water sputters up from the drain, inching brown goo into the sink.

"No, no, no, no, nooo." I fiddle with each knob, twisting the hot, turning the cold. "This can't be happening now."

"What can't be happening?"

"*Eeek*, Mark!" I scream. For a big, burly man, he sure has feet like a cat.

His arms wrap around me, squeezing every last worry to the surface. He looks at the disgusting mess in the sink and *tsks* in my ear. "Someone needs a plumber." He kisses my neck.

Defeated, I eye the sludge. *This* is the one more thing. *This* will be enough for Brian to side with Rex and Cade. Unless I ask Mark for a loan.

Instantly, I shake that thought away.

No. I can't ask Mark for a loan. Everyone is always asking him for something. It's a big factor in why he doesn't trust people. I don't want to be just anyone. With a ton of determination and two ounces of delusion, I know what I have to do.

I have to fix this.

The disgusting goo sludges up higher, bubbling into the sink. "It's just a . . ." I try to think up something scientific. "Freak water reverse-osmosis thing. It comes and goes up here in the mountains." I shrug it off as best I can, but one thing is for sure. Bathing will suck—big time.

"Ah." Mark scrapes his scruff with a plumber's rachet he apparently pulled out of his ass. "I guess you don't need my services, then."

I blink. I never imagined my hot childhood crush slash

billionaire tycoon could become sexier, but here he is—lumberjack flannel, scruffy jaw, and all.

It takes me half a millisecond to respond and offer him something of value. "If you can make everything normal without calling someone, I'll give you the biggest, wettest, deepest blowjob of your life."

Mark's eyes widen to the size of dinner plates. "Deal."

We shake hands, and then he gets to work.

First, he plays with the knobs, the left one and then the right, as my confidence in his ability to fix this shrinks to a grain of sawdust. He even sticks his finger in the sludge and fiddles with it, which is not only pointless but absolutely gross.

"Are you sure you know what you're doing?"

"*Tut-tut*. I can't be disturbed. I'm solutionizing."

"Solution-i-zing? That's a totally made-up word," I mutter, apparently not out of earshot.

"I heard that. Can I help it if I'm too brilliant for Merriam-Webster? And if you keep interrupting my strategic brain at work, you will never get to suck my cock. Is that what you want?"

I drop my head in my hands and actually pray to be able to give him a blowjob later and not have to murder him in his sleep.

"Grab your nana's kettle, will you?"

So, now he wants tea?

Before I can reply, he heads straight out of the house to his sportscar that looks like it should be in a magazine. I assume he's getting tools of some sort. Instead, he returns with several bags. Of groceries.

He rummages through them and finally pulls out what he needs. Holding high a box of baking soda, he cries out, "Yes!"

And now I'm actually wondering if the reason he's been single so long is that he's one buckle shy of a strait jacket.

Mark stares at me as if I'm slow. "Where's the kettle?" he asks with his face buried in the pantry, searching the shelves for who knows what.

The man has seriously lost his freaking mind.

He snaps his fingers. "Chop-chop, Choir Girl. Do you want to give me this blowjob or not?"

My mouth drops to the floor. Maybe he's snapped, and these are the deep, dark demons he's been trying to hide from me.

I need to think of what to do. So, I go and get the kettle just to placate him, and debate sending the 9-1-1 bat signal text to Brian.

When I return, Mark has a box of baking soda out. Because the way out of this mess is to bake ourselves out.

My shoulders slump. Why are all the gorgeous men crackpots?

"Finally," he says, grabbing the pot.

He empties six bottles of water into the pot and heats it on the stove while I take a casual look around for my phone. I know it's around here somewhere. Maybe I left it in the truck.

I hear the kettle whistle, shortly followed by, "Eureka!"

He didn't.

Gobsmacked, I rush back into the kitchen. He's running the water, full force, and cleaning out the sink, which is now empty except for some soap bubbles. "You did it? How?"

"Magic. And by magic, I mean vinegar and baking soda.

When it's mixed with hot water, it'll clean the sludge out of a drain. Sort of like a reverse-osmosis thing." Mark's smile is wickedness personified. "Do I need to do anything for the best blowjob of my life? Stretches?"

He stretches an arm over his head, followed by the other one, like the ridiculous fool he is.

"Do you want me in here, or perhaps I should be lying down? Remember, I have a slight arrhythmia. I might black out." He clasps his hands in prayer. "Be gentle with me."

He chuckles and pulls me against his chest, and I can't help but laugh too.

"If you've come here to win me over by fixing everything that's wrong in this house, you'd better lie down. Because I'm about to suck the life out of you in appreciation."

"Vampire-style?" he muses salaciously, rubbing his chin. "I like it."

I don't know what comes over me. I've never really done this before. Been forward or playful with a man. I'm usually counting down the minutes—and they are minutes—waiting for it all to be over so I can catch the last minutes of *Dancing with the Stars*.

But something about Mark makes me feel brave and sexy. I slide a hand between his legs, caress his balls, grip the hard shaft beneath his jeans, and tease his lower lip with a lick.

He pumps against my hand. "*Mmm*."

His groan sends tingles down my spine and between my legs. The smile he sports shifts to something needy.

"Who are you?" he asks in wonder, looking at me as though for the very first time.

My lips nuzzle his ear. "Your Choir Girl, remember?" I

slide my fingers below the waistband of his jeans and lead him to my room.

As I begin undoing his clothes, his fist wraps around my ponytail.

"Is this what you want, Choir Girl? To suck my dick until I've emptied everything down your sweet little throat?"

He lowers me to my knees, and *yes. God, yes.* This is what I want. Mark Donovan taking me. Dominant and possessive. Thumping his chest, thunderous and hard.

It's clear he's not going to take this lying down. He grips my chin with force, locking his eyes on mine. Arousal pumps between my thighs, and we haven't even really started yet. I'm face-to-face with the tip of his engorged cock, the heavy weight of it held up by my hand.

"Not yet," he says low. "Spread your legs. Show me you want this too."

Goose bumps scatter over every part of my body as I do as he says. I slip a finger beneath my panties, but I know he wants more. I press in, blinking through the sensation as fire strikes behind his hard gaze.

"Yes, that's it. Show me."

Slowly, I lift my soaked finger for him to see. It feels so . . . dirty. When his hungry mouth parts, I paint it up and down his cock.

"*Holy fuck,*" he hisses.

Then I do something I've never done. I suck my finger clean.

His eyes widen, a bonfire behind bright gold. He barely waits for my finger to pull free before his cock presses between my lips, fills my mouth, and steals my breath.

Mark Donovan is a big man. A very big man. His eyes roll to the back of his head, and the grunt that emanates from him is near barbaric as I struggle to deal with every porn-star-worthy inch of him.

He thrusts between each word, my head clutched in his tight, unyielding grip. "You're . . . mine . . . Choir . . . Girl. All . . . mine."

He's forcing his way in, deeper down my throat, and I have to clench my knees together hard before my own orgasm tears free. Watching him—doing this—is my deepest fantasy come to life. I have sucked this man's cock a thousand times in my dreams, but this is a million times hotter. And he hasn't even taken off his shirt.

As he pulls free of my lips, I struggle for air. "What are you doing?" I pant, frustrated. "You stopping is not me giving you the best blowjob of your life."

"You've already done that. And I can't come down your throat. Not now when I know how soaking-wet your sweet pussy is." He's still pumping himself hard, hungry for more pleasure. "Get up here. Now."

His demand is animalistic.

I don't even bother with my top or skirt. I strip off my panties, move to the bed, and spread my legs wide. I want him to see it. To see how hot he makes me. The way no man ever has.

Before I even blink, he's on his knees, burying his face there, the burn of his stubble a contrast to the erotic pleasure of his tongue. It's too hot. Too intense. A violent quake runs through me until my body shakes mercilessly.

Air flies from my lungs in a whoosh when he forces his thick cock in.

This is not sex. This is possession. He hammers himself into me, desperate thrusts, one after the other. One hand on my ass, another on my breast, and his lips at my ear.

"This is what you want, isn't it? Milk my cock, dirty girl."

"Yes!" My cries—his cries—smother into one as his lips take mine.

Again and again, we drive head-on in this collision course, our lust and want ending in white-hot, dirty pleasure. It's never been like this. Where we can't even take half a second to remove all our clothes because our bodies have to connect.

His cock jerks hot inside me before his body collapses on mine.

Our pants are in sync, deep breaths desperate for air, while his hands continue to rove my body, the burn of sensation branding me everywhere. Like he can't stop touching me. Feeling me. Knowing I'm right here with him.

He rolls beside me, peppering my lips, neck, and cheek with kisses, soft and sweet. A stark contrast to the unbridled fucking machine he was moments ago.

This is the other side of Mark. Warm and tender and so loving, I fill with emotion. My heart is too full of him, too wrapped up in a man I'm too in love with to admit.

"Say it, Choir Girl," he whispers.

I slide my leg over his waist, our lips touching. "Say what?"

Sleepily, his eyes zero in for the kill. "Say you're mine."

It's a trap I don't fall into. Can't fall into. Not yet.

With a slight giggle, I nibble at his soft lips and scruffy face as my nose rubs his. "You're mine."

Bang. Bang-bang.

I jolt and rub the sleep from my eyes. Lord knows what time it is. The sun is up, but barely.

Bang-bang-bang-bang-bang.

I look up and hold up my hand to block a beam of sunlight. The blue tarp is gone, with the hole in the roof an unattractive skylight. Did the tarp blow away? The breeze last night was barely noticeable.

A head pops through the opening. "Morning," Mark hollers from up high.

I leap from the bed, grab the only item of clothing in sight—his shirt—and stare up at him. "What are you doing?"

His head disappears from sight, and panic sets in. The last person to go up there was Brian, and he fell.

"Get down!" I shout.

No answer.

Barefoot, I fly from the house, down the porch stairs, and look up.

Mark is standing on the roof, larger than life. He looks freshly showered, which, no doubt, he fixed, too. With a tool belt strapped to his waist, he stands tall, lumberjacked from head to toe in flannel, jeans, and boots.

He holds up both hands. "Don't freak." His tone is irritatingly calm for a man standing on a rooftop, holding on to nothing.

I race for the ladder and grip it with both hands. "Despite your overactive imagination, you are not actually Batman. I am not even kidding you. Get down here now!"

"Yes, ma'am." But instead of taking the ladder, he tosses one end of a rope over the side. He whizzes down it like a superhero, his childhood dream come true.

I smack his arm relentlessly. "Are you deranged? You could've been killed."

Mark grabs both my hands, kissing the palms, then presses them to his cheeks like the idiot he is. He's my big, burly, ridiculously strong man. I can't even bother to pull away.

"I'm a pro mountain climber. It was a pastime I loved between tours, and I've kept it going all these years. Look." He thumbs through the harness I hadn't noticed and gives the dark green rope a good, solid tug. He puffs up his chest. "I've braved ledges twenty times that height."

"So, you really are deranged." I try the rope for myself. You know, trust, but verify. I frown, unable to see what it's leading to on the roof. "What's it attached to?"

"The center beam." He motions over the rooftop. "It's called a ridge beam. A little drill hole won't hurt it one bit."

I tug the rope again. "How much can it hold?"

He shrugs modestly. "About forty-eight hundred pounds."

An embarrassed smile flashes across my face. "So, the weight of your head."

"Nearly." Mark sweeps my hair behind an ear and lifts my chin with a finger. "Can I keep going? Or should I guard my man parts and run?"

Tension forms at my brow as I trace the line of his jaw. "You swear it's safe?"

"Cross my heart." His hand smooths mine over his heart.

After a deep breath, I give in. "Okay. Then, how can I help?"

He pulls me in for a kiss. "I thought you'd never ask. Breakfast is on the table. After you've had a bite, you can record measurements as I call them out. At most, it'll take a week, maybe two."

I look at him, wide-eyed with surprise. "Breakfast and a lumberjack at my disposal? You're too good to be true."

He smiles, and his rugged good looks magnify tenfold. "And you, Ms. Bishop, are a dirty distraction in my shirt. Now, go eat breakfast while I pick out a nice tree to fuck you up against." His lips descend on mine, kissing away all my defenses. "I told you, Choir Girl, we'll make this work."

CHAPTER THIRTY-TWO

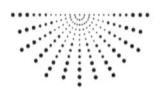

MARK

Lance lashes out, livid. "This will never work."

I don't even know why he's getting all bent out of shape. It's my life. If I want to fly back to the Adirondacks from the city every fucking night, what does he care?

"What's with you?"

"What's with you?" he spits out. "This isn't the time to divert your attention to your latest piece of ass."

My expression turns cold. I steeple my fingers and prop my elbows on the desk, my death glare coming out in full force. "Careful."

He bites his tongue for a moment and rakes a hand through his hair. "You have no idea how much is riding on this IPO."

How is it that I don't have any idea what's riding on this IPO? I'm the fucking CEO. Something seems off. "Then enlighten me."

His hand slams on my desk, a surprising move considering

his nails are usually perfectly manicured, and I don't think the man has done any sort of real labor in his entire life. "We stand to hit a billion dollars."

I shrug. "And if we don't? This company—*my* company—has made more than I could have ever imagined, with not a lot more than hard work, luck, and cutting-edge technology. We didn't go down this IPO path to make a billion dollars. We went down it because you thought it would be a phenomenal competitive advantage, and I didn't disagree. But make no mistake, I couldn't give two shits what the IPO comes in at."

Lance takes a pensive breath, then fiddles with the band of his watch. God, this man changes watches at a rate that outpaces him changing his underwear.

"Sorry, I'm just on edge." He makes his way to the bar, helping himself to a five-figure bottle of bourbon. "I had to let Dean go."

I jump to my feet. In two steps, I'm next to him. "What do you mean, you let Dean go? Dean isn't your employee, he's mine, just as you are. You can't just fire my CFO."

Lance's gaze darts away. "While you were gallivanting through the woods with Snow White, I was catching him in the act of crippling the company. He was stealing. Plain as day."

"Stealing?"

That makes no sense. I've known Dean since Ranger School. The man busted his ass through school, read a library's worth of books on finances, and is now a millionaire ten times over while donating most of it to charity.

"No way. Not a fucking chance."

Lance's face creases, as if he's sorry that he told me. "It's true, Mark. The people you can trust are vastly outnumbered by the people you can't. Most financial crimes aren't motivated by need. They're crimes of opportunity. You were gone. Dean saw an opportunity."

He takes a slow, agonized sip of his drink.

"It's the kind of publicity we don't need, but I like Dean, too. I told him if he left quietly, I wouldn't call the cops or press charges. I know I should have consulted with you first, but you were gone, and I needed to make a decision. I'm sorry if you thought I should have been harder on him."

Harder on him? Confusion spirals through my mind as a thick ball of doubt settles deep within my gut. Lance is talking about grand theft. A felony. He can't mean Dean.

Stunned, I shake my head in disbelief and pat his shoulder. "I'm the one who's sorry. I should have been here. I should have been the one dealing with this." I blow out a frustrated breath. He's right. If I hadn't been distracted, none of this would be happening. "Let me review whatever you have on Dean. I brought him in. I'll clean it up."

Lance shakes his head. "We're too close to the IPO to ignore it. A public statement needs to be made, and the press will be thirsty for blood."

"The press can wait. It's nearly Christmas. Worst-case scenario, I'll take the fall."

He smirks, as if I'm a child. "You have no idea what you're saying. The press is just the tip of the iceberg. The SEC. The Feds. You don't really want to do that."

"No, I don't. But this company was founded on finding truth, exposing theft, and ensuring those who are guilty are brought to justice." I pour myself a drink and take a long sip. "It's my company. If push comes to shove, I'll take the hit."

We both take a mournful look out the window, dark clouds across a gray sky mirroring our thoughts.

Speaking of sniffing out the truth . . .

"Did you ever find out anything on that guy . . . Russ Hensen?"

Lance rubs his chin. "Nothing at all. I went back ten years. Not even a parking ticket. The man is a solid citizen. Why?"

Why does that unsettle my gut? I don't know why, but I don't like the guy.

I rub my forehead, not knowing where I'm going with this. Or anything else right now.

After taking a long breath, Lance eases into the next item on his agenda. "Actually, some good might come out this," he says, setting down his glass. He points to my desk. "I left an authorization there. It's something I held off on, but in light of what's happened, we need contingency plans if we can't get ahold of you and something urgent comes up. The language is standard, but tweak it however you like." He pats me on the shoulder and heads out the door. "Call if you need anything."

"Thanks." Before he can close the door behind him, I holler back. "There is one thing I'd like you to draft up."

"What's that?"

I pause for a long minute, the lowball hovering at my lips. "A prenup."

He nods, frowning. "You never know who you can trust."

The door shuts behind him as I empty the glass, swallowing a shark tank's worth of doubts swimming around in my head.

CHAPTER THIRTY-THREE

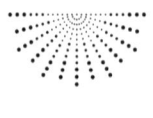

MARK

"Is everything all right?" Jess looks at me with the most endearing eyes.

Is everything all right? I'm reviewing a news article that pegs Dean as corrupt, my company as unstable, and me, the CEO, guilty as fuck. And to top it all off, now there's an investigation by the SEC. So, sure. Fine. Everything's hunky-fucking-dorie.

Fuck.

I pocket my phone and let out a long, tense breath. I've been traveling back and forth for weeks. Leaving before the crack of dawn. Arriving home early enough to make dinner, not that I have to. Jess has not only offered to cook, which I secretly cringe at, but she also offered to bring something home from Donovan's or any other restaurant in the area.

As much as I'm trying, she's trying too. But we're both trying at the worst possible time. The IPO—or what I now refer to as the pressure cooker of shit stew—is crumbling. Projections have plummeted, and saving it is all up to me.

Lance has me hustling at triple my normal workload. Don't get me wrong. Normally, I thrive under pressure . . . *unless, of course, I'm at the fair and there's a gun in my hand.*

Shut up.

And then, there's Dean.

I've left messages. I've sent emails. Hell, I even had a private investigator try to track him down. He might not be my best friend, but he's a close second next to Brian. I've trusted this man with my life countless times, and he's trusted me with his. My mind keeps circling like a vulture, fixated on one question: Why?

Something's off, and I'm ripping my mind to shreds trying to figure out what it is.

Maybe Lance is right. Opportunity was enough of a motive for one of my best friends to pick me off from behind.

I tamp down my tension and move a hand to the back of my neck, rubbing into the stiff muscles. "I'm fine." Even the tone of my voice is tight.

Jess tries to smooth her hand over mine, but I don't want that. Her sympathy. Her pity. Goddammit, I need her. Can't she see that? Not in the Adirondacks. Here. Right here, by my fucking side.

I pull from her touch, irritated. "I'm just . . . hungry," I say, tossing away my mounting frustration like it's nothing.

Jess sets herself on mute for the rest of the ride, primly in one corner of my car's back seat. Which I hate. I hate that for the past few days, all she does is walk on eggshells around me. I hate that I had to ask more than once for her to come out. What do I have to do? Beg?

And I hate—I *hate*—that with my current two-and-a-half

hours of sleep per night schedule, sliding between her legs hasn't happened. At all.

And while I'm on the subject of things I hate, how about the fact that Jess burns the midnight oil more than I do for pennies on the dollar while my million-dollar check still— *STILL*—remains unfucking touched. She works as hard as I do —harder even—but the world is too quick to judge her by her status and her pay. Well, all that's about to fucking change.

With her brothers ready to sell, she needs me now more than ever. Christmas is less than a week away, and Jess has a decision to make. If she chooses right, which she will, then Christmas comes early for both of us.

But what if she doesn't? God, it would just be so . . . Choir Girl . . . to charge the wrong fucking direction. Just to spite me.

We arrive at the restaurant, one of my favorites in the city. The maître d' has a private room waiting for us. It's filled with dozens of red roses and champagne on ice. Jess's response is . . . underwhelming.

"What's the occasion?" she asks, nervously nibbling her lower lip as a waiter helps her with her seat. He fills both our champagne flutes before making himself scarce.

"We are." I tip my glass to hers, which she takes forever to meet.

She has no idea the trouble I've gone through for tonight. I should be working or tracking down Dean, but I've made time for her. Jess is my priority, but does she appreciate it? Is she even happy to be here?

The waiter brings in our first course. Two escargots on a plate with caviar and crème fraîche on toast.

As soon as he sets our plates down, I say, "I'll call you for the next course when I'm ready."

"Very good, sir," he says and vanishes from the room.

Jess keeps her gaze low. "Did you have to speak to him like that?"

Did I? Maybe not. "Don't worry. I'll make it up to him in his tip."

This time, her eyes do meet mine. "So, now you're *that* guy."

"If by *that* guy, you mean the guy splurging on a brat, maybe I am."

Whoa. Where did that come from?

Her ice-blue eyes sharpen and narrow.

Jess is looking at me with contempt. And I'm looking at her like the Pygmalion I am.

She's wearing a new dress. Custom Italian shoes. Hair and makeup done by New York's premium makeup artists. A million-dollar ring is currently burning a hole in my pocket, and this is how I'm treated?

Save your contempt, sweetheart.

But as we sit there in silence, it grates under my skin like steam. In a fit of supreme insanity, I let a little of it off. "This isn't exactly a hotdog stand we're at, Jess."

She raises a brow. "Maybe I'd be happier if it were."

Is she fucking kidding me right now?

"Well, considering this meal costs more than those pretty new shoes on your feet, how about we make the most of it?"

"What's wrong?" she asks so meekly I barely hear her, and it pisses me off more.

"What's wrong?" I ask sharply, repeating her words as if they're in a foreign language. What the hell does she mean, *What's wrong?* "Nothing is wrong." Nothing a little scotch won't fix. I crack my knuckles, then down the champagne.

Jess shrugs. "I don't know. You seem edgy lately. And you're shaking—" I glare as she cuts herself off, moving her gaze from my hands. "Is this because of the news?"

"The news?" My voice rises a notch. Who gives a shit about this week's headlines? My company in a potential scandal—me and my CFO. It's all horseshit. Obviously, I wouldn't expect her to understand.

I begin to pace, realizing I hadn't actually taken a seat. Apparently, I'd been towering over her all this time.

I shake it off. "I'll tell you what's wrong. You. I've been killing myself trying to make this work, and clearly, it's not. You'll be moving in with me. Permanently."

Her eyebrows shoot high. "Moving in with you? I can't. It's happening too fast."

"Too fast?" I scoff. "We've literally known each other forever. If anything, you've been moving too slow. And I've been living with you for weeks. So, I've come to a decision. You're moving in with me. Here in Manhattan. End of story."

Like two ends of a teeter-totter that can't meet in the middle, the second I sit, she stands. *"You* decided?"

"Yes, Jess. I'm a decisive man. It's what I'm good at." I pour myself more champagne, ignoring a small tremor in my hand. I remove an envelope from my blazer pocket and slide it across the table.

"What's this?" Her eyes blink at me before her fingers tear

open the envelope. Her brow knits hard as she reads. "A prenup?"

Out of nowhere, Lance's words come out of my mouth. "It's for our protection."

She looks up, her eyes a fiery blue as they meet mine. "First of all, it's for *your* protection. And news flash, I don't object to any of that. You should protect yourself."

Her words surprise me, though they shouldn't.

Then some dickhead rears his ugly head. The only word out of his mouth is, "Good."

"But I have to protect myself, too." Her hands cover her chest.

This time, Lance's voice comes out of my mouth tenfold. "What do you have to protect?"

You idiot. Stop talking.

"My heart," she fires back. "There are things I don't know about you, and you don't know about me. I'm not marrying you. I can't."

It's as if I've been slapped. "What?"

What the hell is wrong with her?

"Then spit it out, Jess. Release all these deep, dark secrets you've shared with your brothers and even fucking Zac. Just tell me already so you can move on and marry me."

Her whole body shakes with defiance. "Not like this. Not with you barking orders like I'm your . . . what? Employee? I'm not a commodity."

"No, commodities don't talk back."

See? Even as I balance along the quicksand below my feet, I don't tiptoe into dangerous territory. Like a moron, I dive right in.

Her champagne glass slams to the table. "I'm not sure

when you decided you were the boss of me, but let me make one thing clear, Mr. High Powered CEO. You're not."

Who does she think she is?

"My million-dollar donation says otherwise."

The words taste like vinegar as soon as I spit them out. *Shut up, shut up, shut up!*

I know the telltale signs. Narrow eyes. Lips deflated to a hard line. Jess's face reddens with the heat of a million suns. She rips the prenup to shreds, scattering it like confetti before she breaks for the exit.

I jump to my feet. "Sit. Down."

She opens the door and turns back, her eyes blazing. "Go to hell."

Her words burn like fire under my feet. In a second, I'm at the door, yanking her away from it, and slamming it so hard the walls shake.

"Goddammit, Jess, you're not walking out on me. Not on your goddamned life—"

A wall of tears undams from her eyes.

I've seen Jess cry a million times before. Chick flicks. Weddings. That time she broke two fingers in a car door. And the most heartbreaking of all, funerals. But never, not once, have I seen her cry because of me. I just broke my own winning streak, and it kills me.

"Why, Mark? Because the rest of your life is careening out of control, and shoving me into a cage is the easiest option?"

My throat tightens, and I swallow hard. Her stare burns like the sun.

I turn away and hold out my hands, begging. Pleading. "I'm trying to propose, Jess. To marry you. To—"

When the metal hits my palm, everything stops. Time. The Earth. My heart.

Her hand slides from mine, leaving nothing but my dog tags in the palm of my hand. I blink hard, trying to clear the blurriness from my own tear-pricked eyes.

And then she's gone.

CHAPTER THIRTY-FOUR

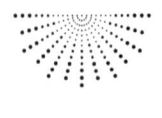

JESS

I stare up at the ceiling, alone in the dark. With a sigh, I slide another Oreo through peanut butter and nibble at it as I look up.

There's no longer a dusting of particles lit by moonlight. No phantom shadows on the walls. No blue tarp flapping in the wind. Mark fixed it. He fixed every last broken thing in this house—except for the two of us. I hate the way we're combustible. Explosive in every way—passion and heartbreak.

He's called a dozen times, but I can't even look at the phone. If I answer, I'll go back to him, and I can't go back. No, all of this happened for a reason. I'm as broken as they come, and loving me will only hurt him in the long run.

My finger is frantic for a moment, scrabbling at my chest, trying to find it, the piece of him I've always had. The necklace with his dog tags has been like another limb. A ward of protection. My lucky charm. And I'm so fucked up, I'm half-afraid to cross the street without them.

A text pings, but it isn't Mark. No, the man pinging me is my sanctuary. Zac.

> ***Hey, is it chocolate chip cookie dough night, or did you pull out all the stops with O&PB?***

I blow out a heavy breath and give him a call. Why not? It's three o'clock in the morning, but he's obviously up. I swallow the mouthful and reply. "I pulled out all the stops."

"I figured as much. Are you going to tell me what happened, or do I have to keep imagining the two of you in a spectacular fight where he rolled his eyes at you, and you ripped out his hair?"

"I'll tell you when we're married," I say, kidding. "Husbands and wives have no secrets."

"Well, we can make wedding plans over lunch tomorrow," Zac says, and I realize that's right. Tomorrow would be our standing lunch. "I just wanted to make sure you'd actually show up."

"Now that you've reminded me tomorrow is Thursday, I'll definitely be there."

"Unless you want to talk now?"

God, why can't I be in love with this man? Zac is sweet and affectionate, thoughtful . . . considerate. And in every possible way, handsome. Like, Hemsworth-level good looks. But it's never been that way. For either one of us.

As soon as I even think about Mark, tears break free. My breath shudders, and I know he's heard it when he says, "Baby. Do you need me to come over?"

I can't even pretend to be brave. It hurts. My heart breaks

all over again, and I can't breathe. All I can do is whisper, "Please."

"On my way."

CHAPTER THIRTY-FIVE

MARK

Fuck me. Fuck my life.

I sit back, chug a mouthful of Scotch, and flip from one news station to the other. I'm fucking trending. And here I am without my social media photographer.

Between Brie painting me as her future baby daddy and me looking as guilty as fuck with Dean, my reputation is like shit on a hot Texas day. Oh, and did I mention I fucked myself straight up the asshole with my girlfriend? So, there's that, too.

On the bright side, bizarrely enough, that ridiculous projection of a billion-dollar IPO looks like it's still in the realm of possibility, just not for me. The shareholders stand to become some of the wealthiest men in the world. Lance has been in front of cameras, exuding trust and confidence, and you know what? It fucking sucks. Twists like a ragged knife through the gut.

You see, I, on the other hand, am treading water against a riptide of accusations, the latest being falsifying documents to the SEC. The accusation is ridiculous and baseless . . . and a class E felony worth hundreds of millions in fines and up to four years in prison. Because my signature came after Dean's every single time. Yet, the fucker has eluded my calls for weeks.

His house is untouched. Bills piling up. Or so I hear, because, God forbid, I wouldn't want to add breaking and entering to my criminal activity spree.

I toss back my glass and fill it again, not minding that it sloshes all over the place like I cannonballed into it. When three knocks sound on the door, I bark, "If you're coming to fuck me over, there's a line."

Zac peers from the other side, a brow popped. "There will be no brother fucking today, thank you very much."

Confused, I sit. "Why are you just standing there?"

"Making sure you're not armed. Or naked." He makes his way in and sits across from me. "Of the two, the naked one is the most alarming."

"It was just the one time, fucker."

"And you were drunk then, too."

I point an accusatory finger at him, spilling more booze. "I am not drunk."

He raises his hands. "No one would blame you if you were."

"Well, I'm not."

"Fine."

"Fine," I snap. "What are you doing here?"

"Trying to be all I can to the people I love."

I stare at him crossways. Maybe I am drunk. I have no idea what he just said.

Zac leans forward, elbows on his knees and hands clasped. "First, you. What can we do?"

I bite back a million snarky remarks. I'm too wounded to tear into him. I already did that with Jess, and look what it got me.

I shake my head aimlessly. "I don't know. The media has been fed documents that were signed by Dean and certified by me. The thing is, I don't rubber-stamp things ever. I don't remember signing these. And I would bet my life Dean didn't do this, but..."

"But what?"

"But everything is pointing to him."

Zac crosses an ankle over his knee, sitting back. "I know Dean pretty well, too. I can't imagine it. Have you spoken with him?"

I rake a hand through my frazzled hair. "It's as if he's vanished off the face of the Earth. Lance has a team deployed looking for him, but there's nothing. Not a goddamned trace. And it couldn't have come at a worse time with the IPO."

Zac stares at me, deep in thought. "This IPO means something to you?"

I look at him like he's sprouted three more testicles. "Of course, it means something. It's my name. My reputation. Mark Donovan: Billionaire." Yup. That tasted like pure horse piss coming out of my mouth.

My brother looks surprised. Maybe he did sprout three testicles. Head quirked and brows raised, all he says is, "*Hmm.*"

"*Hmm?*"

I know that *hmm*. I hate that *hmm*. It's the *hmm* of arrogant knowing. The prick knows something that I don't, and he wants me to figure it out all for myself.

"Aw, just spit it out, for fuck's sake."

"You never lived for any of this, not the money or the fame. You love the chase. You always have. It's why you were a world-class sniper. Yeah, you were an okay shot—"

I roll my eyes at that.

"—but you were great at the hunt. Who gives a shit what people think? To that end, who gives a fuck about a billion dollars if you're going to be miserable and alone?"

"And possibly incarcerated. Don't forget that," I point out, waving a finger at him.

Zac steps over to me and removes the drink from my hand. "You live for chasing bad guys. Stop fighting your gut and follow it." His pat on my shoulder is paternal and affectionate—delivered gently, but just the kick in the ass I need.

I nod, a fire brewing from deep in my gut. "Okay. Yes."

He delivers a soft slap on the cheek. "Good." Our eyes meet in brotherly camaraderie. "Remember this moment when Jess speaks with you."

I step back, combing both hands through my hair to smooth it. "Wait, what? Why is Jess here?"

Zac puffs out a long-winded breath, then shrugs. "All I know is she wanted me to bring her here, to make sure you'd have time for her. She said she wants to speak with you. Alone."

I run my hands down my suit and straighten my tie, puffing air into my palm to check my breath. *Fuck it.* "Send her in."

Zac is only gone a moment before Jess walks through the door.

My heart triple-flips at the sight of her vibrant auburn hair, plush pink lips, and bright blue eyes. Her plain white T-shirt and distressed jeans do more than make her look like the shapely girl next door—the one I'm head over heels in love with. She looks like home.

"Got a minute?" she asks, tucking strands of gorgeous unruly hair behind one ear.

"Of course." I wave a hand in the direction of the sofa. A total dick move that I hope will mean we'll be having make-up sex on it fucking soon.

Instead, she takes a chair. My dick takes the hint and stands down.

I'm too edgy to sit, but I don't want to loom over her again like a creep. So, I take a seat on the carved wooden table in front of her. Her eyes are bloodshot and glistening, and I swear that will never happen again. Not on my watch. I'm done with being a dickhead. Forever.

"I know you're going through a lot," she says, and I hold my breath. "But you keep calling and texting, and I want to be here for you—"

I rush in to kiss her, stopped by her palm on my chest.

"As a friend."

Of all the epic catastrophes that have happened to me today, being friend-zoned reigns supreme as king of the shitshow.

"Liar," I say before I can help myself.

"I don't want you to feel alone, but it's better this way. You and I are no good for each other. Not like that."

I drop to my knees and place my hands on her cheeks. "Not like what? Madly, passionately in love with each other?"

My lips crash on hers. My body overtakes hers. She's mine. She has to know this. Messy and raw, our kiss is deep and erotic. She's here. I can breathe. My arms wrap around her body as her legs shift around me and, Christ almighty, she feels so fucking good. I want her. Need her.

We're tangled in each other—my cock long and thick against her—my hand on her breast—a ball of carnal heat that's nothing but kissing, grinding, needing, wanting—

"Stop." Her panted breath quivers. I stop cold. I don't want to, but my body obeys.

She flies from my hold, distancing herself half a room from me.

"Jess, please. Don't . . . I love you. If this is about the prenup—"

"I came here to tell you I'm here for you. But it's over. I'm marrying Zac."

My next breath comes hard, like inhaling a lungful of kerosene. Before I can move or think or act, she's gone. Ripping my heart from me and tossing it back.

And just like that, it's done.

∽

Slumped over my desk, I sit, destitute and alone. I've watched the sun set and rise and lower, once again ready to set.

The Scotch bottle is drained, and a day feels like a year.

A notification brings my phone to life. Bleary-eyed, I try to make out the words.

Alert!
Check authorization: $1,000,000
Recipient: J. Bishop
To authorize, hit Y.

So, I do what any broken-hearted bastard would do when the woman he loves is running off with his brother.

Fuck her. Fuck him. Fuck them.

Pressing one hand to my chest, where my heart is tearing in two, I reach out with the other to tap a response:

Fuck No!

CHAPTER THIRTY-SIX

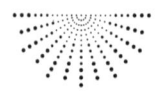

JESS

Hands trembling, I take back the check from the teller, her apology settling like lead bearings in my chest.

I spot the white van with dark-tinted windows. Without money or options, my gut fills with dread. I don't want to return to it. I have to.

I've passed three security guards twice, on the way in and out. I want to say something. Send them a signal. A message. But I can't.

He's watching me. I know he is.

The utility van is parked along the curb with its hazard lights on. The man in the passenger seat holds up a newspaper. I open the driver's door and get in, trying and failing to get a good look at the body slumped in the back.

Struggling to keep my voice steady, I say, "They said no."

The gun shifts from pointing toward the back to pointing at my head. "What do you mean, they said no?"

His voice is muffled by some sort of synthesizer around his throat, and the mask of President Kennedy is horrible. But the check. How did he know about the check?

"I told you, they don't cash checks that big." I try turning toward him, and he cocks the hammer of the gun.

I can't see if Zac is all right. The memory of thick blood draining from his head makes me brave when I'm terrified.

I flip my body and turn. He's still bleeding. "Please," I say to the man in the passenger seat. "He needs a hospital."

Pain bursts in my cheek as cold, hard metal cracks against my face. The pistol hits my cheek with force before pressing its barrel into my gut. "Shut up and drive."

I barely cradle my cheek before starting the ignition and putting the van into gear. "Please let him go. You have me. I'll do whatever you want."

The man scoffs. "It's like I always say: Two heads are better than one. And so are two bodies. You should be more worried about you than him."

I merge into traffic, focusing on his words. *It's like I always say: Two heads are better than one.*

Dammit, I know who it is. I just don't know how desperate he is. I also don't know where we're going.

White-knuckled, I grip the wheel. "Where should I drive?"

The man sits back, relaxing a little. "To visit your boyfriend."

∽

In the heart of Manhattan, we arrive at Mark's building, and I park across the street as instructed. Every minute that Zac lies back there unmoving kills me. He's my best friend ... my only friend so much of the time. I can't lose him.

The masked man scouts the place for a second. "What floor is he on?"

"Who?" I act dumb.

"Donovan."

"The top one. But it's surrounded by surveillance and security. You'll never get—"

"I'm not going anywhere. You are. If you don't return in twenty minutes, you'll never see this van or the bleeding guy in the back again. Understand?"

My nod is slight.

"Understand?" he shouts.

"Yes!" I cry out, praying Zac will be all right. "Yes, I understand."

"Here." He hands me dark sunglasses. "Hide your face. You have quite the shiner."

I slide them high on the bridge of my nose, my hands trembling. "What if he doesn't have it?"

The man sits for a moment and rubs President Kennedy's chin. It's as if he hasn't thought this through at all. "Well, you never know if you don't try." He motions to the back. "And hurry. Who knows how long he'll hold on. Oh, and take this."

He places what looks like an old flip phone in the palm of my hand. Confused, I frown at it.

"It's live. I can hear every word you say. Try anything, and everyone you love dies." He hands me a watch. I notice the inscription. *Our path may change as life goes on, but our bond is ever strong.*

How did he get Brian's watch? Panic thunders through my chest as tears cloud my vision. "Why are you doing this? Where's Brian?"

"Somewhere safe. For now." He taps the face of the watch. "Tick tock, bitch."

CHAPTER THIRTY-SEVEN

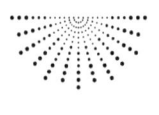

MARK

"Ms. Jessica Bishop to see you sir."

"Jessica who?" I say because I know it's on the loudspeaker and I'm being an asshole. If Choir Girl wants my money, she'll have to suck it from my cock.

"Jessica Bishop?" The receptionist's answer comes out like a question.

Fine. I've been petty long enough. "Send her up."

I've already showered and shaved, put on a fresh suit, and even brushed my teeth. The only way Jess is getting out of here is through me. And when I say through me, I mean through my dick. Because there's no way on God's green Earth she's marrying Zac. It's nonnegotiable. Case closed.

But . . . what if she does love him? It would make sense. They've known each other forever, finish each other's sentences, and buy each other's clothes. I'm not even fucking around when I say they're a goddamned match made in heaven. If it weren't for Zac telling me *repeatedly* that the only thing they attract from each other is lint, I'd have backed off.

But the two of them walking down the aisle feels wrong. Like really, really wrong.

Jess bursts through the door, not bothering to knock. She slams the check down in front of me with a frantic demand. "Give me whatever money you can for this."

I blink. "No."

She checks her watch. Or rather, Brian's watch. What's she doing with Brian's watch?

Jess loses her mind and tears open every drawer on my desk.

"Jess, what the fuc—"

"Money. Goddammit, I need whatever money you have. Now!"

I spin her around, locking both my hands around her arms. "I would've given you the goddamned world, Jess, but you didn't want it, remember?"

But she's not listening. She's patting me down like we're in San Quinten, which I could almost get into, except she stops at my wallet and rips it from the pocket, emptying it of its cash. Openmouthed, I stare in shock.

The second she has it, roughly three thousand dollars in hundreds, she bolts for the door, and I give chase. "Jess!"

She's slams a fist against the elevator door, pounding the button again and again.

I catch up to her, grateful for once that the elevator is taking its sweet fucking time. "Jess, wait—"

I latch onto her arm. She tears it away, screaming as if burned by my touch.

"Jess—" I grab her again, this time harder. "No, no, no.

You're not going anywhere. Explain." It's then that I catch the bruising beneath the rim of her glasses.

Alarmed, I rip them off her face, horrified as I cup her cheeks. Quiet rage simmers beneath the surface. All those crimes the news is ready to nail me to the cross for . . . well, they can add murder to that list. "Who did this—"

Before I know what's happening, her lips latch on to mine —the shock of pure oxygen after going without for a day. Her entire body shakes, trembling hard, so hard in my hold. When a ping hits the air, she pulls away, but I can't let her go. Her kiss is too desperate. Too . . . final.

She slips the watch into my hands and whispers into my ear. "No dancing tonight, Batman."

Huh?

Without warning, my eyes slam shut. Pain. Searing pain. Her knee on my balls might as well be a baseball bat. I'm on the floor. She's in the elevator.

Holding my crotch with one hand, I reach for her with the other. "Wait . . ." The doors close.

She's gone.

CHAPTER THIRTY-EIGHT

MARK

*I*n this very moment, time slows to a halt. My balls are lodged halfway up my windpipe, thanks to my on-again/off-again girlfriend. Which, coming from her, I should pretty much expect and have an athletic cup strapped to my groin at all times.

I suck in a breath and shake the stars from my vision. Jess is in trouble. Serious trouble, and based on Brian's watch in my hand, she's not the only one.

Goddammit, I need my phone. And for the excruciating pain to subside for two seconds so I can climb to my feet and call security.

Fuck. Why does she always have to nail my balls so fucking hard?

I'm still struggling for air when the door opens again. I cock my head sideways to pry my eyes up.

A man grabs me by both arms and lifts me to my feet like a rag doll. Only one man I know is that strong. "Brian?"

Standing but barely upright, I see that Brian has once again come through when no one else could.

Brian beams with pride. "I found Dean." He pats Dean's shoulder. "You might want to listen to what he has to say."

I gimp my way back to my office, one tortured breath at a time. "There's no time. Jess is in trouble."

Brian frowns, his voice a deep *don't fuck with me* tone when he says, "What do you mean, *in trouble?*"

I toss him his watch, my frown grim. "The kind that requires the bat signal." I make haste, calling security. "Jessica Bishop just left. Follow her, but don't be obvious. Report back every ten minutes."

"Yes, sir."

Dean considers us both. "Bat signal?"

"A 9-1-1 we used as kids," I croak out.

"You're Batman?" he asks with a skeptical glance my way.

"We all are," Brian replies.

Like when Cade went missing before an incoming ice storm. Or when I broke my foot trying to flip-kick my skateboard off the roof of the tool shack. And yes, occasionally on a bad date. But never, ever, under any circumstances, did we summon Batman in vain. Anyone and everyone who could respond would, instantly and without question.

I lock on Brian's worried frown. "Someone roughed her up."

Brian pounds a fist to the wall. "That someone is a dead man walking." I know the darkness in his eyes. No doubt, it mirrors mine.

In an instant, Brian goes to work deploying the signal— aka, our group chat—as I tap into the security feeds. Dean rushes through explaining his absence—droning on and on about how he's been away on a five-hundred-mile pilgrimage in Northwestern Spain that can take an entire month to cross.

"When Lance fired me, or rather, fired me on *your* behalf, he offered me an all-expenses-paid trip to El Camino del Santiago if I left quickly and quietly. I figured, fuck it. Why not? Journey the way of the saints. Seek solace."

For half a second, my eyes meet his. "Find any?"

He shakes his head. "Nope. I still want to kick someone's ass. I don't know who set me up, but when I do—"

Brian butts in. "Everyone's ready. We just need to know where."

In a nervous rhythm, my fingers strum the desk. "What was it Jess said? Something about dancing." I close my eyes. Phantom words whisper in my ear. "*No dancing tonight, Batman.* That's what she said."

Brian shifts his attention from the activity on his phone, shaking his head because none of it makes sense. "What does it mean?"

"I don't know. Dancing. We only danced once. At her event. Is she saying she's at the banquet hall?" I pull up the map app.

Dean taps a finger on the keyboard. "If she's under duress, afraid enough to demolish your balls to get away, she's afraid for her life. Or someone else's."

Brian holds up his watch. "Like me?"

Dean goes on. "Maybe she even thinks she won't get out of it alive."

I pound a fist on the desk. "Goddamnit, we have to get her back."

"Hear me out," Dean says. "If it were me, and I had one shot, I'd give you my best card. The cleanest shot possible. Fuck, what if she knows who the son of a bitch is?"

I snap my fingers. "We danced right after she saw that prick, Russ Hensen, but . . . Lance looked into him. He was clean."

"Clean?" Brian scoffs. "The asshole parked in a handicapped spot at a fundraiser for disabled vets. How clean can he be?"

The lead ball in my gut gnaws its way deeper. Fuck what Lance said. I need Dean's help.

"Russ Hensen. Dig everything up as fast as you can. There's no time to reactivate your access. Use my credentials."

I unlock my system and give Dean my chair. His keystrokes are feverish, working our secured databases.

He pauses for a second and gives me a look. "After everything, I'm glad you still trust me."

"At the moment, I can't afford not to. My girl is in trouble. And we're gonna . . ."

My confidence wavers. What if I can't find her? What if I can't save her?

My gaze moves to Brian and his blade. He nearly died that day. We both did. The more I fight to hold on to my self-control, the worse I tremble.

A ping hits my cell. The security team has a lock. I know where they're going.

"We're going to what?" Dean asks.

I do what I always do. I steel my resolve and slide my hand inside my shirt, focusing on the strength of the metal next to my skin. My dog tags. God willing, their luck rubs off on me. "We're gonna deal with this the old-fashioned way."

They both bark back unflinchingly, understanding in a unified response. *"Hooah!"*

The single word echoes a command to my soul. But it can't stop the tremble in my hand. Wasting anymore time grappling with the gun or my desperation is pointless. I toss the weapon back into the drawer and stand.

"What are you doing?" Brian's expression is hard—pained.

My steps grow hasty as I head out the door and into the hall. I can't explain. Not now. "Change of plans."

He lunges ahead of me, blocking my path. "You can't face him unarmed. You'll be walking into—"

My hand lands firm on his shoulder. "An ambush. I know. We've been down this road before." I blow out a pensive breath. "This time, we're ready. You and Dean have my back."

"But—"

"But nothing. He wanted me to see her. To react. He wants me, not Jess. Trust me. This will work." By his expression, I haven't convinced him, and I don't have time to fight, bully, or sway him. Grimly, I layer my tone with conviction and snap an order. "Step aside, soldier."

Jaw tight, he complies. I'm going into battle armed with little more than my demons. God willing, it'll be enough.

It has to be.

CHAPTER THIRTY-NINE

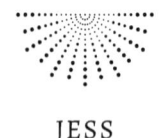

JESS

The longer I drive, the more the pain throbs, tormenting me as it messes with my head. I press a hand against my temple, desperate to unblur my vision.

I've noticed the same dark black SUV now and again nearly a mile back. A rescue party? Or is the small carrot of hope dangling in the distance a mirage? False hope fucking with the unrelenting pounding at the side of my head?

My foot eases a hair off the gas.

The barrel of the man's gun smacks my hand. "Drive!"

On demand, my foot presses the accelerator harder as I choke back the pain. "Where are we going?"

"Turn off here."

His voice is deep and garbled, eerie with every syllable. But his hands, his mannerisms, hell, even his shit cologne, I know it's him.

I speak and wince ahead of the backlash. "You don't have to do this."

"Shut up, you fucking cunt!" He studies the road. "Turn up there."

At this point, I know where we're going. A deep, desolate neck of the mountain woods that I could run through barefoot and blindfolded. I don't have a weapon. I don't even have the protection of Mark's precious dog tags. All I have is the promise that my safe space, my home, will never be safe again.

Is Brian inside? Is that why we're here?

I blink back fresh tears and watch as my family home comes into view and then do the only thing I can. I conjure my strongest wish yet. *Please, Mom and Dad. Protect us. Or if it's our time to reconnect, protect Brian and Zac.*

When the man forces me from the car, I ask, "What about Zac?"

"Leave him."

"No!" I race for the door, my hand on the handle, but his moves are swift, his backhand hits like a brick against my face, throwing me to the ground.

"In the house. Now!"

I struggle to my feet as he shoves me. Inside, I trip and fall again, my eyes locked on a shadow in the kitchen. But a second later, it's gone. Between pain and fear, I latch on to a glimmer of hope that it means something. Anything.

I scramble to get up, but the man's tattered black sneaker crushes my hand. I shriek in pain, scraping at my trapped fingers.

He barely eases up, removing his phone and making a call. "It's done. Now, what do I do with her?"

There's an ominous, drawn-out pause. I twist my body to look up at the emotionless mask and its dark stare back.

"Anything I want?" he asks, repeating someone else's words. "With pleasure." He disconnects the call and sticks the gun at my temple. All I can think is, please, don't let this happen. My body trembles as he runs it down my spine. "It's time for a little fun, *Choir Girl*."

"Hey!"

We both snap our heads in the direction of a voice. Mark's voice.

My breaths stagger as my instant relief drains to dread. Mark is here, unarmed. He needs a gun. A weapon. Anything to protect himself from this fucking madman.

My macho, brave, stupid man takes one step closer, his hands high in surrender. My throat slams shut.

The man yanks me to my feet, using me as a shield. The gun that bruised my skin is now trained on Mark while I'm trapped and helpless. Nerves punch every inch of my gut and chest. All I can do is watch the love of my life stand off against this psychopath and his gun.

"Let her go, Russ," Mark says so calmly, I feel it wrap around me like a blanket. His dog tags hang from his neck, on prominent display, and I calm even more.

It's nothing but superstitious bullshit, but at the sight of them, I feel braver. I'm not afraid like I was a second ago.

"I have your money." Mark slides a backpack from his shoulder. "A million dollars in exchange for Jess."

"I can't fool you, can I, rich boy?" Russ removes the mask and chuckles, loosening his grip. "You think I did this for a measly million dollars? It's like he said, you really are the village idiot."

Mark's ears perk up. "Who said?"

"It really doesn't matter, does it?" Russ cocks the hammer of the gun. His arm grips me tighter, but not tight enough. I do the only thing I can. I bite his fucking hand until I taste harsh, metallic blood. I'm released. In the next second, I'm thrown to the floor.

A deafening crack fills the air. A clap of thunder that strikes my heart like lightning.

CHAPTER FORTY

MARK

*J*fling Jess to the floor, my body, armor for hers. I brace for the shots I know are coming. I just don't know for sure who will fire first.

Brian and Dean are on the perimeter, as well as a dozen of my men. The authorities? Called, but far enough away that this is our fight, not theirs.

The problem is no one had a clean shot. No one except fucking Russ. It's the layout of the house—a security feature built in by Mr. Bishop. It should've been an advantage. It was our worst fucking nightmare.

And Jess . . . what was she thinking? But what my brave girl did, *fuck*, I should have seen it coming. My Choir Girl never takes shit lying down. Biting her way into the fight. But the second she freed herself, a spray of bullets was following, whether she was ready for it or not.

Like Brian on the battlefield, I threw her to the floor with so much force, I must have hurt her. It didn't matter. I learned the last time. *Cover her.* My body locked around hers. My voice against her ear.

"Stay down."

And she did. Cold and detached, like a beautiful statue fallen over in a museum. She didn't move or blink or breathe. It was the battlefield all over again. But this time, not even a jammed gun would warm my grip. I held my breath, waiting out an eternity of gunfire to know if Jess and I would live or die.

The thing is, now my body knows what to expect. Last time, I was hit at point blank range. I stared down my enemy as the white-hot pain seared my chest. Watched as Dean popped him in the shoulder. Even then, the son of a bitch managed to nail Brian's leg twice before Dean cleared a shot to his head.

Even when Russ's body collapsed on the floor beside us, I couldn't lift off Jess. Not with a gun still in his hand.

When the men swarm in, Brian's command is loud. "Get his gun!" Hard footsteps surround us, and as soon as they do, I can move again. Breathe again. I snap to the present, shifting all my attention to Jess.

Her faded blue eyes are cold, lifeless, and dim.

Is she hurt? Shot? "Jess?" My hand moves to her cheek. "Can you hear me?"

I sit her limp body up against mine, rocking her as I inspect her from head to toe. The black-and-blue bruise on her cheek unlocks a world of rage, at Russ and at myself. How could I let this happen?

But I can't think of that now. I need to focus on the lifeless, wilted girl who's just out of reach, but secure in my arms.

"Jess. You're going to be okay." I press kisses to her head. "It will all be fine."

But nothing is fine. What was Russ going to do? Rape her? Kill her? My gaze drifts to the backpack, opened with wrapped hundreds scattered across the floor. If this wasn't about the money, then why?

I move my gaze back to Jess. Her eyes don't meet mine. They're too busy fixed on a lone spot in the distance, a few million miles away.

"Jess," I whisper. She barely blinks, wading through a state of shock. "I'm here."

Brian kisses her head, too. Another blink. He helps us to our feet, but her limbs are rubber. I scoop her into my arms, carrying her from the room, determined to carry her through it all if I have to. Be the man by her side through everything.

As soon as we step outside, she comes to life, bucking from my arms and bolting to the waiting ambulance. To Zac.

My heart thuds to the ground as she rushes into his arms. From a gurney, he pulls her close, with a light shower of kisses to her temple. She isn't the lifeless rag doll she was in my arms. With him, her actions are deep and intense, clutching him for dear life. *Him!*

My steps are numb and heavy. All I can hear is her voice. "You're okay," she says over and over again, sobbing in his arms. "You're okay."

"I'm fine," he says, rocking and consoling her. "We're both okay, baby."

He's okay? I put my life on the line, stared down a dangerous criminal and his loaded gun, shielded her with my own fucking body, and she's running to him? What the fuck?

I look on, dumbfounded, as I stomp out the last beats of my worthless heart.

God, I really am a dick. I should be the bigger man. Grateful they're both alive. Safe and sound and—

No. Fuck all that! They're over there, making a fucking *I'll remember this day for the rest of my life* Hallmark moment, while I'm struggling to hold together the pieces of my life.

I blink back the relentless pricking behind my eyes and swallow hard. I love this woman. Would give my life for hers. But she's too busy taking refuge in Zac's arms to even acknowledge my presence. My existence. *Yes. Fine. Managed to save your life and survive a raging psycho gunman. Thanks for asking.*

I take a bold step over, seconds from going subatomic on their canoodling. My goddamned world just imploded, and the impact was barely a blip on their Richter scale.

My mouth opens, prepared to lay into her—into them. Ready to tear into them until my heart lodges in my throat, stopping me.

What am I doing? Goddammit, I love Jess. Even if she doesn't love me back.

I lift a hand to stroke her hair one last time, a move that slices me in two. Then I clear my throat, forcing determined words past my lips.

"I'm glad you're both all right." Zac looks up, nodding, as I hand him my heart. "Take care of her."

Wounded bits of me are left behind, shattered in the aftermath. I do the only thing that's left to do.

I walk away.

CHAPTER FORTY-ONE

MARK

The phone rings, and I can't take it anymore. With a heavy sigh, I answer. "Hi, Mom."

"When are we going to see you, honey? You know we missed you at Christmas."

It's been weeks since I've talked to anyone outside of The Centurion Group. Why bother? Deflated, I stare at the wedding ring that's become a desk ornament of late.

When my first proposal crumbled in an epic fail, I shoved Christmas to the back of my mind. The last thing I needed was the glittery shower of tinsel and twinkling lights right in my face. Christmas meant watching my brother and the woman of my dreams arm in arm, sharing eggnog and gushing over adorable ornaments and homemade gifts. And mistletoe.

Argh.

I wipe a hand down my face. Don't even get me started on the stupid fucking mistletoe.

"Time's been really getting away with me." It's a total

fucking lie. When your heart breaks, time travels at the speed of airport Wi-Ri. "Sorry, Mom. I've been swamped with the IPO coming up and the press—"

"Of course," she says in her *don't-feel-guilty-but-totally-feel-guilty* voice. "I understand."

"I appreciate that."

"You have a life."

One that's gone to hell in a lead-laden handbasket, but whatever. "And corporate responsibilities," I add, like a businessman. And a dick.

She sighs a motherly sigh. "It's just that, I'm getting older . . ." *Oh, here we go.* "And seeing you this past month was such a blessing, and—"

"It's not happening," I snap with instant regret. My head drops to the back of my chair. "Soon, I mean. It's not happening soon. I'm sorry, mom. With the reporters and headlines, it's best I stay away. But I'll be back as soon as the IPO hits. I swear."

"For my birthday?"

God, she just won't let up. Her birthday. January thirtieth. An event that would definitely have Zac and Jess in elated attendance, no doubt, gifting her with the announcement of pending nuptials as they gaze at each other, dreamy-eyed, and make nauseating plans for Valentine's.

I scoop up that big, fat, eight-thousand-carat diamond and chuck it across the room. *Fuck it.*

"You know what? Absolutely. You have my word. I'll be there. With bells on."

And condoms. Because I'll be bringing a date. Maybe two.

Or a few. The player strikes back. With a fucking vengeance. Hell, I jump to standing. I'm starting tonight.

"Mom, sorry, I have to go."

"Go?"

Yes. The Player's got to get his groove back. Starting right fucking now.

I scoop up my keys and wallet, realizing it's been a while since I've had a condom on me. Which reminds me of Jess. Always of Jess. The last time I held her. Had her. Watched her blue eyes brighten, lit up with ecstasy the first time I pressed through her sweet, tight entrance without a—

"Mark?"

"Huh?" *Fuck.* I wrestle a swarm of Jess-filled inappropriate thoughts from my mind and try to close out the call.

"Yes. I need to go." Grab a hundred-pack of condoms and get Choir Girl out of my life. "I'll call you tomorrow."

"Promise?" Her question is laced with equal amounts of honey and obligation.

"If I don't, you can name your price. Maserati," I offer, then ante up with, "An all-expenses-paid trip to Paris." I swear I've lost my mind. The sum of years of negotiating strength crumbles over a single phone call. One I'll probably blow off.

Her laugh is light. Satisfied for the moment because my mom and I both know any IOU in her hand will be collected swiftly and without mercy. "Oh, I will. And trust you me, Marcus Evan Donovan, you won't get off as cheap as a trip to Paris."

From the recesses of my wallet, my black card cringes. "Talk to you tomorrow."

"We'll see." Her voice is a song. "Love you."

Now, I have two reasons to hit the bar. "Love you, too."

∼

Five drinks in, and Lisa—or is it Liza?—sips her drink through thick, luscious lips before her hand strokes a path up my leg. "You don't say."

"I do say." Because I can't stop talking. "She was—" I blow out a raspberry. "The woman of my dreams. The girl I was going to marry. The love of my fucking life—" I stagger to my feet, extending both hands to the ceiling before slumping back on my ass. "And she left me."

"Oh, no." Lisa's fingers play with the hairs on my chest. Did I undo that button? "Why don't we go back to my place? I'll make you forget all about her." Her hand slides across my length, uninterested as it is.

I watch her lick a finger with the tip of her tongue and ponder her offer. Make me forget Choir Girl? *Eh, why not?* It's not like I have plans, and anything beats suffering through this searing hole in my heart for even a second more.

"Get your hands off my man!" a woman screeches from across the room.

I blink hard, struggling to unblur her. Pink sequin top. Tight black skirt. Six-inch platforms stomping this way. My eyes narrow.

Brie. She was the reason Jess left me in the first place. I mean, the first reason she left me in the first place. Am I making sense?

I face my companion—what's her name—and point an

angry, insulted, fired-up finger at Brie. "I do *not* know that *thrwoman*." Am I slurring?

"Don't know me?" Brie cries like a banshee.

I cover my ears. "Make it stop," I beg to any deity who will listen.

"Is this man bothering you?" Some eight-foot-tall lunkhead strolls up to her side.

I stand. A colossal mistake as I tumble inelegantly back in my chair. "Bothering her?" I say, indignant. "*She* accused *me* of being her man—a flat-out lie." I point to her over-injected face. "She's a yacht-destroying home-wrecker."

Heated squeals erupt as Brie stomps her foot like a toddler, angry fists flying through the air. "I am not a home-wrecker."

"The lies!" I point a finger at her nose. "You wrecked my home. And guess what, sweetheart? That counts."

The lunkhead chimes in. "My girlfriend is not a liar," he says in some foreign accent.

What is that, Norwegian? And seriously? "You mean the girlfriend that says I'm her man?" I toss back my drink. "Just getting this clear in my head."

Confusion furrows his face, a look that seems to suit him.

I deadpan. "I'm. Not. With. Her."

Brie's arm wraps around Lunkhead's. "Kick his ass, will you, babe?"

"Anything for you, babe,"

So, he's kicking my ass to defend her honor? I tear off my blazer. *Fine. Bring it.*

The idiot gives me a *Matrix* hand wave, egging me on.

Oh, it's on. Get ready for your wax-on, wax-off ass kicking, motherfucker. As soon as I can focus on one of him.

My body topples out of my seat as I put all my force behind a massive swing to the air. He clocks me with an uppercut to the chin. On the floor, I notice three shoes facing me and one very familiar blade.

"Making friends, I see."

Once again, Brian lifts me like a rag doll. I'm getting strangely accustomed to it. "How'd you find me?"

He snickers. "I tracked Dean halfway around the world. And you're not exactly stealth." He shows me his phone. Player Mark Donovan and the Yacht Destroyer are trending. Finally, the evil powers of my hashtag are used for good.

We watch as Zac deals with Lunkhead, which doesn't take much. A knock to the cheek. A kick center chest. A kick-flip thing that makes him look like Bruce fucking Lee. *Whoo!* My little bro isn't even breaking a sweat. I might hate that asswipe's motherfucking face, but I love this man.

Lunkhead escapes with Brie in tow as Zac straightens his suit. "You all right?"

"Just licking my wounds with Liza, here."

"Lisa," she says with a frown, correcting me.

Brian takes her hand and kisses it. "Enchanté, Lisa," he says in perfect French.

She giggles and squirms, and it's obvious all her lap dances are now taken. Which by the limp drag of my cock suits me just fine.

Lisa turns to me. "You never said you had such hot friends."

Sorry, I must have been too distracted by your hand running laps up and down my crotch.

Ever the gentleman, I introduce them. "Lisa, this is Brian and Zac."

"Those were some moves," she says to Zac, her smile laced with invitation.

I snap my fingers at her face. "Hey. Zac is taken. Focus on the big guy, Lisa."

He and Brian exchange a look. Brian shrugs and offers to buy Lisa a drink. Which she accepts because she's a fucking camel.

Zac takes a seat beside me, smiling.

I want to punch that grin so bad, my fists tense, but (A) as I said before, I love the motherfucker, and (B) he would clearly kick my ass and not hold back for the sheer joy of it.

He sniffs my half-full drink and takes a sip. "Not that I mind Brian running off with the girl of the hour, but since when am I taken?"

Is he fucking with me? "Why do you say it like that? Of course, you're taken."

Zac sips, a blank expression glazing his face.

I poke a finger in his chest, punctuating my words. "You're with Jess."

He smirks. "How many drinks have you had?"

I rake my fingers through my hair. "Four."

He sips again. "Ah."

"Don't you *ah*, me." I snatch back my drink. "She told me all about it. You proposed. She accepted. End of fucking story. Now, if the only reason you're here is to shove it down my throat, please excuse me while I go play hopscotch in traffic."

When I go to stand, a colossal mistake of dizzying proportions, he eases me to my seat. "Jess and I aren't together."

Now I know he's fucking with me. "She said you were. And my Choir Girl is not a liar."

He rolls his eyes. "Sure, she is. Jess lies all the time. Hell, she's been lying to herself about you since she could talk. Lying to you was probably easy."

Zac orders a round of waters as I sit back, perplexed. He hands me one, and I chug it down. I need a clear head for wherever this conversation is going.

I pound a fist on the table. "Bullshit. If this is your way of weaseling out of marrying the most wonderful girl in the world—"

He shakes his head. "I'm a red-blooded Donovan. I would marry her. In a heartbeat. But not if she's in love with someone else."

I hadn't even considered that. I lean in, almost afraid of the answer. "She's in love with someone else?"

Zac shakes his head. "She's in love with you."

I frown. "No, she isn't. I risked my life for her only to watch her bolt from me and run to you. In my arms, she was unresponsive. One look at you, and she comes to life." I reach for my bourbon again, and Zac flicks my knuckle hard. "Ow."

"Considering she thought you'd been shot, and I was dead, I'd say she did pretty well under the circumstances." He leans in and repeats himself. "She thought I was dead, moron. Sorry, death trumps gunshot when you're coming out of shock."

I press two fingers to my temple. I'm not following. "But I'm fine now. And you're fine, and she's fine. So why haven't I heard a word from her?"

From behind me, a hand claps my back. "That's just

because she's scared," Brian adds dismissively, handing me a basket of steaming fresh pretzels.

"Scared of what?" I chew incredulously. "Me?"

"Of telling you the truth."

"Truth? What truth? Oh yeah, the big secret that everyone knows but me," I say, sarcastic as hell.

In true Brian form, he prioritizes the situation. "Look, uh," he motions to Lisa. "She really wants to see my collection of Harry Potter movies."

I huff out a chuckle. "Is that what the kids are calling it nowadays?"

Brian shrugs innocently. "And she wants to show me her House of Slytherin bra and panties."

Zac lifts his glass. "A match made in cosplay heaven."

I shake my head into my glass of water. "I love how the men closest to me keep stealing my women." I take a sip.

Zac tilts the bottom of my glass so that if I want to avoid a face full of water, I need to chug. "Sober up, asshole. And get this through your thick fucking head: Jess loves you. But she's too stubborn and too wrapped up in her own feelings to act."

"You don't have to tell me Choir Girl is stubborn. I've never had to work so hard to get a woman's attention in my life." I drain my glass. He hands me another. "And fine, maybe she's scared, but so am I. Scared I'm about to lose it all."

He frowns, taking it in. "Your business?"

Hasn't he heard a word I said? Pain strikes my chest. "Jess. I'm scared of losing Jess. Her perfect smile. Big, blue eyes with flecks of amber gold. Every last one of those adorable freckles on her nose." I choke on a mouthful of emotions. "She was mine. I had her. I was happy. For the first fucking time in forever."

He bats me on the head with a pretzel. "Then work it out."

Dismayed, I stare blankly. "How? It's Jess. How are we supposed to work this out when she won't even give me a chance?" I snatch the pretzel from his hand and toss it aside. "*You* are the man she said she was marrying. *You* know all her deep, dark secrets that she's never, not once, bothered sharing with me. *You* are her happily ever after, wrapped up in superhero moves and a McDreamy head of hair."

He doesn't hold back. Zac knocks me so hard in the chest, me and my chair go flying to the floor.

"I'm not marrying her. And not because I don't love her. But because she's in love with you, dipshit." Blinking, I stare as his words sink in. "Hell, I should disavow her for her shit taste in men alone." Frustrated, he works both hands through his hair. "Yes, she has a secret, but so do you. And yes, she didn't kowtow to you when you saved her life."

"A simple thank you would've done nicely." For that, he flicks water in my face. "Okay, okay, I give," I say laughing.

Zac helps me to my feet, and dusts off my shoulders. "She's not scared, Mark. She's terrified. Russ's bullet nicked your blazer. You could've died. She could've lost you. Everything Jess fears has to do with losing the people she loves, especially you. So, in the spirit of self-preservation—or blatant stupidity—she made a preemptive strike." He smacks my cheek—a wakeup call. "She got it in her head that one way or another, you're leaving her. She left you to avoid the pain of her losing you."

I rub my chin, renewed. Is she still mine? *My* Choir Girl?

I smile at the prospect as fire fills me from the inside out. *A preemptive strike?* Now, that's a battle I can fight.

CHAPTER FORTY-TWO

JESS

*E*mptiness is the worst kind of pain. It's dark and suffocating, and there's no getting over it. You can only suffer through it.

Case in point—I have holes in my heart. Big, gaping wounds of excruciating pain every time I breathe. Mom and Dad. Mark. *Even* . . .

I wrap two arms around my middle and stare at my stomach, sinking into a pool of desolate emotions. My eyes drift out the window, studying the stars, wishing for a sign—

A streak darts across the hill—a shadow. *What is that?*

A flicker in the distance glows brighter. My eyes focus, alert to every movement. There it is again. A sudden shift. A shadow. A *person*.

Brian's prophetic words haunt my mind. *And what happens when vagrants and folks up to no good show up at your doorstep?* Panicked, I grab the shotgun, then double back to the kitchen, filling both pockets with snacks.

What? Just because they're vagrants doesn't mean they're not hungry.

I scurry across an unmarked trail. The brush is thick, and areas are pitch black without a moon, but this is my home. It's the back of my hand. I could jog through it with my eyes shut. I skip over every divot, old and new—the land rushing up to meet my feet. It isn't until a twig snaps beneath my foot that I pause.

"Hey, Jess." His voice is warm honey that seeps through my soul. My shoulders relax when I realize it's Mark. "Hope you don't mind, but Brian said I could camp here for a few weeks or so."

Frowning, I glance around. Mark is making himself perfectly at home—Manhattan playboy meets Lord of the Flies. Backpack, pillows, giant marshmallows for s'mores . . . the whole nine yards.

"A few weeks? What is this? A hobo stop?" I shake my head as he stuffs a fist-sized marshmallow in his mouth. "You can't stay here. You have to be in New York City for that all-important IPO. Remember?" Unphased, he blinks. Leery, I step closer and take a suspecting sniff. "You're wasted."

He scoffs heartily. "I am not drunk," he mumbles through a mouthful of gooey food.

"Really? Because you stink of cheap bourbon, and you're missing a shoe."

He looks down as if just now noticing, then meets my eyes again with a grin. "Untrue, Choir Girl. I *was* drunk. I'm now on the path to sobriety." He shakes a bottle of water at me. "And you're so *wrong*," he says with exaggeration. "I only have to be in New York City *part* of the time. The rest of the time I choose to be here. Right here. On this spot." He pounds his finger to the ground. "Unless . . ." Suggestion lights his eyes.

"Unless what?"

He waggles his brows. "Unless you'd like to invite me in."

I don't even know how to respond to that. I ignore the fact that his hair is so beautifully disheveled that I just want to run my fingers through it, or that his smile is delicious, or that he's undressing. "Stop!"

He tilts his head, his dimple sprouting where his growing smile ends. "Why? It's time for bed, and as you well know, I sleep the way the good Lord made me. Naked and unafraid." He unfastens his jeans and, mercy me, I know the dangerous terrain ahead. The dips and cuts and delectable ripped inches of him will beckon me. And by me, I mean my tongue.

I try to reason with him. "You have an IPO launching in a few weeks. A chance to be a billionaire and—"

"Actually . . ." He raises a single finger, pausing mid-striptease to shush me. "It's not public knowledge yet, but I'm canceling the IPO."

Despite the rock-solid dick between us, I step into his space. "You're in no condition to make a decision like that."

"Am so."

"Have you lost your mind? You said yourself you've been building up to this your whole life. That it's the pinnacle of your existence—"

Mark's massive hands cradle my face, not letting go. His lips press hard against mine, possessive and unrelenting. His kiss spreads across me like hot butter and honey. I feel it everywhere. My knees nearly collapse before he lets go.

"I made a mistake." His words press on with urgency.

"None of that matters. Nothing matters. Only you, Jess," he whispers. "Only you."

I blink back tears. It does matter. I know it does. I can't have him choose me over his company or his future. He'll end up resenting me. Hating me. I can't have that.

"You can't choose me when you don't know—" I cut myself off. He needs to know all the facts before he high dives into the deep end of this mistake.

But I can't tell him. Not like this. With him half-naked and three sheets to the wind.

Breathtaking sea glass eyes search mine. "What, Jess? Don't be afraid to say everything you need to say. Let it all out. Give me this one chance to prove to you I will always be the man by your side."

He's right. This is my chance. For once and for all to say it out loud. The problem is I've never said it out loud. Never spoken a word of it to anyone. I feel my heart crack the second I open my mouth. Nothing comes out. Not one word.

"Come on, Jess. Brian knows, and so does Zac. Please, tell me."

He leans his forehead on mine. Why can't I tell him?

Just say it.

But it hurts. I didn't tell Brian and Zac. I've never breathed a word to anyone. They know because they were there. Thank God they were there.

My eyes close, shutting Mark out, sinking into numbness. "You can't choose me over your company. I won't let you."

He reaches for me, catlike but inebriated.

I back away before he unravels me from the inside out with another soul-searing kiss. "It's my property," I say with an ounce of anger I hope sounds convincing. He rolls his eyes. I stomp a foot and wave a stern finger in warning. "You have one hour to be off my property, Mr. Donovan."

"No can do, Ms. Bishop. See, I have Brian's and Rex's and Cade's permission." He wiggles three fingers back in my face. "Three to one. Majority rules. I'm not going anywhere."

With that, two thumbs dip into his jeans, working them down past that sin of his deep-carved V. Lord have mercy, it takes nothing at all for him to unleash his hard, thick, massive cock. Unapologetically, it springs free.

My brain fries a little because it's thick and hard and would be so easy for me to worship.

His eyes melt over me as my body overheats. His wide, cheesy-ass grin brims with satisfaction. "I'm all yours, Jess. Now, be a good girl and get on your knees. I want to fuck that secret from your lips." He strokes himself up and down in a slow rhythm that has me hypnotized.

My lips part in shock. Plus, they like the idea and would kill for just one taste, but mostly from shock.

Annoyed and flustered over what to say, I resort to sneering. "Fine. Stay. But don't come calling for any toilet paper, city boy."

"Why bother? There's a lake right over there." He points, and I cringe. "Mountain living at its finest, Choir Girl." He winks.

To that, I have nothing. Nothing!

Furious with Mark and my brothers and the whole damned world at this point, I march my ass back to the house, shouting, "Go home, Mark!"

He hollers, "See you in the morning, Choir Girl!"

CHAPTER FORTY-THREE

JESS

I've flipped through hundreds of channels, cleaned every square inch of the house, and even skimmed through a stack of those damn ridiculous offers on the property.

Mark has been camped here for days, driving me clear to my wits end. He's like a critter. Too native to the land to evict, and too dangerous to take in.

And make no mistake, taking Mark Donovan in is dangerous. Sinfully so. If he comes in, we'll be all over each other in seconds and humping like bunnies through Valentine's.

I sigh. And then what? Mark will expect things from me. Things that I can't deliver.

I'm stuck in the weirdest social experiment ever. Even if he's off the grid, we both know I was totally bluffing about the toilet situation. I know he comes and goes, though I never see how. If I've left my towel on the sink and miraculously, it's neatly folded and back on the rack. And don't even get me started on my missing panties. I imagine him climbing through windows, stealth-like and shirtless, doing the dirtiest things with them.

Why is that such a turn-on?

There's also the food situation. Breakfast has waited for me on the table every morning, and lunch shows up from out of nowhere at my office. It's as if he's got God's personal Uber Eats at his beck and call. Poof. A meal appears. A heavenly one.

And then there's dinner. It's always piping hot and in the oven. Last night was a macaroni casserole with the cheese perfectly crisped on top. I wanted to have sex with it. Yes, it was that good.

Fresh flowers have started multiplying from every corner of every room, as little heart-filled sticky notes cluster on the fridge.

"Have a wonderful day."
"You look beautiful."
"I love the way you sing."
"You're perfect the way you are."
"I miss your little bear snore."

An outrageous lie. I don't snore.
How dare he.

"I love you."
"I. Love. You."
"I LOVE YOU!"

I've tossed every last one of those notes in the trash. Never mind that his words tug at every last lifeline of my heart. I won't love him. I can't.

Okay, okay, fine. That's a lie. I can't not love him. If I'm honest with myself, I've always loved him. I'm hardwired to love that man. Nothing will ever change that. The issue is that if he knows the truth, he can't love me, even if he thinks he can.

And I didn't trash them all. I saved the last one. The prominent *I LOVE YOU* in all caps, punctuated by an exclamation point, underlined twice, and every O in the shape of a heart. I've hidden it under my pillow. I love him so much, it hurts. Every day that he's here hurts. It's why I have to push him away.

Frustrated, I angrily toss aside another offer and pick up the next. I skim over the jargon-ese and flip through to the bottom line. A stupid amount of money that would set each of us Bishops up for life.

My brothers want me to sell. And if there's even a shred of sanity left in my brain, I have to do it. But I don't have to like it.

Something on the news catches my eye—the flash of a headline. I snatch up the remote and raise the volume.

"In breaking news, Manhattan multimillionaire Mark Donovan seems to be missing. Though documents have been obtained this morning that clear his name and stamp out any further delays on the IPO, Mr. Donovan was unavailable for comment, and all his social media accounts have gone black. In a baffling twist, he was spotted a week ago in an unprecedented altercation at a nightclub. Witnesses speculate it to be a love triangle gone wrong . . ."

Oh. My. God.

CHAPTER FORTY-FOUR

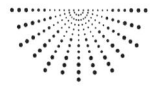

JESS

I rush from the room, blast through the door, leap over the patio steps, and storm up the grassy hill, cursing his name every step of the way. "Marcus Evan Donovan!"

"Here!" he bellows out.

I block the afternoon sun with my hand, barely making him out in bright, reflective stars that dance along the lake. My steps freeze in awe. He's fishing. I haven't watched Mark fish since he was a teen. A flood of memories rushes through my thoughts. It's enough to pump the brakes on my freakout and warm my lips to a grin.

My steps slow as I take him in. Soft mahogany hair and masculine scruff. Broad shoulders on an olive-toned body that could've been chiseled by Michelangelo himself. Mark always manages to steal my breath. Like a glorious work of art for me alone to treasure.

His loungy flannel pants are too thin to leave anything to

the imagination. As heat licks my neck and cheeks, I can only stare. Stunned speechless.

His smile is pure joy as he recasts his line far into the lake. It's a Mark I haven't seen in so long—relaxed and carefree. And happy.

"You're fishing. Just like old times."

"Yup." He glances over, amused. "And you're gawking. Just like old times," he repeats, popping a knowing brow.

My gaze turns sentimental, remembering how he and Brian would spend hours out here, on this exact stretch of shore. I'd stay a safe distance away, planted on a branch of the old maple, eavesdropping. Watching him with keen interest, hanging on his every word.

"It was either that or cling like a mini-creeper," I reply without a lick of shame. "Gawking from afar was the more civilized option."

"I'm sure it was."

I stand there for another moment, taking him in. Every muscle, every line, every dip. It's as if he was always destined to carry the weight of the world. I want to touch him. Kiss him. I want what I can't have.

I want him.

My trance is broken when the breeze kicks up, and my slight shiver is followed by his. I scoop his soft shirt off the ground. "Aren't you cold?"

"Freezing," he openly admits. "But if I put on a shirt, I'll never get Jess to come out and play."

He might be right. But that doesn't stop me from flinging his shirt at his head. "You're an idiot."

"A desperate fool in love. What can I say?"

My heart squeezes hard. When his eyes catch mine, they're a rich shade of caramel, though I can see flecks of pine green as I draw closer. I have to swat away the butterflies he manages to send fluttering in my chest.

He sets the pole aside for a moment and slips on his shirt, not bothering to button it. With an inviting smile, he pats the ground beside him. "I promise, I won't bite."

"Liar."

His hearty laugh is a rumble. I feel it from my head to my toes. When I don't budge, he pulls out all the stops, luring me with the one thing I can never turn away from.

A dandelion. A big, fluffy, white dandelion held up between his thumb and forefinger. "Come on, Jess. Your wish is waiting."

I take a seat beside him, bringing my knees to my chest. His arm blankets me—a strong, tender heat so natural, I can't help but lean in.

God, he feels like home. I don't know what comes over me, but in this moment, I need him. His warmth. His strength. Even his closeness as I prepare to burn the bridge between us to the ground.

He holds it to my lips as the heat of his breath wreaks havoc along my neck and ear. "Make a wish, Choir Girl," he whispers.

I close my eyes and do as I'm told. I blow. Blow out a big, defiant, unimaginable wish before I could help myself. This was my last wish on Bishop Mountain, and I wasted it on the impossible. I wished for us.

With the next gust of wind, the feather-light whisps scatter to the sky, and for a long while, we say nothing. We just sit, letting our gazes drift out over the lake.

"Warm enough?" he asks, wrapping an arm around me.

I nod against his neck. "Mark," I breathe.

"Yes," he whispers.

I love you. I need you. For a brief second, I imagine telling him everything I want to say. Then, I sweep all that crazy talk under the rug and refocus on what brought me out here to begin with. "You're missing."

His chuckle is light. "You found me."

"No. Seriously. It's all over the news. *Multimillionaire Mark Donovan Missing.*"

"Good." He pulls me snugly against him, completely unfazed by this revelation.

I don't understand. "Good?"

Our hands connect as his thumb rubs delicate circles over my knuckles. "Yes. Good. I've needed to be missing. I've needed time to clear my head and figure a few things out. Why it felt like my company was crumbling away beneath my feet. Why, after I've been everywhere in the world, the only place I've ever had any peace at all is right here. And why the love of my life can't open up and talk to me."

My jaw tightens as I chew on his words.

"I figured out two of the three, Jess, and I'm not budging from Bishop Mountain until I figure out the third." He kisses my temple. It sinks into me like lava. "And I don't give a flying fuck what the rest of the world thinks of it."

The sun, a bright ball of orange, plummets slowly behind a lake of indigo blue. I can feel the day ending. My time on this mountain ending. *Us* ending.

My lips tremble. "I'm taking the deal. Selling the property."

With a single finger, he lifts my chin and meets my gaze with a frown. "Why?"

I have to turn away. "Because it's time. Because it's right. Because I—"

I taste the tear before I feel it. The ball of his thumb forms gentle strokes on my cheek. God, why can't he just be an asshole? Make me hate him. Break my heart and never look back.

"Jess?"

"Because I don't want to keep fighting with everyone I love, okay? I love it here. I do. It's the only home I've ever known. And the thought of leaving it, well, it's ripping me to shreds." Sobs choke my words, but I forage through. "Everyone is right. It's a crutch. A tether."

"But it's not."

"Yes, it is." My whole body begins to shake. I curl up into myself, a puddle of tears. "I've been swimming against the current for so long because I didn't want to face the inevitable. But I've failed. Failed this house, failed my family, failed you."

"You haven't failed. Not at all."

My head shakes, defeated. "It's over."

Both his arms knot around me tightly, locking me against his chest. "You don't have to do this alone, Jess. I'm here. Whatever you need. Tell me."

Agony trembles through me. He needs to know the truth. Tears come on harder as I fight to free myself. Distance. I need distance for this.

"Jess?" His soft voice drifts between us, swallowing me in

grief and regret. He takes one step closer. I take two determined steps back.

"There is something I need you to do for me. For us." I suck in my pain before releasing it in a slow, staggered breath. "I need you to leave."

"What?"

My next words slice their way out through my heart. "I can't have children, Mark."

Silence descends between us like a wall of ice, and it kills me. I know he must have questions. He'll want answers. An explanation. But rather than ask or say anything at all, he just stands and stares, letting me wilt beneath his unbearable gaze.

"Severe endometriosis compounded by fibroids." My own voice doesn't register. It feels distant and clinical. "When the pelvic pain became debilitating, I was rushed to the ER . . ." I swipe fresh tears from my face and press on. "The blessing in all of it was that Brian was here when it happened."

Mark's face twists, dazed. "When?" He answers for himself before I can breathe a word. "That last mission. It was before Brian and I left for our last mission, wasn't it?" I nod. "We were supposed to leave together, but at the airport, he got a call. He left without a word."

"I made him swear not to tell a soul."

"And Zac? You told him? But not me?" His eyes are full of pain.

"He was there, Mark. We were at the park. Our regular lunch. The pain hit so fast, he had to carry me to the car. By the time we arrived at the hospital, Brian was waiting."

The dam lifts, releasing years' worth of pent-up tears

down my cheeks. The anguish in Mark's expression only makes it worse.

He reaches out for me, but that's just his sense of loyalty. Responsibility. I know he wants children. He's always wanted them. Hell, he used to make bets with his brothers that he'd have the most, and he should. I want that for him. He deserves it. All the joys of having a precious family all his own.

As if reading my mind, realization bleeds through the lines of his face. "That's why you ran. It wasn't that the sales clerk was talking about Brie, it's because she said that word. Family." This time, there's no escape. His arms are around me, holding me still. Locking me in place. "Jess, none of that matters."

I stare up at him, his gorgeous face wet with tears. God, he would do this. Give it all up for me. "Liar," I whisper, my chest tight, my heart aching. "You deserve so much more than I can give you."

"I deserve you. You will always be more than enough." He cups my cheeks tight, almost painfully. It's too much. "Jess, there's something I have to tell you—"

I don't let him finish. "Don't follow me. Don't stay. Don't make this harder than it already is."

His lips devour mine, owning me. Possessing me. But it's a mistake. I can't let him make the biggest mistake of his life. When his lips soften—sweeten—I wrench from his arms and let him go. "Goodbye, Mark."

His expression falls. I've wounded him; I know I have. But it's for the best.

If only one of us can hitch our wagon to a star of happily

ever afters, it has to be him. Because I love him. Love Mark Donovan with all my heart.

   End of story.

CHAPTER FORTY-FIVE

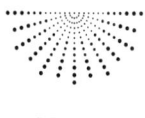

MARK

"Goodbye," I say, calm and controlled—almost sedately as I focus. It's early morning, and I'm a man on a mission.

I line up the high-powered helicopter for a landing. With the sun in my eyes and the wind at my tail, I bite back my nerves and focus. Flying a helicopter? Piece of cake. It's the whole landing it that's a bitch and a half in the heart of Manhattan.

A sea of concrete spindles fills the sky as the crosswinds wrestle with me. Not gonna lie . . . it makes my brow, palms, and balls sweat the entire fucking time.

"Goodbye?" Brian shouts, his loud word setting off a deafening feedback squeal. I tear off my headset. The helicopter tilts fucking near sideways. The angle—pucker-factor-ten.

"Fuck!" we cry like a chorus from the top of our lungs.

Heart racing, it takes both hands and all my strength to stabilize her, lulling the wild beast back to center. A heart attack and a half later, I set her gently on the pad, landing her as if my life didn't flash before my eyes and nothing had happened.

It takes a beat before Brian and I are howling with crazed laughter and deep breaths of relief.

"*Whoo!*" Brian cries, both fists bumping the ceiling. He socks me in the arm. "What a rush!"

Pulse spiked to oblivion, I clutch my chest. But it's not fear kicking it up to a thousand beats per second. It's euphoric adrenaline. I feel... alive. Free.

Everything makes sense. This was exactly the Ebenezer Scrooge wakeup call I needed.

As the rush subsides, we head into the elevator of one of the tallest buildings to grace the Manhattan skyline. Brian edges back to our original conversation. "So, Jess. You said your goodbyes." He air-quotes. "Now, what's the plan?"

"The plan?" I hit the elevator button and mull over his question for a moment. I feel the center of my brow pinch.

The Jess Dilemma: How do you hold onto a vexing little someone who won't stay? I'd have better luck hauling an Egyptian pyramid across the Brooklyn Bridge than swaying Jess a millimeter before that made-up mind of hers is ready.

I lift a shoulder with an uncertain shrug. When I left Jess this morning, I didn't exactly have a plan.

And no, I didn't slither away in the night like a douchebag and abandon her. Jeez, what kind of asshat would do that? Fuck, if I'd had my way, I would've stayed with her all day, waited until I was sure she wasn't going to launch a full-on attack of my nuts, and held her until I squeezed every last deluded cell from her brain.

Instead, I gave her space. A selfless act of love that my dick still laments. His answer for everything is to bang her into submission. But yesterday wasn't about lust. It was about love.

As I did every morning, I gave her the second-best thing next to sex. Food. A biscuit with ham, egg, and cheese might seem simple, but when I cook for her, each meal—each bite—is a symphony of ingredients prepared with small pieces of my heart, gift-wrapped for her soul.

And I knew when she was hungry, she'd eat. Whether she'd admit to it or not.

Alongside her breakfast sat a pile of offers—six and even seven figure ones for Bishop Mountain. I pressed a sticky note to the strongest offer of the lot.

"Take this one."

Then, I dressed. As I worked a cufflink into my sleeve, Jess looked up from the bed. But her stare wasn't just on me. It was in me. I felt her from the inside out. Behind those Bishop blue eyes, my girl was there. Somewhere.

"I have to head back to the city today. I won't ask again, Jess. You sure you won't come?" I knew it was a long shot. My ultimatum was weak at best.

Her smile waned, and her head only shook once.

"Okay," I whispered, kissing those perfect pink lips one last time before everything between us changed. And *thank fuck*, she kissed me back.

I slipped a hand beneath her pillow, capturing my little *I LOVE YOU!* note. I held it to her stubborn, beautiful face.

Her words ghosted across my lips and heart. "Goodbye, Sharpshooter."

Exasperated, I had nothing more to say except, "Goodbye, Choir Girl."

"*Ahem.*" Brian clears his throat.

I haven't answered him. What did he ask? Oh, yeah. My plan. My *How to Unfuck my World with Choir Girl* Plan.

I straighten my stance, the answer hitting me like an arrow to the heart. My entire face is smiling. "I'll just do what every self-respecting, grown ass former sniper does in a position like this."

"Which is?"

"I'm breaking out the big guns." I whip out my phone, chuckling. "I'm calling my mother."

CHAPTER FORTY-SIX

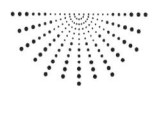

JESS

I couldn't stop staring at the note. Mark had read through a dozen proposals, annotating each one with professional thoughts and opinions. He'd scribbled his way through all of them with professional advice and words of encouragement and dozens of big loopy hearts. And love.

He'd poured all his love into this—into me—and like an idiot, I sent him packing. I let him go.

Rather than kick myself repeatedly in the ass, I stood on my own two feet and made a decision. I took the offer.

I chose the one Mark recommended because he was right. The offer was good. It also made my realtor's day. Kristie Mae with Make Your Day Realty.

Mark had left her business card along with two others. But hers had a picture—a lovely black woman with a cheerful smile and a logo with a heart. If I had any doubts about who she was, the coupon on the back for a free dinner at Donovan's erased all doubts. Kristie was Anita Mae's sister, and I was more than happy to repay the tip she so generously shared with me all those years ago.

Twenty minutes later, she was on my doorstep, offering me a hug, a hot cup of coffee, and a beautiful basket of blueberry streusel muffins—homemade by Anita herself.

Clad in my pink monkey-and-bananas pajamas, fuzzy, mismatched ankle socks, and a worn flannel robe, I welcomed her and the promised pain relief she offered. With an unconvincing smile, I opened the door wide. "Come in."

I'd given up on the rat's nest crowning my face and hoped she and her beautifully tailored suit could overlook my current state of despair.

She came in with a wholehearted, "Thank you." Kristie was a ray of light on my gloomy day, armed with a sympathetic smile and a notary public. I grab a pen and focused on signing every form presented to me without hesitating once.

Maybe I was hoping for one last reprieve—a way out—when I ask, "Don't my brothers need to sign, too?"

Quick as a bullwhip, Kristie reassures me, her hand on mine. "I'm visiting each of them next. Everything has been arranged."

And there it was. The deal was as good as done. Within the next hour or so, my dreams of holding on to this land would be over, crumbling into nothing more than a memory. Like Mom and Dad.

And Mark.

My heart aches with sadness as I sign the last dotted line. This is it. There's no going back. I have to move on.

Kristie and her notary make their way out. I swallow hard

as the walls close in. Quick breaths send the room spinning. Air. I just—I need air.

In a frenzy, I make my way out the door and rush to the far end of the field. To that isolated expanse of space where the treeline ends and the lake begins, and I'm free to shout and scream and cry.

My heart cracks wide open, and I need my mother so badly, it hurts.

I drop to the base of a hundred-year-old willow and sob at the loss of her all over again. This was our spot. It was here that she placed that first dandelion in my hand. Taught me to read. To chart the stars. To sing.

A cold gust of wind sweeps my hair from my face as I stare helplessly at the sky. My chest is heavy with pain and loss, and every breath is a shard of glass through the heart.

Please, Mom. Send me a sign. I need you—to dry my tears and stroke my hair and promise me, just once more, that everything will be all right.

A guttural sob breaks from my throat. I've lost everything, and it all feels so final.

The way a death always feels.

CHAPTER FORTY-SEVEN

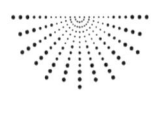

JESS

After hours of memorizing every blade of grass and storm cloud in the sky, I blow on one last mountain dandelion and toss the universe one more wish: I wish everything would be all right.

Eventually, I make my way back. To the house. My home . . . at least for a few more days.

My steps slow as I notice someone on the porch, waiting patiently for my return. And like the ragamuffin I am, my steps hasten, robe, slippers, and all. And let's just ignore what's going on with my hair.

I wave a hand in approach. "Mrs. D.? What are you doing here?"

Her cheery giggle warms me in an instant. "Oh, Jessica. You really must call me Delilah." Her smile brightens. "I was just in the area dropping off a casserole—" She pauses, as if searching for her words. "For someone up the road."

Uh-huh. I pop a hand on my hip, amused. There is no one up this road. We're it. Or, at least, I am.

"Well, I thought it was time I dropped by. So we could catch up." Her jubilance wavers. "I hope you don't mind."

I point to the grocery bag beside her. "Happened to be in the area and needing a place to cook?"

She shrugs guiltily, though her bright eyes dance with mischief. "I'm sort of in a bind. I need a few shots. For a magazine." Thank God she cooks better than she lies. If I know Mrs. D.—or Delilah, rather—as well as I think I know her, news of the sale flew to her doorstep like a Texas wildfire in July. But she's not here to gossip. She's here for me.

Her honey-laced tone lifts expectantly. "Can I come in?"

I take a look inside the bag. "What's the password?"

She doesn't even think it through. "Bourbon caramel brownies."

God, that is definitely the password. "You may enter."

The split second I'm in arm's reach, I'm wrapped in the biggest, hardest, warmest hug of my life. It crushes every last emotion out of me.

I have no defenses against her. Anything I've ever needed, she's given. Maybe it's why I try not to impose or take advantage of her outrageously generous spirit. Not once have I wanted to burden her with a myriad of unimportant things that I needed to figure out on my own. But I'm glad she's here.

With her tight arms around me, I break down. My words come out small. "I'm sorry."

"For what?" she asks, stroking my hair. Is it any wonder this woman birthed the most amazing men in the world?

I smile through tears. "How about for being the biggest blubbering mess?"

Delilah snags a tissue from her pocket, wiping my cheeks and dabbing my nose. "Everything will be all right."

I hoist the heavy bag to my arms—which weighs a ton—as I hang on to those hopeful words. "What did you say?"

With a hand on the knob, she says it again, like a messenger straight from heaven. "Jessica Marie Bishop, I promise you, everything will be all right."

There it was. Someone to give flight to those exact words. The ones I needed to hear. And I don't know why, but they make me feel better. Lighter somehow.

∽

For the next hour, she cooked, and I ate. I admired her the way I did as a kid—wide-eyed and fascinated. She commanded a knife with flair and grace. Single-handedly flipped a grilled-cheese sandwich from the pan to my plate. Whipped up a meringue with ease, creating the perfect topping for her delectable brownies.

Her food never required a recipe. It was made with all-natural ingredients and a whole lot of love. And I sank into each bite as if it were my last.

After a ravenous meal of mostly eating and very little talking, I finally came up for air. "Thank you for this."

She set her plate aside, her expression twisting with discomfort. "I know I'm not your mom, Jessica. But I've always thought of you as one of my own." Her lips tighten into a line, guarded as she studies me. "It's not my place to pry . . ."

My smile widens. "You let me ugly cry all over your cashmere coat. Consider yourself entitled."

"My son is in love with you."

My heart squeezes for a beat. What do I say?

When I say nothing, she assumes the worst. "I see. You don't love him."

What? "No. I do, but—"

"You're worried about him being a player?"

My head drops to my hands. Memories of Mark flash through my mind—a high-powered CEO standing on a balcony, declaring *I am not a player!* to the entire freaking world. I smother a snort. "No, I'm not worried about Mark being a player."

Her hand pats mine. "No one would blame you if you were, Jessica. We've all warned him. He's been far too reckless with his social media." She air quotes. "Hashtag Player Mark Donovan," she mocks with exaggeration.

Oh, my God. This has to stop. I drum up enough insistence to defend him. "He isn't reckless. And it isn't his fault we're not together. It's mine." I bite back another set of tears and brace myself, prepared to tell her the truth. "Mark deserves a woman who can give him everything."

It's clear she's not following when her voice lowers. "Everything?" She pauses. "Like . . . sexually?"

My eyes fly wide. "What?"

Geared up and raring to go, she leans in, ready for girl talk. "Is he a selfish lover? Because you're absolutely entitled to your slice of satisfaction." She nibbles a brownie without a care in the world, while I wither below a heat lamp of embarrassment. "Do I need to have a talk with my son? Because I will."

And I'll be praying every minute of that talk ends with the earth opening up and swallowing me whole.

I stammer a response. "No. Not . . ." I stare at her, my mouth agape. This conversation cannot be happening. Horrified, searing heat floods my face as I go utterly mute.

Patiently, Delilah studies me. She tops off my coffee when what I really need is booze. Finally, I figure out what to say, and all without bringing Mark's lovemaking into question. "Your son is absolutely wonderful. In every way. No complaints."

She continues, unphased and keen with interest. "Then, if he loves you, and you love him, what more could you possibly need?"

"A family," I utter before I can help myself. "I—" I can't even meet her eyes when I blurt out my confession. "I can't have children."

There's a long, silent pause before she says one word. A question really. "And?"

And? What does she mean *and?* By this point, my heart sinks like lead. How can she not understand?

Hands clasped tight, I'm barely holding myself together. Another wave of tears threatens as I trudge on. "Mark deserves a family. And you deserve grandchildren. And I—" Tears blur my vision, my throat choking out the words. "I can't—" God, why do I have to keep saying this? It's salt on a fresh wound, saying it out loud. "I can't have a baby."

Her chin dips to meet my gaze as both her hands clasp mine. "And?" she asks again, followed by, "What did Mark say about that?"

I shake my head in remorse and despair. "Nothing. I told you, he's an amazing man. But it matters. I know it does."

"Jessica Marie Bishop, look at me," she gently orders. And I do. Her eyes are wet with tears but loving. "It doesn't matter. And the reason I know it doesn't matter is because one of my own sweet boys was adopted."

I blink, absorbing her admission. It takes me a moment to take in what she just said. Ty, Mark, and Zac . . . I've known them my entire life. As a family. As brothers. "I . . . I had no idea."

In a maternal way, she forks a good size piece of brownie and feeds it to me. A Donovan trait I've grown accustomed to. Fond of, even. Grateful, I take a bite and smile, listening.

"It's not something that comes up in idle conversation, so of course, you didn't know. Because it doesn't matter," she repeats again, her gentle sway of persuasion, urging me to really listen to what she's been saying.

And I do. I'm not sure I would've believed this coming from anyone else, but I believe her. It doesn't matter. Who knew three little words could speak volumes to my soul?

Even now, I can't imagine which one it could be. There are traces of Donovan-angled good looks and witty charm in all of them. It's impossible to tell.

"You see, my dear, I am their mother. And they are my sons. Period. Believe me when I tell you a family isn't made from the birth of a child. It's made from the love for one."

And for a split second, my mouth nearly gets ahead of me. I almost ask who. Could it be Tyler, the tallest and blondest of them? Or Mark, the renegade? Or Zac, the man with more fashion sense in his little finger than half the straight men on earth?

But the truth is, it wouldn't change a thing. I don't need to know which one to know they're all amazing in their own rights. And I don't even want to know because it changes nothing.

Not one thing.

After a good, long time of letting my mind run free, she keeps going. "Do you know what the boys call it?"

"What?"

Delilah turns her glassy eyes up, her laughter light. *"The Donovan Secret.* But in a way, I guess it is. Not because we have anything to hide, but because we haven't had a reason to share it." Her eyes twinkle as they dance with mine. "Can you imagine my three rugged boys romanticizing it as if one of them were the Count of Monte Cristo or the Scarlet Pimpernel?"

"The Donovan Secret," I say, romanticizing it myself. Somewhere from the smallest corner of my heart, a spark lights, and I wonder if it's a secret I'll keep . . . or carry on. "Thank you for trusting me with this."

She pats my hand. "Of course, Jessica." Her warm eyes fill with emotion. "And I know no one can replace your sweet mother." For a beat, my breath hitches. "But I hope you know you can always come to me for anything." Her smile dwarfs into a shy line. "I've always wondered what it would be like to have a daughter."

And, oh, I miss having a mom. Someone to go shopping with and gab on and on about romance novels and *The Bachelor* while we pick out colors for our nails. I try not to let my mind run away with me, but perhaps I've been quiet too long.

Delilah begins slipping her hand from mine. "If I'm overstepping—"

"No." I squeeze her hand. "You're not. I'd like more of this."

Hope lifts her smile to her eyes. "I would, too. And no matter how your life with Mark twists and turns, maybe you wouldn't mind me dropping by every now and again?"

I wrap both arms around her neck. Her presence—her wonderful, motherly force—it feels good. So good, it elevates me from the inside out. She's showered me with perspective and understanding, and I never realized how much I needed this until now.

"I'd love that."

"And if you ever need me to talk to my son about how he treats you in bed—"

Oh, God. "No. Really, I'm good."

Another hour later, my nails and hair are done, courtesy of Delilah's handiwork. The sides of my auburn hair are swept up in elegant, loose braids, accented with bright yellow dandelions she plucked from the backyard. It's elegant and romantic—a stark contrast to the pajamas I'm still in. But I love it.

So much so that when she slips a peek at her watch and prepares to depart, I threaten to hold her against her will. "So soon?" I ask in bitter disappointment. "What if I chain you to the refrigerator?"

Her hand pats my cheek gingerly. "Next time, my dear. So, clip your hair, and collect your strength. Maybe take a nice, hot bath."

"In the middle of the day?"

"Why not? It gives you time to focus on you. Think of what you really want, and then go after it."

We hug our goodbyes, and I wave at her until her Lexus disappears behind a thick stretch of pines.

She's right. A soak in the tub will do me good. I'm done licking my wounds. It's time to muster up the courage to charge into my future.

Even if it is one baby step at a time.

CHAPTER FORTY-EIGHT

MARK

Dean meets us in the hall, a thick binder in his hands. He salutes smartly. "Ready for war?"

I salute back. "Fuck yeah, I am."

He hands me the folder, and I'm off to Lance's office. Dean will make sure things run smoothly on the outside, while I square off against Goliath.

When I get to the door, I don't knock. I kick it in and stroll through it.

"Jesus." Lance looks at me as though he's seen a ghost. In a frenzy, he saves whatever he was working on and slams his laptop shut, then slides every last piece of paperwork into a drawer. "Wha-what are you doing here, Mark? I didn't expect you back so soon."

"So soon? Or at all?" Frozen, he stares back. I ease up. There's no fun in it if I can't fuck with his head a little. "Yeah, I'm back early. Change of plans."

"Oh." He stands and walks over to shake my hand. "Uh, what changed?"

I commandeer his desk, bouncing my butt in the big, cushy, ten-thousand-dollar seat. He fidgets with his cuff, nervous and not sure what to do with himself.

I notice the authentic Chopard Imperiale desk clock with solid gold finishes, three violet cabochons, and delicate baton hands. A small token of my appreciation to him after he badgered me about it relentlessly.

I prop my hands behind my head and lean back, kicking the damned thing over as my feet slide comfortably to his desk. "Nothing changed, Lance. See, I wanted you to think I'd be out for a while. Maybe for the count. *That* was the plan."

Confusion knits his brow. "I don't understand."

"I know. If only ignorance was bliss," I say, and he scowls with just enough venom, I know he's catching on. "See, Lance, I couldn't get this case out of my head."

"What case?"

"The one I personally took on. When you build a company by taking on some of the toughest, most intriguing cases of financial fraud, I wasn't put off when I made headlines. I was fascinated."

He lowers to his seat near the desk as if keeping up the conversation. "Fascinated?"

"Yes. You see, both Russ and Brie knew her nickname."

His voice raises as he shakes his head. "Whose nickname?" I gage his irritation by the vein of his forehead. He's pissed. I'm delighted.

"Jess's. They both called her Choir Girl. Which is odd because only three people in the world know I call her that, and my own brother didn't know until a few months ago." I drop my feet to the floor and lean over the desk, lowering my voice in confidence. "See, truth be known, she wasn't exactly keen on it when I first started calling her that. Hence the secrecy."

Impatient, Lance huffs. "As interesting as this is, Mark, I really do have quite a bit of work to do. What with the IPO tomorrow and all."

"Don't worry, I'm getting to that next. But back to what I was saying. I kept asking myself, 'What does a trust-fund princess from Manhattan and a low-life letch in Saratoga Springs have in common?'"

When I stare at him expectantly, he shrugs. "I give up. What?"

My smile curls up. "An attorney. I checked every public document Brie and Russ have ever filed."

His face drains of blood. God, what a rush. That moment when they know I know. Where's a fucking camera when I need it?

"Mark, look, I can explain."

I cut him off, palm to his face. "*Cui bono*, Lance. It's etched across spaces all around this building, but you never bothered to translate it, did you? See, you forgot my cardinal rule. The foundation for every brick the fortress of this company was built on. Why The Centurion Group is the unbeatable best in the world." I stand and lean across the desk. "Who does it benefit? Or more loosely translated ... Follow. The. Money."

Lance blinks, then goes on the offensive. "You're making a big mistake, Mark. I don't know what you think you know or don't know, but I've been an attorney to hundreds of companies and hundreds of thousands of people."

"Which is why it was even more perplexing that all roads

lead to you. What was your advantage? Why try nailing Dean to the cross? Or me? You stood to make millions, but that wasn't enough, was it? You wanted it all. If two of the top three seats goes down before the IPO, you are the CEO. You'd have everything."

He begins to move for the door. "You're delusional."

"And you were too greedy to stop while you were ahead. It's why you helped Russ buy the luxury condo Brian Bishop lives in. It was formerly owned by Renaissance Holdings, which is why all the streets are names for renaissance artists."

He attempts to speak.

I cut him off. "At first, it was just to spy on me, wasn't it? You knew where I was staying. It was easy enough. That's how Russ got Brian's watch. He broke in, snooped through my shit and Brian's. Maybe he just liked it at first, but then he used it. Gave it to Jess. And thank God he did, because it's the only thing that ties the two of you."

Lance shrinks uncomfortably and moves slowly for the door while I continue.

"The biggest issue was that if I had a wife, ousting me becomes ten times harder because Jess would be entitled to a portion of my shares. You knew Dean would go quietly, and I never cared about the money, but Jess? If she got a whiff that someone was trying to screw me, she'd come out, guns blazing. So, you had to smear her good name, too. Make it look like she was trying to personally cash a million-dollar check, which either made me look complicit or like an idiot. People had to see her go to the bank, then come back to me. And then?"

"Then?"

"Then what happens to Jess?"

He stands there and doesn't reply.

That pisses me off. I pound both fists on the desk. "Answer me!"

When he still says nothing, I lunge for him and stop short when he pulls out a gun.

Lance's evil smile is pathetic, but I play along. "It's a nice story, but you and I both know I can spin this any way I want. I'm the face of this company. Have been for months. With the IPO and all the media attention—"

That makes me laugh. "It's as if I've taught you nothing. Try getting this through your dumbass head: There is no IPO."

He takes his time analyzing what I've said, the lines of his brow furrowed in disbelief. "You're bluffing. You wouldn't give up a billion dollars."

"Wow. It's like you don't know me at all. I don't love the money. I love the chase. Which, I need to thank my little brother again for that epiphany." I shrug, nonchalant. "I rushed the cancelation. The Centurion Group will stay private. Everyone stays right where they are . . . well, except for you, of course."

He struggles to cock the hammer of his pistol. Amateur hour at its finest.

"Look, before you break a sweat trying to work that antiquated gun that will probably misfire and take out your eye, perhaps you should look down, asshole."

Confused, Lance does and notices the pretty pattern of lasers targeting the center of his chest. Like a dumbass, he tries swatting them away. "What is this?"

"Sniper lasers. It's good to have friends with rifles. And since my future brother-in-law can shoot a fly off a turd at two hundred meters, I suggest you stop moving and have a seat." I lean closer, offering a few words of wisdom. "He's eager for any excuse to shoot your ears, nose, or dick off. He's sort of taking the attack on his sister personally."

Petrified, Lance glances out the window. I take the opportunity to snatch the gun from his hand. Fuck, where did he get this? A civil war reenactment?

He falls slowly to the chair as I lay out his options. "The choice is yours, asshole. Confess to the cops and face prison for fraud and conspiracy or..."

His eyes veer up, hopeful. "Or?" I bet he's praying for the sweetheart deal he made Dean. An all-expenses-paid trip to Spain if he goes quickly and quietly. Ha! Fat fucking chance.

"*Or* face the boys of Bishop Mountain and possibly die. Don't worry, they'll give you a good head start." He blinks in fear, looking to me for guidance. I simply shrug. "I'm oddly good either way."

Okay, so I lied. When he agrees to confess, I admit, I'm disappointed. Bitterly so.

Especially since I now owe Brian a hundred bucks because I lost the bet.

CHAPTER FORTY-NINE

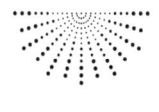

JESS

I dial Mark's phone. Again. It's been going to voicemail nonstop. Which means he's knee-deep in work or he's ignoring me. My stomach sours, thinking how the bridge I lit on fire might be burned beyond repair.

A second later, my phone lights up with an incoming call. But the second I see the caller ID, my shoulders deflate. "Hi, Kristie." My soon-to-be six figures richer realtor.

"Jess." She's panting. "I'm so glad I caught you. I ran to the car so we could talk. They'd like to meet with you."

"Me?" I immediately add, "Who? And why?"

"*They* are an investment firm. With the sale final, they want to speak with you. Apparently, your knowledge of the land is legendary. They value your opinion. On the development."

Development? I let out a sigh.

Giddy with excitement, Kristie's voice climbs an octave. "They're willing to pay, and they are willing to pay a lot!"

My opinion. I swallow a lump the size of this mountain as

my heart sinks to my gut. When I agreed to sell, I didn't think to ask about the buyer. Call me naïve, but I thought it would be a nature conservatory, or at worst, a residential builder.

But what if they're industrial? What if they're here to rip out all the trees? Pollute the lake? Crush the land to oblivion?

What if I've made a terrible mistake?

"I told them it was fine if they dropped by this evening. Around six-thirty," she offers, her voice practically screaming, *please say yes.*

I check my watch. It's only a few hours away. I'm barely out of the tub, but at least I'm not still in pajamas. "I guess so. But I can stay on the property through the end of the month, can't I?"

"Absolutely."

～

"When do you close?" Zac asks, sitting on the stoop, staring off.

"Technically, I already closed. Today," I say with an exhausted breath. "An all-cash offer. With the agreement, I could stay on the property for a few more weeks."

I'm swaying in Mom's old rocking chair, losing my gaze over the land. Golden flecks of sunlight catch the tip of each tall grass and flower as the lush green blankets the hillside. Tree branches and lilies seem to wilt a little more today as sadness weighs down the sky.

"I understand why Rex and Cade couldn't come, but I wish Brian were here."

Zac takes my hand but still isn't facing me. "I know."

Over the horizon, men in suits are in a cluster of conversation, a buzzing that loudens with each nearing step. As much as I'd like to grab the shotgun and pick them off like ducklings at a fair, I agreed to this chat. But it was my decision to make, so there's nothing I can do but step up to the guillotine and face the consequences.

I shouldn't give a damn what these turdwads do with the land. But the truth is, I do. I want to know if this will be a soccer plaza or a big-box store. God help me if they make it into a water park.

I drop my head to a hand as I realize they're all in dark glasses and hard hats. What a bunch of dipdorks. Like, what's going to fall on your head, Chicken Little? Rain?

Zac tugs my hand, luring me to my feet. "Come on. Let's go meet them."

His smile is brimming, far too happy faced for the occasion. I smack his arm. "Read the room, Zac. Nothing to smile about, okay?"

He rubs his arm and flattens his lips. "Okay."

I make my way to the half dozen or so of them. Instantly, they part so I can meet with Mr. Big-Wig Alpha, I guess.

He stands, his back straight as an arrow, as the rest of them circle around. In his hands is a stack of blueprints, which he drops to the ground.

In his too-expensive-for-real-work suit, he gets on all fours, smoothing out each corner and securing them with rocks. I'm tempted to tell him there's a table in the kitchen, but then again, perhaps they should all be on their knees, appreciating this land and God's gift that it is.

Once the blueprint is spread wide, I lean over it, arms

crossed. I try to make out the drafter's lines, comparing them to the natural landmarks to understand the size and scale.

To my surprise, it's not a store or sports center or any flavor of amusement park at all, though it appears as big as one. It's a house. One massively colossal house. And now, I'm wondering if I've just sold out to the mob.

"Is it a resort? Or a wellness center?" I ask, studying it harder. I mean, it has to be ten times the size of the house on the property now. "Like, somewhere people can stay and unwind? Meditate?" My mind gets ahead of me, swimming laps around the potential. Even if not, it's a great idea for our vets.

No one is answering me, though. I look at them, wondering if I've said something wrong.

The man on the ground clears his throat and balances on one knee. "Yes, Jess. It's a sanctuary. Our sanctuary."

He removes his hard hat and sunglasses and latches on to my hand. For a second, his thick waves and golden amber eyes steal my breath. "Mark?"

Everyone removes their hard hats and glasses—their costumes. Brian, Rex, Cade. Tyler and Mr. and Mrs. D.—I mean Delilah. All of them in suits. While I'm in a pair of scuffed-up jeans and a vintage Coca-Cola T-shirt. Is this why Delilah did my hair and nails? Confused as all day, I blink through tears, beaming like a loon.

Zac snuggles up beside me. "Sorry, I had to keep this from you."

I smack his arm. Twice. "You couldn't throw me a bone and pick out a dress or something?"

A small roar of laughter erupts as Mark presses a sweet

kiss to my hand. "This morning, when I asked you if you were sure you wouldn't come with me to the city, I wasn't trying to move you there, Jess. I was making sure you wanted to be here. Right here, on Bishop Mountain. This blueprint is just a first draft."

"First draft?" I ask, wiping my cheeks. I lean over to get a closer look.

"Of our sanctuary. Our home. Where I'll come home every night and fix us dinner and kiss you every morning before work."

So happy I could burst, it takes every last shred of willpower to rein in my jubilation. I shake my head. "No. That's insane. You'd be running yourself ragged. You can't keep this up."

"Watch me." He stands, pressing so close, my heartbeat connects with his. "Someone once said that giving love a second chance is like giving them an extra bullet because they missed the first time."

"I take it that's a sharpshooter saying."

"*Shh.*" He presses a finger on my lips. "Trying to propose here."

I bite the smile on my lips. Like a warm blanket on a crisp day, the family that surrounds us closes in.

He removes the ring from a box he pulls from his pocket, but not some big, showy ring he picked up at a store. I know this ring. When I was very young, to quell my crying from a scraped knee, Delilah once let me play with it. It's his mother's, and she beams with pride as she nods, teary-eyed.

Fidgety, he clasps my hand to his chest. "As I was saying . . ." He clears his throat. "Giving love a second chance is like giving them an extra bullet because they missed the first time. But maybe, just maybe, Jessica Marie Bishop, it's not a bullet at all, but an arrow. A Cupid's arrow."

Zac makes a face, hushing under his breath. "A Cupid's arrow?"

Brian adds helpfully, "Maybe it's a boomerang."

"No, no, no." Flustered, Mark works a hand through his hair, justifying his well-rehearsed speech. "It's a Cupid's arrow. I can't believe I have to explain this." He lets out a grunt. "I've thought this through, long and hard, and—"

"Can we talk?" I ask sheepishly. Beg, really. My voice is barely above a whisper, as if the Circle of Trust can't hear every word happening.

He smiles, confident as he answers. "Of course. Jess and I might be a while," he says, not looking at anyone but me.

Rather than walk off hand in hand, he tosses me over one shoulder like a sack of potatoes and marches straight for the house. My squeals shatter into giggles.

He barely shuts the door when I'm flipped around and pinned against it. His lips sink into mine, and this kiss—it's everything.

But I have to be sure. "Mark." I press him back, hard, determined to meet his gaze. "You'd be giving up kids of your own. Maybe if you'd known from the beginning—"

"Jess." He pecks me sweetly. "I have known. Since the night of your charity event."

I blink. "Zac? Brian?"

Mark shakes his head. "Zac and Brian would never betray your trust. Numbnuts Lance. After I asked him for a check for your charity, he did what lawyers do. He did a thorough, if somewhat invasive, background check on you. Including medical history. I'd barely skimmed the report before I deleted it, but I couldn't unknow what I'd already read."

A small smile breaks through my nerves as my mind connects the dots. "That's why you didn't use a condom."

He rubs his nose to mine. "That's why I didn't use a condom."

I shake my head, at a loss. "But if you knew my secret all this time—"

"I didn't. I mean, I read the outcome of a medical procedure. I had no idea *that* was your big secret. The way you were acting, and with Brian and Zac hinting about a big ass elephant in the room, hell, I had no idea what it was. My money was on some weird fucking kink."

I roll my eyes, giggling in his hold. "You wish."

He kisses me again, sucking my lower lip before nibbling his way to my neck. "Don't you want to know my secret, Jess?"

His secret? Challenge flashes across his sea-glass eyes. Their gold-tones mean happiness. The greener shades, desire. He wants me to know it, to figure it out. And I do know it. The reason he has no doubts. No questions. No worries when it comes to us—to our future. I rub the scruff of his jawline and breathe out the truth. I say it as his smile meets mine. "You're *Donovan's Secret*."

"I'm *Donovan's Secret*, Jess. Adopted at eighteen months. Mother, deceased. Father…" He blows out a breath. "Who knows. But those people out there, the Donovan's, they're my family. They chose me, and I choose them back a hundred times over. The way I choose you, Choir Girl."

I smooth a hand through his hair and look at him as if for

the first time. There are no walls. No doubts. No more secrets. And the smile that brightens his face lights up my entire world. "I choose you, too, Sharpshooter."

He lifts me, my legs wrapping around his waist as I settle into his hold.

"Jessica Marie Bishop, I can't imagine a single day without you. Marry me."

I'm dizzy as my heart somersaults to the sky. In my mind, he didn't ask. He commanded. And I've already said yes.

But I haven't actually said a word. Not with my outside voice. Because someone's been kissing me relentlessly. After another long, deep, passionate plea of a kiss that tilts the world on its axis, he comes up for air. "Stop torturing me already," he whispers to my lips. "Tell me you're mine."

Seriously? I swear, this man makes it too easy. My lips brush his. "You're mine."

A masculine growl escapes his chest, and he spins me around. "That's it. You're getting it now." Heated, he stomps to the bedroom and tosses me onto the bed.

Giggling, I play coy. "Getting what?"

He rips down his slacks clear to the floor, showcasing his enormous erection in all its glory. "My dick," he says, proud as all day. And damn, does he have a lot to be proud of. "The gift that keeps on giving."

Does it ever.

We strip off each other's clothes and go in for our millionth kiss before Mark stops short. His brow is hard, creased with concern. Dismayed, he shakes his head and blurts out, "What am I thinking?"

My breath screeches to a halt. "Huh?" Panic whips through me, and I wonder if it's just hit him. All he'd be giving up.

"This is all wrong." My heart sinks like the Titanic as I fumble for what to say.

I watch as he stumbles back a step, snatching his pants from the floor. But before I can summon enough strength to say something brave and selfless, the crisp snap of his fingers cracks the air.

In a flash, he's shoved a fist in his pocket, removing it slowly. The familiar chain dangles from his grip. With a world of love in his eyes, he lowers it over my neck until his dog tags slide securely between my breasts.

Approving, he nods, and tilts my chin until my eyes meet his. "Now, Choir Girl, you may have my dick."

∽

Two hours and several earth-shattering orgasms later, Mark and I settle into the grace of each other's arms.

His eyes meet mine, his pants, still heavy. "You're killing me, Choir Girl. Is that a yes?" he asks.

I kiss the hard plane of his chest and bat my biggest puppy-dog eyes at him. "If I marry you, I can't take your name."

"What?" He leaps from the bed, outraged. Playfully so. "What's wrong with Donovan?"

I snap to sitting. "What's wrong with Bishop?"

A smile quirks up the side of his face until two dimples sprout at his cheeks. Like a panther in the wild, his chiseled body moves gracefully over mine. "Absolutely nothing."

I feel the telltale throb of round seven at my entrance when three hearty knocks thump on the door. Our eyes shoot wide.

We've been at it for hours, and quiet we were not. Mortified, I cover my face with both hands. "Oh my God." We both yank on whatever clothes we can find and rush from the room.

The living room is a lively place, filled with his brothers and mine, making themselves comfortable in front of the game. Mark's parents stand, arms wrapped around each other, both sporting aprons.

"Sorry," she says, her expression ripe with apology. "But dinner is ready, and the way the two of you were going on, I was worried you might be, *er*—"

"Famished?" Mark says, wrapping a strong arm around my shoulders as his kiss lands on my head.

I die on the spot, burying my face in his shirt. Or is he wearing my shirt?

Zac clears his throat and pockets a hand. "I'm guessing that's a *yes*. Or should I keep our chapel reservation in Vegas?"

Nostrils flared, Mark growls possessively.

All eyes are on us, the air frozen with bated breaths. Mark presses a tender kiss at my temple. "Well, Choir Girl?"

I stare up at this incredible man as he looks lovingly back. Then I meet the gazes of the most important people in my life, prepared to face this future, head on. "It's a yes."

Everyone flocks to us, a frenzy of hugs and well wishes, and more love than I ever imagined possible. My heart overflows with so many emotions, I can only imagine my parents are here, now, surrounding us, too.

A warm breeze sweeps through the open windows of the house, my mother's voice echoing along it. Her presence circles all around me, warm as a campfire and soft as a cloud.

"See, baby girl? Never underestimate the power of a wish."

～

Thank you for reading MARKED, the first in BOYS OF BISHOP MOUNTAIN series.

Next in the series is **CUFFED**
Where Zac Donovan is about to meet his match.

Hannah
The second I saw him walk through that door, I knew he was trouble.
Men like him always are.
The dark hair.
The smoldering stubble.
Those piercing green eyes that might as well be a flame thrower between women's legs.
Oh, and the fact that he's in a gentlemen's club.

What am I doing here, you ask?
It's my job to be here.
No, not that job.
My job is to put away bad guys, like the elusive mob hitman I've been tracking for months who's now somewhere in this very club.
You see, I'm a woman on a mission,

And this is a raid.

Zac

For heaven's sake, I was hosting my brother's bachelor party,
Is that a crime?
(Seriously, asking for a friend.)

I mean, considering my brother is about to walk down the aisle,
I'm just doing my best man duties.
And sure, technically, it's a gentlemen's club...
A private, exclusive, highly coveted one where everyone is supposed to be protected and completely anonymous.
Oh, and did I mention that it's six-figure stupid expensive?

Whatever.
At least there's one silver lining to this cluster of a night...
Agent Hannah Evans.

Even as she slides the cuffs around my wrists,
And her fiery eyes meet mine,
It's clear we both know the truth:

My name isn't James Smith.
My attorney will have me free in under an hour.
And that kiss...
The one I couldn't help stealing...
Won't be our last.

GRAB IT NOW>> **CUFFED**

Need more?

The Alex Drake Collection >> **1-CLICK HERE**

Ruthless Billionaires Club >> **1-CLICK HERE**

Sinful Soldier's Series >> **1-CLICK HERE**

SINS of the Syndicate >> **1-CLICK HERE**
>> *Keep scrolling to read an excerpt.*

Join Lexxi's VIP reader list to be the first to know of new releases, free books, special prices, and other giveaways!

Join to receive hundreds of FREE romance books a year! All retailers - 100% FREE!
https://www.lexxijames.com/freebies

SINS OF THE SYNDICATE

BOOK ONE

1
IVY

"I'm here to see Ms. Palmer."

The man's voice is deep, with an authority that makes me wonder why he requested his tour of the assisted living center with me. His suit is expensive but not overly fitted. And the dark gray is a stark contrast to the clear blue of his eyes. The silvery accents in his well-trimmed salt-and-pepper hair give him the air of distinction, with professional charm brimming from behind what seems to be a practiced smile.

It's not unlike the smiles I'm used to from people clinging to their courtesy as they navigate a world of decisions. How will I care for my loved one? Will they be safe? Is this covered by insurance? How much will it cost?

If money is no object, the ones with the deepest pockets land here. Except for me. It took two years for me to work off my mom's debt, and it gave me a lifetime's worth of watching people in return. I remind myself that I'm here to ease them into a relationship of trust and support. Not to pressure them with a hard sell, despite those very words from my boss.

"I'm Ivy," I say, stepping out from behind the long reception desk. I hold out a hand, meeting his solemn smile with one of my own as he takes my hand for a brief shake. "And you're Mr.—"

"Sin," he says, scanning the lobby and halls. I can't tell if he's overwhelmed or underwhelmed, but he avoids meeting my eyes as he glances around. "Call me Sin."

"All right, *Sin*."

I've already seen the roster, noting that the tour request was made by a Bryce Jacob Sinclair, Esquire. The formal name suits him as equally as the nickname Sin. A gravity and authority harden the lines of his face, hiding whatever's lurking just below the surface.

The heaviness that drags him down threatens to pull me with it, an occupational hazard to a career dependent on emotional connection and empathy. When his expectant eyes meet mine, I snap back to work.

Handing him a visitor badge, I gesture down the north hall. "This way."

Along our tour, Sin asks the usual questions: How many occupants are there? What's the caregiver-to-resident ratio? If the staff live on the premises—which feels more like he's asking if *I* live on the premises.

No matter how many times I give this tour, I'm delighted when he asks about the one thing that always connects us, though it never seems to at first. Mr. Whiskers.

The small fluffy toy is weightless in my hand as I tug it from the pocket it's been peeking out from and hold it up.

I'm not the only one beaming at the sight of him. Even the stone-faced Sin cracks a smile, albeit a very small one. It creases his face enough that I peg him to be about sixty, which makes me wonder if he's looking at the facility for his mother or possibly his wife.

"This is Mr. Whiskers."

"Your stuffed animal?" Sin's studious eyes move from it to me, the intensity of his gaze so much harsher than is warranted by my crazy talk.

Unnerved, I take in a breath. "Mr. Whiskers is so much more than that. He's a therapy stuffed animal. You can even pop him in the microwave to warm him up."

I avoid talking about my past or that Mr. Whiskers has been my personal security blanket for nearly twenty years.

Sin nods. "Do all residents get a toy? Or just the bad ones?"

His contempt doesn't bother me. He doesn't understand, and it's my job to help him understand.

"Sparrow Wellness and Assisted Living is unlike any facility you may have seen. Our occupants range in age from twenty to eighty-two. Sometimes, a little non-threatening toy is a great way for people to open up. I didn't have to say a word about him, and you asked."

His face is stone. No hint as to whether he's annoyed or amused. His eyes wander through the opening to a vacant room. "Continue."

"Even if they aren't interested in a little support from a cuddly friend, he's a big hit with the children who visit. We keep a small stockpile in the back."

"Trauma victims?" He mutters the question under his

breath in a way that sounds less like distaste and more like hope.

"We cater to a wide range of conditions, trauma being just one of them. Some residents have degenerative conditions that require more care than their families can provide. Others don't have families, in which case we become their family if their physician recommends us."

Sin takes several steps into the room, moving his gaze from the warm cream walls and big bay window to me. "Looking for a family, Ms. Palmer?"

His tone is sharp and icy, with enough condescension that I have to remind myself that people in pain tend to inflict pain. He's just hurting, and I'm the closest target within striking distance. But it's not directed at me. *Even if it is the truth.*

"Just looking to help as many people as I can." I hold my smile as I step away, shooing off a flurry of emotions that I'll need to deal with later. For now, Sin is in his role of distrustful client. It's up to me to win him over.

His brisk footsteps close in quickly from behind.

We stop at the courtyard, where a few residents have opted to spend their morning lounging on lawn furniture, enjoying the sun. We walk in silence. He takes an interest in a resident, Angie, lost in the strokes of a painting she's creating. I use the time to take a closer look at his paperwork, only now noticing he's left several areas blank.

It's not uncommon. People tend to be guarded their first time walking through. It's a long way from *nice to meet you* to *I trust you with my loved one*, but it's a familiar road I've traveled many, many times.

"It's you," Sin says, and I look up.

Seeing the painting this close, I realize the resemblance is uncanny. I'd almost believe it was me if not for the elegance of the off-the-shoulder gown Angie has painted her in, or the delight in her eyes that could never radiate from mine. It's how I want to look. Confident. Complete. Happy. Instead, my heart is riddled with so many holes, half the time it feels like it's about to collapse under all the damage.

Taking a closer look, I see the white curl in her subject's curly black hair—identical to the one that inexplicably grows at my right temple. Angie nods, beaming with a grin as she silently lets me know it is me.

It's a version of me that could only happen in Angie's beautiful imagination.

Grateful, I hug Angie, being gentle to avoid overdoing it. Her muscles are weak. Every word from her lips is a fight, but they're always worth waiting for. Especially today as she sounds out two words.

"H-h-hap-p-py b-b-b-irth-d-day."

My heart leaps as she completes the short sentence. It's the most she's said in a week, and I find myself speechless, if not a bit teary-eyed.

"Sorry, do you mind if I steal Ivy for a second?"

Derrick interrupts, probably to keep me from outright blubbering. He's more than my boss, though no one would know it. We've been a couple for nearly a year but keeping our relationship under wraps was his idea as much as mine. Sort of.

I keep one eye on Sin, watching as he carries on a one-sided conversation with Angie. He doesn't seem concerned that she isn't responding. On the contrary, his smile is genuine, even though he receives nothing more than a few polite nods back. But I'm ready to jump in if he demands any more.

Derrick's hands stay pocketed, the way they always do when he's hiding something. Maybe it's a surprise. Like dinner at a fancy restaurant on the waterfront. Or cuddling together in front of a romantic bonfire on the beach.

Between his work schedule and mine—which is a result of his—it's been weeks since I've had any action. I'm bursting at the seams with sexual frustration, so if my birthday celebration is a beer, a grilled cheese, and twenty solid minutes of hitting it hard during whatever sci-fi show he can't live without, I'll take it.

I'm grinning like an idiot when he says low, "I really need you to bring this one home, babe. Seal the deal. The numbers need to look good. I've got a big meeting tonight."

"Tonight? But—"

His cell phone buzzes, and he takes it, mouthing, "Gotta go," as he winks and rushes back inside.

"Why are you in this, Ms. Palmer?" Sin asks as he sidles up to me.

"What?" I scoop my jaw up off the ground, realizing he isn't referring to my conversation with Derrick.

Sin means my work. Of course, he does. His thousand-yard stare roves across the lush grounds, taking it in while not focusing on anything at all.

"The same reason everyone works here. It's personal. We've all been here. Helping family members who need assistance."

He turns, narrowing his eyes. "Family?" The way he says the word is strained, as if he doesn't believe me.

It compels me to share more than I normally would. "My mother had a degenerative condition. There was a lot of pain in her last years of life. I did all I could."

I don't talk about the specifics. How by the time a doctor diagnosed her liver disease, nothing could be done. That it never stopped her from the drugs or the alcohol. Or that despite the unbearable pain she suffered every second of her last days of life, she pushed me away until she was too weak or too tired to put up a fight. There's no way I can explain how you can love a person with all your heart when they seem to hate you with all of theirs, so I don't try.

By the look on Sin's face, I've already given him an uncomfortable amount of information to unpack. So, I wrap it up, quickly finishing. "I did what I could to make her comfortable."

The hard lines of his face soften. "I'm sorry for what you've been through."

"Thank you." The practiced smile I use in times like these emerge, and I nod appreciatively, steering our discussion back where it belongs. On him. And not because Derrick wants me to close the deal, but because this man and his family need me. And that's why I'm here.

"The first steps are never easy," I say as a gentle reminder. "We have different levels of care and service. Can you tell me more about the person who brought you here today?"

He spends another moment looking me up and down, torment storming behind his eyes as they finally settle on mine.

I don't know what to make of it, but situations like these can be delicate. With all my encounters, I'm patient as I let the client drive the discussion, deciding for themselves if they'll tear the bandage off bit by bit, or rip it off all at once.

With an abrupt huff, he steps away, his large, determined strides taking him inside the facility and back toward the lobby. I rush after him, but don't shout out his name or make a scene, not wanting to draw attention from the residents or staff... especially Derrick.

Sin wastes no time depositing his visitor badge on the desk, and I nearly break into a jog to catch up to his mile-long stride. When he bolts out the front doors, I'm right behind him, struggling to catch my breath.

"Sin," I say, winded but compassionate. He stops but doesn't face me. "If I've said anything—"

"You haven't."

His reply is so matter-of-fact, I feel silly for suggesting it. So, I reclaim my smile, if only for my own benefit.

"I know trust takes time. My card," I say, holding it out and feeling doubly foolish when he doesn't take it.

Instead, he sneers.

This is the point where others might give up, but I don't. It's the people who push you off the most that are in the most pain. At least, that's the excuse I've always given myself.

He eyes the card, then casts an amused glance to the sky. After an awkward second of silent conversation between him and a few puffy white clouds, he faces me. The hand he places on my shoulder feels paternal. "I don't need your card, Ms. Palmer. The person who brought me here today was you."

Unbuttoning his blazer, he fishes a thin envelope from the

inside pocket and hands it to me as a dark car with tinted windows pulls up beside him. "Someone recently told me the first steps are never easy, Ms. Palmer."

A well-dressed chauffeur rushes around to open the back door, and as soon as Sin is seated inside, the man returns to the driver's seat.

The darkened window rolls down, and Sin's smile widens. "Happy birthday."

He slides on a pair of sunglasses as the car rolls away.

2

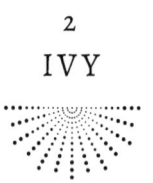

IVY

The black town car makes a left at the end of the drive, disappearing behind a thicket of birch trees, and I'm left there scratching my head. What just happened? I take another look at the plain white envelope in my hand, ready to open it until I notice Derrick. He's been watching from the large window of his office, a practice of his I've come to accept.

There's an intensity to his expression, one I meet with a cheerful smile. It takes him a moment before he returns it, waving me over. Maybe there's a surprise waiting for me. Like gathering the staff over to sing "Happy Birthday." Or an intimate cupcake with a single candle for me to wish upon.

"Everything all right?" Derrick asks as I enter. It's just him and me and the ever-growing clusters of paperwork and folders covering his desk. My hopes for a cupcake are instantly dashed, and it's a wonder he can find anything in the small space. For every new meeting with his accountant, the mounds of paperwork are only getting worse. He closes in from behind me, though the door remains open.

"Yes. He's going to think it over," I say as I slip the envelope into the roomy pocket of my cardigan. I want to remind him that sales aren't made in a day. That trust must be earned. But the irony is enough for me to bite my tongue.

I should tell Derrick about the envelope. For once, trust him. Really let him in. It feels self-sabotaging not to.

As often as I repeat the usual mantra, *I should trust him*, over and over again in my head, I can't deny the parts of my mind and heart that don't . . . and it's not for a lack of trying. Or admitting to myself that I'm damaged goods, the byproduct of an absentee mother and father unknown.

But Derrick is my ticket to a normal relationship, even if things between us have felt a bit uncomfortable lately. It's just a hiccup, one every couple encounters. He's stable. Sweet. A bit of a workaholic, which means I haven't seen him much in the past three weeks. But at least he has a J-O-B, and that should count for something, right?

Still, I can't help but shove the envelope deeper into my oversized pocket, hiding it from both my boyfriend and my boss. No matter how hard I try, distrust slithers between us, threatening to pry us apart.

Let's face it, I have issues, and trust is just the tip of the iceberg.

One of his arms wraps around me. Instead of giving him the usual elbow to the ribs, I nuzzle into him, and it feels . . . nice. Warm and caring and . . . nice. That is, until he releases me. And just like that, I second-guess everything.

Am I like Goldilocks complaining that my man is too nice?

Derrick's shirt is perfectly fitted, the navy blue tapering over his chest and abs before disappearing into his slacks. It looks professional and sexy, though I still prefer his lucky polo. His sweet superstition is that whenever he wears it, luck lands in his lap. As if I was a manifestation of luck.

"Chase another one off?" he says, only half-teasing me.

With his half smile and adorable gaze, maybe he's ready to finally make it official. "Aren't you afraid someone will see us?" I playfully ask, wondering if we can finally stop hiding our status from coworkers and Facebook alike. Be a couple in the actual light of day.

I know I agreed to keep our relationship under wraps, but maybe this is a baby step in the right direction. Hope blooms from deep within my chest that maybe, just maybe, I'm finally learning to trust.

"You're probably right," he says, pulling away to bring us back to a proper boss-employee distance apart. When my frown catches his eye, he lowers his voice. "Hey, it's not forever. Just for now. Meeting you was my destiny."

His sweet words and wink revive my smile, but before I can slip him a kiss, he steps back.

Noticing the envelope, he asks, "What's that?"

It would be so easy to tell him about the tour with Sin. The strange encounter and Sin's bizarre escape. Why can't I take the envelope out and open it with Derrick? Share something, *anything*, with my boyfriend of nearly a year.

I slide the unmarked envelope from my pocket, flipping it aimlessly. "Just a letter."

"I'm running to the post office after work, then I've got a meeting. Need me to mail it for you?"

"I've got it," I say, forcing a smile. "Meeting?" On my birthday?

Derrick has taken several meetings this week away from the office. And another dinner meeting? This can't be good.

His nod is reluctant, and I know when to back off. But I offer him all the support he needs, cuddling Mr. Whiskers against his neck. And like Sin before him, Derrick can't help but crack a smile.

"You and that . . . cat."

I don't know what word he mentally used to fill in the blank between *that* and *cat*, and I don't care. I'm tired of being ruled by my stupid doubts. And they are stupid.

But I tuck Mr. Whiskers back into my pocket, leaning closer to Derrick's rigid stance. "I need something for luck. I mean, we can't all have a lucky polo."

3
IVY

"*T*able for two. Under Brooke Everly," my best friend says, rescuing me from a birthday dinner for one of mac and cheese.

"You reserved a table?" I ask as we're seated, surprised because we never get a table. We always sit at the bar.

"The strongest they have . . . so we can dance on it. It's your birthday!" She squeals loud enough that absolutely everyone is looking. "And just because your boyfriend has to work doesn't mean we celebrate less. After this, it's karaoke time."

Her elbow nudges mine, and I know she's serious. My throat dangerously tight, I choke down the ball of fear with a few sips of the chilled water our waiter has placed in front of me.

Brooke instantly demands two tequilas. Both for her. "And keep them coming," she tells the waiter.

We've plowed through our first basket of chips as she tosses back her second shot.

"So, let me get this straight," Brooke says as she taps her lip with her index finger. "Some mysterious good-looking guy books a tour with you just to deliver mail and check out your ass?" She slurs the word *ass* and motions for the waiter. "Tell me he at least offered you a lap dance."

"He did not."

"Fucker. So, what did the letter say?"

I shrug. "It's still in my pocket. I got busy, and—"

Her eyes widen. "You didn't want to open it in front of Derrick in case it's a dick pic."

I deadpan. "Who would print out a dick pic?"

"A man who fills the page. You can't open it until after dinner. Birthday present number one."

Laughing, I shrug and dunk another chip into hot, gooey cheese. "Good-looking, yes. But more than twice my age, at least. And we all know twice my age is my hard limit."

"Really? I'll bet he's still hotter than Derrick. You rarely spend the night at his place, and we both know he's never at yours. Plus, he never takes you out. Ever. What kind of eighty-year-old boyfriend is he?"

"For your information, he's thirty. And I'm trying to be supportive as he builds his career."

"For a year? And when's the last time you've had sex?" she shouts, trying to be heard above the lively Mexican music.

Our waiter refills my water, grinning broadly. Sweltering heat rises up my face as I melt into the seat and die of embarrassment. Brooke roars with laughter, planting herself face-down along the bench.

"This coming from a woman whose face is kissing an area

where someone's ass has been. After they've eaten their weight in Mexican food."

I ball up my napkin and toss it at my drunk friend's head, which does little good. If anything, it eggs her on, as she moves on from laughter to a perfect whale-song combination of howling, raucous heaving, and silent squeals.

She rubs the flood of hysterical tears from her face before pointing a finger straight up, conveying how she needs a moment to catch her breath.

Hushed, I lean over. "I've had sex," I say, arguing with the giddy drunk girl. "For your information, I have it regularly."

"Like as regularly as when the salmon swim upstream?"

The waiter brings our food—two shrimp quesadillas for me and a taco salad the size of my Honda Civic for Brooke. I glare at her over the rim of my water glass as she orders a margarita.

"Virgin?" she shouts, having lost all control over the volume of her voice.

I scowl at her until I realize she was talking about a drink. Which actually sounds good.

Turning to the waiter, I ask, "Can you do a pineapple margarita with no alcohol?"

He nods and heads off.

"And more nachos," Brooke hollers after him.

In an instant, her elated happy face drops. Despite the fact that she's a champion lush who can usually out-shot or out-chug any man, I'm almost afraid she's about to be sick.

"You okay?" I ask, ready to rush her to the ladies' room.

She merely points past me, and I turn to see whatever zapped every last drop of happy-go-lucky from her face.

Lo and behold, it's Derrick.

I'm elated that he made it to my birthday celebration after all, until I see he's not in the professional button-down shirt he was wearing earlier at work. And he's not alone.

This version of Derrick looks freshly showered, his hair still damp and curled in a pretty-boy style that actually makes him look younger. Wearing his faded jeans that are my favorite, he's seated at the bar, relaxed as his spread-eagle legs give easy access to let a sloppy blonde slide in between them. She's made herself perfectly comfortable, smoothing her fingers against his chest and shoulders and pretty much all over his lucky fucking polo.

I square my shoulders, and before I know it, I've crossed the length of room, vaguely aware of Brooke huffing, "Shit," as her footsteps stumble behind me. I'm seconds from yanking the blonde by the hair—southern style—when I come to my senses and realize it's not her I'm pissed at.

"Oh, fuck," Derrick says like a dumbass because that's what he is. A worthless, dickless dumbass. He fumbles his way from behind the body of a woman whose perfume smells way too familiar because, like the man she's draped all over, that's also mine.

"Is 'oh, fuck' all you have to say? I guess she's your destiny, too." I frantically search the bar for the biggest drink within reach to toss in his face.

"What's going on?"

When his companion turns to face me, I realize it's none other than his accountant. Which explains all those closed-door and after-work meetings.

"Hey. Iris, right?" she says with the charm of a pole dancer, and now I'm searching the bar for two of the biggest drinks I can find—preferably crammed full of ice.

"Don't make a scene, Ivy," Derrick says calmly like a total idiot. "We're hardly exclusive."

"Excuse me? You're the one who was talking marriage and kids. You're the one who's always asking what cut of diamond I prefer and where our honeymoon should be."

His lips tighten, and his words come out cool. "You can't pin this on me. I need passion. Spontaneity. A woman who will throw caution to the wind. The most I got out of you was your toothbrush."

He means a girl who will throw condoms to the wind. "And that's my fault? You're the one who wanted to keep our relationship on the down-low, and now I know why."

"Grow up. You don't want exclusive. You want to roam fast and free and with whatever guy rolls up. Like Limo-man this afternoon. What was in that envelope he gave you? Cash? A hotel room key?"

"What the fuck, Derrick? No."

At least, I don't think so. Besides, Derrick's so-called accountant is two seconds from sucking him off at the bar, so why am I the one on trial?

Derrick crosses his arms over his chest. "Yeah? Prove it."

He casts an arrogant glance at the pocket of my cardigan because, unlike him, I didn't have time to shower and change clothes before going out. I was actually working.

"I have nothing to prove." Which now looks like I have everything to prove. *Dammit.*

When I feel a tug at the envelope, I whirl around.

Brooke waves Exhibit A suggestively in the air. "And what

if she hasn't been cheating on your sorry ass, Dare-dick? What are you willing to wager?"

At least my ride-or-die has my back, though I feel a bead of perspiration trail down the nape of my neck at her suggestion. And since there's no backing down now, I square my shoulders and pray to God that Derrick is wrong.

Derrick waves her off. "It's not like you didn't already destroy the evidence."

"It's still sealed," I say, not certain if I'm making the situation better or worse but not willing to let my friend hang in the wind.

His expression sours. "Fine. What do you want if I'm wrong?"

"Your fucking car, jackass," Brooke says.

Wow. Her balls get all kinds of big after that much tequila. And when my bestie dives in headfirst, demanding his shiny new Mercedes convertible, there's only one thing to say.

"Yeah, Dare-dick," I say, repeating her insult because it's kind of catchy and totally spot-on as he plays fast and loose with Sluts-R-Us over here.

That's not jealousy talking. That's his accountant's cherry red lips now printing a path up another guy's neck before her tongue lands in his ear. It sickens me to remember that you've had sex with everyone your partner's had sex with. Perhaps a few weeks of no action with Derrick is just enough time to avoid a collision course with a round of STDs.

"Fine," he says, bellying up and stepping into my space. I anchor myself in place, ready for whatever he's got. Until he says, "Then if I win, you quit."

"Quit?" I squeak out.

I can't quit. What I do isn't just a job. It's my life. For years, I've cared for every single person in the center. Working evenings. Weekends. Christmas fucking morning. And now he wants me to quit?

Derrick is going too far. I'm not quitting my job over a stupid bet or even a breakup. No way. Not a chance.

I'm about to tell him so when Brooke cracks open the seal of the envelope and pulls out an old-looking photograph. Who in the world has photos anymore?

She flips it around and trombones the square to and from her face in the booze-filled hope of reading it. "Who's Olivia?"

"What?" Carefully, I take the delicate photo from her hand, staring at it hard, as hard as I can. My heart pounds wildly against my ribs, and I stand there, stunned. I blink before I regain my senses and can move.

Brooke slaps the empty envelope on Derrick's chest. "Ivy doesn't need your job. She's an overqualified badass who's tired of taking your shit."

Oh. My. God. Brooke really needs to stop talking now.

"Fuck both of you," Derrick spits out. "I'm not giving you my car."

As Derrick storms off, Brooke shouts after him, "Way to be a bad loser, Dare-dick."

It isn't until she wipes my cheek that I realize I'm crying.

"Hey, don't cry. He doesn't deserve you," she says, stroking my hair.

"It's not that," I say, staring at the image of my mother. At least, I think it's my mother. It's as if Angie's magic wand has brushed alchemist strokes across her image. Her dark curls are thick and full, framing round cherub cheeks and a big, beautiful smile I've never seen her wear. I almost didn't recognize her.

Next to her stands a man I don't know. His dark wavy hair is the perfect crown to his tall stature and confident stance. His lips are a line that barely tips up, and his dimpled chin could have been molded to form mine. But it's his eyes that draw me in. Instantly I want to know him, and it bothers me that I don't.

On the back is a riddle, one I reread again and again . . . and again.

For
Olivia Ann Palmer.

"What is it?" Brooke asks with a side hug that wraps me tight and squeezes out my reply.

"It's me. I'm Olivia Ann Palmer."

~

1-CLICK NOW >> SINS of the Syndicate

To the outside world, I'm known only as Z. The enforcer. A widower with nothing to lose. An ex-SEAL sworn to keep one vow: protect the D'Angelo's at all costs.

I'm not a good man, and I never claimed to be.
Protecting her was second nature. Nothing more.
Claiming her was just a one-night escape.

But she made one mistake ... a cardinal sin.

Slipping away on her terms. Not mine.

No strings.
No commitments.
No names?

No way.

There's just one price for my protection.
And it's her.

<u>GET SINS NOW!!</u>

∾

Looking for another sexy billionaire? Meet Davis R. Black ... aka Richard. Some know him as a tech mogul. To Jaclyn, he's the King of the A-holes. Which is why this billionaire is hiding *his* in plain sight. Check out the first book in the Ruthless Billionaires Club.

<u>Get RUTHLESS GAMES now!</u>

ABOUT THE AUTHOR

As a USA Today Bestselling author, Lexxi James has hit the top 50 bestseller lists on Amazon, Apple Books, and Barnes & Noble, with books sold in over 26 countries. Best known for seductive romantic suspense, she loves matching smoking hot heroes with their soul mates. Her signature style is witty banter, high heat, and a whole lot of heart.

She proudly calls the Midwest home where she lives with the man of her dreams and the sweetest daughter in the universe. Her pastimes include reading, loading up on unhealthy quantities of caffeine, and binging Netflix and reality TV. She's a sucker for kids selling cookies and pretty much anything on Etsy.

www.LexxiJames.com

Printed in Great Britain
by Amazon